the
secrets
we keep

ALSO BY KATE HEWITT

A Mother's Goodbye

KATE HEWITT

the secrets we keep

bookouture

Published by Bookouture in 2018

An imprint of StoryFire Ltd.

Carmelite House
50 Victoria Embankment
London EC4Y 0DZ

www.bookouture.com

ISBN: 978-1-78681-630-6
eBook ISBN: 978-1-78681-629-0

To my children: Caroline, Ellen, Teddy, Anna, and Charlotte.
I hope you always know you are loved exactly as you are.
Love, Mom

PROLOGUE

You are so silent, so still. I can barely hear you breathing, and I don't think I'd know you were except for the barely there rise and fall of your chest under the starchy hospital sheet, visible only when I lean forward and look for it, for a desperately needed sign that you're still here, that you're holding on, despite what the doctors say, the way they shake their heads.

It all happened so quickly—a blur, the blood, screams and shock. So much shock. My mind is still spinning with disbelief, that this happened to *my child*, but I know if it stops spinning the guilt will rush in, along with the terror. *This is all my fault.* I can't escape that awful reality, that I could have stopped all of this if I'd seen it coming... I could have kept you safe, and I didn't.

All around me the hospital is quiet, the long, lonely hours of the night ticking by as I wait for the verdict. The doctors say they'll know more soon... whether you will wake up or not. Whether you will live or die.

I stare at you, willing you to open your eyes. To smile sleepily as recognition dawns. I crave that, the unutterable relief of it, because I can't stand to think that you might not be all right, that a moment was all it took, a moment when I wasn't watching, when I didn't see.

Because no matter what I try to tell myself now, I'm sure, I'm so sure, that I could have kept all this from happening if only I'd been strong enough. If only I'd been different.

CHAPTER ONE

TESSA

Six weeks earlier

"We're almost there."

I crane my head around, taking my eyes off the winding road for a split second, to give Ben and Katherine what I hope is an encouraging smile. Ben isn't even looking at me—his eyes are glued to his Kindle Fire tablet, as usual—and Katherine is staring out the window, twirling a strand of hair around one finger. Both of them already seem bored, and our summer vacation has barely started.

I turn back to the road, unsure if the clench of my stomach muscles is from excitement or terror. I'm doing this. I'm really doing this. Three months away from the city, away from Kyle, away from a life that has finally become unbearable. Three months alone with my children, in the wilds of Upstate New York, reconnecting with them and myself or whatever mindful approach made me think this was a good idea back in March. And it is a good idea. It has to be, because it's the only one I've got left.

We've been driving for over an hour from Syracuse, where we picked up our rental car for the summer after taking the train from New York, down winding, country roads, the rolling fields and clumps of trees—what are they? Oak? Maple?—interspersed with occasional buildings—long, low, shed-like barns that sell tractor parts, or speedboats, or animal feed.

The cute little antique shops and local wineries I've been daydreaming about haven't quite materialized yet, but I'm sure they will. This is the Finger Lakes, after all, a major tourist area, even if most New Yorkers probably consider it on par with Antarctica.

Suddenly Ben throws his tablet across the seat, making Katherine let out an irritable "ow" as it hits her leg, before he presses his nose to the window. "Mom, there's a paintball place over there. Can we go? Please? Now?"

I picture my nine-year-old son pelting my body with paintballs and try to give him a bland look. "Not now, Ben, we're on our way to the cottage, but maybe later. We'll see."

Ben groans theatrically and starts kicking the back of my seat. Katherine throws the Kindle back at him and they begin to bicker; before I can so much as offer a "hey, stop", Katherine is in tears and Ben is back on his game. I'd close my eyes if I weren't driving. *This summer is going to be good,* I remind myself. *Really. It has to be.*

The trees on either side of the road feel as if they're pressing against the car as we inch along; after spending the last twenty years in New York City, I'm not used to driving, and I'm probably being a bit over-cautious. I've been passed by at least a dozen pick-up trucks and SUVs, two of the drivers flipping me the finger, but never mind. We'll get there.

And then what?

I can't quite see how this is all going to unfold, how I'm going to turn it all around. All I know is I couldn't stand another day back in Brooklyn, feeling like a ghost in my own life, with everything piling on top of me, making it hard to breathe—Katherine's sulky shyness, Ben's boisterousness, Kyle's heavy silences, the tension that covers everything, thick and toxic. Sometimes I catch Kyle looking at me, his eyes narrowed, his lips pursed, and I feel a chill penetrating my body all the way through. What happened, that made him look like that at me, his wife?

At least here there will be no frowning school teachers giving Ben yellow cards for being too rough. There will be no supposedly all-class birthday parties where Katherine is the only one who isn't invited. There will be no smug mothers on the school playground, slyly rolling their eyes when they think I'm not looking.

And there will be no Kyle. That brings the most relief. There will be no silently accusing looks, no suppressed sighs, no endless tension that leaves me feeling as if I'm constantly making missteps, only I don't know what they are and I'm afraid to ask.

Escaping it started to feel like the best option, the only option. So I went online and rented the first affordable place I could find for the summer—Pine Cottage, on the shores of one of the Finger Lakes, three months away from Brooklyn, from PS 39, the children's school… and from my husband.

I wanted a place where we could put down the devices and let go of the worry and fear, where we could reconnect over barbecues and late-night swims and… other stuff. In my mind, it was a hazy mirage of happiness for the three of us; Kyle was never in the imaginary picture. Now that we're actually approaching our summer destination, however, I'm not sure what the reality is going to look like, or more importantly, how to make it happen.

But that feels as if it's been my story since I lost my own mom; I feel like her death cut me adrift, and I'm still trying to find something to anchor me back to my reality, to connect me to my children, both of whom feel impossibly distant sometimes. If my mom were still alive, she'd show me how to do it, I'm sure of it. She'd laugh and hug me and tell me not to worry so much. She'd remind me of stories from my own childhood, how moody and impossible I was when I was eleven, how I didn't get invited to this or that birthday party. Stories I've forgotten, because I need my mother to keep telling me, to ground me in my own past, so I can help Katherine with her present.

"When are we going to get there?" Ben demands as he kicks the back of my seat again, making me let out an *oof* in response.

"Soon." As if my answer is the magic word, we suddenly break free of the dense forest, to emerge on an open road with a glittering, endless expanse of lake before us. I nearly stop the car to take in the magnificent sight—endless blue above and below, the sun sparkling over everything, the world shimmering with promise, a picture postcard of what life could be like. Neither Ben nor Katherine seems particularly impressed, though, so after a second's glance I keep driving.

I continue along the narrow road that hugs the lake, past gorgeous, sprawling log cabins and three-story lake houses with their own boat launches and docks, huge, rambling places with friendly front porches hung with American flags and Adirondack chairs scattered on the velvety grass; they all look like something from a photo shoot for Eddie Bauer or Abercrombie & Fitch.

Foolishly, I start to imagine that this is the kind of house we're renting, even though I've seen the picture and read the description myself, online, three months ago, and I know our rental doesn't look anything like these dream homes.

We are renting a two-bedroom ranch house with a scant twenty-five feet of lake frontage, a kitchen and bathroom in 1970s avocado green, and a screened-in porch with a couple of frayed wicker chairs. It was what was in our budget, even then just barely, but at least it will be ours.

Kyle muttered about it being a waste of money and he didn't think we should go at all, giving me a dark look that I couldn't interpret and chose not to try. I'm glad to escape him for a little while—except the realization, now that we're here, suddenly seizes me with anxiety. Am I really doing the right thing, leaving my husband for nearly three whole months? Leaving my *life*?

"Which one's ours?" Katherine asks as we pass a three-story mansion covered in brown shingle, complete with a Rapunzel-

like turret. My stomach clenches a little more. How are we not
going to feel disappointed by our shabby reality, with all these
gorgeous behemoths around us? But that's not how I want to
start our summer—with disillusionment rather than hope. I've
had enough of that already.

"Let's see…" I peer at the signs staked in front of various
cottages with their playful, curlicue script, like each one is the
entrance to a personal fairy tale. Ten Maples… Cove View…
Twilight Shores… "Ah, here it is. Pine Cottage."

My children are silent as I pull into the dirt track that serves
as a driveway. Pine Cottage sits huddled against the shore of
the lake as if it is ashamed of itself, which perhaps it should
be, considering its neighbors. Painted a drab olive green that is
peeling off in long strips in various places, the cottage squats in
the looming shadow of a huge, gorgeous lake house of dark blue
shingle with a massive deck jutting right over its hundreds of
feet of lakefront, and a three-story picture window overlooking
the sparkling water.

On the other side of our cottage, a bit farther away, is a sprawling modern house of white stucco with three different terraces
and a dock that extends far out into the lake, a gleaming red
motorboat moored at its end. How on earth did poor, pathetic
little Pine Cottage survive the arrival of all these showy upstarts?
I feel a surge of protective affection for it, simply for being there,
for clinging to hope, if only just. Kind of like me.

"So, shall we go in?" I ask brightly.

Katherine and Ben still haven't moved or spoken as I get out
of the car and stretch, my back aching. I glance at my children;
Katherine is chewing a strand of hair and Ben is back on his tablet,
thumbs moving so rapidly they practically blur.

"Come on, guys." I can't keep my tone from turning the tiniest
bit frustrated at their lack of involvement in this moment. "Let's
go check it out."

"Let me finish my level," Ben grunts, and something in me starts to fray.

"*No*, Ben." I yank open the back door of the car and then reach in, managing to snatch the tablet from his sweaty hands, a move I've practiced over the years, although admittedly it has a limited success rate. "Let's go now. You can play this anytime." Although not that often if I can help it.

I pocket the device and walk across the scrubby little yard to the cottage's front step, a slab of cracked concrete. From behind me the car doors slam. At least the kids are following me. I fish in the FedEx packet I was sent a few weeks ago for the keys, and then a second later, I open the door and step across the threshold of Pine Cottage, blinking in the gloom. The pine trees that gave the cottage its name droop over the house, making it feel a bit like walking into a cave. There is a smell of must and damp in the air, but once we open the windows I'm sure it will be fine.

"So," I say as I flip on a few lights, illuminating the small living room with its orange sofa and fake wood coffee table, "at least it's clean."

Ben snorts and Katherine hovers in the doorway, a strand of hair still trailing out of her mouth as she looks askance at our summer home. I can't blame her, but I still feel a little frustrated, a little sad. I want us all to share in the excitement of this summer.

I head into the small kitchen with its laminate cabinets and cracked linoleum, determined to see the bright side of everything. So the house is shabby? Big deal. The kitchen feels like a tacked-on afterthought, and the fridge is making a wheezing sound that suggests it is not long for this world, but none of this matters. I peer out the back door, which leads to the little porch, that, unlike in the photo online, is filled with junk and, for the moment, unusable.

I breathe in deeply, clinging to my optimism. We'll be outside most of the time anyway, enjoying the sand and the sun and the lake. We don't need a gourmet kitchen or acres of indoor space.

"I saw mouse poo in the bedroom," Ben announces from behind me. He sounds gleefully disgusted. "On the *bed*." Katherine lets out a little shriek at this, and I try for a smile.

"Don't worry, we'll get traps." And marshmallows to toast, and citronella candles, and a blanket for picnics. I'm holding on to that hazy montage, trying to make it seem more real, the kind of life I always thought I'd enjoy, once I had kids. The kind of life I'm sure I had once, even if I don't feel as if I can always remember when things were different. Before my mom got sick, before she died. "Let's go take a look at the lake."

With Ben and Katherine trailing behind me, I leave the cottage and make my way across the yard, the scrubby dirt turning to sand, until I come to the shore. Pine Cottage is no more than twenty yards from the lake, and as I kick off my sandals and let the cool water lap over my feet, digging my toes into the pleasingly squishy sand, I feel the tightly held parts of myself finally start to loosen.

"Look," I say. Ben and Katherine are huddling by the shore, as if the water might be toxic. They're city children, no doubt about it. Grandly, I sweep out an arm to encompass the shining waters stretching nearly to the horizon, a fringe of evergreens darkening their edge on the other side, dotted with lake houses. A raft bobs about fifty yards out. "Isn't this amazing? This is why we came. This is all we need."

"Can I have my tablet back?" Ben asks after a few moments when he's been kicking the sand with his sneaker. Katherine is sitting down, her knees clasped to her chest, looking woebegone.

"Why don't you get your swimsuits on? We can christen the lake with a dip."

Katherine crinkles her nose uncertainly. "Christen…?"

"I just mean, let's go swimming." I'm suddenly seized by a near-panicky determination to make this into a moment. "Why not? Let's do it! Right now!"

Ben and Katherine simply stare as I hurry past them to the car. I open the trunk and yank our suitcases out, opening them right there on the drive.

"*Mom.*" Katherine sounds both fascinated and appalled. A pair of her underpants has spilled onto the driveway, and she snatches it, mortified even though no one's looking.

"Here." I throw the pale pink suit we bought at Target last week and it hits her squarely in the chest. "And here." I toss Ben his blue-and-white striped board shorts and then grab my poor, faded tankini—I wasn't able to find a suit I liked this year, surprise, surprise. The ten extra pounds around my middle are not going to shift, no matter what I keep telling myself. Still, I don't want to buy a new suit and admit defeat, and in any case until now there hasn't been much point.

We change inside the house, Katherine barricading herself in the bedroom and shrieking when Ben rattles the doorknob, cackling. Over the last few months she's become increasingly self-conscious about her budding body, and Ben torments her over it. I shout at him to stop as I wriggle into my tankini in the minuscule bathroom, avoiding my reflection in the foggy mirror above the sink and what I know I'll see there—frizzy hair, eyebrows that need some serious maintenance, and a body that reminds Ben, as he so kindly told me once when he poked my stomach, of dough.

We emerge from the cottage, each of us like a shy caterpillar from a shabby chrysalis, blinking in the sunlight, conscious of all the bare skin. Or at least Katherine and I are. Ben lets out a primal yelp and barrels toward the lake, letting out another one as his feet touch the water.

"It's *cold!*"

"You'll get used to it."

Ben shivers theatrically and I laugh. This is what I dreamed of. This is what we all needed. Ben starts wading into the shallows, his city skittishness abandoned, but Katherine stands by the edge like a shy foal.

I glance at her, as ever unsure what she is thinking or feeling. My firstborn, my only daughter. She's been an enigma to me for so long, and I can't help but feel like it is my fault. Where is my mother's instinct when it comes to Katherine? Where has it ever been? We always seem to be reaching for each other and missing, and it's become more and more noticeable as she's got older.

"Come on in, Katherine," I say, my tone hopelessly cajoling. "It's not that cold, really."

Katherine looks away without replying, making me wilt inside, although I try not to show it. It feels like it's always been this way between us, from the time she was a baby, first refusing to nurse no matter how much I tried to bring her to my breast, and then later maintaining stony silences even as a hurt toddler, with a scraped knee and tears drying on her cheeks.

Sometimes I almost prefer Ben's manic boy energy compared to Katherine's wary stillness; now, as ever, I don't know how to handle it. It frustrates and saddens me at turns, and the worst part is, I think she knows, no matter how hard I try to hide it.

In any case, Ben breaks the moment by splashing me, dousing me in water which, no matter what I just said, really is cold.

"Ben!" My voice rings out, half-laughing, half-scolding. He grins and splashes me again. Katherine, still on the shore, sits down on the damp sand and clutches her knees to her chest.

While Ben splashes around I float on my back and stare up at the azure sky, the world around me fading to nothing but this sunlit moment. I'm not going to worry about my children, or how we'll occupy the next three months, or the fact that I ought to call Kyle, even though I'm dreading one of our tense conversations. I'm simply going to let my mind empty out as I revel in the perfect peace of this moment, the sense of possibility that still remains, shimmering and endless.

I'm aware of something changing more from a strange, prickling feeling than anything else; I don't think I've heard a sound or a voice. But for some reason I stand up, my feet touching the bottom of the lake, which out here, up to my shoulders, doesn't feel as nice. My toe brushes something slimy and I jerk my foot away from it.

I blink water out of my eyes to take in the sight of a little girl standing by the shore, hands planted on her hips. She looks to be about eight or nine, with glossy blonde hair in an expensive-looking pageboy cut and impossibly bright blue eyes. She wears a tiny string bikini that looks incongruous on her sturdy little child's body.

"This is our beach," she announces. Ben and Katherine simply stare. I start wading back toward the shore.

"Sorry?" I say, adopting that slightly jolly mother's tone that is meant to convey both friendliness and authority. The little girl doesn't even blink.

"This is our beach." She takes one hand off her hip and waves it toward the hulking lake house of blue shingle in the distance. Of course she comes from there. "We have five hundred feet of lake frontage, and I've been measuring it." She points to Pine Cottage's pitiful twenty-five feet of said frontage. "This is ours."

"Oh, really?" I smile with a certain kind of adult condescension. Her determined gaze doesn't waver. "Well, actually, this is our cottage, and the lake directly in front of it is ours too, at least for the summer. Anyway," I add, afraid my voice may have been a bit too hard, "I'm sure you have enough for yourselves. The lake's big enough for both of us, don't you think?" I give the girl what I hope is a friendly smile.

"That doesn't matter. My mother said we had five hundred feet, and the brochure said it too, and so that's ours." She blinks, her gaze fastened on me. "You shouldn't be here."

Ben and Katherine are still silent, watching this exchange with a kind of morbid fascination. I grit my teeth, holding on to my mom-friendliness with effort. Who *is* this kid?

"Well, this is our cottage and our beach," I say, trying to keep it light and friendly, "so maybe *you* shouldn't be here." I temper my words with a smile. "Unless you'd like to swim with us?"

"*Swim* with you?" The girl looks practically revolted.

"Then maybe you should go? Find your parents, maybe?" Too late I realize how unfriendly I sound, but *good grief.* I guess we won't be hanging out with our neighbors, not that I ever imagined such a thing.

"Zoe!"

I look up to see a woman coming down a worn dirt path snaking between the drooping pines; it leads to the big lake house, although why there should be such a path between these two impossibly different residences I have no idea.

"Zoe, you gave me such a scare. What are you doing over here?" The woman glances at Pine Cottage, her nose wrinkling, her guileless gaze taking it in and undoubtedly assessing it as a dump in less than three seconds before she turns to me with a wide, sunny smile. "Hello, I'm Rebecca Finlay. We're renting over there." She gestures toward the grandiose lake house.

I manage a smile, although everything about this situation is making me tense. Rebecca Finlay is exactly the kind of woman I dislike, and yes, I know that makes me sound judgmental, but I'm basing it on unfortunate experiences of women just like her back home who blanked me, and worse, did the same to my children, at school or the park. Who meet each other's gazes over the top of my head, eyes rolling just a little. Who give tinkling laughs as they look away dismissively.

She's also everything I've never felt myself—confident, self-assured, elegant, at ease. She is tall and willowy, her impossibly blonde hair cut in an expensive-looking bob like her daughter's, and now caught back with a pale blue cloth-covered headband. Her hair is gleaming and perfect, expertly highlighted in a pale rainbow of golds and silvers, just as everything else about her is perfect—her nearly wrinkle-free skin, her manicured nails, her thin-as-a-stick figure. She wears a crisp, white sleeveless blouse with a pair of pale blue capris—they match the headband—with knife-edge pleats.

In this moment I am horribly conscious of my nubby bathing suit, faded and stretched out from years of reluctant use. "Hi," I manage as I wade out of the water. "I'm Tessa McIntyre. We're renting here."

CHAPTER TWO

REBECCA

Of course, I go upstairs for three seconds and Zoe disappears. I can't have a moment to myself here. I should have hired a nanny for the summer, but Josh said the kids were too old for one and anyway, that wasn't the point. What the point is, I have no idea. To be tidied away? To not embarrass him any more than I already have? I don't know which is worse—having Josh disapproving of me, or having him worried about me. The children suspect something is wrong, I know. Charlotte has given me looks.

Zoe, of course, is angry; she misses her gang of summer friends from the Hamptons, and of course she blames me for taking her away from them. Charlotte seems indifferent about whether we're in the Hamptons or Hicksville Finger Lakes, and there is no denying that Max is relieved. Yet whatever my children feel, whatever I feel, the fact remains we're in exile, even if it was somewhat chosen.

I glance now at Zoe and then at my neighbor, this Tessa, with her two awkward-looking children behind her. No one says anything, but I feel the tension in the air, which is practically crackling. Zoe glares at Tessa while her two children stand by the water's edge, completely mute and still. I know how to handle this, of course; I'm an expert at handling these tedious situations, making socially awkward people feel comfortable and liked. Whether it's a school fair or cocktail party, I'm your woman. At least I was. I'm sure some people would disagree now, and I know Josh would. I've definitely let it all slip in the last few months, but it doesn't matter anyway, because I don't even feel like making the effort right now.

We arrived here a week ago and it's already felt endless, even though I'm relieved not to face a summer of judgment and whispers in the Hamptons. Josh's words keep replaying in my mind: *Maybe it's better for you to be away from it all. Give you time to think. How about Wisconsin?*

Three months with my parents. Absolutely not. And the last thing I want is time to think. Just thinking about thinking sends memories flitting like shadows through my mind, along with the treacherous doubt. I feel like my mind has splintered into spinning fragments and there's no way I can put them together again. It's a miracle that I've managed, for the most part, to seem as if I have. I've fooled Josh far more than he realizes. That much I know, at least. Sometimes I think I've managed to fool myself. *If I act like I'm okay, I will be.* The biggest lie but I'm buying into it for now because I don't know what else to do.

I don't want to think about all that now, though, and so I focus on Tessa and her children.

"You're renting too? Oh, how wonderful!" My voice is bright and carrying, full of enthusiasm. "How long are you here for?"

"The whole summer." Tessa has come out of the water and stands on the beach, round-shouldered and shivering. "What about you?"

"The same."

"Oh. Wow. Great." Tessa's words fall like stones into the stillness, and I know she is thinking the same thing as I am. Nearly three months of being neighbors. We could politely avoid one another, but it will be awkward, a summer of apologetic smiles and stilted chitchat as we clamber into our cars. We're clearly very different people.

"So where are you from?" I ask in the same friendly voice. "Very far away?"

"New York City," Tessa says, and I give a semi-squeal.

"Oh wow, us too! Which part?"

"Park Slope."

"Oh, I love Brooklyn." I haven't actually been there, except to drive through. "It's so hip and trendy, isn't it? Everyone's moving there." One of the moms at Stirling Prep, the children's private school, moved to Brooklyn and honestly, it was as if she'd died. We went out for drinks the night before her move, and it felt like a wake.

"Yes, well, the rental prices certainly reflect that." Tessa lets out a little laugh and I nod, as if I know anything about rental prices in Brooklyn. We've owned our own apartment, a four-bedroom on Fifth Avenue, for ten years.

"Mommy, this is our beach." I glance down at Zoe, taking in the familiar gleam of obstinate mischief in her bright blue eyes. Maniacal child. Exhausting, maniacal child whom I can't help but adore, simply for being so stubborn. Charlotte and Max are both ridiculously easy compared to her, and yet if I had to have a favorite, which of course I don't, it just might be Zoe.

"Zoe, what on earth are you talking about?" I let out a laugh and share a glance with Tessa, who looks heartened by this seeming complicity between us. *Kids these days.*

"We have five hundred feet of beachfront," Zoe says, her tone determined now. "It said so in the brochure. I've been counting it out, and so this part has to be ours, because we only have four hundred and fifty."

I glance back down at my daughter, too exasperated to be embarrassed by her ridiculous assertion. She's just trying to cause trouble, although why she'd pick on our hapless neighbors I have no idea. Easy targets, I suppose. "Oh, Zoe, honestly. You are too much. We have plenty of beach, we don't need to go grabbing other people's."

I glance back at Tessa, shaking my head, inviting her to share the joke even though I know Zoe will be furious later. Zoe is so often furious.

Tessa manages a smile. "Maybe it goes five hundred feet the other way," she suggests to Zoe, who glares at her.

"That's in the woods," my daughter says scornfully. "It's not really beach so it doesn't count."

"Yes, but it's still lakefront." I can't believe I'm bothering to debate this ridiculous point. "That's what they're counting, not whether it's beach or not. The sand is all driven in, dumped by a truck. There's no natural beach. Anyway…" I give Tessa a farewell kind of smile. "It's been *so* nice to meet you."

"You, too." She glances back at her children, who have been shuffling by the shore. "Sorry, I should have introduced my kids. This is Ben and—and Katherine." For some reason she sounds almost uncertain as she says her daughter's name.

"*So* nice to meet you." I give them a wide smile as I glance at them appraisingly. Katherine has hit that gawky stage of girlhood, her breasts two noticeable bumps under her bathing suit, and Ben's shaggy hair hides his eyes. Neither of them speaks.

A shiver of apprehension runs through me as it hits me all over again—nearly three months in this place. Good grief, what are we going to *do*? We went to the tennis and pool club for the last few days, for the children's lessons, and we have sailing twice a week, but rubbing elbows with the provincial version of the Upper East Side at the club was even more exhausting than I expected. But what's the alternative? Becoming best friends with Tessa McIntyre?

"Ben, Katherine…" Tessa sounds both annoyed and embarrassed, and trying not to be either. "Say hello, guys. Introduce yourselves."

They both mumble something unintelligible, and I give yet another wide, sunny smile; my cheeks are starting to hurt. "So how old are you, Katherine?"

"Eleven."

"The same age as Charlotte!" I clap my hands as if in delight, the sound startling both children so they jerk a little. "And what about you, Ben?"

"Nine." He glances up at me from underneath his shaggy hair, clearly bored by grownup conversation.

"The same age as Zoe here!" Zoe stares at them both, unimpressed. "And Max is eight."

"You have three children?" Tessa says, dutifully doing the arithmetic, and I nod.

"Yes. Three." Conversation is clearly going to be hard work, but at least it keeps my mind engaged. "I know," I say, as if I've just had a sudden and fantastic idea, "why don't you all come over for dinner tomorrow night?" They all stare at me blankly. "It will be so much fun."

"Yes…" Tessa says, sounding uncertain. You'd think she'd be grateful for such an invitation.

"I'm afraid we're out in the afternoon for swimming lessons, but I could order a bunch of pizzas and you can come over and hang out." The two words—hang out—seem to remain there, hovering awkwardly in the air, before they fall, silent, to the ground. I cannot exactly see our five children hanging out together, but they're young, they'll get along eventually. Kids always do.

I turn to Ben and Katherine, lowering my voice in a conspiratorial whisper. "You'll both be lifesavers to my three. We've only been here a week and they're already bored to tears." Zoe snorts in derision, showing my words for the lie they obviously are.

"Thank you," Tessa says at last. "That would be great."

"Perfect." I give a little satisfied nod. "Shall we say five?"

Tessa nods jerkily. "Five it is."

After a flurry of goodbyes, I head back down the path to our house, Zoe trotting behind me. I feel strangely, surprisingly exhilarated by the conversation, which is something new. Everything social has exhausted me lately: the endless routine of conversations and gossip, the sneaky sniping, the careful quips. It seems so utterly pointless now.

At least Tessa is different; she's the kind of person who will no doubt be grateful for my friendship. As arrogant as I know that makes me sound, it's still true. I won't have to watch myself with her, which is a relief. And she's a distraction, which I desperately need.

"Why did you invite them to dinner?" Zoe asks as we reach the set of steep, wooden stairs that lead to the deck. They must be a nightmare in winter. "They're boring."

"Why did you go on about the beachfront?" I retort, my annoyance slipping through. "Honestly, Zoe, what a bratty thing to do."

Zoe juts her lower lip out, and I turn away, unwilling to deal with her theatrics right now. Let her be furious. "We need to be at the club in ten minutes. Go get ready, and tell Charlotte and Max as well."

Zoe huffs as she goes off, and I am alone in the huge, gleaming expanse of the kitchen. I place my hands flat on the granite-topped island and breathe in deeply.

I think back to Tessa, slumping where she stood, an apology for herself. She could use a makeover, or at least a decent set of tweezers. I toy with the idea of helping her make the most of herself; that would certainly be a project, and might keep me busy. Then I glance at my phone and see that Josh has texted me yet again. *Everything okay?*

I grab the phone and thumb a quick text. *Yes. Fine. Just met the neighbors!* Smiley face and a heart. I toss the phone back onto the counter, disgusted with both myself and my husband, at the charade we're both willingly enacting because it's so much easier than admitting the fault lines that have appeared in our marriage, the cracks that are growing wider with every passing day.

Josh has texted me every morning, afternoon, and evening since I've been here, but he doesn't want to *talk*. He just wants to check up on me, the jailer rattling my chain, making sure I'm still suitably tethered.

He's called Charlotte on her phone, and talked to the other children nearly every day too, but not a proper word for me. Not a conversation, not that I'd even know what to say, how to begin. We've been trying *not* to have a conversation for months.

Upstairs, I hear the children shuffling around, getting ready for tennis. I walk to the fridge, leaning my cheek against the cool stainless steel for a few seconds before I open the door and take out the bottle of white wine I picked up in Geneseo during the last grocery trip. There's a quarter inch left, after two days. Not bad. I quickly swig right from the bottle, the cool, crisp taste zinging on my tongue as I swallow and then sending up a needed glow in my stomach.

By the time Zoe stomps downstairs, dressed in her gleaming tennis whites, the bottle is in the bottom of the recycling bin and I am smiling, car keys in hand.

"Hey, there. Are Charlotte and Max ready?"

"Almost," Zoe says in a bored voice, and as she fetches her tennis racquet I give my reflection a quick glance, noticing the deepening crow's feet by my eyes. I can see a few gray strands amid the careful highlighting. Maybe I'm the one who needs a makeover. Not that a makeover is going to help me now.

For a second I feel that now-familiar consuming wave of dread, as if I'm being sucked down a hole and there is nothing I can do about it. Oh, I could go the usual route of the bored housewife—mindfulness, yoga, Valium. The trinity of self-care that everyone in my world does. The trouble is, I don't think anything will help me now. I'm drowning, and no one can save me.

CHAPTER THREE

TESSA

We are all a bit subdued as we head into Pine Cottage after our interaction with Zoe and Rebecca Finlay. The house feels strangely quiet, my ears practically ringing the way they would after a rock concert, when you're plunged into sudden, breathless stillness. Katherine barricades herself in the bedroom and Ben sprawls on the sofa in his wet swimsuit.

"Ben! Change."

He groans but at least he gets up. I change out of my suit and as I hang it up with Katherine and Ben's on the frayed line strung between two trees outside, I see Rebecca and the kids getting into a shiny, enormous SUV parked in the driveway of their house.

Standing here, I realize just how much I can see of their house, their lives—the big picture window is practically like a movie screen; I can even see the shape of some sofas and chairs in the room beyond. It all looks sumptuous and comfortable, the best of both worlds.

Only a few straggly trees separate our properties, so I have a clear view of their deck and the steep stairs up to it, as well as the manicured lawn leading down to their lakefront, with its manmade beach and long dock. I squint and make out a tall, slender girl drifting toward the car from the deck—that must be Charlotte—and a small, slight boy with glasses following behind, who must be Max. Then Zoe struts out, carrying her tennis racquet like a rifle over one shoulder, and as I watch, she turns her head and her eyes narrow. I realize she's looking right at me.

I duck out of view, behind my dripping suit, but it's too late. She's seen me spying on them, and will no doubt tell her mother. This is going to be a long summer.

Back inside, Ben has found his Kindle Fire in my bag and is stretched out on the sofa, hard at play. Katherine stands uncertainly in the doorway of the bedroom she will share with Ben, looking, as ever, as if she doesn't know where or even how to be.

"Do you want to help me get the bags from the car?" I suggest and she shrugs. I glance at Ben. "You too, Ben. Come and help."

Ben grunts in reply. I hesitate, wondering which battle to pick as I feel like I am always doing. I used to simply not bother, because I was too tired, too sad, too worn down by life. But in the last few months I've been trying more, before my children slip away from me completely.

So now, despite the resistance I'm sure to meet, I plant my hands on my hips and take a stand.

"Come on. *Now.*" I stand over him, my hands on my hips, waiting. Ben gives another one of his groans.

"Fine."

Outside Katherine is struggling to get a bag out of the trunk and with a snort of derision, Ben elbows her aside and hauls it out, catching the side on the latch of the trunk and creating a big rip in the side. Perfect.

"You hurt me!" Katherine squeals resentfully, and Ben just shrugs. I sigh and take the bag from him before it gets battered further. Maybe this wasn't such a good idea.

The honk of a horn makes all three of us jump, and I turn to see Rebecca at the wheel of her SUV, the window down, expensive sunglasses hiding her eyes as she waggles her fingers. "Remember," she trills. "Tomorrow at five!"

As if I could forget.

"Why do we have to go there for dinner?" Katherine asks once all our bags are inside and I am starting to unpack, putting my t-shirts and shorts in the drawers of the dresser in my bedroom. The boughs of the pine trees completely cover the window, making the room gloomy and dark.

"It's nice of them to invite us, Katherine." Even if I'm dreading it almost as much as I think my daughter is. I know women like Rebecca Finlay. She might live on the Upper East Side but there are plenty of women like her in Brooklyn, which has become so gentrified in recent years that it's hard to believe we moved there to be arty and cool, back when we were young and idealistic and the rent wasn't astronomical. It feels so long ago now it's like looking through the wrong end of a telescope, everything fuzzy and distant. Was that me? Was I really like that?

In any case, no matter where they live, women like Rebecca are experts at seeming friendly while making subtle digs. Making you feel inadequate—hell, she only needs to show up to make me feel that—while acting like your friend. Sort of.

Uneasy guilt creeps through me, because I know I'm being at least a little judgmental. I'm painting Rebecca Finlay with the same colors as the moms I know in Park Slope—the ones who smile vaguely at me from a distance, as if we're friends, and then "forget" to include me in the Friday night social at the local wine bar. I never expected motherhood to be so hard, in so many ways. If I'd had my own mom to guide me, or at least to complain to…

A lump forms in my throat, even after two years. I feel like I should be past it now, I should be able to move on a little more. My mother's death, two years on, shouldn't make me cry, but in these unguarded moments I feel like I could sob. I miss her. I need her.

As if to drag me out of my encroaching self-pity party, my phone buzzes and I see it's my best friend Rayha, no doubt checking in to see how I'm doing.

"So, is it fabulous?" she asks as soon as I swipe the screen to take the call. I glance at Katherine still standing in the doorway of my bedroom, and Ben back on the sofa.

"We just got here, but I think it's going to be really good." I give Katherine a quick, reassuring smile before I slip past her and step outside for a little privacy. The glare of the sun hits me all over again and the air smells fresh, of pine and sunshine. "The lake's right on our doorstep. We've already had a swim."

"Wow, I can't even imagine! That's great, Tessa. I'm so happy for you." Rayha's voice is full of warmth; she knows a little bit about how I've struggled, especially after my mom's death, although she doesn't know it all. No one does, because I'm too ashamed to admit how lost I feel when it comes to my own daughter, how helpless when it comes to my son, or how my marriage feels like something that's broken. And I don't talk about my mom at all, because it hurts too much.

But I've told Rayha some things, and she's always sympathized. "I think this could be really good for you all," she continues. "Exactly what you need. A reset button, a new perspective."

"Yeah." She's echoing back what I told her in April; back then Rayha was worried and disappointed I was going away for the summer and she tried to hide it from me. She's a single mom with a full-time job and a special needs son, and the hectic chaos of her life has reduced our friendship over the years to phone calls, texts, and the very occasional night out, but she liked having me around in Brooklyn, just as I have needed to know she was there. Three months apart felt like a long time.

We met in a baby group when Ben was born, before her son Zane was diagnosed with childhood disintegrative disorder, one of the most heartbreaking conditions I've ever known or heard of. As a baby, Zane was cheerful and normal, with his drooly, toothless grins, his excited squeals. I don't know exactly when he started to lose his social and motor skills, but Rayha says she thinks it was around two years old. The diagnosis came a year later, and six years on, Zane is unable to walk, talk, make eye contact, or hold things.

When I think of what Rayha has to endure, and how much she loves her son, I feel nothing but humility and shame for my own petty problems. And yet she's a generous enough person to be concerned about them on my behalf, while my own efforts to help her have sometimes felt paltry by comparison.

"Have you met anyone? Any nice neighbors?" Rayha asks, and I think of Rebecca, but for some reason I don't say anything. Rayha, being such a sunny person, won't see Rebecca the way I do. She'll take her friendliness at face value, which would be easier for me to do if I hadn't been there before, time and time again. I saw the way Rebecca's lip curled when she looked at Pine Cottage, and more tellingly, when she looked at my children.

I wonder what on earth she is doing stuck here in the Finger Lakes, instead of in the Hamptons or somewhere else that's upscale and ritzy. Or perhaps the real question is, what is she doing with *me*?

The screen door bangs behind me and Katherine comes out and sits next to me on the sand. I end the call with Rayha, promising to talk later, and slide the phone into the pocket of my shorts.

"Hey!" I touch Katherine lightly on the shoulder and she shies away, just a little, but enough for me to notice. To feel it. Has she always been so distant, or has it become worse with age? She's only eleven; surely the teen angst shouldn't start now?

"So, what do you think of this place?" I ask and she shrugs, staring out at the water. "I think if we give the cottage a bit of a clean, open a few windows…" I feel optimism buoy gently in my soul, like waves lapping the shore. I need to feel it, after the fog of the last few years, when it was hard enough just to get through each day. "It could be great, Katherine." Just like Rayha said.

"Do we have to go there?" Katherine asks in a low voice, her gaze still on the water.

I don't pretend not to know what she's talking about, even though I am a little bit tempted. "It's just dinner, Kat," I say, using a nickname Kyle gave her that never quite stuck. "A couple of hours at most." I can't fault her for dreading another encounter with the mutinous Zoe, just as I am semi-dreading seeing Rebecca again, noticing how her smile doesn't reach her eyes. "If it's really terrible, we don't have to see them again."

Katherine turns to look at me suspiciously, as if she thinks I might be making a promise I can't keep. Of course we'll see the Finlays again; they're our neighbors for the summer. And perhaps I shouldn't be making such promises in the first place. Shouldn't I be encouraging Katherine to give it a chance, to make friends in a new place? I tried to when she started at school in Park Slope two years ago, but it was so hard for both of us. I want it to be better now.

"Don't worry so much," I say softly, and while I mean it as encouragement, I can see from the flash of hurt in her eyes that Katherine takes it as a criticism.

The sand feels hard and cold underneath me and so I get up, extending a hand to my daughter which she hesitantly takes, her palm sliding away from mine before they've barely touched.

"I thought we could drive into Geneseo and pick up some groceries. See the town."

Katherine hunches a shoulder. "Okay."

A few minutes later, having roused Ben from the sofa, we pile into the car and head down the narrow road around the other side of the lake, to the small town of Geneseo. I drive slowly down its main street, charmed by the faded Victorian buildings, the fountain in the middle of the street. On the other side of town we find a Walmart as big as several city blocks, and far bigger than the C-Town Supermarket we shop at in Brooklyn.

Ben and Katherine's eyes goggle as we push an enormous cart into the store, passing six-foot-high stacks of donuts in plastic containers, huge tubs of candy and caramel popcorn, sugar bomb after sugar bomb. When they were little I was much better about sugar intake; I made my own baby food and I bought organic when I could afford to. I cut up carrot sticks and julienned red pepper for their preschool snacks. At some point I stopped, maybe when my mom had her first stroke and everything started to feel like too much effort.

At some point I gave up on that persona, the mom who bustles around, volunteers endlessly, who makes homemade cakes and sneaks broccoli into brownies. And at some point Ben started inhaling sugary snacks like a junkie in need of a fix. I try not to buy them, but inevitably, exhausted, I break.

Today, though, I tell Katherine and Ben they can have one sugary snack each that will last them for the week. I wag my finger, speaking sternly, hoping to imprint this on their young minds. To show them I mean what I say, for once. "Choose carefully," I warn. "It's the only one you're going to get."

And I tell myself I'll keep to it as I load our cart with healthy vegetables and little tubs of hummus, because the only way to be different is to start doing different things.

Back home I wipe the inside of the cabinets with a damp cloth before stacking our newly bought groceries away; there is something inherently satisfying about making this place a home, even in such a small way. Katherine asked if we could buy some plants, and even though I'm no gardener, I agreed to an azalea bush in a plastic tub that we can take back to Brooklyn with us, assuming I don't kill it before then.

Twilight is settling over the lake as I clear up after our admittedly uninspired meal of frozen pizza straight from the freezer. I'll cook tomorrow, or really the day after, since tomorrow we're going to dinner at Rebecca's.

Rebecca. I picture her tall, slender form, the knife-edge pleats on her capris, the easy, enthusiastic way she had of talking. Everything about her was effortless and elegant, like she didn't have to try with anything. Life just comes to people like that, like fruit falling into your hand.

I wonder how much we'll see of her and her family this summer. Our houses might not be far apart but our lives, our worlds, surely are. I'm not sure how we'll manage to fill an evening with conversation, never mind a whole summer. But perhaps we won't see the Finlays very much.

While Katherine and Ben get ready for bed, I slip outside onto the darkened bit of beach and sit down on the hard, cool sand. I can't put it off any longer, I need to call Kyle.

His cell rings four times, and with each shrill, persistent ring I get more and more tense. We didn't part on the best of terms, although I can't say it was particularly acrimonious. It simply was—the silence, the sighs, the feeling that I'm letting him down again somehow.

The decision for me to go away for the summer was entirely my idea and it ended in a standoff, with Kyle, exhausted from working a nine-to-five job he hates, seeming bitter that I'm spending more of his money on something he won't even enjoy, and then shrugging his agreement. I know he resents that I don't work a nine-to-five job like he does, but I wanted to be there when the kids were little, and childcare was so ridiculously expensive, it wasn't even worth it for me to go back to work. Now they're in school someone still needs to be able to stay home when they're sick, and go to the school plays, and pick up the dry-cleaning, and all the rest.

Finally, just when I think it's going to switch over to voicemail, Kyle picks up. "Tessa? Are you okay?" His voice sounds abrupt.

"Hey! Yeah, I'm fine." I gaze out at a few distant, twinkling lights on the water; someone is out on a boat, enjoying the dusky, purple twilight. "We made it."

"How is it?"

"Fine. Good. The lake is beautiful." Kyle doesn't answer and I close my eyes, wondering how to navigate this moment, as with so many others. Even from hundreds of miles away the tension feels unbearable, hostility tautening the silence. "Thank you for making it happen," I say stiltedly. I feel I owe him that much at least, despite his reluctance to spend four thousand dollars on a summer rental. "I know you weren't that keen, but I think it will be really good for the kids to be here."

"I hope so," he says. "I hope it's good for all of you."

There is a subtext to the sentiment that I can't discern. Is he saying it spitefully, or is he implying that we've needed this break from each other, that he'd rather I wasn't there? Oh, the minefields. Rayha has told me that all marriages go through rocky patches; her own marriage lasted for five years before Zane's issues drove her husband away. He lives in California now and never visits. Again, I feel like I have nothing to complain about. Nothing to feel unhappy about. And yet… I can't shake the nebulous yet insistent feeling that something is very wrong. Something has been very wrong for a while, and I don't know what it is or how to fix it.

"What have you been up to?" I ask.

"Work." *What else?* is the implication, and for some reason that stings a little. I know he will miss Ben and Katherine, but he's got a lot of freedom… freedom to watch what he wants on TV, eat what he likes, take up the whole bed. *And who knows what else?*

That treacherous little voice unsettles me, because I haven't let myself think that way. I know things are bad with Kyle, but surely we haven't hit that low, I hope.

"Are you going to relax on the weekend? Go for a bike ride?" The bike that takes up half our living room and which Kyle hardly ever uses. I didn't mean it as a dig, but belatedly I realize it could sound like one.

"Maybe. It's over ninety degrees, though, so I don't know." Kyle lets out a sigh. "I'm glad you got there safely and that you're okay. Are Ben and Katherine around? I'll say hi."

I walk back inside to hand the phone to Katherine, and then Ben, half-listening to their monosyllabic replies as I wipe down the kitchen counters. Kyle hangs up, or Ben disconnects the call, I don't know which, before I can talk to him again and say goodbye, which is more of a relief than a disappointment.

"Why doesn't Daddy come here for the weekends?" Katherine suggests when she and Ben are tucked in their beds. Moths hurl themselves against the window screens with a rat-a-tat-tat sound and in the distance I hear a motorboat's engine being suddenly cut. Compared to the noise of the city, it feels eerily quiet, deathly still.

"It's expensive." I sit on the edge of Katherine's bed, one hand resting lightly on her shoulder. I made up the two narrow camp beds in the second bedroom with the mustard-yellow sheets in the linen cupboard, after airing them outside for a little while. Ben is lying on top of the sheets, already sweaty even though the night is turning cool. He radiates heat like he's full of atomic energy.

"Still." Katherine pleats the sheet beneath her fingers and I let my hand drop. "He could come up some weekends, couldn't he?"

Yes, he could, and I suggested as much when I first floated the idea of a rental past him. He agreed it was a good idea, but we made no firm plans. "Why don't you ask him? Maybe he can come up for Fourth of July, in a couple of weeks."

Katherine finally smiles properly—the first time she has since we've been here—I don't let this hurt me. She has always been closer to Kyle than me, although his affection sometimes feels easy, careless. He used to toss her up in the air and tickle her; he buys her and Ben cupcakes on Saturday mornings; he effuses praise over her spelling test without bothering to notice the mistakes.

Everything difficult falls to me—the discipline, the cleaning up, the worry. And while I admit I might have dropped the ball for a little while, wallowing in my own grief, I've picked it up now while Kyle has never really bothered, at least not the way I have.

I give Ben and Katherine a quick hug goodnight before I close the door to their bedroom and then stand in the middle of the living room, listening to the stillness, trying not to feel lonely.

Now what?

I brought all my card-making supplies here—the cardstock, the fine-tip markers, the glitter and paint and sequins. I'm in the middle of working on a congratulations card, and this would surely be a good time to finish it.

Last year, when Kyle kept telling me I needed to do something, I suggested I try my own card-making business, make use of my art degree. He was cautiously encouraging, and so I started small, setting up my own online shop on Etsy, filling a few orders. Admittedly, after buying all the supplies, I don't turn much of a profit, but it's something, and Kyle no longer asks me to take up the kind of corporate job he's suffered in since I got pregnant with Katherine.

We met, twenty years ago now, as freshmen at NYU. I was into art, Kyle into music, both of us determined to live the bohemian lifestyle, or at least a twenty-first-century version of it. Unfortunately, as we both discovered over the years, idealism didn't pay the rent. Neither did busking or selling sketches in Central Park, fun as it all was.

But the people we were then—determined, dreamy, truly believing the world was ours for the taking—have long ago left the building. I don't know where they are now.

From the bedroom I hear Ben tossing and turning, the springs of the cot creaking beneath him, and Katherine's irritated sighs. They share a room back in Brooklyn, but it's bigger than theirs here. It's hard to believe this place is a step down from our small sixth-floor walk-up, with the kitchen tacked on the back and a bathroom you can barely stand up in, but take the lake out of the equation and it is. I walk outside, breathing in the cool night air, trying to recapture some of the optimism I felt earlier. But instead worries pluck at me as I realize the hugeness of the decision I've made. A whole summer in a strange place. How are we going to fill our days? What friends will we make? What is Kyle going to do all summer?

I sit on the sand and rest my chin on my knees, gazing out at the dark water, fighting the sweep of loneliness that always threatens to crash over me in moments like this. When I feel alone and lonely, I wish I could talk to my mom, because she was always ready to listen, always got where I was coming from. She'd put her arm around my shoulders, touch her head to mine. Just thinking about her brings the sting of tears to my eyes, and I can almost imagine I am breathing in her scent—Shalimar, the citrusy notes of lemon and bergamot.

A movement from next door catches my eye, and I turn to see Rebecca silhouetted in the picture window overlooking the water. I watch her slender, willowy form; she's standing still, her head tilted upwards… what is she thinking? Feeling?

For the first time, I feel a flicker of genuine curiosity about who Rebecca is and why she's here, as well as a reluctant tug of fascination. Is her life as easy and effortless as it seems from the outside? Is she feeling lonely, standing all by herself in that big house, an evening stretching out in front of her just as it is in front of me? I feel like I'm being fanciful, that someone like Rebecca Finlay couldn't possibly feel the way I do, ever. Of course she couldn't.

CHAPTER FOUR

REBECCA

By four thirty the next day I am starting to regret my invitation to Tessa and her kids. Zoe has been particularly difficult, throwing a tantrum about missing sailing that morning, and for some reason deciding to take it out on Charlotte, who couldn't care less about being in a boat. Max was quietly, desperately relieved; sports of any kind terrify him.

And the truth is, I wouldn't have missed their sailing lessons if I hadn't been hungover. I'd ended up picking up a bottle of wine on the way home from the country club yesterday, popping it in with the milk and bread we definitely needed, ignoring Zoe's sharp gaze. She's nine years old. She probably doesn't even know what it is.

I'd only meant to have one glass, but the evening felt endless and it was a surprisingly good red, so I had three. I wasn't *drunk*. I wouldn't get drunk, not when I'm the sole caregiver for my three young children. I'm not that far gone. Not yet, anyway.

In any case, it was enough to take the edge off last night, and then for me to feel regrettably hungover this morning, so when I heard the children getting up and clattering downstairs for breakfast, I simply rolled over and put the pillow over my head. I think Charlotte must have crept in at some point, and then returned downstairs to get cereal for the others. But at ten minutes to ten Zoe came in, banging the door shut behind her, and stood at the end of my bed, scowling, her hands on her hips.

"Our sailing lesson is in *ten* minutes."

I blinked up at her blearily, feeling woolly-headed, thick-tongued. "Not today, Zoe. I can't."

"But we only go sailing twice a week!" Her voice came out in a shriek and I winced. "We'll miss it!"

"Yes," I snapped, making my head pound, "you will." And then I rolled over, my back to her. It was mean, I know, and completely unmotherly, but I didn't have it in me to do anything else. I really didn't.

I winced again as Zoe slammed the door behind her, feeling worse than ever. It was hard to believe that once I'd been a smug and complacent mother, so sure I was getting it all so very right. I didn't have a single qualm, not one. I sailed through life, and everyone followed in my wake. I started losing that person nearly four months ago, and now I feel like I'll never get her back. Like she never even existed.

After another miserable half-hour in bed, I manage to drag myself out of bed and to the shower, and then downstairs. The children are sitting in the huge family room off the kitchen, watching TV and looking morose. Bright sunshine spills through the huge picture window, a reprimand. It is a day for going outside, breathing everything in.

"Well, then," I say gaily, once I've poured my first cup of coffee and taken a much-needed sip. "Isn't it nice to have a lazy morning?"

Zoe turns to stare resentfully at me, and none of them utter a word. "Why don't you all get your suits on and we'll have a swim?"

We haven't actually done much swimming in the lake yet. We've been so busy with sailing and tennis and swim lessons at the club, using the house as little more than a place to sleep and eat.

"We're swimming at the club later," Charlotte points out with a long-suffering sigh. She is sitting on the sofa, managing to look both beautiful and bored, and very slightly disdainful.

"We can swim here too. That's why we're on the lake, isn't it?" My head is pounding but I force a smile to my lips. "I'll come in, too."

I haven't actually yet been in the water, but guilt over drinking too much and then missing sailing lessons propels me into the pale pink tankini that still has its tags, and then to walk down the dock with Charlotte, Max, and Zoe, staring uncertainly at the smooth, ripple-less expanse of lake.

"Jump in, Mommy!" Max entreats, and Zoe dares to give me a push, enough that I almost lose my balance.

I gaze down at the three faces of my children—the people most important to me in the world—and feel a sudden, strong spasm of love, momentarily blotting out the numbness that has served as a thin veneer over the swirling depths of my interior life. The warmth of the feeling reassures me.

"All right!" I take a deep breath and then a running leap off the end of the dock. The cold water closes over me, shocking my system, dragging me under. For a second I am back in Wisconsin, at the lake house where I spent all my summers, a rambling place a lot like this one, with a lake colder and deeper. I can hear my brothers' laughter, my little sister Taylor. The memory is drenched in sunshine, tinged with darkness.

I emerge from the water with something close to a gasp; Max and Charlotte are cheering and even Zoe looks vaguely impressed. It's so wonderfully easy to please children sometimes, and so woefully difficult at others. I'm glad I got it right this time.

We swim for about an hour, out to the raft and back, flipping onto our backs, diving deep, cavorting like seals. It's fun but also exhausting, and after a while I haul myself out of the water and lie belly down on the sun-warmed dock for a few moments, my legs still in the water, like a landed fish. I haven't worked out in a while, and it shows.

"Mom, are you all right?" Charlotte calls, caught between anxiety and amusement at my clumsiness, and I manage a laugh. Of course I'm all right; I have to be.

"Just need to do a few more sit-ups, I think, sweetie." With what feels like superhuman strength I manage to drag the rest of my body out of the water. I sit on the dock and watch the three of them splash around for a bit, but without me there jollying them along, they lose interest. Max has never liked the water very much, and when Zoe splashes him, he crawls onto the dock with silent dignity, shivering. Charlotte floats on her back, in her own serene world as always, above everyone and everything else.

We troop back inside to have lunch and get ready for swim lessons. And then after swimming, Tessa and her children are coming for dinner… a prospect that now fills me with weariness. I don't have the energy to perform anymore today.

But somehow I plow through the lessons, the meaningless chitchat with several club members, and even being cornered by a well-intentioned, beady-eyed forty-something who invites me to the ladies' doubles morning on Wednesday. I demur, telling her I have a long-term wrist injury.

As soon as we're out in the parking lot, Zoe turns to me and demands in a loud voice, "Why did you lie to that woman, Mommy? You don't have a wrist injury."

Both Max and Charlotte look at me curiously, Charlotte's eyebrows slightly raised, waiting for my answer. I try not to grit my teeth. "Because I don't want to play tennis but it was too difficult to explain that to her."

"Why not?"

"It's a grownup thing, Zoe. You wouldn't understand."

"You always say that when you don't feel like explaining something," she snaps, flouncing off.

God help clever children. "Get in the car," I order. "The McIntyres are coming in less than an hour."

"You could have just *said*," Charlotte says, so quietly I almost don't hear, "couldn't you? To that woman?"

I meet her calm gaze in the rearview mirror and feel a ripple of unease. All of my children are far too eagle-eyed, too sharp. "Yes," I say after a second. "I suppose I could have."

By the time five o'clock hits I'm feeling edgy and fragile. Zoe, as usual, has picked up on my mood, and has started a fight with Max, her easy target. Charlotte tries to placate them, and ends up getting in a fight with Zoe; loftily, she says she's not going to fight with babies, sending Zoe into a frenzy. In a near panic I banish them all to the playroom so I can pace the kitchen in peace.

I bought a bunch of frozen pizzas for dinner but now it feels lazy. I should have cooked some gourmet, all-organic meal. I should have made some cookies, at least. What kind of mother am I?

That's a question I try not to ask these days, much less answer. For the last few months I've just been drifting, pulled by a relentless current I can't control. But the tide is getting stronger, pulling me out into the wide open sea, and then what kind of mother will I be? What kind of woman? Still, right now I'm treading water at least, if only just.

None of the children seem particularly enthused to meet the McIntyres. Zoe's fury aside, they've been fairly nonplussed about our living arrangements here in the Finger Lakes, a place they'd never even heard of until I recklessly booked the cottage, after Josh suggested I spend the summer in Wisconsin, under the eagle eye of my parents. The Hamptons, clearly, were out. Josh agreed with my plan reluctantly; I could tell he wanted someone looking out for me, keeping me in line, but I assured him I would be fine. He wanted to believe me.

My insides clench as I picture his face, the way his mouth turned down in disappointment, his eyes clouding, every time he looked at me in the last few months. I'm failing him, I know I am. But what he doesn't realize, what I haven't been able to explain to him, is how he is failing *me*.

At exactly five o'clock I see, from the huge picture window, Tessa and her two children troop out of their house and down the path toward ours.

"Zoe, Charlotte, Max, they're coming," I sound, unintentionally, as if we're bracing for invaders.

The deck stairs creak under their combined weight and I hear their light tread: *thump, thump, thump.* Then they are standing on the deck in front of the sliding glass door, all looking rather morose, although when Tessa sees me she smiles.

She's clearly tried to make a bit of an effort with a pair of wrinkled capris and a t-shirt that has a scalloped edge, but she still looks rather dowdy, and now that I've seen her hair when it's dry, I realize what a frizzy nightmare it is. Has she not heard of straighteners?

"*Hello!*" My voice rings out in a merry peal as I open the door and step aside so they can come through. "*So* nice to see you! Thank you so much for coming."

Katherine thrusts a plate of cookies at me, mumbling something, and I continue to effuse.

"Oh, you *shouldn't* have! We'll gobble these up, I have no doubt." I laugh, the sound tinkling, crystalline. I feel myself relax into the role; my weariness slides off like a snakeskin. I've done this so many times before. It's still easy, thank God.

"Thank you for having us," Tessa says. She is standing in the middle of the family room, trying not to look uncomfortable. "It's really kind of you."

"It's no trouble, honestly." I put the plate of cookies on the counter; they look like they came out of one of those prepackaged tubes. "Just pizzas."

"We had pizza last night," Ben says, and Tessa shoots him a dagger-like look.

"You can never have too much pizza, can you?" I say lightly. "Now, my three are upstairs in the games room, why don't I show you the way?" Ben and Katherine don't move and Tessa nudges Katherine between her shoulder blades, giving her an encouraging smile while Ben starts kicking the sofa legs.

"Come on, you two," I say cheerfully. "There's a PlayStation and a pool table and air hockey, I think."

"Goodness," Tessa murmurs as we all head up to the top floor of the house, to the large playroom full of sunshine pouring in from a huge skylight. Max is sitting on one edge of a leather sofa reading, his knees drawn up to his chest, and Charlotte is on the other, her hands folded in her lap, that slightly remote, slightly superior look on her face that I know so well. Nothing fazes my oldest daughter. She's almost more in control, more cool, than I would like. Zoe stands in the center of the room, chin thrust out, defending her domain.

"Hey, everyone, Ben and Katherine are here!" I announce this as if it is the best news ever, and receive blank stares in response. Ben and Katherine lurk behind me, along with Tessa. Good grief, do I have to do *all* the work?

"Cool, air hockey!" Ben says, and he pushes past me to start sliding the puck along the table with a dangerous level of enthusiasm. Max eyes him warily, and Zoe looks furious that he's touching our stuff. Katherine and Charlotte both stay still and silent.

"Well, then." I clap my hands lightly. "I'll leave you all to it. Have fun, all right? I'll call you for dinner in about an hour."

"An hour!" A yelp from Max, who immediately looks woebegone.

"Have fun," I repeat firmly. I'm not deluding myself that they're all going to become best friends over the course of a single evening, but how hard can it be to endure an hour together?

"Do you think…" Tessa begins, but she trails off before finishing that thought as I march gaily downstairs, breathing a sigh of relief as I come into the kitchen and open the fridge.

"Now, on to really important matters. Red or white?"

"Um..."

I hold up an unopened bottle of Sauvignon Blanc from the fridge with a determined smile. "We have this or a Pinot Noir..."

"Oh, uh, white, please."

"Perfect." I take two wine glasses out of the cupboard and fill them to the brim. This is what I've been waiting for all day—that first refreshing sip. My hangover of the morning has disappeared, leaving me craving and restless.

I'm not an alcoholic, not even a high-functioning one, no matter what it might seem like right now. If I have to have that label slapped on me, then I'm a temporary, expedient one, because I know what I need to get through this period of my life. And hopefully it is just a period, and not the rest of it. Alcohol is nothing more than my finger in the hole of the dam, plugging the dark tide I'm not ready to deal with. "Cheers," I say, and hand Tessa her glass.

We move toward the sofas in the adjoining family room, and I relax into the buttery suede as I take another sip and feel the wine already start to relax me.

"Cheers." Tessa perches on the edge of her seat, her glass clutched to her chest. Her gaze keeps darting to the stairs.

"They'll be fine," I say. "Kids always get along eventually, don't they?"

"It would be nice to think so." She lets out an uncertain laugh.

"So, Tessa," I ask, settling back into my seat and taking another sip of wine, "what made you rent in the Finger Lakes?"

Tessa looks startled, as if I've asked her something personal. Perhaps I have. Who knows what sent her to Upstate New York—a worried and disappointed husband, like mine? A doomed affair? A desperate bid for freedom?

"I don't know, it just seemed like a nice place. And... the rent was cheap."

"It certainly is. About a tenth of the Hamptons." Last summer we spent nearly a hundred grand on our summer vacation, and I have friends who spend even more without blinking an eye. Not that I'd be so crass as to name actual figures.

"Oh, I bet!" Tessa manages another laugh. She obviously doesn't have money, just as I obviously do. I'd feel guilty if it weren't so glaringly apparent, a fact that doesn't need stating, even in an oblique way.

"So, tell me about yourself," I invite. "Have you lived in Brooklyn long? Do you work?" I smile, lean forward as if I'm about to hang onto her every word, because the truth is, I am interested. I want to hear about someone else's life, and I need to forget about mine. "I want to know everything."

CHAPTER FIVE

TESSA

I sit on Rebecca's sofa as she waits expectantly for my answer, seemingly interested in me. Fascinated by me. My children have been at the public school in Park Slope for a year, and I've shown up every single morning and afternoon, smiling hopefully, trying to make chitchat, and no parent there has shown as much interest in me or my life as Rebecca Finlay has. It's weird, but it's also nice. More than nice. It feels a bit like stumbling upon a sip of water when you've been in an endless social desert.

"I don't know what to say," I tell her with a laugh, because the truth is I'm too dazzled to think of anything clever. Yes, I am dazzled by Rebecca. I judged her a snob; I dismissed her as someone I could easily hate, and yet I can't help but admire her effortlessness—and envy her life. Who wouldn't? This house is huge. She's so skinny. And her children seem perfect too—a dreamy boy, a lithe, self-contained girl, and of course Zoe, who might be bratty but at least she's self-assured. I wish Katherine had a tenth of her self-confidence.

And the fact that Rebecca is interested in me… it's the icing on the cake. Almost too sweet to be true, and yet also irresistible. I am pulled in by her smile, her raised eyebrows, everything about her engaged and interested… in *me*.

"Tell me anything," she says with an insouciant shrug of her slender shoulders. She's wearing a black maxi dress that would make me look like a fat, frumpy widow, but on her it seems the height of chic. Her legs are tucked up, her feet, with magenta-polished toenails, bare. Her hair is loose about her face, and falls in a corn-silk waterfall nearly to her shoulders. Her blue eyes are wide, eyebrows perfectly plucked. She practically looks airbrushed. "I want to know it all."

Of course my mind is a blank. I know I must look slack-jawed and stupid, staring at Rebecca, while she is the poster child for a perfect mother. How could she possibly be interested in me?

"Well, you—you know I live in Brooklyn," I finally stutter, and she nods as if I've said something scintillating. I kind of love her and hate her at the same time.

"Right... which part? Not," she adds with one of her tinkling laughs and a cutely wrinkled nose, "like I know Brooklyn all that well, to be honest."

She's probably never even been there, no matter what she said yesterday. "Park Slope."

"Ooh, Park Slope. A mom from school moved there, I think..." Her forehead wrinkles.

"It's nice. Really... pretty. The Brownstones are gorgeous." I'm annoyed with how stupid I sound. I wasn't always like this. In college I had plenty of friends as well as confidence. I was so sure of myself, in a way I haven't felt in years. Where did that go? *Why* did it go? Was it motherhood, or losing my own mom, or the failure of my artistic dreams? All three perhaps, and more besides. Somehow I've ended up here, a dismal shadow of myself, but at least I am trying to step back into the light.

"I'm sure, I'm sure it is beautiful." Rebecca has almost finished her wine and her head is lolling back against the sofa. She seems utterly at ease, totally relaxed—is she not worried about our children upstairs? I've heard several thumps that have put me on edge, and I'm as worried about Ben pummeling her son as I am about Katherine being bullied or at least overshadowed by Zoe, and even Charlotte, whose quiet stillness radiates confidence rather than fear. But maybe I'm being ridiculous; maybe I'm being the kind of helicopter mom I'd assume Rebecca to be, except she doesn't seem that bothered right now.

"So, have you lived in Park Slope long?" she asks, and I get the prickly sense that this conversation is akin to pushing a boulder uphill for her, but I'm not sure how to help.

"We've been in Brooklyn for fifteen years, since we got married, but only in Park Slope for one."

"We?" One eyebrow delicately arches.

"My husband and I. Kyle." I smile, almost apologetically. I don't really want to talk about Kyle, or the way I've caught him looking at me, as if he's wondering how he ended up where he did, with someone like me. Or am I the one wondering that? I don't know anymore; I don't know what went wrong between us, only that something did. He texted this morning, just to check in, and also to ask if I'd picked up the dry-cleaning before I'd left. I hadn't.

"Kyle," Rebecca repeats, rolling the syllable around like a fine wine.

"What about you? You live in Manhattan…"

"Upper East Side." She makes a face. "Couldn't you guess?"

I laugh, surprised. "Yeah, I suppose I could."

Rebecca stretches her legs out, toes pointed like a ballet dancer. "Well, I'd hate to surprise you by being different. We've lived there for fifteen years."

"We?" I echo her, even if I can't quite manage the eyebrow arch.

For a second Rebecca's expression freezes, like she's been caught in a spotlight or even a trap, but it's so faint and fleeting that I think I must have imagined it. She tucks her legs back underneath her, the black dress floating out around her in a gentle bell shape.

"My husband, Josh. He works on Wall Street. A summer bachelor."

Summer bachelor. I think I've heard the term for Manhattan men who make a lot of money while their wives and children hightail it to the Hamptons. "I guess Kyle is one, too." I really don't like the phrase; it makes it seem as if I've been forgotten. Erased.

"Hopefully he won't get into too much trouble."

Another prospect that fills me with alarm. "So why the Finger Lakes?" I ask. I feel bolder now; perhaps it's the wine. "Because that does surprise me. I would have expected you to go to the Hamptons." Religiously.

"Oh, but I can't be that boring, can I? Anyway, I wanted a change. Something a little more low-key." Rebecca laughs, giving an easy shrug.

"Do you know anyone here?"

"No, but there's a club for swimming and tennis lessons, and the lake is right on our doorstep. What more do we need?"

"My thoughts exactly." Minus the club. Still, I am surprised. I would have expected a woman like Rebecca—although perhaps I don't actually know who a woman like Rebecca is—to demand a full summer social life, complete with cocktail parties and charity balls. Maybe she is different, deeper, than I first assumed. Maybe, just maybe, she could actually become a friend. The thought is so surprising and novel that it makes me smile.

"*I* know," Rebecca says, in that over-jolly tone she used when she invited us for dinner. "Why don't you join the club? It's a lifesaver for lessons, and keeps the kids busy. Tennis, swimming, sailing…"

For a second I wonder if she is being spiteful, like the women on the playground, eyes rounding innocently. *Oh, were you not invited?* But Rebecca is smiling at me so openly and expectantly that I realize she isn't. She just has no idea that something like that would most definitely not be in my price range.

"I'd love to," I answer, although I'm not sure I would, "but I'm sure it's way out of our league."

"Oh, trust me it's not. Honestly, the men are all in plaid pants and golf shirts. It's *ridiculous*." I stare at her, unsure how to reply, and then her expression changes. "Oh, you mean the membership fees…?" I sort of nod, and she dismisses the finances with a flick of her fingers. "Honestly, it's not that much. Peanuts compared to Manhattan." I can't think of anything to say and Rebecca shrugs, smiling. "Well, think about it, at least. You could come just for the day, as our guests, try it out. I suppose I should put the pizzas in." She uncurls herself from the sofa and moves across the room with fluid grace, the long black folds of the dress whispering about her endless legs. "Sorry it's just pizza," she calls as she takes out half a dozen gourmet pizzas, the kind that are too expensive for me to buy, from the freezer. "Especially since Ben had it last night." She says his name carelessly, like she's known him a long time, as if he's a friend.

"How were you supposed to know that?" I answer with a laugh. I walk over to the huge granite island, my half-drunk glass dangling from my fingers. I feel deliciously relaxed all of a sudden; it must be the wine. I've never been much of a drinker, and half a glass goes to my head.

"Anyway, kids never mind pizza, do they?" Rebecca rips open the boxes with quick efficiency and then slides the pizzas into the huge double oven built into one wall. She nods to my glass. "It looks like you need a refill."

"Oh, no…" I must sound halfhearted—I know I feel it—because Rebecca wags a finger at me and heads over to the huge, subzero fridge.

"Now, now! It's summer, time to relax." She tops up my glass as well as her own, dancing around the kitchen with it for a second, her eyes sparkling, her dress flaring out around her legs. "No one to impress, right? No school run, no awful PTA meetings, nothing. We're finally free. Free to be you and me." She laughs, tilting her head back so I can see the elegant column of her throat as she takes a deep sip from her glass.

I find myself smiling back and taking a similar sip; there's something wonderfully contagious about Rebecca, something that makes me want to be like her. That wonders, incredulously, if I already am, at least a little bit. It's as if her sparkles rub off, shower over me. I bask in her light.

And it's both difficult and encouraging to think that, like me, Rebecca sometimes dreads the humdrum life of the stay-at-home mom. We wouldn't change it, of course we wouldn't, but it can still feel like a life sentence. Like me, she came here to be free, to be different. And that *we* is so wonderful, the idea that we might be complicit in something. We might actually be friends. It's been a long time since I've had a friend, the kind I see every day, kick back with coffee or wine, walk home from school together. Rayha is great, but her life makes it impossible to see her very often, and texts and phone calls don't always feel like enough.

Rebecca takes another long swallow of wine. "Tell me the truth, Tessa. Aren't you the tiniest bit relieved to be away from all of it? The city, school, friends, even your husband?" She smiles mischievously. "Honestly, now. Confession time, since it's just the two of us."

"Well…" I feel nervous, shy, like a girl on a first date. "Yes, actually. I needed to get away from it all, husband included."

"Tell me about it." She groans theatrically, the sparkle still in her eyes. "*Men.*"

"What did you want to get away from?" I ask. "I mean, the most?"

"Oh, I don't know." Her gaze slides away from mine, her answer deliberately vague, and I feel disappointed by her prevarication. Then she turns back with a smile and a shrug. "Just… the whole slog of life, you know? The endless running around, the social calendar, the afterschool clubs, all the demands and endless expectations… It's all so tedious, isn't it, really?"

"Do you have any help here? Besides the lessons, I mean?"

She purses her lips. "No, not here. I had a nanny in New York, before the children were in school. But we could hardly justify it afterwards, you know? It's not like I work." She laughs and takes another sip of wine.

"Did you work before kids?"

Rebecca shrugs dismissively. "Oh, you know, nothing much. I was the receptionist for an art gallery for a few years, although my title was 'assistant curator' or something." She rolls her eyes. "My father knew a friend of a friend and got me the job. I didn't do much more than answer phones and file—my nails." She lets out a trill of laughter and then drains her glass before heading to the fridge.

"More wine," she announces, even though I haven't touched mine since she topped up our glasses, and my head is already swimming.

"None for me," I protest, and Rebecca shrugs and fills her own glass, a challenging look lighting her eyes for a second. I wonder what, if anything, seethes beneath her insouciance, because right now it feels as if something does. But then we all have secrets, don't we? Parts of ourselves we want to hide, things we don't want to remember? Even someone like Rebecca Finlay. It makes me feel even closer to her, to know that she's not actually perfect. That there might be a few hairline cracks in her life, just as there are a few gaping craters in mine.

"It's summer," she says with another expansive shrug. "Time to relax, right?"

"Right." Of course it is. I smile and Rebecca smiles back and raises her glass in a toast. A sudden thud from upstairs, followed by noisy wailing, has me freezing, a familiar panic flooding through me, and Rebecca puts down her wine glass.

"Sounds like someone had a bump," she says cheerfully, but I can't answer because my panic is turning into an icy dread.

I've been in this position before, too many times. Called into classrooms, or arriving after playdates or birthday parties, back when we still had invitations to those. A teacher's pursed lips, a mother's disapproving frown. A child's tears. And, as ever, Ben had been too loud, too rough, too rude, and didn't seem to realize—or care.

I always made him apologize, always explained he was just a little boisterous, because that's what the pediatrician said, and what I wanted and needed to believe. There were a few teachers through the years who were determined to slap a label on him, prescribe pills for what others called "natural boy energy".

I think I might have actually felt reassured by a prescription, a solution, but Kyle didn't want to go down that route, and really, underneath my fear, neither did I. Once a child is diagnosed, labeled, he never escapes it. And Ben isn't so difficult that he needs a label, or so I continue to tell myself.

When we get upstairs, Max is in the corner, cradling his hand in front of him, tears streaking his little face. Katherine is standing by the door, looking alarmed, and Zoe and Ben are in a standoff, fists clenched, glaring at each other. Charlotte is presiding, her hands flung out in a dramatic fashion as she glances quellingly between them, graceful and superior.

"Mommy, he hit Max!" Zoe screeches as soon as we appear.

"I told him he had to apologize," Charlotte says. She sounds admirably calm and adult.

"Oh dear, I'm sure it was an accident," Rebecca says as she places a placating hand on Zoe's shoulder. "Wasn't it, Ben?"

Ben shrugs and doesn't reply, and my heart sinks even further. Couldn't he have at least *said* it was? "What happened, Max?" I ask as gently as I can. *Please, please, let him say it was an accident.*

"It wasn't an accident," Zoe seethes. She is incandescent with rage, her face flushed, her eyes glittering. There is far too much emotion for her little body, just as there is far too much energy for Ben's. Perhaps they are more alike than they realize, these infantile adversaries. Max sniffs.

"He hit him with the air hockey puck," Charlotte explains. "While they were playing."

"He aimed it right at his hand," Zoe adds, her tone as vicious as her glare aimed at my son.

"I wasn't trying to hit him," Ben says sullenly. "I just wanted to play."

"Well, then," Rebecca says, as if somehow this makes it all better. She pats Max on the shoulder. "You're all right, aren't you, sweetheart? We'll put an icepack on it, just in case."

Max sniffs and nods, and then forlornly follows Rebecca downstairs. I pause, wanting to say something to smooth it all over, willing Ben to look at me, but he refuses, and so does Katherine. Zoe, however, makes it up for me by giving me a full-on glare.

Downstairs Max is sitting at the kitchen table with a pack of frozen peas pressed to his hand, looking miserable. Rebecca seems unbothered as she checks on the pizzas, and really, I'm not sure what to make of it all.

My experience with other mothers—mothers I assumed were like Rebecca—has been a groveling walk of shame, apologizing for Ben, for myself as a mother, even for existing, or at least that's what it has felt like over the years. Rebecca, however, isn't giving me the flinty-eyed glare I've come to expect and dread; she's buzzing around the kitchen, humming under her breath.

"I'm sorry…" I begin, and she gives a little laugh.

"Oh, don't worry about it. Boys will be boys, won't they?"

"I suppose." Although Max and Ben seem polar opposites in terms of how boys act.

"Max is fine, aren't you?" She tosses him a glance. "Nothing some pizza and ice cream won't cure." She takes out a stack of brightly colored plastic plates and plops them on the counter.

"Let me do something," I say. I feel the need to be useful.

"You can get the cups…" Rebecca glances around vaguely, and then the landline rings, the loud, bright trill seeming to split the air. Rebecca stills, and for a second I think she's not going to answer it, but then before she can, the ringing stops.

She is just sliding the pizzas out of the oven when we hear the sound of someone thudding down the stairs, and then Zoe comes in, brandishing a cordless phone.

"Mommy, Granny is on the phone!"

A strange look comes over Rebecca's face for a moment, and then she smiles. "All right, Zo." She throws me an apologetic glance. "Do you mind slicing the pizzas? I'll only be a minute."

"No, of course not," I say, but Rebecca is already gone, disappearing down the hall. I hear the click of a door shutting, the sound strangely final.

"Okay, then." I turn to Zoe and Max, determined to appear competent and cheerful. Zoe, at least, is not fooled. She scowls at me, her arms folded. "Why don't you call the others, Zoe? I'll start slicing."

For a second I think she's going to resist, her lower lip jutting out, but then she shrugs and stomps upstairs. I find a pizza cutter and start making slices.

A few minutes later Ben, Katherine, and Charlotte come downstairs, and I breathe a silent sigh of relief that they're all in one piece and no one is crying. Ben glances at Max and then punches him lightly in the shoulder. Max flinches, but I know Ben meant it as a sign of solidarity.

"It doesn't look too bad," he says, and I can't tell if he's trying to cheer Max up or make him feel wimpy.

I am doling out slices onto plates, the children silent and rather morose, when Rebecca comes into the kitchen, the phone in her hand, her eyes bright, her smile hard and wide.

"Right," she says, and tosses the phone aside, where it clatters onto the counter. There is something contained yet manic about her, something that feels almost feral, and apprehension ripples through me. Her eyes glitter as she nods toward the table. "Shall we eat?"

CHAPTER SIX

REBECCA

I am barely aware of my movements as I get plates and pizza and drinks, not looking anyone in the eye. Not daring to. I feel if I make contact, I might split apart; I might shatter.

"What did Granny want?" Zoe demands once the children are all, thankfully, seated around the table. "And why didn't you let us talk to Grandad?"

"Zoe, they were busy. Grandad was about to play golf." I shake my head, smiling. At least I think I do. I feel like I have to check, make sure I'm acting the way I think I'm acting. Coming across the way I need to. In my worst moments over the last four months, it's been like this—as if I am two people, checking on my visible self, making sure she still seems normal and sane, the surface as smooth as ever. I really don't know if I've succeeded.

"Why did they call?" Zoe persists. She never, ever knows when to stop. Never gauges a mood or heeds a warning, or at least chooses not to.

"Just to say hello." There is a definite edge to my voice, not that my youngest daughter notices. I'm not ready to tell her more than that. I want another glass of wine, I crave it, but I think Tessa was looking at me a bit oddly when I poured the last one, and the truth is, I am feeling more than a little buzzed. I don't need any more; never mind the craving.

"Where do your parents live?" Tessa asks.

"Wisconsin," Zoe answers for me. "On a much better lake than this one." She shoots me one of her challenging glares, which I choose to ignore.

We all sit down to eat, but if there ever was a mood, it's definitely gone a little sour. Max continues to look completely woebegone, and Zoe is still angry about Ben hitting him—whether it was by accident or not, I can't tell. Ben is only a year older than Max but feels almost twice his size, nine going on fifteen, by the looks of him. As for Katherine... she keeps darting shy looks at Charlotte, who seems to be unintentionally—or maybe not—ignoring her. They're the same age, both quiet and contained; there's no reason they can't be friends. Why does it have to be so *hard*?

Suddenly I feel impatient with everyone, ready to snap. I barely touch my pizza and I almost debate whether it's worth getting the ice cream out after; I just want everyone gone. But at the same time, I can't bear the prospect of being alone with my own thoughts, my own self.

So I pull out the tubs of ice cream and the cones and sprinkles and squirty bottles of chocolate and caramel sauce I bought on the way home from tennis, and it's enough for the kids to start looking cheerful. They make their cones and a mess along with them, and then I shoo them outside, watching them all loiter on the deck before I tap on the glass and point to the yard, with the trampoline and hammock, the grass jewel-green and soft, the dock in the distance. The sun is starting to sink to the horizon, so the lake is shimmering with golden light; it's a beautiful evening, a beautiful place. Surely five children between the ages of eight and eleven can think of something fun to do?

"Are you okay?" Tessa appears at my elbow as I'm dumping pizza crusts into the trash. She touches my arm hesitantly, like the brush of a wing, a look of concern on her face.

"Oh, I'm fine." I give a rather brittle laugh. "Parents, you know. They can be so exhausting, so full-on. My mother especially." I don't know why I feel the need to say that.

"Yes…"

"Where are your parents?"

"My dad lives in Pennsylvania, my mom has passed away." She speaks quietly, with dignity, and I get the sense of an old but deep wound, one that still pulses with pain.

"I'm sorry. When did she die?"

Tessa swallows hard. "Two years ago, but she wasn't well for a few years before that. She had a stroke six years ago, which left her paralyzed on one side, among other things."

"I'm sorry." She nods, looking down; clearly this is still hard for her. "I'm sorry," I say yet again. "That must have been tough."

"It was. But…" She draws a quick, raggedy breath. "I do know what you mean. Parents." She gives a little grimace. "My dad and I don't really get along."

"Don't you?" It's so much easier to talk about Tessa's life than think about my own. "Why not?"

"Oh. Well." She shrugs. "I left home to study art and he didn't agree with that. Said I was going to end up penniless, living in his basement."

"Well, you proved him wrong, I suppose?" Park Slope is not Pennsylvania.

"Yes, but not really." Tessa's gaze slides away from me. "I mean, I never made it as an artist, you know? Not even close."

"Not many people do." I think of the horrendous paintings and abstract sculptures in the gallery where I worked. The stuff was awful, like something a five-year-old would make with playdough, but some of them were worth thousands. "Do you work? Besides kids, I mean?"

"I have my own business, making greeting cards. Which sounds a lot more impressive than it is."

"Don't apologize for it. It's more than I do." I am reluctantly impressed. "You'll have to show me one sometime." I glance at the children, who are milling aimlessly around the yard. Charlotte tugs on Katherine's hand, whispering to her, and a shy smile blooms across her face. See, maybe it's not so hard, after all. At least not for kids.

"I'm sure you're very busy, though," Tessa says, sounding loyal even though she has no idea about my life.

"Oh, of course I'm busy," I trill sarcastically, rolling my eyes so she can share in the joke, although maybe she doesn't even know what I'm talking about. I gesture to my body. "This doesn't come easy."

"Oh." She actually blushes. "Right."

"And I do the usual charity stuff. Fundraising, galas, that sort of thing." It all sounds so boring and shallow, even to me. Especially to me. Tessa nods slowly, and I realize, not for the first time, of course, how completely different our lives are.

"So, your parents?" she asks after a moment. "What's the deal with them?"

"Oh, you know. Just the usual stuff. Bossy mother, distant dad. Well-meaning, but they love me too much." Tessa doesn't respond and I'm not willing to say more. The kitchen is clean and I want wine. "What about you, do you see your dad much?"

"Thanksgiving, Christmas." She shrugs. "The usual."

"What about your husband's family?"

"Not much there. Kyle's parents divorced when he was little. His dad moved to Abu Dhabi for some corporate job and his mom moved out to Arizona. She's got a new husband and is kind of... I don't know, wacky."

"Power crystals and positive energy kind of thing?"

Tessa laughs, a little relieved that I seem to get it. "Yeah."

"My aunt was into all that for a little while." I shake my head in memory. "We went to her house for Christmas one year and

we all had to sit in a circle, holding hands and feeling the energy."
Although none of that sounds all that bad now. Maybe it would
help. Before Helen got into all that New Age stuff, she was a
manic-depressive. Now she's got to be doing better than I am.

"So, will your husband come visit during the summer?" Tessa
asks, startling me out of my brief reverie.

"Josh? He'll come up for part of August." Although we haven't
talked about it since he paid for this place. "He's busy, you know,
making money." I laugh, rolling my eyes, inviting her to share
the ridiculousness of it all once again, the over-the-topness of my
life, but Tessa just smiles faintly.

"Looks like the natives are restless," I say with a nod outside.
Ben is trying to start a game of tag but nobody's interested, and
in a minute I suspect Zoe is going to deck him.

"Yes, I should get back." Tessa gives me a quick smile before
hurrying outside. I feel guilty because I think I made it obvious
that I wanted her to go, but I can't handle any more. I know I
can't. The phone call was the last straw, the damn nail.

*We'd love to see the children, Rebecca. And Josh called... we're
worried about you, up there on your own. He is too... what if we
came for the weekend?*

It doesn't take long for Tessa to tear Ben and Katherine away,
and within a few minutes they are saying their dutiful goodbyes.
Some guilty urge makes me reach for Tessa's hand, surprising her.

"Think about coming to the club with us tomorrow," I say,
squeezing her fingers. "It would be fun."

Tessa murmurs something noncommittal in reply, and then they
are gone, shuffling down the meandering path between our cottages.

"I don't like them," Zoe announces before they've cleared
the trees.

"*Zoe!*" I usher the children inside, where they can't be overheard. "Where are your manners?"

"Ben is a bully."

"So are you," I return before I can think better of it, and Zoe's face crumples before her chin lifts a notch. "What happened upstairs, anyway?"

Zoe launches into a diatribe about how Ben forced Max to play air hockey, and then slammed the puck into his hand on purpose, and I glance at Charlotte for confirmation. She shrugs.

"I think it was an accident, but you know Max. He didn't want to play and Ben said he had to."

"Couldn't he just say no?"

Charlotte shrugs, and I sigh. Max is a pushover, the opposite of Zoe, both challenging in their own ways. He probably wanted to please Ben, or maybe just appease him.

I turn to Max, who has just come inside, for a final opinion. "What happened with Ben, Max?"

"I shouldn't have had my hand there," he whispers, and my heart contracts with guilt and love. Poor little Max. I pull him into a quick hug, and he burrows his head into my stomach. "Are they going to come again?"

I stroke his silky hair, the same rumpled chestnut brown as Josh's. "You might all learn to get along, you know. They are our neighbors, we should be friends."

"*Friends?*" Zoe sounds utterly disbelieving.

"What about you, Charlotte?" I ask. "You and Katherine are the same age. Did you get along?"

"Yeah, I guess." Charlotte doesn't sound convinced.

"Katherine is *weird*," Zoe declares. "She kept chewing her hair, and that is just gross. Plus, she bites her nails and it was disgusting. She kept spitting little bits out, and her fingers were all raggedy and bleedy."

"Really, Zoe, you're being a bit critical, don't you think?" Zoe pouts and I press my fingers to my temple. It's only seven o'clock, ages until they go to bed. Another endless evening, trying to get through it, minute by minute.

"What did Granny and Grandad want?" Charlotte asks, and my temple throbs.

"They want to come visit."

"Really?" Charlotte's face brightens, as do Zoe and Max's. They love, love, *love* their grandparents. Mom is all about the presents and dinners out, and Dad is full of fun and jokes, tickles and games of hide and seek. My stomach cramps at the thought of dealing with it all now.

"When are they coming? And for how long?" Zoe demands, firing the questions like bullets.

"For the Fourth of July weekend." Which is only in two weeks, and I'm definitely not ready to see them. It was hard enough telling them back in the spring that we wouldn't be coming to the lake house for a week in August, the way we always did. That we wanted to stay here. Josh made it harder by first floating the idea by them of me coming for the whole summer. When I refused, he thought it was because I didn't want them to know I'd been drinking too much, as if I have a problem I need to hide. As if *I'm* the problem.

We argued over that; he insisted I'd be better with my parents, and I told him I wouldn't. "Are you actually worried?" I challenged. "Do you think I can't cope on my own, just because I drank a little too much at one stupid party?"

I held his gaze, defiant and a little sneering, even though inside I wanted him to say, *Yes, Rebecca. I am afraid of that. I see something is wrong, I want to help you.*

But of course he didn't. He's not a mind reader and I can be a very good actress.

"No, of course not, Rebecca," he said. "I know you'll be fine. I just want you to have some support..."

"Maybe I just need some time on my own. Time away from this rat race, all the gossip and one-upmanship. And trust me, being with my parents would *not* help. It would just make everything more difficult, managing them as well as the kids. You know that, Josh."

And so he relented, as I knew he would, and I felt both relieved and more alone than ever. I can never win.

"Why don't you all get ready for bed?" I suggest now, an edge of desperation creeping into my voice.

"But Mom, it's only seven." Charlotte frowns, her eyes narrowing as she looks at me. "Are you okay?"

"Yes, yes, I'm fine. Sorry, it just feels later to me." I turn away, mindlessly swiping at the already clean counters.

After a few restless minutes the three of them drift upstairs to watch TV, and I finish needlessly tidying the kitchen, taking the time to get at the grease under the stove's edges, by the sink. By some extreme force of will I do not finish the bottle of wine in the fridge. I want to, God knows, but I'm not an alcoholic and I'm not going to wake up hungover tomorrow. Again.

When the kitchen is gleaming and spotless and I can't put it off any longer, I head upstairs to my bedroom. It's an ocean of cream carpet and Holiday Inn décor, but at least it's spacious, and the adjoining bathroom is luxurious—and private.

I close the bathroom door. Lock it. Take a deep breath. My heart is starting to drum, the blood surging through my veins in a way that almost feels pleasurable. The anticipation is almost the best part, although with it comes a healthy dose of shame. This is not who I am, not remotely, and yet it is. Now it is.

It only started a few months ago, and then partly by accident. I remind myself of this as if it's a justification. As if it makes a difference. I was washing some crystal wineglasses—ones I wouldn't trust to the housekeeper—and one slipped and shattered in the sink, a shard sinking into my palm. I watched the blood well up in a dark crimson crescent and something in me eased and expanded.

Since then I've tried to keep myself from moments like this, and mostly I succeed. Half a dozen times at most have I succumbed. I'm not some angsty teen obsessing over her Instagram likes, after all. But tonight my parents' phone call has nudged me over the edge—my mother's determined cheer, the underlying note of reproof.

She loves me so much, and right now I'm such a disappointment. As for my father... he was as jovial as ever, easygoing in a way that doesn't cost him anything. "All right there, Becky?" He's the only one who has ever called me that, an endearment from my childhood that I used to love.

I run the water to cover any noise and then carefully, almost reverently, I take a razor blade from the top drawer of the vanity unit, hidden behind a box of tampons. Guilt and anticipation churn inside me. I take another breath and gaze at myself critically in the mirror.

After studying the few faint and not-so-faint lines on my arms and legs that have appeared over the last few months, I finally choose the curve of my hip. It's covered by my swimsuit, so no one will see it. My little secret. One of many.

I honestly don't know why it feels good—the quick, sharp pain, the welling up of blood, a crimson line stark against my pale flesh. It's a release of pressure, I suppose; as soon as I make the cut, I feel the flood of relief, a post-adrenalin rush, and I nearly sag with it. My eyes flutter closed as the stinging pain sharpens to an exquisite point and then recedes to a dull throb. I need this. I know it's stupid and wrong, but I need this.

I press my thumb against the cut to absorb the blood and let my breathing even out. I try not to think how bad this looks, how sick it should feel. I'm thirty-eight years old, for heaven's sake. I know, I absolutely know, I shouldn't be doing this. I shouldn't even be thinking about it. The shame floods in, following the relief. *What is happening to me?*

A sudden pounding on the bathroom door has me jerking upright, and a few drops of blood splash onto the white tile. I cut too close to the bone; it's going to bleed a lot. More than I meant it to.

"Mom! Mom!" It's Charlotte, sounding panicked. "Zoe and Max were fighting and Max hit his head on the corner of the air hockey table. There's blood everywhere."

"I'm coming." I feel as if I'm coming down from a high, not that I've ever taken drugs. I grab a Band-Aid and stick it on my hip, but blood soaks through it almost immediately. I stick another one on and then I pull down my dress, unlock the door, and run upstairs, Charlotte following behind.

Poor Max is on the floor, his face white, blood pouring from a cut above his eye. Zoe is looking both terrified and mutinous.

"Oh, Max. Maxie." I cradle him in my arms as I inspect the cut, feeling queasy. You would think I'd have a stronger stomach for this, considering what I was just up to, but it's different when it's mine. When I'm in control of that one thing, at least.

"I didn't mean to," Zoe says in a high, thin voice. "I really didn't, Mommy."

"I know you didn't, sweetheart." I give her a reassuring smile; she looks sick with guilt. Looking back at Max, I realize I'm going to have to go to ER, because the cut needs stitches, just as I realize after three glasses of wine I probably shouldn't drive. *How* did I end up in this place? It's so ridiculous, so not me, I'd almost laugh but of course I can't. There's nothing remotely funny going on here.

"Mom?" Charlotte bends down to peer into my face. "What are you going to do?"

All three of them wait for me to answer, to act. To take care of everything and make it all better, because that is what mothers do, what children expect, and yet I feel paralyzed; my head throbs and my hip stings. I know I can't drive.

"We'll ask Tessa to drive us to the hospital," I say.

Zoe lets out a sound of disgust. "Why can't you just drive yourself?"

I take a deep, steadying breath. Max is bleeding onto my hands, looking paler and more miserable by the second. "I had some wine with dinner, Zoe. It wouldn't be safe."

"What do you mean? Why wouldn't it be safe?"

"Because..." I'm at a loss.

"Because she's had too much alcohol to drive," Charlotte fills in. I can't tell anything from her tone.

"You're not *drunk*?" Zoe exclaims.

"Of course I'm not drunk, I'm just trying to be safe." Charlotte's eyes have narrowed, her look calmly assessing. "We need to go," I say as decisively as I can. "Poor Max is bleeding everywhere, and we're just sitting here talking." I scoop him up in my arms, noticing the bloodstain on the cream carpet I'll have to deal with later.

I hold Max all the way to Tessa's, half-amazed at how light he is. Charlotte and Zoe trail behind me, and we all skid to a halt in front of the cottage's shabby front door.

Tessa's jaw drops almost comically when she opens the door a few seconds later. "Rebecca... what's happened?"

I realize that holding Max might be a little extreme, and I gently put him on his feet. "Max hit his head, and I think he needs stitches. And... well..." I try for something like a smile, but I don't think I manage it. "I had a couple of glasses of wine..." So did Tessa, although I know she didn't drink as much as I did. Surely she's up for driving?

Then, way too late, I realize I could have called a cab. Why didn't I think of that earlier? I could have avoided this whole messy awkwardness, this sense of being beholden to a near-stranger.

"Of course, of course," Tessa says quickly. "But I'll have to bring Ben and Katherine, and my car's not big enough..."

"You can take mine." Too late now to backtrack. "Thank you so much. I can't tell you how much I appreciate it."

"Okay, just let me get the kids."

Katherine has appeared in the doorway of her bedroom like a shadow, staring at us with wide, dark eyes. She'd be pretty if she didn't look so abject all the time. Why is she so shy? Ben lets out a near-roar of protest when Tessa tells him he has to move off the sofa.

After a few minutes of scuffling they are out the door, and we are heading back toward our house and car.

Now that I'm out in the fresh air, I feel sober enough to drive, but maybe I'm not and I can hardly tell Tessa I am, can I? Still, I don't like having to depend on her kindness and charity. That wasn't how I envisioned our quasi-friendship working.

While everyone clambers in the car I run in to get my purse and keys. I catch a glimpse of my reflection in the sliding glass door; I look a little crazed. But maybe that's expected, considering the situation.

Tessa is waiting behind the wheel when I return and hand her the keys. The children are all in the back, everyone silent and in various bad moods, judging by their expressions. No one wants a trip to ER, especially on a night like this one, the sky dark and starry, the air like warm velvet. It's a night for sitting outside under the stars, tilting your head up to the sky and soaking it all in.

"Are we going to Geneseo?" Tessa asks, her uncertain voice breaking the tense stillness.

"No, Dansville. That's where the hospital is." I swipe my phone and open the map app. "I'll get directions."

I realize I need to do some damage control, especially with Tessa looking at me so uncertainly. I can't have her guessing what's going on, or seeing who I really am. Who I've become, messy and desperate and splintering apart. Somehow I've got to prove to her that I'm still okay. Still me... whoever that is.

CHAPTER SEVEN

TESSA

I can't believe I'm driving Rebecca's absolutely enormous SUV, the five kids in the back, Max bleeding quietly into the leather upholstery by the looks of it. And Rebecca looks as if she's lost in outer space. I didn't think she had that much wine, but maybe she had.

I'm not even sure what strikes me as so odd; she looks as elegant as ever, not a hair out of place, her maxi dress floating around her in a dark cloud. When Charlotte asks her how long it will take to get to the hospital, she answers in a cheerful voice and gives her daughter a reassuring smile, in control even of this anxiety-ridden moment.

Maybe it's all in my mind, this weird sensation that something is not quite right with Rebecca. That something feels… off. It must be all in my mind, because how could Rebecca be anything but perfect? She practically sparkles.

"I'm so sorry about this," Rebecca says, sliding me a quick, knowing smile. "Honestly. If I'd ever thought something like this… and you know, I actually think I could drive. I mean, I'm not falling down, am I?" She lets out one of her crystalline little laughs. "But better safe than sorry, right? Especially when children are involved." Her voice catches a bit, and when I glance over, she gives me a slightly watery smile. I smile back.

Of course nothing is off here. I'm probably the one who is acting weird, because everything about this evening has been beyond my admittedly limited realm of experience. Rebecca turns toward the backseat.

"Everyone all right back there?" she calls cheerfully, and receives a couple of monosyllabic replies.

As soon as we'd left the Finlays' house, I grilled Katherine about what happened upstairs. I meant to wait a bit, see if the topic came up naturally, but of course it didn't. Katherine just muttered something about Ben playing too rough, and Ben refused to say anything at all, except that Max was a "total girl".

"Don't *say* that. And how did you hit his hand, was it on purpose?" I couldn't keep from pressing.

Ben gave me a disgusted look. "Why would I hit his hand on purpose?" he said, heartening me a little. "He couldn't play with me then."

I decided to leave it. "And what about you, Katherine? Did you get along with Charlotte? She seems nice, doesn't she?"

"I guess so," Katherine answered dubiously.

Back in the darkened cottage, which felt even smaller and more depressing after spending the evening in the grandiose luxury of Rebecca's house, I felt the vestiges of sadness swirl around me in a mist. I always get like that when talking about my mom. Remembering how hard it was while trying not to admit the depths of my grief, because somehow that doesn't feel appropriate. People don't really want to know, even if they ask.

Katherine curled up with a book while Ben pinged around the house, a pinball of energy, and I drifted. I felt as if I couldn't settle to anything; memories flitted through my mind, of my mom and me painting my first car blue with daisies all over the hood; and then, ten years later, that first stroke, the look of confused shock in her eyes as she struggled to speak, to regain a fraction of all the capabilities she'd taken for granted.

The memories feel twined together, so sometimes I can't remember when my mom was healthy, and when she wasn't.

Sometimes I picture her sitting in the kitchen when I was a teenager, waiting for me to get home from school and tell her about my day, as I always did. But in the memory her face is frozen in that paralyzed rictus and her speech is garbled, even though she didn't have her first stroke until I was in my late twenties, just after Katherine was born. It's bizarre, how the memories shift and slide, and everything feels cloudy and uncertain. What happened before, and what happened after? She was in the delivery room when I had Katherine, her stroke still something unimaginable, and yet I picture her there with her shuffling, one-sided walk, only able to move one side of her body. It scares me, how things blur together. Why can't I remember her the way she really was, the way I want to?

I'd just started getting the kids' pajamas out when Rebecca knocked at the door, and now I'm here, torn from my sadness.

We don't speak much on the way to the hospital; I'm concentrating on maneuvering the huge car along the darkened country roads, a nerve-wracking proposition at the best of times, and Rebecca keeps looking back at the children and chirping some motherly encouragement. Max's forehead has stopped bleeding, but it still looks like an ugly gash, and it will almost definitely need a couple of stitches.

We finally make it to the hospital, and in we troop, to find it half-full of people in various degrees of distress. With a sinking sensation, I realize we could be here for hours. All night, even. It hadn't occurred to me that we'd have to wait once we got to the ER, but what else are we going to do? I can't afford a cab back to the cottage, and in any case, it seems callous just to leave Rebecca and her children the minute we've arrived. It also feels a little weird to stay. How well do we know each other after one night?

We perch on plastic chairs while the minutes tick by, everything feeling endless. Finally, Max's name is called, and I wait with Charlotte and Zoe, Katherine and Ben while Rebecca takes him in.

"How did he cut his head, anyway?" I ask, just to fill the silence, and Zoe glares at me. Clearly that was not the right question to ask.

"He fell and hit his head on the corner of the air hockey table," Charlotte says, and then looks away. Fell, or was pushed? Zoe's lips tremble and she presses them together. I almost feel sorry for her, whatever she did or didn't do. For a second she looks vulnerable rather than angry.

"Accidents happen," I say, and too late I realize it sounds as if I am reminding them about Ben's *accident* with Max. Maybe I am.

Another half-hour drags by and then finally Rebecca comes out with Max; he is sporting a gauze bandage over his forehead that covers half his eye.

"Six stitches," Rebecca says with a quick smile. "Not too bad. They'll come out in a week."

"How are you doing, Max?" I ask, and he gives me a wobbly smile. I feel a sudden burst of affection for this quiet, shy boy, so unlike my own son with all of his boisterous energy. I smile back and pat his shoulder. "You're very brave, you know."

"Thanks," he says in a small voice.

"Can we go now?" Zoe asks, and we all troop back to the car.

It's after ten o'clock now and I am exhausted. By the time we reach the lake, it's nearly eleven, and Max, Katherine, and Charlotte have fallen asleep in the car; their heads all drooping, and only Ben and Zoe are awake, seeming, as ever, to bristle with energy.

"Thank you so much, Tessa," Rebecca says. "You've been a lifesaver. I realized too late that I should have called a cab." She rolls her eyes in good-natured bemusement. "It would have been so much easier for you—"

"No, no," I say. "I was glad to help. Honestly."

Rebecca reaches over and clasps my hand, her nails digging into my skin a little. "Come with us to the club tomorrow," she says, a note of urgency in her voice. "Try it out for a day." She smiles and squeezes my hand, lowering her voice. "To tell you the truth, I feel like you might be my lifesaver this summer."

It's such an unexpected comment that I don't know how to respond. I feel pleased, and flattered, and also a tiny bit wary. Lifesaver? Me? *How?*

"Please do come," Rebecca says, and so I smile and nod.

"Sure, of course. We'll check it out tomorrow."

"Wonderful." One more hand squeeze and then she gets out of the car. "Thank you."

It feels as if I am doing her a favor, rather than the other way around. Something warm blooms in my chest; maybe Rebecca actually needs me. Maybe this friendship won't be as one-sided as it has felt so far; we will both have something to offer the other.

It's so late that Ben and Katherine don't protest as I usher them to bed, Katherine still half-asleep from the car. Even though I'm tired, I can't sleep. I lie in bed and stare at the ceiling, listening to the gentle sounds from outside—the lap of the lake, the hoot of an owl, the rustle of the wind in the pine trees. It's so peaceful, and yet I feel all jumbled up inside—apprehensive and excited for tomorrow, for the whole summer that lies in front of me, now shimmering with a new and yet unknown possibility.

You might be my lifesaver this summer. I feel like double-checking she said that, asking her again. *Did you really mean that?*

Eleven years into motherhood, and I still don't really get why friendship hasn't come easily to me. It did before, and there have been so many opportunities post-kids—baby groups, toddler groups, Mommy and Me swimming, singing, dancing, and pottery. Basically, whatever you want to do with your child in tow, you can. And there are plenty of mothers around.

Brooklyn is filled with women with a baby or two or three, in slings and Bugaboo strollers, walking with determination and purpose down the sidewalk, their Starbucks skinny lattes anchored firmly in their strollers' drink holders, smartphones pressed to their ears.

Maybe that's been part of the problem. I've never felt nearly as busy and self-assured as those other moms, and even less so since my own mom's death.

I looked to her for reassurance, the knowing laugh that yes, all mothers felt the same; she helped me when Katherine was born, told me that nursing never came easy, comforted me that every new mother felt as if she was floundering in the deep and the dark. But then she had a stroke when Katherine was just a few months old; she spent the next nine years trying to get herself back and losing more all the time, hope battling despair and eventually losing.

I felt as if I were losing myself at the same time; I dropped everything to be with her when she needed help with recovery and rehab, because my dad was hopeless. He hated hospitals, and he didn't know how to deal with a wife who had to learn how to talk, to walk, to *be*. When she needed him most, he let her down, and I find that unforgiveable.

But it was hard, harder perhaps than I can even remember, to balance small children with a mother who needed me desperately; to beg babysitters to stay a little bit longer while I made the two-hour trip to Pennsylvania, or keeping Katherine or Ben in a baby carrier while I took my mom to rehab, helped her to stagger along or try to hold a spoon. Kyle, to his credit, picked up the slack where he could.

In any case, I tell myself now, motherhood hasn't been as isolating as it has sometimes felt—there's Rayha, who has been *my* lifesaver for the last eight years, and a few other moms along the way—a friend in Katherine's preschool, a mom whose son went to the same Minecraft club as Ben last year. I've managed, and I've learned along the way, but it hasn't felt as natural or easy as I'd expected, as I'd hoped. At the center of myself I've felt a deep, dark well of loneliness that I'm scared to peer into, frightened even to acknowledge. I watch the busy moms bustle down the street and wonder if any one of them ever knows what that feels like.

Does Rebecca?

I almost think that she does, at least a little, and then I tell myself I'm being fanciful, crazy even. How could someone like Rebecca ever feel the way I do?

In any case, I'm not that alone. I have Kyle… except lately he's made me feel more alone, the way he looks at me, like he doesn't know how we ended up together, how we got here. It's a relief to be away from him, even as that thought makes me feel guilty. I know it's not how I should think about my husband.

But I'm here now, trying to be different. Trying to find the hope that has eluded me for so long. And this summer I am determined to find it.

Eventually I fall asleep, to waken with sunlight streaming through the windows, as I forgot to close the curtains last night. As dark and gloomy as this little cottage can be, at seven in the morning, on a perfectly sunny day, it seems lovely. The whole world does.

Ben and Katherine are still asleep, so I tiptoe to the kitchen and make a cup of coffee as quietly as I can, not wanting to wake them, or have this moment of stillness and peace be shattered.

I take my coffee outside, dragging one of the plastic chairs toward the lake, where I can catch the sunshine. The morning is cool and fresh, the sand slightly damp with dew, everything sparkling. I feel filled with possibility, buoyant with hope. Maybe this summer will be the best thing that's ever happened to me. To us.

Two minutes later, Ben's demanding cry splits the air: "Where are the Froot Loops?"

Rebecca didn't give us a time to meet to go to the club, so I spend the morning in a dither of waiting, unsure whether we should head over to their house or wait to be summoned. With every passing moment, I start to doubt.

Do I really want to go to some ritzy country club? We won't fit in. I don't even know what to do in a place like that. And what if the kids fight again? It seems all too likely.

Katherine certainly doesn't want to go to the club; she's asked me all morning whether we have to, if she can stay home by herself. I'm tempted to let her, simply to put her out of her misery, but I don't. Some hard kernel of determination inside me insists that Katherine, just like me, needs to step outside of her little comfort zone, spread her fragile, still-damp butterfly wings, and see what happens.

But for the moment, nothing is. I glance over at Rebecca's house throughout the morning as the kids mooch about, and it remains silent, a hulk of slate blue perching on the tranquil water. No kids come running out; there's no slap of a screen door or splash into the lake.

Then, in the middle of the afternoon, when I'm lazing on our little strip of scrubby beach, flipping through a self-help book on living in the present that Rayha recommended, with the children closeted in the cottage, Katherine reading a fantasy book and Ben playing some shoot-everything-that-moves game, Rebecca leaves her house and marches over like a mama duck with her three ducklings behind her.

She's wearing a fitted pink linen sundress that looks expensive and immaculate, designer sunglasses covering her eyes. Max, Charlotte, and Zoe are all in swimsuits with terrycloth cover-ups over them, holding monogrammed tote bags for their towels.

I scramble up from where I'm sitting on a beach towel, a flurry of nerves swirling in me. After the long, empty stretch of the morning, I had half-convinced myself that Rebecca had changed her mind, that she wouldn't be coming after all. Now I wave before hurrying inside and barking to Ben and Katherine to get ready, that we're going.

"But I don't *want* to go," Katherine protests, and Ben doesn't move from his sprawled position on the sofa.

"Come on, come on, it will be fun." I'm starting to sound frantic as I grab beach towels and swimsuits and check my reflection all at the same time.

"Hello…?" Rebecca's voice is light and musical as she gives a perfunctory, pretend knock on the door and then steps inside. "Hey, gang!" she says, and part of me boggles yet again at how effortlessly she can carry anything off. Who calls anyone "gang" these days? She sounds like she's in an episode of *Scooby-Doo*, and yet somehow it works. *She* works. She looks beautiful, glowing with health and confidence, her smile beamed right at me.

"Hey, Rebecca! We'll be ready in a sec."

"Perfect." She ushers her three in, smiling all the while, white teeth gleaming. "Do you want to come with us, or follow me in your car?"

"Oh, um…" My mind is spinning. "We'll follow you, I guess."

"Great." She waggles her fingers at Ben and Katherine, who are simply staring at her. "See you soon."

The Finlays leave in a drift of flowery perfume and coconut-scented sunscreen. When she's gone, I deflate a little. Somehow, being in her presence feels like stepping into the light, or a magnetic force field, helplessly compelled toward her, basking in the rays. When she leaves, I step back into the shadows, whether I want to or not.

"All right, so, we'd better get a move on—"

"Mom, I really don't want to go." Katherine gazes at me imploringly, her fingers knotted together. "Please. Please don't make me. I don't even like swimming. I don't want to take lessons."

"It will be good for you. You need to get out there, Katherine—"

"*Please*." She looks anguished, but I harden my heart. Katherine has never wanted to do anything in her life, ever. No lessons, no afterschool clubs, no friends over, no sleepovers. All she has ever wanted, it seems, is to be left alone, which is its own brand of neediness. Sometimes her solitariness was a godsend, when I had to cope with my mom, when grief overwhelmed me, but now I know I need to help her come out of her shell.

"We're going," I say, and my voice comes out firm. "Get your things."

We drive in silence to the club, a sprawling complex of shingled buildings with endless manicured lawns on the opposite side of the lake. I am intimidated before I even set foot in the place: it reeks of money and privilege. Rebecca sails through the doors, pausing only to briefly look behind and see if I am following.

I hesitate, at a loss. Then Rebecca smiles, and for a second I feel like she understands my uncertainty. Maybe she even shared it, once upon a time.

I take Katherine's hand, which is cold and clammy, and give it a squeeze. We can do this. It's just a country club, after all. Not a field of lava, no matter how Katherine is acting.

By the time I walk through the doors into the plush lobby, with its leather club chairs and glass cases of trophies, the noticeboards full of glossy photos and announcements of golf and tennis championships and champagne charity evenings, Rebecca is at the membership desk, looking animated. When I walk up to her, she turns to me with a bright smile.

"So, it's all sorted. All you need to do is get your photos taken and we're good to go."

"Photos…?"

"For your membership cards."

"Oh, but…" This is all going so fast. "Do we really need cards just for the day?"

"Oh, what's the point in one day, really?" Rebecca answers with a laugh. "No, I've already paid for you to have a summer membership, just like us. Ben and Katherine are booked into swimming lessons every day, and tennis three times a week."

Next to me Katherine stiffens, her face resembling Munch's *The Scream*. I stare helplessly at Rebecca.

"I can't let you do that…" A summer membership is surely in the hundreds or even thousands of dollars, plus the cost of all the lessons on top of that. I'm stunned by how easily she seems to have arranged and expected it, to have our summer plans fall completely in line with hers. Stunned and a little bit annoyed. What if we had other plans? Or does she simply assume that of course we don't?

"You can," Rebecca replies briskly. "I just did it. And really, you're helping me." I have trouble believing that. "Plus, all the kids can be together." Even if they don't want to be. I have no idea what to say, or even what to feel. Still, I try.

"Rebecca, it's too much, really. I can't possibly—"

"Right." Rebecca steamrollers over me as she claps her hands. "Zoe and Charlotte, show Katherine where the girls' changing room is. Max, you can show Ben." Max and Katherine are both looking horrified by this prospect, Charlotte and Ben nonplussed, and Zoe, as usual, furious about something. It's clearly her default setting. "And we can go to the bar and get a cocktail," Rebecca says and starts to steer me away.

"I think I should just check on them," I finally work up the gumption to say, as we reach the tinted glass doors of the bar area, with its upholstered leather and gleaming mahogany. My head is still spinning at how fast everything has seemed to be sorted. "You know, first time for them and all that. And what about Max? Can he swim with his stitches in?"

"Max will be fine. I told him not to get his head wet. But you go check on your two if you like." Rebecca waves a hand toward the outdoor pool behind the main building. "Go ahead, I'll order our drinks."

"Okay, thanks." I'll talk to her afterwards, I decide, and tell her that I can't possibly allow her to pay the membership. Maybe I can offer to pay some of it, although I doubt I can afford even that. I wander down several plushly carpeted hallways before I find a bank of French doors leading out to the pool area. There are about forty kids getting ready for lessons, all sitting on the edge of the pool, dangling their legs into the sparkling blue water. Sunlight glints off everything, making my eyes hurt.

It takes me a few seconds, but I see Ben and Max, and then Charlotte and Zoe lining up for their lessons. Katherine is not with them, and my stomach cramps. I walk up to them, trying for a smile.

"Hey! Where's Katherine?"

"She didn't want to come," Zoe says, jutting her chin out. "Can she even swim?"

"She's in the changing rooms," Charlotte adds. "We did ask if she wanted to come with us."

This always happens to Katherine. She's always being left out, left behind, and yet I tell myself now that it's not a big deal—it doesn't have to be a big deal.

"I'll just go have a look." I find the women's changing room; it's empty of people, filled with neatly or not so neatly piled clothes—t-shirts, shorts, sneakers, and flip-flops. I don't see Katherine anywhere.

"Katherine?" I call softly into the humid stillness. "Sweetheart?" There's no answer, but then I hear a loud sniff from one of the changing cubicles. I knock softly on the door. "Katherine? Is that you?"

"Yes." Her voice is small and wobbly and my heart twists within me. My poor, miserable daughter. Why does everything have to be so hard for her? I can't help but feel like it's my fault somehow, even as I battle a sense of frustration at her inability to just *try*.

"Come on out, sweetie. It's just a swimming lesson."

"It's not just a swimming lesson," Katherine practically whimpers. "I don't know anyone here—"

"You know Zoe and Charlotte."

"I hate Zoe."

"Katherine, you can't hide in there forever. Some things in life are tough, but they are worth doing." I feel like I'm spouting cheap sayings but I believe them; I try to. "I know you think I'm being mean by making you do this—"

"You *are* mean."

"Katherine, at some point you've *got* to try." I sound exasperated rather than encouraging, and inwardly I cringe. This is as hard for me as it is for her. "Please come out. It will be worse for you if you don't, you know, because then everyone will wonder what happened. You can do this, sweetheart. I know you can."

"For the whole summer?" she flings at me, peeking through the crack in the door.

"Let's take one day at a time, okay?"

"But I never even said I wanted swim lessons!"

"But you never want to do anything, Katherine." I can't keep a slight edge from my voice, and Katherine notices; she always does. She gives me a silent, wounded look and I take a deep breath, gathering my patience as well as my persuasiveness. "Look, you can't hide in the locker room all afternoon. That would be worse than going out there and making a fool of yourself, which you won't. I know you won't. Please, sweetheart. Do this for me, but more importantly, do it for yourself. I know you don't get along with Zoe, but Charlotte is nice, isn't she?" Katherine jerks her head in what I decide to take for assent. "Come on, then. Before the lesson has started."

What feels like an age passes and then slowly, so slowly, Katherine comes out of the locker room and slouches toward the pool.

Her face is blotchy and her swimsuit is both baggy and tight in the wrong places. I almost relent, even though I've won; I almost spirit us all back to the car, away from this shiny, new world, to a place where we were lonely but safe. But then I don't, because I can't be in that place anymore; it was suffocating me. It was suffocating all of us. I need to be somewhere different, to be *someone* different, and maybe, just maybe, Rebecca Finlay, of all people, can help me achieve that.

So I square my shoulders and give Katherine what I hope is an encouraging smile. "The teacher will be waiting for you, sweetheart. It's going to be fine."

Five minutes later, after making sure both Katherine and Ben are settled in their lessons—Katherine abject and Ben hyper—I find my way back to the bar. Rebecca smiles and waves gaily before gesturing to the two piña coladas she's ordered, complete with paper umbrellas and maraschino cherries on sticks.

I feel a burst of relief, a chance to escape the tension and the worry. To have fun with a friend. I smile back as I join her at the table and reach for my drink.

CHAPTER EIGHT

REBECCA

I can't sleep. Again. I lie flat in my bed and stare at the ceiling, the house silent and dark all around me. My fingers pluck at the sheet and my legs twitch. I can feel my heart beating. Alcohol won't help; nothing will. I'm too restless to settle to anything, even my own darting thoughts.

There's no reason to feel so edgy. The day went well, mostly; Tessa and I had a relaxing time over piña coladas, while the children swam and played tennis. Poor Katherine has even less sporting ability than Max, and admittedly looked miserable as she swung at ball after ball without hitting a single one. Zoe, who has been good at just about everything she tries, looked supremely scornful, although she did deign to show Max how to serve.

Still, I think this summer will be good for all of the children, to be with kids who are different from themselves, to learn to get along. And it's good for me to be with Tessa, as tiresome as she can be sometimes, with her stammering uncertainty and her endless worry over her kids. Still, she feels like both my security blanket and human shield; she protects me from other people, as well as the worst of myself, at least for now. I wonder how long it will last.

The moon slides in and out between clouds and sends bars of silver light through the curtains. It's only eleven. I could get up, read a book, watch TV, have a drink. But I don't want to do any of that, not even the drink; I feel a deep, abiding loneliness, like there is a well of cold, dark water inside of me. I don't want to be alone with myself.

I tried calling Josh tonight but his phone flipped to voicemail. Nine days we've gone now without talking, just the stupid surveillance texts he sends. What is he trying to tell me? That he's still angry, or that he doesn't care?

Too restless to stay in bed now, I get up and walk to the window. The lake stretches nearly to the horizon in a smooth, silent stretch of darkness; none of the cottages have their lights on. Everyone goes to bed early here, it seems. No one is living in the cottage on the other side of Tessa's; I don't know if it is a rental or for weekenders, but it remains empty, the deck furniture covered in plastic sheeting, all the blinds drawn. Sometimes it feels as if we're the only two people on this lake, even though I know that's not true. I've heard laughter in the distance, seen motorboats far out in the water. Still, I feel alone. But then I have for a while now.

The moon slides from beneath a cloud again, and my eye catches sight of a lone figure on the scrubby beach in front of Pine Cottage: Tessa. She is sitting out there alone, her knees drawn up to her chest. She looks lonely, the way I feel. And before I can even consider what I'm doing, I run downstairs and out the sliding glass door; I nearly slip on the steep stairs from the deck but I grab the railing and right myself, and then I am skimming lightly across the pine needle-strewn path to Tessa's bit of beach.

She looks up as I approach, still half-running, and I can see that she is shocked by my sudden appearance.

"Rebecca—"

"I couldn't sleep." I sprawl on the beach next to her, breathless, suddenly exhilarated. "I saw you out here and I wondered if you felt as lonely as I do." Too late I realize how revealing that sounds, but I don't care.

"Lonely? Do you feel lonely?" She sounds curious, almost eager.

"How can I not? Stuck up here for three months, away from everything…" I let the thought trail off, leaving Tessa to fill in the blanks as she chooses.

"But I thought you wanted a change."

"I know, I know, but still… Nothing turns out as you expect, does it?" The words feel heavy with meaning, but she doesn't seem to notice. "My husband Josh didn't want me to go to the Hamptons this year," I say recklessly. Tessa looks at me in surprise.

"Why not?"

"He wanted me out of the way, where I wouldn't embarrass him." I regret the words almost instantly, but then I give a mental shrug. Screw it.

"I can't imagine you embarrassing anyone," Tessa says and I pause, wondering how much to confess. Wouldn't it be nice, wouldn't it be *wonderful*, to have someone know at least some of my secrets? And Tessa is such an easy person to talk to, in part, I suppose, because she doesn't really matter. After this summer, I'll never see her again. She's my summer friend, and I can tell her anything. Almost.

"Well, I did." I try for a laugh. "The truth is, I got drunk at a party. One of Josh's office dos." I wince slightly at the memory, blurry as it is. Josh has told me all the cringe-worthy details, so unfortunately, I have been able to fill in the awful blanks.

"That doesn't sound so bad."

"Oh, trust me, it was." I lean back, bracing myself on my hands, and stretch my legs toward the dark ripples of the lake. "I'm a sucker for Prosecco, and I hate office parties, so a pretty deadly combination, as it turned out." I try to keep my voice light, and I'm not sure I manage it.

"What happened?"

"Apparently I started dancing on top of a coffee table. A bespoke designer piece that cost twenty thousand, but at least I took off my heels, right?" I glance at Tessa; she is struggling between shock and amusement. It is kind of funny, isn't it? Can't it be?

Josh was coldly furious when it happened; I remember that much. I was high as a kite at the party, and stone-cold sober seconds later when we went home in the taxi, Fifth Avenue flashing by.

He didn't talk to me that night; like a naughty child, I went to bed with nothing but silence and disapproval. No, it was the next evening that he confronted me, after the children had gone to bed. I was flicking through one of the highbrow architecture magazines we have around the house, which are deadly dull, all glossy pictures and ridiculous posturing, trying not to think.

"Rebecca," Josh said. "We have a problem."

"Houston…?" I joked, but he didn't smile. He took off his glasses and ran a hand through his hair, rumpling it more than it already was. I put down my magazine.

"If you mean last night…" This said in a tired, here-we-go-again type voice, which Josh ignored. He's so calm, my husband. So steady. I love and hate him for it in equal measures. I'd discovered that it's both hard and wonderful to be with a rock when you feel as if you're about to shatter.

"Rebecca, you embarrassed me. You embarrassed *yourself.*"

"I had a little too much to drink. It happens." Irritable now, like he was the one who was being unreasonable, even though I knew, of course I knew, that I'd been over the top. Unacceptable. But Josh didn't even care about why. He didn't ask, and I wouldn't have answered anyway.

"Not like that," Josh said.

"Like what, then?" A challenge.

"Dancing on top of a table, for heaven's sake—"

"A coffee table."

"*Rebecca!* It was a reception for new partners. No one was drinking more than a glass or two, no one else was drunk. There wasn't even any music playing."

I felt cold then, as if ice was coating my insides. The way he made it sound… I was more than an embarrassment, I was a joke. A cringe-worthy, pathetic *joke*. And I couldn't even remember how I got there, how it happened.

"I'm sorry," I said at last. "You know what I'm like with Prosecco."

"You've never been like that before, Rebecca." Josh's voice is quiet and sad. "Not really. It… worries me." The last said as a confession, one that demanded my own, but I had nothing to say. Nothing I could bear to say.

I looked down, not wanting to see the disappointment and confusion in his face. I ran my thumb over the first scar on my inner arm, two days old, already faded to a pale pink line. At that point I'd only just started cutting, and the shame boiled within me. It was March, three weeks after I'd got back from Wisconsin, a quick trip for Presidents' Day weekend.

"Do you need help?" Josh asked gently. So gently it made me angry and want to cry at the same time.

"Help? What do you think I am, Josh? An alcoholic?" Might as well get the A-word out there, have done with it.

"I don't know," he admitted. "No, I mean I never thought… you're a social drinker, certainly."

"So are you." Whiskey neat and the occasional glass of Pinot Noir. Not exactly on my level. In any case, I'd stopped being a social drinker in the last few weeks. I'd become, to my own shame and horror, a secret drinker, replacing empty wine bottles in the cupboard with new ones I'd bought on the sly.

A trick of the trade, but the thing is, the really true thing is, I know I can stop. I *know* it. Just as I know every alcoholic says that, but it's different with me, it really is. Because I didn't start drinking like this until I felt as if I needed to, and when I've got my life back under control, when I've figured out what is true and what isn't, I know I will stop. Absolutely.

"So, your husband was angry?" Tessa ventures, startling me out of my thoughts.

"More disappointed than angry, which of course is much worse. He felt I needed a break from all the 'societal pressures', as he put it. So here I am, exiled to Hicksville." I glance at her, unrepentant. "Sorry if that offends you."

"Why should it?" She shrugs. "I'm not from around here."

"Right." I stare out at the dark lake, trying to ignore the pain pulsing through me. I shouldn't have brought all that up, I shouldn't have told her. It makes me feel exposed in a way I hate, as if my scars, the real as well as the invisible ones, are all on display for her curious perusal.

"So, do you think it will help?" Tessa asks after a moment. "Being here?"

"Who knows?" I nearly shudder at the possibility that things might not get better. Might not change. If being here doesn't help, what state will I be in at the end of the summer? "If it doesn't..." Too late I realize what I've admitted. That I need help. That Josh is right.

"Rebecca..." Tessa pauses, and I have an awful feeling she's going to say something both trite and true. Something like, *I'm here for you if you need to talk* or *you seem so unhappy, can I help?*

"I know," I say quickly, cutting her off. "Let's go swimming."

Tessa looks blank. "Swimming?"

I nod toward the water, still and dark. "Skinny-dipping. No one's around."

"Skinny..." She looks both surprised and horrified, and I laugh.

"Come on, dare you."

"I don't..."

But I'm already up on my feet, pulling my shorty nightdress over my head. I toss it onto the sand, standing naked under the moonlight. I feel liberated; I'd much rather reveal my body than my fear. Tessa gazes up at me, transfixed.

"Come on, Tessa. Haven't you ever done this before?"

"About a million years ago, when I was eighteen or something."

"Don't be a dinosaur. No one's looking."

"*You* are."

"We're both moms. We've both given birth, and more importantly, had God only knows who looking up our lady bits. I think I had six doctors in the room when I had Zoe." She was a difficult birth, surprise, surprise. I turn away from Tessa, toward the water, conscious now of my pale scars, the one on my hip still angry and red, a jagged, condemning line. Hopefully she won't see them with just the moon for light, and really, there aren't that many.

Tessa lets out one of her uncertain laughs. "Okay," she says. "All right. Fine."

I turn around to see her shyly undoing the drawstring of her shorts. She shrugs them off, and then after a second's hesitation, pulls her t-shirt over her head. She's wearing a worn bra and granny pants, both of them an indeterminate well-washed beige. Her skin is dimpled and doughy; she's got to be at least fifteen pounds overweight, at least by Manhattan standards.

"Excellent," I cry, and clap my hands. "Bravo!"

Even in the moonlight I can see Tessa is blushing as she unclasps her bra and shimmies out of her underwear. Now we're both naked, and it seems more than a little ridiculous. What are we *doing*?

"To the water," I shout, and we both race in. It feels like cool silk at first, but by the time I'm in to my knees, I realize it's actually freezing. I wade in to my waist and then dive in, arcing through the air before I plunge below, that moment I've always enjoyed when the whole world falls away. If only I could stay like that forever, insulated from everything, encased in ice.

Then my head starts to throb and my lungs burn and I burst through the surface like coming through a wall of glass, droplets of water shattering all around me.

Tessa is crouching in the water up to her neck as her lips turn blue.

"Come on, you big chicken," I call as I flip onto my back and float. "Come out and swim."

"It's cold!"

"You'll get used to it." I haven't been skinny-dipping in years, since I was a kid, at the lake in Wisconsin, happy and carefree. At least I think I was. I can't trust my own memory anymore, and that hurts as much as anything else. How much of my life has been a lie?

I lift my head to check if Tessa is coming; she's waded a little farther into the lake and is now treading water, but she still doesn't look committed.

"Come on!" I shout, my voice echoing through the stillness. "Don't be a chicken! A scaredy cat! A total wuss!" I laugh, and that echoes too, the sound otherworldly.

"Fine, fine," Tessa says, half-grumbling, half-laughing, and she starts to swim toward me. I can see the whiteness of her naked body through the dark water. I flip onto my stomach.

"Why don't we swim out to the raft?"

"Out *there*?"

"It's not that far." A hundred yards or so, tops. I start to do a free stroke, my arms cutting through the cool water. I don't look back until I've reached the raft, my arms aching, lungs burning. It was farther than I thought, but it felt good.

I haul myself onto the raft, wincing as the rough wood hits my stomach. Who knows where I will have splinters? Another heave and I'm up, flat on my back, staring at the stars. I can hear the gentle splash of Tessa swimming toward the raft.

"Come on!" I call. "You're almost there."

Moments later the raft creaks and dips as Tessa climbs up. I glance up to see her in a most ungainly position, struggling. She catches my eye and flushes, and I sit up and stretch out my hand.

"Come on, I'll help you."

After a second, she takes it, and I pull her onto the raft. We collapse in a pile of limbs, our naked bodies nearly entwined, until Tessa pulls away, tucking her knees up to her chest, trying to hide herself.

I stretch out in a starfish, determined to enjoy this moment. Above me the sky is full of stars, the night air like cool velvet. Even a mosquito buzzing by my ear and then landing on my shoulder doesn't bother me. I slap it away and let out a sigh of contentment. If only the rest of my life could be like this. If only I could always forget.

CHAPTER NINE

TESSA

We lie on the raft in silence, staring up at the stars, as I struggle not to feel self-conscious. Rebecca clearly isn't; she has stretched out, arms and legs spread wide, her naked body on brave display. Or perhaps not so brave, since there isn't an ounce of fat on her, never mind a single stretchmark. I feel like a lumpen pile of unformed clay next to her, and I am trying not to mind, fighting the urge to dive back in the water and swim to shore.

"Don't you wish we could stay here forever?" Rebecca asks dreamily, and I almost laugh. Um, no, I don't. It's cold and there are mosquitoes and I'm *naked*. But at the same time, there *is* something almost magical about this moment—the night sky, the stars, even our nakedness. Rebecca looks ethereal and otherworldly, moonlight coating her skin in lambent silver, her hair a damp, blonde nimbus about her upturned face. She's like a mermaid without the tail.

She turns to me suddenly, rolling over on her side. "Do you believe in God?"

Now that's unexpected. "Umm... sort of? Maybe?"

Rebecca wrinkles her nose. "I know what you mean," she answers, as if I've said something deep. "It's hard not to believe there's something up there with all this." She throws out an arm to gesture to the stars spangled above us.

"I suppose," I say after a moment. I don't really think about this stuff too much, but I don't feel like I can say that to Rebecca. She seems so *intent*.

"But at the same time," she continues, her voice suddenly turning low and savage, "I can't believe there is some loving God upstairs when so much *shit* happens in the world." She practically spits the words out. "Unless he's asleep at the wheel, which he probably is. Isn't everybody?"

"It's... hard," I venture, knowing my sentiment is inadequate. I feel like we're in far deeper waters than those that lap at the raft; the mood has shifted, and I feel the tension in the air, like electricity before a storm, a veritable crackle.

Rebecca lets out a shuddery sigh and flips onto her back. "You have no idea," she says quietly, and for some reason that is more powerful, more frightening, than anything else she could have said.

"Rebecca..." I hesitate, feeling for words. For courage. "Is everything... okay?"

"Of course it is." Her voice is high and bright, a deliberate, mocking falsetto. "Look at me, look at my life. How could everything not be absolutely wonderful?" She lets out a hard laugh and then scrambles up from the raft. She dives into the water and I watch her silvery form slide through the silky waves, sinuous and lithe, before I lumber upwards and jump in myself. By the time I reach the shore Rebecca has already thrown on her clothes and is hurrying through the path to her house, like some woodland nymph afraid of being caught by the dawn.

"Rebecca..." I call, my voice echoing through the trees, across the water.

"Thanks for the swim," she calls back, sounding as energetic and enthusiastic as ever. "It was so much fun! I'll see you tomorrow!"

*

By morning, with Ben and Katherine bickering over the last of the Froot Loops, it feels as if my midnight swim with Rebecca was a dream, or perhaps a figment of my imagination. I can't believe it really happened, or that she seemed so strange for a little while, manic and desperate. Surely I'd imagined that, or maybe Rebecca just has a flair for the melodramatic?

As the kids split the cereal down to the last loop, I mull over her words. What could really be wrong? Everything about her life is so privileged, so charmed. Even she acknowledges that.

I can't keep my mouth from twisting sardonically as I imagine what Rebecca's first-world problem might be. A lack of meaning amid her endless round of social calls and cocktail parties? The desperate need to keep herself looking toned and beautiful for her mega-rich Wall Street husband? Plain, simple boredom? Is that why she drinks? Why she danced at that party? I feel sorry for her even as a part of me thinks, *big, lousy deal. Poor little rich you, Rebecca Finlay.* Try being me, with an estranged husband, estranged father, no mom, no money, and children I love so much but don't understand. Then I feel guilty for my little pity party, because I know I'm lucky, especially compared to some. Even if I don't always feel it.

"Mom, Ben got more than me!" Katherine's voice is high and plaintive, and I stand up from the table, cradling my coffee cup.

"You guys work it out between yourselves. I'm going outside."

It's another gorgeous day, bright blue skies and hard, lemon yellow sun. I stand on our scrubby bit of sand, tilting my face to the light. Inevitably, though, I lower my head and my gaze trains on the house next door. Why am I so fascinated by Rebecca Finlay? Is it just because she's so out of my league?

When I was younger, I didn't want to be part of the in crowd, so smug and certain of their status. I had my own thing going—my art, my ambition, my cool-in-a-nerdy-way friends. I genuinely didn't care. But now I do, and not just for my sake, but for my children's.

A lump forms in my throat at the thought. Rebecca really has no idea how lucky she is. If my kids were like Charlotte or Max or even Zoe…

The thought slips in like a treacherous little serpent, winding its coils around my heart. Surely I'm not envious of Rebecca's children? I love my own, of course I do. Desperately. Urgently. With every part of me.

And yet… how many times have I wished that Katherine could make just one friend, or Ben could calm down at least a little bit? How many times have I felt frustrated and impotent, unable to help them be their best selves?

A few years ago Rayha told me how we had to let go of our dream children. She was really talking about herself, and of course I understood that, because Zane has so many heartbreaking issues. I didn't apply it to myself then, and I'm reluctant to do so now. Is it really so much, to want my children to have friends, to be healthy and happy and well? Do those basic things have to be nothing more than illicit dreams?

We moved to Park Slope to give the kids a new start, a new school, especially after the difficult years of my mom's second stroke and then her death. Kyle was particularly insistent we all start over, saying we needed a clean slate, but it hasn't worked out the way he hoped. Nothing ever does, and I can't keep from wondering, how much of that is because of me?

"Mom, do we have to go to the club again today?" Katherine joins me on the beach, winding one leg around the other like a stork.

"We have a membership now, and you enjoyed the swimming and tennis lessons, didn't you?" I'm not sure why I'm asking. I know she didn't, but at least it wasn't quite the hell-on-earth experience Katherine had been bracing herself for. Baby steps. Baby steps for all of us.

"I don't want to go."

"Katherine, couldn't we just—"

"You *promised*." Her voice takes on a wild, ragged edge. "You promised that if I didn't like it, I wouldn't have to go again."

"I didn't actually promise." I feel both guilty and stubborn, not a good combination. "Katherine, swim lessons are good for you—"

"I *know* how to swim. And I don't care about tennis."

"I don't just mean swimming, or tennis. I mean…" I hesitate, not wanting to hurt my shy, fragile daughter, yet knowing things need to be said, in order to help her. Maybe they should have been said a long time ago, but it's only recently that I've realized how much of a push Katherine needs—and that I've got to be the one to do it. "I mean, being with people," I explain as gently as I can. "Getting out there. Making friends. It's important, a skill you have to learn—"

"Seriously? *You're* telling me this?"

I stare at her, startled by the slightly sneering tone I haven't heard in my daughter's voice before. I feel as if she's referring to something I should know about but don't. "Yes, I am—"

"Whatever." Katherine's lower lip juts out as she folds her arms protectively across her body. "So, you mean at a country club, with stupid strangers I'm never going to see again, ever?"

"They could be your summer friends—"

"Summer friends?" Her voice is filled with scorn as well as fear. "Who has those?"

I glance over at Rebecca's house again. "Lots of people do."

"Well, I don't," Katherine snaps, her lips trembling and her eyes filling with angry tears. "And I'm not going swimming again." She slams back into the cottage and I deflate. Another battle fought—and lost. But we *are* going to the club.

In the end, we all go in Rebecca's car, I'm not even sure why. She suggested it, all beaming bonhomie, as if last night never happened. She tosses our towels in the back and the children climb in silently. You'd think we were going to the dentist instead of the pool.

Then Rebecca cranks up the radio and rolls down the windows as we drive along the road that winds around the lake. She belts out the lyrics to "Firework" by Katy Perry, and Zoe is right there with her, singing along with a powerhouse voice, both of them grinning as they go for it. I've never seen Zoe look so happy, her smile transforming her usual sulky expression into something lovely to see. I feel that treacherous flicker of envy again, nebulous, persistent. *If only I could be that carefree with my children. If only I could be different. If only they could.*

Katherine, of course, is silent, as am I, and Charlotte is just smiling faintly, her gaze on the blurred view from the back window, as if she is thinking of something else and is slightly above us all. Max has inched over to the window, sitting as far away from Ben as he can, shooting him furtive glances.

I glance at Rebecca, and wonder why or how she doesn't notice the often painful dynamic between the two boys. Or is it that she simply doesn't care? I wish I had an ounce of her insouciance, her immediate ability to switch off, not to worry. I know I worry too much. It eats at me from the inside out, an emotional parasite.

It started soon after my mom died; at least I think it did. I don't think I worried nearly as much before then as I do now, always obsessing about their happiness, their social lives, whether they're doing the right things or enough things or anything. Before, all my emotional energy was sucked up by my mom—the near-weekly trips to Pennsylvania, the endless hours and days in hospitals and then rehab as she tried to get just a little bit of her life back.

But when she died, it was as if a big emotional vacuum had formed in the center of my life, and I filled it with worry for my children. Worry feels like the natural by-product of love, but sometimes I wonder if it's merely a poor substitute. It never seems to help.

At the club the kids all head to the changing rooms, Katherine giving me one last pathetically beseeching look, which I return with a smile that is both sympathetic and steely. I wonder if Rebecca will head to the bar again—surely she doesn't have a cocktail every afternoon?—but she goes outside instead, and I follow her, trotting at her heels, waiting for who knows what.

She drops her big straw bag next to a lounger in the pool area, before collapsing into it with a theatrical sigh.

"One hour of peace," she announces as she slips her sunglasses over her eyes. "Thank God!"

"I know, right?" The gems I come up with. I sit next to her, the lounger creaking beneath me as Rebecca rests her head back against the wooden slats.

"It's sailing tomorrow," she remarks with her head still tilted back. "That's another whole hour, three times a week, at the yacht club."

Is she assuming we'll go along to that, as well? Will she pay for it all? Maybe she already has. I feel the familiar prickle of unease as well as guilt at the thought of how much she is paying for. I shouldn't let her. I know I shouldn't let her. Yesterday, while we were having our piña coladas, I offered to pay for some of the membership, but Rebecca waved me away and I let her. Guilt sours in my stomach. Accepting so much feels both weird and wrong.

I know Katherine is not going to like sailing any better than she likes swimming or tennis. I dread the thought of dragging her along to even more activities, and yet Rebecca makes it all seem so obvious, so easy.

"How do you do it?" I blurt, and Rebecca raises her head.

"How do I do what?"

"I don't know, everything." I shrug, semi-regretting my impulse to ask her I don't even know what. "You seem so relaxed about everything. And your kids seem so..." I hesitate. "Well adjusted."

"Do they?" She lets out a little huff of laughter. "Zoe's a handful, that's for certain."

"Yes, but she's confident. That's a good thing."

"Yes, I don't think I'd have her any other way, really."

"And Charlotte…" I can't quite contain a note of near-longing in my voice. Charlotte is the same age as Katherine, has the same quietness, and yet she radiates a kind of inner calm and stillness. A confidence that's almost beatific, as if she's so certain of her place in the world, as if she doesn't need to impress anyone, isn't worried about how she measures up.

"Yes, Charlotte's easy," Rebecca agrees. "I'm lucky there."

"And Max." Now I do hear the envy. What I wouldn't give for a boy who isn't bumping into everyone, hitting or pushing people "by accident", getting yellow and red cards in school. I bet Max plays chess and collects bugs.

"Oh, Max!" Rebecca sighs. "The grass is always greener there, I think, Tessa."

"What do you mean?"

"Max is…" She purses her lips. "Quiet."

Blissfully quiet. "Yes…"

"And he hates sports. Hates gym class at school. Can't stand getting messy or dirty or wet."

Whereas Ben is always in motion and is constantly dirty. Things that usually make me exasperated, but for a second I see how they can be of a certain value. "Yet he takes swimming?"

She shrugs. "You've got to know how to swim."

I sit back, rolling over all she's said in my mind. Of course I knew her children weren't perfect, and yet…

"Still, you don't seem bothered by anything," I say at last.

She lets out another laugh, this one with a slight edge. "Don't I?"

I know she has problems, even if she won't tell me what they are. I know she probably drinks too much, and she danced on a table, and sometimes she seems a little wild and desperate. But even so… I can't believe it's that bad. That her life in any way resembles mine, no matter what I've thought before.

"I mean, you always seem to have it together," I stumble to explain. "With your kids. I feel like I'm constantly worrying about mine. Their lives. Their moods. Whether they're doing their homework or—or making friends." I admit this guiltily, a confession. I feel as if I'm betraying Katherine. "It eats me up inside sometimes."

Rebecca glances over at me, her eyebrows raised. "I didn't take you for a helicopter mom."

"I'm not. Not like that." I've seen those manic mothers at school, always hovering, bleating about organic this or that and zero screen time. I'm not that kind of mother at all. Ben is practically surgically attached to his electronic device, and we had SpaghettiOs for dinner last night. *So what kind of mother am I? Why does it always feel so hard? Would my own mom have made that much of a difference?*

"I don't know," I say after a moment. "I just feel like I'm doing it wrong."

"We're all doing it wrong in one way or another," she says, her face slightly averted as she gazes at the shimmering blue of the pool. "Sometimes more wrong, sometimes more right. Either way, kids grow up. They survive."

"But surely you want more than just survival for them?"

"That's a start," Rebecca says, and she sounds so grim, I feel as if we've plunged into that ice-cold water again and I don't know how to get out.

"So, are you having anyone come up for Fourth of July?" I ask in an obvious attempt to change the subject. "Your husband or…?"

"My parents." She speaks flatly. "They want to visit."

"Will that be stressful?" I feel like I'm going to get a well-duh answer, but I don't know what else to say.

"Oh, the usual over-the-topness. Over-sugaring the kids, subtly critiquing my parenting. At least my mom will do that."

"And your father?"

Rebecca purses her lips. "I was a daddy's girl growing up," she says after a moment. Her gaze is trained on the pool. "I'm not sure I know how to be anything else." She leans her head back against the lounger. "I'm not sure I can be bothered to deal with them coming, to be honest."

"So, what will you do? Tell them not to come?" I am fascinated, because it's so far from my experience. I haven't seen my father in two years, and he hasn't seemed to mind. The distance that had always been between us became a yawning chasm when my mother died.

Rebecca turns to me suddenly, grabbing my arm, her manicured nails digging into my flesh. "They'll be here for the whole weekend. You can't leave me alone with them, Tessa. I'll go crazy."

I stare at her, shocked by the desperate urgency in her voice.

"Seriously," she says, her nails still digging into my arm. "I need you guys hanging around all the time. Otherwise it's going to be a nightmare." Her lips tremble as she tries to smile, and I feel a sudden, surprising surge of compassion for her.

"It can't be that bad, surely, Rebecca?"

"Oh, I know." She releases my arm and looks away, making me feel like I've said the wrong thing. "I'm overreacting. They can be irritating but they mean well, right?" She draws a shuddery breath. "It's just, it would be great to have you around."

"Okay." I'm not sure what I'm agreeing to. "What about Josh? Will he come too?" It feels a little strange to say the name of a man I don't know, have never met.

"Josh?" Rebecca lets out a humorless laugh. "He's not actually talking to me right now, so…" She shrugs.

Not talking to her? The cracks on the gleaming surface of Rebecca's life are starting to show more deeply, hairline fractures starting to look more like deep fissures. "He'll want to see the kids…" I venture, even though I have no idea.

"Oh, yes. The kids, he'll come for them." Her face hardens for a second and then she nods toward the pool. "The lesson's over. We'll need to get them ready for tennis." And then she's gone, striding away from me, leaving me wondering yet again what is really going on with Rebecca Finlay.

CHAPTER TEN

REBECCA

A few days later I finally work up the nerve to leave Josh a voicemail. It's been two weeks since we arrived here, two endless weeks of those awful daily texts and nothing else. My parents are coming in five days, I can't cope.

Tessa has helped, at least a little. She tries to be nice, and she goes along with whatever I say. She's a distraction, but not enough of one. She's not here all the time, she's not inside my head.

When the kids are in bed, the house quiet, a glass of wine in my hand, I call him. My husband. My jailer.

"Josh, it's Rebecca. You know that, of course." I let out a brittle laugh. This has already gone badly. "I wanted to talk to you. I haven't… we haven't…" I'm at a loss for words. *Me.* I hate the woman I'm becoming. "Please call me," I say simply, and then I hang up.

I pace the family room off the kitchen, feeling restless. The last few days have been okay, really. We've had our tennis and swim lessons, sailing too, although Tessa backed off on those, and said they'd stay at home. I decided not to press, because the sailing is expensive, and Josh will look at the bills and wonder what on earth I'm doing.

Still, I've spent a lot of time with Tessa. I've listened to her go on about her card-making business and actually, when she brought over one of her cards at my request, it was surprisingly good. I would have bought one if I'd seen it in a store.

She offered to bring over some of her card-making stuff on a rainy day, and the kids spent an afternoon sprinkling glitter on cardstock and using all her nice felt-tip pens and she looked on, laughing a little, not seeming to mind. It was really rather sweet.

The kids have started to get along, at least a little. Ben and Max have seemed to bond, if only slightly, over his gaming device; Max watches and murmurs encouragement while Ben plays with a maniacal frenzy. Sometimes he puts it down and they do something outside; I watched, touched, while Ben pushed Max on the tire swing outside, eventually pushing him far too high, but still… I think he was actually trying, in his own clumsy way.

Katherine and Charlotte have also reached a hesitant understanding; Katherine follows Charlotte around, copying her shamelessly, and Charlotte doesn't seem to mind. In fact, I think she enjoys it. I've seen her give a secret little smile as Katherine tries to copy her, whether it's her clothes or her hair or even just the way she stands, one hip jutted out.

Zoe remains alone, sometimes clinging to me, always watching everyone, and I think she prefers it that way.

But now it's nine o'clock at night and I feel like I'm going to crawl out of my own skin. I need something; I crave it, anything to blunt the sharpness, to blur the edges. It doesn't even matter what.

So I prowl around the house, picking up a magazine, tossing it aside, curling and uncurling my hands into fists, fighting this awfulness inside me. Memories. That's what I'm fighting. The dark, dark tide of memories that pull me under.

I slump onto the sofa as I feel the fight leave me. I hate that I'm not strong enough, and yet there is a strange sweetness in defeat. In letting the tide sweep over me, letting myself drown. To choose to stop fighting… is there a strength in that? Can there be?

And so I sit there, and the memories come. They creep at first, blurry and unfocused, as if they happened to someone else. Maybe they did. They remind me of mist—ephemeral, barely there, and yet obscuring everything. A twinge, a twitch, a sudden, sharp sense of fear or wrong, and then a memory will slide into place, startling in its clarity, perfectly envisioned, and it's way too much.

I lurch upright, my skin prickling with cold sweat, my stomach heaving. There is no sweetness in this. The phone rings, saving my sanity. It's Josh. Thank God.

"Hey!" My voice comes out in almost a gulp of relief.

"Rebecca?" He sounds concerned, a little impatient. "What's up?"

It's so good to hear his voice. I want to cry, I want to sob, but somehow I keep it all in as I take a steadying breath. "Nothing's up, really." It's all down, down, down.

"You sounded as if you wanted to talk to me urgently."

"Have you been avoiding me?" I blurt the words.

"I've texted you every day, Rebecca—"

"I mean, *talking*. We haven't talked in two weeks, Josh. What's going on?"

Josh sighs. "I'm sorry. I just haven't been sure what to say to you."

"'How are you?' would be a start."

"Okay. How are you?"

I bite my lips, unable to answer, knowing I can't admit one iota of how I am to him. "Okay. We've made some friends."

"The neighbors, right? Charlotte told me."

"Oh, what did she say?"

"Not much, just that you'd been hanging out with another mom and her two kids. I'm glad." I still have nothing to say. "How is it there?" he continues. "Charlotte seems to like it."

"Charlotte likes everything." Nothing bothers my oldest daughter; her interior life is a placid sea compared to my own endlessly churning waves.

"Do *you* like it?"

"It's fine, I suppose. It's just…" The breath trickles from my lungs as I continually come up against this ever-familiar impasse.

What I can't say. The words that won't come, because I'm so scared to let them out. Scared they'll be dismissed, and just as scared they'll be taken seriously, and make things real. Which would be worse? "I was hoping you could come up here for the Fourth of July weekend."

Josh is silent, which tends not to be a good thing. "You know the first week of every month is the busiest," he finally says.

Yes, I do know this, even if I don't really understand it. For some reason, in Josh's investment banking firm, something happens in the first week of the month that forces him to work a lot of hours.

"But Fourth of July," I persist. "The whole city empties out, Josh. You know that."

"I thought I might come up a bit later. Aren't your parents coming up then, anyway?"

"How did you know that?"

"Your mother called." Josh sounds wry; he doesn't dislike my mother, and he pretty much gets along with everyone, but still. My mother. Overwhelming at the best of times, if generally well intentioned. At least, I've always thought she was, but now I wonder. Now I wonder about everything.

"So, do you need me there?" Josh asks, to which there seems to be only one answer. "Since you'll have a full house anyway…"

Which is exactly why I need him there, but I don't want to beg. I close my eyes. Take a deep breath. "It would be nice if you were there too, Josh. The kids want to see you. It's been a long time."

"I know it has." He sighs, as if he is so burdened—by me. "I'll see what I can do."

I know it's the most I can ask for, but it feels like so little. What happened to us? What happened to *me*?

"How are you, Rebecca?" Josh asks quietly, surprising me. "Really?"

"I'm okay." I don't feel like I can say anything else, not on the phone, with these tortured silences between us. Still, I try. "I'm… I'm not looking forward to my parents coming."

Josh chuckles. "They're full-on, that's for sure."

"Yes, but…" Words clog in my throat, and a pressure builds in my chest. "It's more than that," I say, which feels like a huge confession.

"Do you mean your drinking?" His tone is gentle yet matter-of-fact, with a hint of the never-ending disappointment.

"No, I don't mean my drinking," I practically snap. "Can't you just get over that, Josh? You act as if I've been knocking back bottles of vodka in the kitchen every night." Which I haven't been. Not exactly.

"I don't think that, of course I don't. I'd hardly let you go somewhere far away with our children if I did." Which makes me feel guilty. "But I am concerned. You haven't been yourself, Rebecca. If you need help…"

"I don't need *help*. Not that kind of help. But what if I did? What if I really had that kind of problem?" My voice nearly breaks and by some superhuman effort I manage to pull back. "Would you be there for me then, Josh?" I know he doesn't even understand what I'm asking. I'm not sure I do, either.

"Of course I would—"

"Funny, because it doesn't feel like it. Not right now, when I'm all the way up here in Bumblefuck, New York." Even if it's where I chose to go. I know I'm not being fair, but that's because nothing feels fair. I can't manage Josh on top of everything else. And so I disconnect the call, because I'm trembling all over and I can't take any more. I toss my phone across the room, willing it to shatter—I need something to break.

Which is why I find my way upstairs, to the sumptuous bathroom with its double sinks and sunken tub and razor blades. I despise myself when I do this, and yet it's the only pressure valve

I have, the only way to keep me on this side of the knife-edge of sanity.

The cut on my hip is healing well, but after four months of sporadic cutting, I'm running out of places to cut without looking like I rolled around in a bath of shattered glass, a fact that makes me cringe inwardly. It's getting harder and harder to say my choices are aberrations, necessary one-offs. They've become a lifestyle, a way of being, and that is intolerable.

I decide on the underside of my arm, near my shoulder, which will be covered by my clothes. I pick up the razor, light glinting off its straight edge, the tension of this moment both exquisite and painful. I can't believe I'm doing this again, and yet I have to. I *have* to. I take a deep breath and raise my arm.

"*Mom?* What are you *doing?*"

The blade slips on my thumb, creating an instant deep welling of crimson blood across the pad, and then clatters to the ground. Charlotte is standing in the doorway, looking stunned. I forgot to lock the door, damn it, because it's nearly ten o'clock at night. I thought everyone was asleep. I thought it was safe, but of course nothing is safe. *Nothing.*

"I'm not doing anything, sweetheart." My voice comes out high and bright. *False.* I grab some tissues and press them to my thumb, trying to think of a reason I would be holding a razor blade, but my mind is a complete blank. And Charlotte is staring at me, her eyes wide as her gaze darts from my thumb to the razor blade now gleaming on the floor, a silver indictment.

Her mouth is open, as if she doesn't know what to think. As if she can't believe what she's seeing. She couldn't guess, could she? She's so young, only eleven. She couldn't *know.* And yet if she did… if she figures it out… I am icy with horror at the thought. My stomach writhes.

"I was just going to remove the caulk from the bathtub," I say finally, my words tripping over themselves. It's a nonsensical excuse, but it's the only thing I can think of. "It's covered in mildew and I wanted to recaulk it." Charlotte glances at the tub, which has only a few specks of mildew on it. She says nothing.

"What's up, sweetheart?" I ask, the tissue pressed tightly to my hand. "Why aren't you in bed?"

"I couldn't sleep."

"Why not?" Charlotte shrugs, and I stare at my daughter, wondering how to get in her head, not that I've needed to try too hard before. Charlotte has never given me any trouble. Model baby, angelic toddler, easy tween. She gets good grades, is able enough at sports, can play the piano. Everything seems, if not easy for her, then easy enough. She has a couple of friends at school, but she's not obsessed with them or with boys, and she hasn't touched social media yet, although she has a phone. She's self-contained, observant, calm. Why can't she sleep?

Lightly, I touch her shoulder. "Everything's okay, isn't it?"

"I guess." Another shrug as her gaze slides away from me. "Is Daddy coming for Fourth of July?"

"I just spoke to him, and he's going to try." Which might be stretching the truth a bit, but I want to believe it.

"And what about Granny and Grandad?" A shadow passes over her face, so brief I think I might have missed it, and everything in me freezes. Something I haven't let myself think of, and yet…

"Don't you want them to come, Charlotte?"

"I guess."

"You usually love seeing Granny and Grandad." I keep my voice casual even though it's physically hard to say the words. Charlotte just shrugs again, her gaze sliding away from me again. *What is she hiding?* I hate the thought that my little girl is hiding anything, that she has something to hide, just like I do. Too many secrets. Far, far too many secrets.

"I think I'll go back to bed," she says, and with the blood still dripping from my thumb, I watch my beautiful, graceful eleven-year-old daughter walk out of the room. Fear clutches at me, a new terror that overwhelms me, a tsunami I didn't even see coming and is now crashing over my head as I think of what Charlotte might not be saying. How could I not see it? *How could I not?*

And what am I going to do?

The next day Tessa notices something is wrong. We've fallen into a comfortable habit of sitting on sun loungers while the children swim, although I'd rather have a cocktail.

Tessa, as usual, is obsessively worried about her own children, although she tries to hide it. She keeps peering over at the pool, a deep frown scoring her forehead. A few days ago, I felt a gentle scorn for her needless compulsion; her children are *fine*, they're going to be fine. So, Ben is boisterous, and Katherine is gawky. They'll grow out of it. They'll grow into themselves; they'll become wonderful, functioning adults.

But now I sit and stare at Charlotte and Zoe perched on the edge of the pool, and I feel just as worried. I feel terrified. What if they're in trouble? In danger? What if I've made it worse? I keep thinking of Charlotte looking at that razor blade, her expression stunned, and I hate myself.

"Rebecca?" Tessa's voice is hesitant. "Is everything okay? You seem… preoccupied."

"I don't want my parents to visit." I blurt the words. "I really don't want them to visit."

"Okay." Her anxious gaze scans my face, searching for clues. "Then why don't you just tell them that?"

I drum my fingers on the armrest of my lounger, restless, like I'm going to jump out of my own skin. "It doesn't work that way."

"Why not?"

I shake my head. I can't go into the dynamics now—my mother's bossiness, my father's determined bonhomie, the way they operate together, a benevolent bulldozer you can't stop. You just have to get out of the way, if you can, or lie down and take it. And I can't do that, not now. "It just doesn't," I say impatiently. "They'll come anyway, or they'll reschedule, or they'll get all worried and disappointed and it will be worse."

"Then what are you going to do?"

"I don't know." I try to summon a smile, but this time I can't. "I'll figure something out."

"Okay." Tessa smiles, and I stare at her, feeling a sudden, overwhelming envy for her uncomplicated life. She has it so easy. So, so easy, and she doesn't even realize it. She envies me, and I understand that, but can't she see how I'm coming apart at the seams? Does she not see my scars, both the literal and the invisible? How can she not?

She's so worried about her children, but I could sort them out in a minute. A *second*. Find a doctor to prescribe something for Ben and give Katherine a mini-makeover, find her an activity where she feels confident. Boom. Done.

As for Tessa herself…

"We should give you a makeover," I announce and Tessa draws back, startled.

"Sorry, what?"

"A makeover." The idea fills me with sudden determination. I need a project. "It would be so, so fun. We can go to Syracuse, find a spa… do it all properly."

Tessa is still looking stunned. "I can't…"

"Oh, come on, Tessa, it would be amazing." I lean forward, favoring her with a smile. "New hairstyle, some serious eyebrow shaping… maybe a little Botox if you want it? And new clothes, of course." Too late I realize how insulting I might sound, as if she needs to change everything about herself, but surely she realizes she could make more of her looks? I mean, come on. It's obvious.

"I don't think so," Tessa says, sounding surprisingly firm. I can usually cajole her into almost anything.

"Imagine Kyle's shock when he sees you again," I persist. I really want this now; it feels like a mission, a focus. "Is he coming for the Fourth?"

"I… I don't know."

"We don't have to go crazy," I continue. "If you don't want to. It can be a girly day, just the two of us. God knows I could use a touch-up, at least." I pat my hair. I can tell Tessa is considering it now. "And a manicure. Look at my nails!" I hold out my hands; one fingernail is chipped. "It really would be fun."

"What about the kids?"

I've got her now; I can feel it. "I'll arrange a sitter, there are plenty of college girls waitressing here at the club who would do it." Tessa doesn't say anything, and I press the point. "How about tomorrow? We can stay out, have dinner."

"Okay," she says at last, and I feel like she wanted to all along, but didn't want to let herself. Is she worried about the money? I know the club membership was probably overkill, but surely she realizes it's pocket change to me? And I'm glad she's here. I think she must be too; how could she not? The kids are getting along, and the long summer days are filled.

Last night we all ate out on the deck as the sun set; the kids had an impromptu game of tag, and Tessa looked almost tearful with happiness at seeing them dart across the grass, their laughter echoing in the summer air. It was a Kodak moment, precious and perfect. I could practically caption it.

"I'll arrange it right now," I say, and reach for my phone. Someone at the club gave me the contact numbers of a couple of girls who babysit. And I need to find a decent beauty salon in Syracuse, of all places. I feel filled with energy, with purpose, and it's such a relief. Today is going to be okay, after all. Today is another day I am going to survive.

That night I call my parents. I've had to steel myself with just one glass of wine for it, and I wait until I know, absolutely, that the children are all asleep. I peek in their bedrooms—Max huddled under the covers, knees drawn up to his chest, Zoe sprawled out in a starfish, Charlotte lying perfectly still on her back. Even in sleep their personalities reveal themselves.

Downstairs, I pour myself a second glass of wine and dial the number. My mother answers after the first ring, sounding concerned before I've even said anything.

"Rebecca? Is everything all right?"

"Yes, why shouldn't it be?" I wonder how much Josh has told her.

"Because it's nine forty-two at night," my mother says, sounding far too worried. "A bit late for a regular call."

"Well, actually…" Too late I realize my kneejerk reaction to say everything is all right was wrong. I've messed up my plan before it's even begun.

"Yes?" My mother's voice is sharp; Josh must have told her about my drinking, or at least hinted at it.

"I don't think this weekend is going to work out." I try to sound regretful even though my heart is thudding in my chest. "The children have stomach bugs."

"Stomach bugs?" I can't tell if she sounds skeptical or simply nonplussed.

"Yes, pretty bad ones. Max hasn't ventured out of the bathroom all day." I will, of course, be caught out in this lie at some point; one of the kids will say there never was a stomach bug while on the phone. It was a stupid idea, to lie so obviously, but I haven't got anything else and I really don't want them to come.

"I hope he's not dehydrated, poor thing."

"I don't think so, but you know how contagious these things are."

I can practically hear the hum of my mother's thoughts. "The Fourth isn't for another few days. Surely they'll be over it by then?"

Surely not. "I think it's going to run through us all, honestly, Mom, and the last thing you and Dad need is to get some awful bug. Why don't we just reschedule?"

"Oh, but we were so looking forward to seeing you all. Daddy especially…" I do not reply and my mother sighs. "Well, if we must, but you know things are quite busy for the rest of the month. There's a charity fundraiser at the club…"

I stay silent, because I can't make myself suggest an alternative weekend or act like I want them to come. I hear my mother flipping through the pages of her planner. "I suppose we could do a weekend in late August."

Which is over a month away. It feels like an unbelievably wonderful reprieve, and yet that's all it is. A reprieve. Eventually I will have to face them. I will have to face everything.

After I've said goodbye and hung up the phone, I press my forehead against the wall, letting out a shaky breath as the post-adrenalin rush hits me. My legs feel weak and I stumble over to the sofa and practically collapse on it.

I have a month. A month to get my act together, to figure out what I'm going to do to get myself out of this pit, because clearly something has got to give.

The question is, what? What can help me now? I can't even picture myself in a month—where I'll be, what I'll be feeling. I can't picture any way out, and that's what terrifies me.

CHAPTER ELEVEN

TESSA

The salon in Syracuse is very upscale. I feel out of my league as soon as we cross the marble threshold, past a tinkling fountain that has streams of water splashing over rocks that look like speckled ostrich eggs.

Rebecca is buoyant, as she has been since we climbed in the car two hours ago, now sailing in with a gracious smile for the elegant woman behind a crescent-shaped desk.

"We're booked in for ten," she trills. "Facials, massages, hair, eyebrows... the works!"

The attendant smiles pleasantly and my stomach cramps. Why did I agree to this? *How* did I agree to this? I'm really not sure how it happened, how it ever happens, but somehow when it comes to Rebecca I constantly find myself caving—whether it's a cocktail, a club membership, or now a makeover. I can't say no to her, to the shimmering world of promises and possibilities she offers, even as I know, as she's *shown* me, that something is wrong in her world.

But how wrong can it be?

The attendant ushers us to a couple of plush leather sofas and offers us sparkling water and thick, glossy magazines, the kind that I never buy, that are full of ads for designer clothes and perfume.

"Nia will be with you shortly," she says, and Rebecca, clearly accustomed to this world, merely flicks open the magazine and starts reading. I sip my water, feeling nervous for a whole lot of reasons. One, I've never actually been in a spa before. I've had ten-dollar manicures in hole-in-the-wall places in Brooklyn, and once, when I had a crick in my neck, I had a massage from a woman who worked out of her home… but this? The works, as Rebecca said? It makes me feel uncertain and exposed. I won't know what to do, and I don't like the thought of these shiny, airbrushed attendants seeing me in all my blemished glory.

The second reason I'm nervous is because I've left my children with Rebecca's and Ana, a nineteen-year-old whose phone appeared to be superglued to her hand, in charge. Not that I'm expecting quality time from her with my kids, but… something could go wrong. Something *will* go wrong; it's just a matter of how bad it will be. Will Ben push Max? Will Charlotte ignore Katherine? Will Zoe explode? The kid is a walking hand grenade, ready to be hurled into any situation, yet none of it seems to bother Rebecca.

"Relax," Rebecca chides as she reaches over to pat my hand. "This is going to be fun."

I smile, trying to take heart from this little bit of encouragement. Haven't I dreamed of something like this when I've watched a bevy of mothers stroll down the street from PS 39, all heading for a big confab at Starbucks, while I'm clearly uninvited and invisible? Or when I've overheard them talking about a girls' night at the new wine bar on Seventh Avenue, haven't I wanted to be involved and included? And now I finally am. I feel like the gawky twelve-year-old inside me is squirming with delight, even as I battle a nameless apprehension.

"Mrs. Finlay?" A woman in white scrubs, looking more like a surgeon than a spa attendant, appears in front of us. "Right this way."

We follow her into a darkened cave of a room that has pan flute music piped in. I recognize "Can You Feel the Love Tonight".

"Feel free to handle the serenity rocks," the attendant says, and I nearly choke with laughter. *Serenity rocks?* Seriously? Rebecca nods as if she is about to do exactly that, but as soon as she's left, she rolls her eyes.

The attendant has left thick terrycloth robes on two lounge chairs, and we change into them, Rebecca as unselfconscious as ever, whereas I try to hide my worst bits even though she has already seen me naked.

While she positions herself on one of the loungers I take a glance at the serenity rocks—they're the same speckled ostrich eggs as in the lobby, but these are placed over some kind of heat lamp that's meant to look, I think, like a volcano, and when I touch one it's actually pretty hot. I certainly don't want to *handle* one, as the attendant suggested.

"I know, I know," Rebecca says, even though I haven't said anything. "All this Zen stuff is pretty ridiculous. But just go with the flow, it's a chance to relax."

"True." I sit on the lounger next to her and lean my head back, determined to let go of the worries that keep my stomach muscles in a constant clench. Rebecca certainly seems relaxed, idly flicking through another beauty magazine.

My mind reels relentlessly back to saying goodbye to Ben and Katherine this morning; it's true that over the last few days they've been getting on better with Rebecca's kids, but it still doesn't feel completely natural or easy. But maybe it never does, at least for us. For me.

Then I think further still to the tense conversation I had with Kyle last night. He'd called to tell me he couldn't come up for the Fourth as I'd hesitantly suggested the last time we'd talked—he was going out with some college buddies to some indie rock gig at a bar in the Bronx; they were even hoping to play.

I was speechless; Kyle never did stuff like that. I thought he'd lost touch with his old friends, or at least most of them. They'd all drifted off to either dull careers or penniless jobs, depending on how committed they were to their music. Now they were *playing?*

"Couldn't you go to a music thing another weekend?" I asked, trying not to sound judgmental, but Katherine really wanted him to come.

"It's only this weekend, and I can come up there anytime," he answered. "I already talked to Katherine about it, and I'm planning to come up the next weekend, or maybe the one after that."

"You did?" This surprised me, since she didn't have her own phone. "When?"

"She called me on her friend's phone while I was at work. I promised her I'd come up soon."

And Katherine had said nothing of it to me. That wasn't surprising, really, and yet I still felt wrong-footed… and both disappointed and relieved that Kyle wasn't coming.

"Anyway," he said, "you're doing okay, aren't you? You seem well."

He made me sound as if I constantly struggled, and maybe I did, sort of, but I still *managed*. I still cooked and cleaned and cared for our children, and I resented how inept he often made me sound—and feel.

"Yes," I snapped. "I'm fine."

A few minutes later, another attendant comes into the darkened room, giving us both a purposeful smile. "So," she says briskly. "Which one of you is Tessa McIntyre?"

"Umm… me?" I have no idea why I make it a question.

"Time for your power facial."

"My… what?"

Still smiling, the attendant leads me away from Rebecca, into a bright, white room that reminds me of a doctor's office. "First, we're going to start with an exfoliating retinoid peel, followed by some intense pulsed light, which will target those broken capillaries." She brushes a finger across my nose and cheeks. "Then we'll finish with a microdermabrasion with antioxidants and some radio frequency to tighten those saggy spots." She gestures to my chin and eyelids. I am speechless.

"I'm not sure if I understood what any of that meant."

"Don't worry," she assures me, "you don't need to."

And so I let myself be led to the examining chair like a lamb to the spa slaughter. I close my eyes and brace myself for who even knows what, but actually none of it is that bad—a little heat, some stinging. Somehow I find myself relaxing into it all, carried out on a bobbing sea of enforced tranquility. I don't need to think; I don't need to understand. And I'm not going to let myself worry... about anything.

I try to glance at my reflection as I'm led from my facial to a full body massage and seaweed wrap, but irritatingly, there aren't any mirrors around.

"Can't spoil the big reveal," the attendant tells me with a laugh, and I feel a flicker of alarm as well as one of anticipation. What on earth am I going to look like?

From the seaweed wrap and massage—both of which take some getting used to—I'm led to stylist after stylist to see to my eyebrows, my chin hair (cringe) and my hair. I don't get so much as a glimpse of my reflection all day long, and I only see Rebecca in passing, as she waggles her fingers at me on the way to a massage, looking as luminescent as ever.

I feel both uneasy and excited, way out of my comfort zone, and by four o'clock, when I've finished the day with a manicure and pedicure, I am eager to have people's hands off me, and get out of here.

Strangely, or perhaps not, Rebecca sees the new me before I do. "Oh, *Tessa!*" She beams at me, her hands clasped in front of her. "You look fantastic, like a whole new person."

Not quite a compliment, but I decide to take it. I know I didn't look great before. It's been a long time since I've really taken care of myself.

Now I want to know what I look like. I feel shiny and new, my skin soft and pink, and I know my hair, normally an uncontrollable frizz, has been straightened to glossy sleekness. But I have no idea what will actually greet me when I look in the mirror, how the sum of the parts will fit together.

"All we need is a couple of new outfits," Rebecca says as I search for a mirror. "Kyle won't recognize you."

"Ta da!" The attendant leads me to a full-length mirror and positions me in front of it. I stare. I blink. Is that *me*? It's the quintessential Cinderella moment, the ugly duckling flapping her swan-like wings. I am amazed.

"Don't you love it?" Rebecca says as she stands beside me. I can barely tell she's had anything done. Her skin is a bit shinier and tauter, and her hair gleams even more than it normally does, but… Rebecca is still Rebecca. Rebecca will always be Rebecca, I suspect, timeless and perfect, no matter what.

"I do love it," I say, although I'm still trying to take it all in. When I move my head, my newly straightened hair swings in a single, glossy sheet. My eyebrows are thin, dark arcs that make me look a little surprised, but perhaps that's just because I *am* surprised. I definitely look younger, not much more than thirty. I sparkle.

"And now clothes," Rebecca says, and leads me from the spa.

"But we haven't paid…"

"I took care of that," she dismisses with a wave of her hand. I knew she would, and yet I feel like I have to protest.

"Rebecca, I could have—" I *should* have.

"No, you couldn't," she says matter-of-factly, and I don't know if she means because she wouldn't let me, or because it was too expensive. I saw one of their brochures—the retinoid peel that was only part of my power facial was two hundred dollars. She's right. I couldn't have paid for it, even if I felt like I had to make a token offer.

It makes me squirm inwardly to think of all the money Rebecca has been spending on me—the club membership, the cocktails, and now this. She genuinely doesn't seem to mind, but I know in my gut—in my heart—that it's not right to take so much so freely. At the very least, it creates even more of an imbalance of power between us.

Rebecca leads me by the hand to an upscale department store, weaving her way through racks of designer clothes until she gets to a section I've never been in—Personal Style Services. I balk, tugging at her hand. I have to put a stop to this, I know I do.

"Wait…"

"Come on, come on!" She grabs for me again. "It will be great."

"I can't let you…"

"Why not?" For a second she looks petulant, hands on hips, lower lip jutting out. She reminds me of Zoe. "Tessa, if this is some kind of misplaced pride or something…"

"It doesn't feel right."

"It feels right to me. I want to do this, and I can."

"I know, but—"

"Look, not to be crass, but this is nothing to me. Absolute peanuts. Last year, Josh's bonus was two million. Okay?"

For a second all I can do is goggle. Two *million*? I knew she was rich, and yet the blatant number still shocks me. That's silly money.

"So, no more protests, okay?" Rebecca says, and I nod. She marches me through to the personal stylist's area, and I sit on a velveteen sofa while a sleek-looking stylist bustles about, bringing outfit after outfit that have been preselected.

"When did you arrange this?" I ask, because it's obvious Rebecca made some calls beforehand to set up this whole day for us.

"Oh, you know, whenever," she answers with one of her airy shrugs. "There's no point wasting time searching through racks of clothes for something that looks good. Much better to have someone know what you need."

And, according to the stylist, I need flowing tops to cover my admittedly thickened middle and make the most of my "shapely legs". I feel like a piece of meat, a trussed-up turkey, when I emerge in an outfit for the stylist and Rebecca to rate—a tunic top and capris, both of whose price tags make me wince, two-million-dollar bonus or not.

Then I glance in the mirror and I am stunned by the woman I see—a woman who is recognizably me, and yet so not. It's not just the straight hair, or the sculpted eyebrows, or the shiny skin. It's not the expensive clothes or even the "shapewear" the stylist has promised takes ten pounds off, even if it feels like my body is being squeezed like meat into a sausage casing.

No, it's the whole, promising package—the vision of the kind of woman I look at from afar, the kind who spends sunny afternoons outside Starbucks, or weekends at wine bars. Who is confident and self-assured, easygoing and relaxed, instead of lonely and lost inside, struggling to emerge from a cloud of grief. Yes, I can be that woman.

By eight o'clock I'm exhausted, and I don't even make one of my token protests when Rebecca swipes her credit card for the huge amount of clothes she's just bought me. It's wrong. I know it's wrong, no matter how much her husband makes.

As we pick up the bags—six—I stammer a thank you. "Really, Rebecca, you've been so kind. So generous. I should have said no…"

"And deprive me of the pleasure? I've had so much fun." She throws me a careless smile. "I love seeing you like that! Don't you feel fantastic?"

"Well, yes," I admit rather shyly, and her smile widens.

"I know you do! You're on fire, Tessa. Let's celebrate with something fabulous to eat."

"Let me pay for dinner. It's the least I can do."

"Now that I'll accept," Rebecca says, and even though I know it's nothing in comparison to what she's done, I feel as if we're on somewhat equal footing, or at least as equal as we can be, perhaps.

We end up at a run-of-the-mill Italian place with granite tables and lots of glass, the bags all piled at our feet. As we peruse menus I realize I haven't checked in on the kids all day. Neither Ben nor Katherine has a phone yet, even though I offered to buy Katherine one, wanting her to try to connect with the other girls in her class. But she didn't want one, and there wasn't really a need.

"Have you heard from the sitter?" I ask. "Or Charlotte?"

"Hmm, what?" Rebecca glances up from her menu. "Oh no, but that can only be good, right? I'm sure they're fine." She wags an admonitory finger at me. "Relax, Tessa. Today's for you. You don't need to worry about the kids."

"Okay." I want to ask her if she can just send a single text to put my mind at ease, but I don't. When it comes to Rebecca, I'm a coward as well as a pushover, and besides, she's right. One day for me. For us. Surely I can handle that?

"Seriously, they're fine, okay?" Rebecca leans forward. "I know you think Ben is too boisterous, but he's *nine*. He'll calm down."

"Right." I'm not sure what to say to this, because I've never actually told her that, have I? I suppose it's obvious.

"And Katherine just needs to grow into herself. Eleven is such an awkward age, isn't it? Not a teenager, not a little girl."

"It's not… just that."

"She's shy. Let her be shy. There are worse things, trust me."

I nod, feeling both exposed and reassured. Yet I can't help but feel that Rebecca doesn't really get it. That she doesn't understand how isolated I feel, day in and day out, wishing my mom were around, wanting some friends to moan and worry to, needing to feel like I'm getting it right for once.

I wonder how many friends Rebecca has back in Manhattan. I picture her as the leader of a gaggle of skinny blonde crows, everyone being vicious behind each other's backs. Maybe she's glad to be away from them.

"So, what shall we order?" she asks, and plucks the drinks menu from between the salt and pepper shakers.

"We are driving," I remind her, even though she's the one who is driving, not me. Rebecca glances up, her eyebrows raised. "Exactly, so I'll limit myself to one cocktail." Her smile is easy, innocent, without even a glimmer of self-consciousness.

It's not that I think Rebecca has a drinking problem, I really don't. I know she drinks a fair amount, and over the last few weeks she has definitely been at least a little buzzed on occasion, when she's kicked back with a glass of wine—or three. And of course there was the dancing-on-the-table incident she's mentioned, but still, an *alcoholic*? Rebecca? That's taking it several steps too far, surely? She's way too in control for that.

"What are you going to have?" she asks, and hands me the drinks menu. As I take it, I catch my reflection in a mirror across the room—the swing of hair, the sculpted brows… they both surprise and thrill. I'm different now, I'm finally different.

"I think I'll go with a Sex on the Beach," I say recklessly, and Rebecca laughs.

"It's not like we're having much of that, is it?"

"I'm not having much sex in Brooklyn," I quip back, and Rebecca gives a grimacing nod, although her eyes are smiling.

"Tell me about it! Upper East Side sex isn't happening much, either."

Although her tone is light, as mine was, I think we're both aware of how much we've just confessed, although maybe we haven't admitted all that much. Neither of our marriages is in a good place. That's at least part of why we're here in the first place, surely?

"So, is Kyle coming for the Fourth?" she asks, and I shake my head.

"Busy with work." I don't want to explain about the music gig, or how uneasy it makes me feel. "What about Josh?"

"He hasn't decided yet." Rebecca drums her fingers on the tabletop. "My parents aren't coming though, so that's something."

"They're not? When did that happen?"

"Oh, last night." Rebecca shrugs, seeming unconcerned. Considering how a week ago the prospect of their visit filled her with dread, I am a little nonplussed by her lack of reaction now. "I told them I wasn't up for it, and they decided it was a bit long to drive just for the weekend."

"Oh. Wow." This is so different from the way she was talking about her parents before that I'm really not sure what to make of it. "I guess that's... good?"

Rebecca's smile is hard and bright as she reaches for the cocktail the waitress has just delivered. "Yes," she says. "It is."

In the end Rebecca has two cocktails, and I drive home. Somehow I expected this, and it feels almost normal. We don't talk much; Rebecca dozes and I focus on maneuvering this huge vehicle that's twice as big as my rental. I realize I am looking forward to Katherine and Ben's reactions to my new self.

When we pull into the drive of Rebecca's house, it's after eleven. During dinner, the babysitter called to say Katherine and Ben wanted to sleep over, a prospect that filled me with hopeful surprise. Maybe they were all getting along a lot better than I realized.

We tiptoe into the house and Rebecca pays the sitter, who is, amazingly, still on her phone, thumbs moving as fast as Ben's do.

"Let me pay for some of that," I offer, but Rebecca predictably waves me away. "Where are all the kids?" I ask once the sitter has clattered down the steps from the deck.

"Let's go see." Rebecca lets out a slightly tipsy giggle. Together, like a pair of kids ourselves, we creep upstairs and peek inside the bedrooms, which are all huge, with soft, cream carpets and built-in wardrobes. They're also empty.

"What…?" My stomach plunges icily. Surely the babysitter wasn't so incompetent that she lost five children?

"Tessa, look!" While I've been staring sightlessly into Charlotte's empty bedroom, Rebecca has gone up to the playroom. I follow her upstairs, and then draw my breath in surprise when I see the five of them all laid out on the floor like a row of sausages, fast asleep in sleeping bags.

"Don't they look angelic?" Rebecca whispers.

Ben looks as if he hasn't washed his face or brushed his hair all day, and Katherine is sucking her thumb in her sleep, but still, it's a lovely sight.

"Yes," I whisper back, "they do."

"Why don't you sleep in the guest room?" Rebecca suggests when we head back downstairs. "It's already made up and it seems a shame to wake Ben and Katherine to go back to yours."

"That's really sweet…"

"I'll make pancakes in the morning. We'll all have a slumber party!" She giggles, and I find myself laughing along with her, her playful enthusiasm catching. It's been a fun day, and this feels like a good way to end it.

"Okay, sure," I say. "Thanks, Rebecca. Thanks for everything."

"Thank *you*," she says, and presses her smooth, perfumed cheek to mine. "Seriously. I've enjoyed every minute."

"I have too," I admit. I feel a warm glow inside at the thought.

Alone in the guest room's sumptuous ensuite bathroom, I take the opportunity to study my reflection. I run my hands through my silky hair and trace the smooth lines of my eyebrows. On impulse I take a mirror selfie and send it to Rayha. *What do you think?* She won't answer now, she'll be asleep. But I am smiling as I climb into bed.

CHAPTER TWELVE

REBECCA

I wake up to Zoe peering at me, her face about two inches away from my own. My heart is thudding and there are tears on my cheeks.

"Mommy," she says, and her voice trembles. "You were crying in your sleep."

I roll onto my back, willing my heart rate to slow. "It was just a dream, Zo." My voice comes out in a croak. I feel shaky, the dream still enveloping me, smothering me.

"Mommy…?" Zoe's voice sounds little and scared, so unlike her usual feisty self.

"Why don't you get into bed with me, Zo? We'll have a cuddle before we get up."

"Okay." She climbs in, and I fit her sturdy little body next to mine, wrapping my arm around her waist as I rest my chin on her hair and breathe in her sleepy, little girl scent. I close my eyes, savoring this moment. For a few seconds I can simply be—I can try to forget my nightmare, my memories, the disappointment I am constantly feeling with myself. Zoe's fury, Josh's distance—it all fades away right now. Zoe relaxes into me and I think she's fallen asleep. I almost feel like the mother I used to be—loving, warm, present. Will I ever be that woman again? It's like looking through the wrong end of a telescope, a tiny, blurred vision of something I can barely discern.

"Are you going to make pancakes?" Zoe asks, startling me out of a semi-doze. I remember my extravagant promise last night, how this would be like a slumber party. Now, in the morning, my body aches and I can't let go of that damned dream, although I try—I've got to try.

"How did you know I was thinking about it?"

"Tessa told me."

"Tessa? She's awake?" I'd sort of forgotten she'd slept over, that I'd invited her to.

"Yes, she's been up for a while. She made us hot chocolates."

"Hot chocolates and pancakes!" I give Zoe a little squeeze. "Sounds like it's going to be a pretty spectacular day." It comforts me, to know Tessa is downstairs, manning the kitchen. I don't have to do this on my own.

A few minutes later Zoe wriggles out of my arms, and then I get up and barricade myself in the shower, letting the water stream over me. In the mirror my reflection is pale, my eyes a bit dark and dazed, but it's nothing a little concealer can't fix. I glance at my naked body and notice new hollows in my shoulders, my hips. My biceps look scrawny. Well, you can never be too rich or too thin, right?

By the time I make it downstairs, the last shreds of the dream are dissolving; I can almost shake it off.

The kitchen is full of sunlight and laughter; miraculously, or maybe not, the children all seem to be getting along, more or less. Max is watching Ben play on his device, peering over his shoulder at the neon, animated blur, and Charlotte and Katherine are painting their nails with one of my bottles of polish. Zoe is outside on the deck, staring out at the water, fists planted on hips, queen of her kingdom.

And Tessa… Tessa is in the kitchen, unloading the dishwasher. Bless her.

"Thank you *so* much," I say as she looks up with a smile. Her appearance startles me; foolishly, I'd forgotten that she got her hair straightened, her eyebrows done. It's amazing how much difference it all makes. She's also wearing some of her new clothes—a floaty sundress in deep red that makes the most of her dark hair and eyes, her curvy figure. She looks alive and lush, while at the moment I feel like a pale, feeble ghost. It's slightly disconcerting.

"It's no problem." She straightens, swiping a strand of silky hair from her face. "Everyone seems to have had a good time yesterday." She glances at Katherine and Charlotte, her expression softening with both hope and love. "They're really getting on well, aren't they?"

"Yes, they are." I feel a surge of affection for her and her easily fixed problems. If only mine were of that variety.

"Oh, and these came." Tessa crosses the room to pick up a huge, showy bouquet wrapped in white tissue paper. The sickly-sweet scent of gardenias and white roses floats out and I blanch, taking a step back as if the flowers are poisonous, as if they'll hurt me. "Rebecca…?" Tessa frowns, the bouquet outstretched, as I simply stare. The smell surrounds me, invading all my senses. I'd forgotten about those flowers. How I used to love them. They were in my prom corsage, my wedding bouquet, sent after the birth of every child. *My* flowers.

"There's a card…" Tessa fumbles among the waxy petals for a small, stiff white card. I take the card from her with numb fingers, forcing a smile to my lips.

"Thanks, Tessa." I nod toward the expanse of gleaming granite. "Just put them on the counter." She does, and I turn away, unable to trust the expression on my face. I don't want to open the card but I do, scanning the lines written by a local florist in an unknown hand.

Hope you're all feeling better! Lots of love, Granny and Grandad.

I exhale quietly, feeling something like relief. What did I think it was going to say?

"Mommy, aren't you going to make pancakes?" I turn to see Zoe standing in front of the sliding glass door that leads to the deck.

"Close the door, Zoe, you'll let the mosquitoes in." Discreetly, I put the card in the trash before turning to everyone with a bright smile. "Now, who wants pancakes?"

We sit around the table in a warm glow of syrup and sunshine, everyone eating pancakes and seeming to get along. Katherine is still copying everything Charlotte does, watching her covertly, or really, not so covertly. Their nails sparkle silver and when Charlotte flips her hair, Katherine does too, or tries to, desperate to make sure she's got it right and not quite managing it. Charlotte notices, I think; occasionally I see her give Katherine a slightly superior and pitying smile.

Ben and Max seemed to have found some sort of common ground; as far as I can tell Max is aping Ben in the same way Katherine is Charlotte. He watches Ben nervously, flinching a little at the bigger boy's expansive movements; in the course of one meal Ben has overturned his glass of juice and the bottle of syrup, and put his elbow in the butter dish. It doesn't bother me the way it does Tessa, because I can tell he's simply at that age where his body is too big for him. Like I told Tessa, he needs to grow into himself, and I know he will. He's not unkind, just careless, no matter how Max flinches.

As for Zoe… she sits alone, watching everyone with slightly narrowed eyes, faintly pursed lips, occasionally looking to me for some kind of reassurance. I smile at her and pat her arm, and for a second she leans in to me. I close my eyes briefly, savoring the moment, rare as I know it is.

Tessa is seated at the other end of the table, listening to the general chatter and drinking coffee. Every once in a while she glances at her reflection in the sliding glass door, and a little, secretive smile flits about her lips. She's like a woman who has fallen in love with herself for the very first time.

Everyone is having fun but I can't relax fully, soak in the sunshine. I feel restless, the smell of the flowers overpowering and unpleasant, but I don't want to draw attention to them by throwing them out in front of everyone. It would make far too much of a statement, and yet I am desperate to get rid of them.

"We need to go to sailing," Zoe announces, and as I glance at the clock I realize it is ten minutes until we need to be at the yacht club. "And," Zoe adds, unable to keep a sly note of triumph from her voice, "Ben and Katherine can't come since they don't have a membership."

I'm about to reprimand Zoe or insist that they can come, even though they haven't before—I'm not sure which—but somewhat to my surprise Tessa interjects before I can so much as open my mouth.

"It's okay, Zoe. We're not much of sailors, really. I think we'll just see you at the club afterwards, okay?" There is something casual, even offhand, about the way she says it—"the club", as if it's hers. Of course it is hers, she's a member—I made sure of that.

Tessa stands, stretches, and then starts clearing plates. "Ben and Katherine, why don't you guys run back and get your swim stuff while I clean up?"

I watch as her children stand up and then obediently file out. They clatter down the deck steps while I simply sit there, feeling as if there has been a subtle yet tectonic shift in our world that I don't quite understand.

"Thanks for everything," I say to Tessa as she begins rinsing the sticky plates in the sink.

"I'm the one who should be thanking you, for yesterday," she replies. Which is true, of course. The spa treatments and the clothes cost more than I expected, but money has never been an issue, and so I didn't care. I still don't. "Really, Rebecca." She turns to me with a tremulous smile yet with a spark in her eyes, a new, blossoming confidence about her that unnerves me somehow. "You've done so much for me, I'm so grateful."

"It was my pleasure." I finish the dregs of my coffee, caught between satisfaction at how changed Tessa is—totally my doing— and the slightest prickle of unease whose cause I can't put my finger on. I still need to throw out those flowers.

Zoe, Charlotte, and Max come back a few minutes later, with tote bags and boat shoes, and I grab my purse and my keys. Tessa is still loading the dishwasher.

"Just leave it," I tell her. "I'll get to it when we're back."

"Oh, you're leaving already?" She straightens, tucking a strand of hair behind her ear. "Sorry, I'll go."

"You don't have to. I leave the house open usually." I fall silent, and we stare at each other for a few seconds, both of us waiting for something, but I'm not sure what. Then Tessa smiles and shrugs. "I'll just get my stuff."

"We'll see you at the club?"

"Yes, absolutely." She smiles, a beam of light across her face. "Can't wait."

I smile back, heartened by her easy cheer. I'm glad our spa trip boosted her confidence. It's nice to know I've helped someone, even if I can't help myself.

"Mom." Zoe pulls on my hand, and I realize I'm just standing there, staring.

"Get in the car," I tell her. "I'll be there in a few secs."

Zoe pouts but then goes, as do Max and Charlotte. I can hear Tessa upstairs and in one quick movement I seize the bouquet of flowers and take it to the black bin in the adjoining garage. I stuff it down as far as I can, under some empty pizza boxes, thorns snagging on my skin, leaving a smear of blood on my palm.

I close the lid of the bin with a clatter as well as a deep sigh of relief, and then I head outside to the car.

"Sorry," I say as I get in the car. "I just had to do one little thing. We won't be that late, Zoe, I promise."

Tessa still hasn't left the house, but there's no reason to wait. We'll see her later, and it's not like I have anything to hide—anything she could find out, anyway, by poking through my house, not that she would.

"Mommy, let's *go*," Zoe says, a strident tone in her voice, and shrugging the last of my unease aside as best as I can, I reverse out of the driveway.

CHAPTER THIRTEEN

TESSA

Ben and Katherine are waiting by the car as I stroll over from Rebecca's house, enjoying the sunshine on my face. I've enjoyed everything this morning, from the ping of the text from Rayha that woke me up in the sumptuous double bed in Rebecca's guest room, to the surprising flutter of pleasure I feel now at going to the club this afternoon, on my own. This is the new me, and I like it.

Rayha was impressed by my new look; at least I think she was. *Wow!* she'd texted, followed by several different emojis—laughter, amazement, smileys. *I barely recognize you?!?!*

I barely recognize myself, I'd texted back. And that was a good thing. I liked this glossy version of myself, this image of a woman who can stroll through life, who can take it all in her stride, who has never felt anchorless and adrift. I felt like the Instagram version of myself, airbrushed and at ease.

The whole morning felt touched with a kind of magic; when the children came down a little while later, tousle-headed and sleepy-eyed, their jaws all dropped rather comically when they saw me, even Zoe's.

"Mom," Katherine breathed, and stroked my shiny hair. "What did you do to yourself?"

"Had a haircut," I answered with a smile and a shrug. "And a few other things. Do you like it?"

"You look beautiful," Katherine said, and her words sent a glow spreading through me like butter on toast. She touched my hair again, letting her fingers slide through the silky strands.

"I think you look weird," Ben said, but he was smiling, and I just laughed, letting everything roll off me because somehow now I *could*.

"Truth be told, Ben, I feel a little weird." A little different.

"I think you look nice," Charlotte said frankly, giving me a thorough once-over, and Zoe said nothing at all, which I counted as a win.

"You guys all seemed to have fun yesterday," I remarked, although I didn't know for sure. This was greeted with a variety of shrugs and smiles, which I also counted as a win. Zoe wasn't glowering; Ben wasn't pushing; Katherine looked happy. Things were finally changing. "Now," I chirped with a Rebecca-like clap of my hands, "who wants hot chocolate?"

Somehow it felt natural, pottering around in Rebecca's kitchen, finding milk and mugs, cocoa and sugar. The six of us sat out on the deck, sipping our hot chocolates as the morning mist rose from the shimmering water and a few loons set off with a flapping of their great wings, no one feeling the need to say anything. Even Ben was relatively chilled, doing nothing more than drumming his legs against the rungs of his chair as he slurped his cocoa.

I felt more content than I had in a long time—really, since I could remember. The air was cool and fresh but the sun was warm, the morning suffused with the dreamy, Technicolor light that was better than any Instagram filter, because it was real.

As we sipped our hot chocolate Katherine leaned her head against my shoulder and I patted her arm, reveling in the simple affection that for once felt uncomplicated, savoring the moment.

Could a day at a beauty spa really make that much difference, or was it being here, even being with Rebecca, as part of her world?

Somehow this summer at the lake, for whatever reason, was providing the reset button I'd so desperately needed. That we'd all needed.

Rebecca came down a little while later, looking both tired and surprised at the sight of us all. She made pancakes while I set the table, both of us seeming at ease as we moved around each other with a pleasing synchronicity.

The only slightly awkward moment was when I showed her the flowers that had arrived earlier that morning; I'd assumed they were from Josh but she didn't look too pleased to see the huge, gorgeous bouquet. I didn't ask for details, and she most definitely didn't offer, and the moment moved on.

Now I find I'm actually looking forward to an afternoon at the club, and Ben and Katherine seem to be as well; at least they're not complaining about it. Maybe we'll feel more like we belong there today, because, just maybe, we do.

"You had fun yesterday?" I ask, even though I've asked them this already, several times this morning. I want details; I want proof. But Katherine just shrugs and smiles faintly, and Ben gives one of his boy-grunts. "You all seem to be getting along a bit better now," I offer, and Katherine nods.

"Yeah," she says. "I think so. Charlotte's nice."

"And Ben? You and Max…?"

"He's not a *total* wuss," Ben says grudgingly, and I smile. High praise indeed, from Ben.

At the club the receptionist greets me with a smile and I walk in with a swing in my step. After we've all changed, I settle into my lounger while the kids have a free swim before the start of their lessons, the sun sparkling off the pool water. I slip on a pair of sunglasses and flick through one of the magazines the club offers its members, glossy and thick as the ones in the spa, with photos of the kind of life I never thought I could have.

A few minutes later the shriek of a lifeguard's whistle splits the air and I look up to see a red-shorted teenaged Adonis marching toward two boys in the middle of the pool. One is choking and spluttering and sobbing, and one is my son.

Tossing the magazine aside, I scramble off the lounger, my heart beating with hard thuds. I hurry over to the side of the pool, leaning down to address the lifeguard, who is wading through the water, toward the crying boy.

"What happened?" I ask, but he doesn't seem to hear me as he pats the boy on the back, while Ben looks on, nonplussed.

"You," he says to Ben in a tone of total authority. "Out of the pool."

Ben shrugs before clambering out of the pool and shaking the water off him like a shaggy bear. I hurry over to him, conscious of the stares boring into my back as I touch his arm.

"Ben," I whisper urgently. "What happened?"

"He's a sissy," Ben says, his voice far too loud, and I hiss at him to be quiet as I take his arm and lead him away.

"Don't *say* things like that."

"Why not? It's true—"

"*Ben.*" I give his arm a little shake. "What *happened?*"

"We were playing a game and he chickened out. He's stupid." I stare at him desperately, needing more, and then someone behind me clears her throat.

"Excuse me, but are you this boy's mother?"

Slowly, I turn, trying not to flush or squirm as I face down a bustling, busty woman in a brightly patterned tankini, who must be the other boy's mother. She is clearly furious, practically vibrating with it, as the boy cowers and snivels behind her. I've been in this place so many times before, and yet I thought I was different now—I thought we all were.

"Yes... I'm so sorry about what—what happened," I stammer, trying to hold my ground even as I apologize and grovel. "I guess they got a little rough..."

"A little *rough?*" The woman's voice bounces off the concrete walls surrounding the pool area, carrying to every single person who is watching this scene unfold with morbid fascination. "I don't think so. Your son is a complete menace. Toby has told me about him, how disruptive he is during the lesson times." She points at Ben with one trembling, accusatory finger. "He deliberately held Toby's head under the water. He was *drowning* him."

"I'm so sorry," I say with as much dignity as I can. "I don't think Ben knows his own strength sometimes. I don't think he meant to do any harm to—to Toby." The woman snorts in derision and I force myself to continue as civilly as I can. "Ben, say sorry to Toby."

"Sorry," Ben says without an ounce of sincerity in his voice.

Toby's mother fumes at us for a few tense seconds, and then she turns on her heel and marches away, dragging her son behind her. I can still feel everyone's stares, rubbernecking at the little drama that has played out on the poolside. Tears sting my eyes and I blink them back. I'm stronger than that now—at least I want to be.

"Come on," I say to Ben, "let's get dressed."

"But I still have my lesson—"

"Not today," I snap, and I beckon to Katherine, who has been watching us from the other side of the pool. My fingers are shaking as I change back into my sundress in one of the cubicles, the air smelling damply of chlorine.

"Why do we have to go?" Katherine complains in a complete about-turn as I comb through the tangles in her hair and she flinches away from me. "I was waiting for Charlotte…"

"We'll see them later." There's no way I can stay at the pool for another hour while everyone stares at me, condemning, judging. I'm not that different.

"The lifeguard would have let Ben go to his lesson," Katherine persists. "He was just telling him to get out for a few minutes, like a punishment."

"I know." Just as I know I need to clear my head, away from this goldfish-bowl atmosphere. "We'll come back tomorrow, Katherine, don't worry. And we'll see the Finlays later today."

"But why—"

"I'm glad you're enjoying your lessons." I try for a smile, keeping my voice firm. "But right now, we need to go."

"This is all your fault," Katherine hisses, turning to Ben, and he doesn't answer. "Why are you so rough with everyone? Why do you have to be such a bully?"

"Katherine—"

"Well, it's true—"

"I'm not a bully!" This explodes out of Ben, and he looks mutinous. "That stupid Toby is such a wimp. It wasn't my fault." Then, to prove it, he shoves Katherine so hard she falls back off the bench and lands on her bottom, letting out a cry of surprised pain before she bursts into noisy wails. Ben storms out of the changing room.

"See what I mean?" Katherine demands, wiping her nose with her forearm as I help her from the floor.

"You provoked him, Katherine—"

"You never see how mean he can be!" She glares, turning her fury back toward me. "You never see *anything*." I feel like there's more behind that accusation than she's saying, some veiled reference or old hurt, but I have no idea what it could be.

"I'm trying," I say quietly. "I'm not sure what else I can do."

Katherine huffs and pushes past me, and I gather up our swim things and hurry after my children.

Ben is thankfully waiting in the lobby, and he and Katherine follow me sullenly toward the front doors when a sudden trill stops us all in our tracks. "Tes-*sa*! Ben! Katherine! Where are you all going?"

I turn to see Rebecca smiling at us, sunglasses perched on her newly smoothed forehead. "We were just coming to look for you."

"Oh. Uh…" My mind, predictably, blanks.

"Ben misbehaved and got called out of the pool," Katherine announces, with another glare aimed in her brother's direction.

"Some of these lifeguards are a little overzealous, aren't they?" Rebecca remarks with a dismissive flick of her fingers. "Eighteen years old and full of themselves, as well as way too much testosterone." She laughs lightly. "Come on, don't run away. We were so looking forward to seeing you all here."

"I know, but I think we probably should just call it a day…"

"Nonsense!" Rebecca clearly won't hear of it. "You can't let the bullies win," she says, giving Ben a conspiratorial wink. "And I think those lifeguards *are* bullies."

"Really, Rebecca…" I feel I should explain the situation since she wasn't there, but I don't know how to begin.

"Come on, everybody." Rebecca is smiling, in charge, sailing through the lobby, and somehow I follow in her wake, letting myself be propelled back toward the pool. We all change back into our suits, and then we return to the pool area, Rebecca slipping her arm through mine.

"So many bitchy women," she whispers as she steers me toward a couple of loungers off by themselves. "Don't pay any attention to them. *I* certainly won't!"

I nod, feeling a bit better with Rebecca by my side. Running away wasn't really an option. Not a good one, anyway. Maybe we can redeem this situation.

Ben has waded into the pool, with Max edging in behind him, and Charlotte and Katherine are sitting on the side, heads bent together as they splash their feet in the water. Zoe is by herself, swimming with dogged determination as her strokes cut through the water.

I feel myself start to relax. I overreacted, clearly, because of past experience, and I'm glad I came back to see it out. I'm glad Rebecca made me. I even agree to the Mai Tai she orders for me, insisting I need some "medicinal support". And of course she joins me in it, clinking my glass with hers before sucking the maraschino cherry off the straw.

A couple of thankfully uneventful hours later we are heading back out of the club when Rebecca stops by a poster propped on an easel for a Fourth of July party on Saturday.

"We should go to this," she exclaims. "How much fun would it be to dress up?"

I eye the poster uncertainly. A formal cocktail party with dancing at the club, two hundred dollars a head? Definitely not my thing. "I'm not sure…"

"Come on, Tessa," she coaxes. "Don't be such a stick in the mud."

"What about Josh? Isn't he coming for the weekend?"

"He doesn't think he can." Rebecca speaks carelessly. "He says he'll try, but he has too much work, surprise, surprise. Come on." Her smile is easy, inviting. "Be my date."

"I don't have anything to wear…"

"We'll find something, and we won't go all the way to Syracuse for it. There are some cute stores in Geneseo."

"What about the fireworks?" Zoe interjects, sounding stubborn. "You promised we could go see those."

"And so we can," Rebecca returns gaily. "The fireworks are on Friday. We'll have a full weekend planned! It will be so much fun."

Her smile is wide and engaging, her eyes glittering with an almost fevered enthusiasm. I've seen it before, but it feels even more pronounced now. Why is she so determined? Is she cross that her husband isn't coming? Now I look at her properly, I see that despite the spa day, she is looking a little pale, even gaunt. Her skin seems to be stretched tightly over her bones, and her legs look like tanned sticks poking out from under her cover-up. She tilts her chin upward, reminding me of Zoe, as she looks at me.

"Well? Shall I buy the tickets?"

"No, I'll buy them." I can't afford the four-hundred-dollar price tag, but neither can I have Rebecca buying me any more stuff. Even I have my limits.

With everyone watching, I march up to the receptionist's desk and hand over my credit card, my stomach churning as I picture Kyle's reaction. But then he's having his own fun, isn't he, going out to bars, playing his gigs? Making a life without me. So I'll do the same. The new me will be on full display.

"There we are." I brandish the pair of tickets at Rebecca with a smile as determined as her own. "I can't wait."

Later, when we are back at home and the Finlays are back at theirs, Ben and Katherine relaxing inside, I wander out to the lakeside with my phone and call Rayha.

"At least you sound the same," she jokes as soon as she answers, and I laugh.

"I know, I know, it's crazy how different I look, right?"

"It really is." Rayha sounds pensive and even a little sad, which isn't what I expected.

"What?" I ask as I sit down on the sand, my legs stretched toward the water. "Don't you like it?"

"Of course I do. You look like a model, Tessa—"

"Hardly," I scoff, but Rayha is insistent.

"No, you really do. Curvy and sexy and gorgeous. And so glamorous. I don't think I've ever seen you with nail polish."

"I've worn it to weddings and stuff." I glance down at my magenta nails, flexing my fingers to admire the smooth sheen of the polish.

"I guess that's part of what makes me... I don't know, wonder," Rayha says slowly. "It's almost like I don't know you. Stupid, I know, but... why did you feel the need to change so much?"

"I'm still the same," I protest, a little stung. "An eyebrow threading and hair straightening doesn't do that much." The afternoon at the pool showed me that. I may look shiny and confident on the surface, but underneath I'm the same hesitant, uncertain mess. I sigh, feeling dispirited by the thought.

"Good," Rayha says, "because I want you to be the same. I like you the way you are, Tessa."

"At least one of us does, then," I joke, except I'm not really joking.

"Don't run yourself down, Tessa. And don't try to turn yourself into someone you're not."

"Is that what you think I'm doing?"

"I don't know." Rayha backtracks quickly. "It's just this neighbor of yours…"

"What about her?" I haven't actually told Rayha much about Rebecca, besides that she's rich and thin, but maybe that was enough.

"I don't know," Rayha says again. "She seems like a personality, I guess, that's all. An influence." I am silent, because I don't know what to say. Rayha is right, Rebecca *is* an influence, but does that have to be a bad thing? "I'm sorry," she says, "I'm just feeling lonely without you here. I know we don't see each other all that much but it helps knowing you're around." She lets out a shaky laugh. "I miss you."

"I miss you, too." I realize, in an instant, that my friendship with Rebecca is nothing like my friendship with Rayha. It's not even close. And yet…

As ever, my gaze wanders toward the lake house up on the hill. I'm drawn to Rebecca, mesmerized by her and her life, in a way I never have been with Rayha or anyone else. She still has a magnetic pull on me, one I don't even want to resist. "How's Zane?" I ask, and then listen to Rayha try to downplay her daily struggles, reminding me how lucky I really am.

CHAPTER FOURTEEN

REBECCA

I'm going to be good. I've been good since the spa day, involved and excited and completely sober. I haven't had so much as a sip of wine, no cocktails at the club—well, just that one. And I've stopped my evening entertainments in the bathroom, as well. When I think of Charlotte coming in, maybe even realizing what I was up to, everything in me cringes and cowers with the shame of it. How could I expose her to that? I am ashamed and guilty, but worse, I am scared of the damage I might have already done.

I *have* to get a grip on myself, and I will. For my children's sake, I will. I tell myself it's easy, mind over matter. I'm a strong person, I can do this. But I feel like I'm sprinting through life and if I stop, if I pause for one second...

It started when we got back from the club, after Tessa had purchased the tickets for the Fourth of July party. I felt bad that she'd done it, but also a little bit self-righteous. I'd paid for a lot, after all, and four hundred dollars wasn't that much, although maybe it was for her.

I was in the kitchen trying to think of what I could throw together for dinner when Zoe came in from the garage, my parents' bouquet in her hands, her whole body bristling with indignation.

"Why did you throw these out?" she demanded, her voice quivering. I stared at the now-crumpled flowers with their browning petals and struggled to think of something to say. What reasonable excuse I could give, what lie I could tell.

"The smell is a bit overpowering, sweetheart, that's all. It was making me feel a bit sick." I tried to smile.

"It never made you sick before," she shot back. "Why would they now?" She flung out the words; they seemed to hover in the air, reverberate through the room. I had no answer. "I'm going to keep them in my room," Zoe said, her chin tilted at a defiant and dignified angle. "*I* like Granny and Grandad's flowers."

As she marched upstairs, I stood in the center of the kitchen and felt helplessness swamp me. It's clear that Zoe suspects something is wrong. Wrong with me. And Charlotte knows, from the bathroom episode, and Max probably knows too, or at least suspects. I've been pretending they don't, they couldn't possibly, convincing myself it can still all be fine if I just keep acting like it is, but it can't.

And yet still I try, because I don't know what else to do. I inject energy and enthusiasm into everything; I race around, everything on hyper-speed, whether it's baking cookies or going to swim lessons, or simply sitting outside on the deck and watching the sun set over the lake. Everything feels frantic. Everything *has* to be frantic, because if I slow down, I'll be like the spinning top that finally falls over. And then I might never get up again.

But it's fine, it's all fine, because I can keep myself busy— cooking, cleaning, running to and fro. There are so many things I can do.

The day after the flowers incident, Tessa and I traipse into Geneseo to look for dresses. We've left the kids with a sitter, another college girl from the club.

We end up in a strip mall on the edge of town, trying on cheap off-the-rack dresses at a no-name department store with clothing stacked in bins and hanging on circular racks. It could be worse. Maybe.

"Occasionally you find something good in a place like this," Tessa says with a smile as she swipes through a rail of dresses, hangers clattering. "You just have to look hard."

"So it seems." I've never shopped in a place like this in all my life, and truth be told, I don't know where to begin. Everything looks tacky and cheap.

Tessa looks different today, though; she's washed her hair, so it's not as straight, but she must have done something to it because it's not as frizzy, either. It falls in gentle waves about her face, softening her appearance. She's wearing a pair of old cut-off jeans shorts and one of the new t-shirts I bought her, in emerald green with gold embroidery, and somehow the pairing works. She looks, I realize, less like the stranger formed in the spa, but not back to her old, boring self. Something new and better.

"Ah-hah! What about this?" Tessa brandishes a slinky dress in deep burgundy. I eye it askance.

"It's not really my color." I generally stick to pastels for day and black for eveningwear.

"I was thinking for me, actually," Tessa says, and holds it up to herself.

"Is it your size?" I ask skeptically, realizing too late that I might sound spiteful, but she'd have to pour herself into that dress. Spanx might not do the trick.

"It is, actually," she returns, flushing a little. I feel mean. "I'm going to try it on."

She heads to the fitting rooms at the back of the store and I wander through the racks, determined to find something for myself. I pick up a couple of dresses that aren't the ugliest things I've ever seen, but a far cry from what I'd normally wear on an evening out. I've just draped them over my arm, heading for the fitting rooms, when Tessa comes out.

"What do you think?" She sounds shy, but somewhat to my surprise she looks fantastic. She *is* poured into the dress, but her curves are sexy and the slinky material flares out around her calves. She blazes like a jewel. "Is it too much?"

"No, it's amazing," I answer honestly. "You look like a brunette Marilyn Monroe. Seriously, Tessa, you should get it."

Her smile blossoms across her face like a flower in sunlight and I hurry to the fitting room to find my own diamond in the rough. Except, as I stare at my body in the three-way mirror, I realize, with a sudden, sickening jolt, how absolutely awful I look. I'm a scarecrow, clothes hanging off me, the angles of my elbows and collarbone sharp and jutting. I didn't realize how much weight I've lost in the last few weeks, even though I've looked in the bathroom mirror countless times. Several pale pink lines crisscross my upper arms and thighs, more than I realized. I look like some kind of victim, someone you'd see in one of those depressing war documentaries.

Quickly I turn away from my damning reflection and yank on the first of the dresses. It's black and it hangs like a bag on me, looking terrible. I hurry to take it off, trying to avoid my reflection from three different angles, but I keep catching glimpses and they make me wince.

"Rebecca?" Tessa calls. "Find anything good?"

"Not yet." I try for a light laugh and grab the second dress, a pale pink confection that looks like it belongs on a bridesmaid. No, no, and another no. It's just as awful. I look like Jane in *What Ever Happened to Baby Jane?*, a deluded geriatric acting like a little girl. Tears sting my eyes; this is ridiculous, I don't need to get upset about this. And yet I am, because I look and feel awful, and nothing is going to change that. Certainly not a cheapo dress from a bargain basement department store.

I don't even bother with the third dress. Instead, I slip on my clothes and bundle the dresses up, thrusting them into the corner of the dressing room like garbage. Then I take a deep breath and step out of the cubicle to where Tessa is waiting, her dress already bought and bagged.

"Well?"

"Nothing I really liked, I'm afraid."

"Let's try somewhere else. Maybe one of the smaller boutiques on the main street?"

I'm not in the mood anymore, not remotely, but I need something to wear and Tessa jollies me along, chatting about the history of Geneseo, of all things—apparently, she read some booklet somewhere. The name comes from the Iroquois, she tells me, for beautiful valley. I pretend to listen, to care, but inwardly I am still seeing how awful I looked in the mirror. Does Tessa see it? Do my children? Maybe I'm not hiding nearly as much as I think I am. And with another sickening jolt, I realize I must not be, not even close.

We drive to the main street and then stroll down the sunny sidewalk until Tessa pulls me into a small, homely boutique. It's not at all the sort of place I'd normally go, a mix of boho and boring, with plastic trays of bangles and jumbled-up necklaces on the counter. I simply stand and watch as Tessa browses through the racks before coming up with a sheath dress in lilac.

"And check this out," she says, flipping the dress around to show the deep V in the back, so it would skim my tailbone. "Sexy, huh?"

It is sexy, although I'm not sure I'll look sexy in it. But I agree to try it on, and when Tessa insists I model it for her, I do. I feel distanced from myself, acting out a part in a play. Thankfully I know my lines, even if I'm uttering them in a near monotone.

"You look amazing," Tessa exclaims. "Like a model. A flapper."

"Is that the in look these days?" I quip. I glance at myself in the mirror, trying not to notice the dullness of my hair and eyes, the painful jut of my shoulder blades, like chicken wings. Can't Tessa see how awful I look? Is she just pretending not to notice? We only went to the spa a few days ago. Did I look this bad then? I feel like I don't know anything anymore, like I can't trust myself—not even my own eyes.

I buy the dress, mostly because I don't want to shop any longer, and then we have a coffee at a quaint little place on Main Street.

"Has Josh decided if he's able to make it for the weekend, after all?" Tessa asks as she sips her latte.

I shake my head. "He's decided he can't come. Too busy, after all." He told me for certain last night, sounding genuinely regretful, which is something, I suppose. I didn't say anything in response; I just let it go. The conversation was short, flat; we really have so little to say to each other, but then I wonder if we *ever* had that much to say. Life was always so busy—children, work, parties, fundraisers. When we talked, it was usually just about everyday details, or meaningless gossip. Nothing deep. Nothing real, at least not that I remember now, when something horribly real is threatening to overwhelm me.

"So, we're both single for this party," Tessa says with a little laugh. "You really will be my date."

"We'll have to laugh it up." I force a note of enthusiasm into my voice. "Dance the night away."

"I haven't gone dancing since my college days." I hear a note of nostalgia in Tessa's voice that makes me think she must have been different, back then. More carefree. Weren't we all? I try to think of my twenty-two-year-old self, swanning about Manhattan, the whole glorious world my oyster, and I almost laugh in disbelief. Was I ever like that? Was I really like that, just a few months ago?

"Rebecca…" Tessa's voice is both warm and hesitant as I blink her back into focus. "Is everything…" She gives me a smile full of sympathy. "Well, is everything… okay?"

I tense as I stare at her, wondering why she is asking, how obvious it is. How obvious I am. And for a few glorious, liberating seconds I imagine telling her the unvarnished truth, whatever that really is. *I think I'm going crazy but I'm not sure. I hope I am, because it's worse if I'm not.* My throat thickens and I feel that dizzying sense of expectation, like when you're about to jump off a diving board. Everything inside me tenses, springs…

And then I gaze at Tessa, her hair curling about her face, everything about her so warm and vibrant, and I think, *I can't. I just can't.*

"I'm a little down, I suppose," I say as casually as I can. I know I have to admit to something. "Things haven't been too easy lately… I mean, back in New York."

"Because of Josh?" She looks so serious, so intent.

Bizarrely, I almost want to laugh. As if my marriage is the only problem I'm facing. "Yes, a bit. Just… everything." I take a sip of coffee and look away, willing this to be over. I have nothing more to give. But apparently Tessa does.

"I've been going through a hard time too, you know," she says quietly. Each word seems to be chosen with care, said with reluctant yet deliberate purpose. "For a while now." I wait, saying nothing, because for once in my life I don't actually know what to say. My easy social glibness has no place here. "I suppose it started when my mom died," she continues, and her voice hitches. "Or really, when she got sick. She had a bad stroke, years earlier, when Katherine and Ben were both little. It was really hard. And then she died two years ago, when Katherine was nine. We moved to Park Slope a year after, from farther out, for the elementary school. I thought that would make it easier, but I don't think it did."

I nod, intrigued now. "Did something… happen?"

"No, nothing big anyway, and that was part of it. I thought it would be easy, making friends, fitting in, but it felt so hard—for me, for Katherine. Ben, as well." She pauses. "People weren't as friendly as I thought they'd be." Another pause, as she presses her lips together. "They weren't friendly at all. I felt like I was invisible, as if it didn't matter what I did…" She shakes her head, lost in those sad memories, and I try to comfort her.

"It sounds like it was a tough time, Tessa. But at least you got through it." Which is more than I can say about me right now.

"Well, all I'm trying to say is, I get it. Life can be hard, even if we have it easy compared to some. To most."

I let out a hollow-sounding laugh. "I know I do." My oh-so-charmed life.

"I don't know what's going on behind that perfect veneer, though," Tessa says quietly. "What secrets you have, or hidden sorrows. But just because your life looks pretty good from the outside, doesn't mean it always is." I stare at her, my heart beating painfully, my throat tightening like a vise. I say nothing. "So all I'm saying is, I'm here. If you need me, if you want to talk."

"Thanks," I manage, and we finish our lattes in silence.

The next night is the country fireworks on a point at the other side of the lake, and I pack an extravagant picnic, blankets, and folding chairs, determined to make it as much fun as possible. Tessa's heartfelt words rubbed me raw, and that's one thing I don't need. I'm trying to stay on an even keel, and her sympathy has the power to tip me right over.

"Can we stay for the whole thing?" Zoe asks, not for the first time, as I load the car. "Right till the end?"

"I said we could, sweetheart." The fireworks don't end until ten, but it's summer, and the night is warm and sultry, the sky slowly darkening to violet. "It will be so much fun, won't it?"

We're all in a good mood as we head toward the point. Charlotte has insisted that Katherine come with us, and Max has gone with Ben in Tessa's car. I turn on the radio and start singing along to Miley Cyrus's "Party in the USA". Zoe joins me, and we share a complicit smile as we belt out the lyrics.

The point is busy with people—families stretched out on blankets, kids and dogs running around. The sun is sinking below the lake, the surface placid and golden, the sky now indigo at the edges. I breathe in the warm night air, inhale the not-unpleasant scents of hotdogs, cotton candy, and citronella candles. Laughter drifts on the mild breeze.

Ben barrels by me, followed by Max, and Charlotte and Katherine are giggling together. I smile at Zoe. "Help me set up?"

"Okay."

We find a spare space in the field and spread the blanket out. I start unpacking our picnic, handing each item to Zoe, and then Tessa joins us, spreading out her own blanket next to ours.

"Here, try this." I dip a strawberry in whipped cream and pop it into Zoe's mouth. Her eyes go round with delight and she grins, whipped cream on her chin. I smile back, glad to have made her happy, to have this moment. I can still do this, I can still be a good mother. I can give this furious, uncertain daughter of mine what she needs, at least in the little things.

"Now it's your turn," Zoe says, and picks the biggest strawberry and stuffs it into my mouth so I practically choke. She grins and I burst out laughing, wiping strawberry juice from my chin as I force the fruit down.

"You never do anything by halves, Zoe."

She nods proudly, a point of honor. "No, I don't."

Later, as we lie on the blanket, our bodies pressed close together, and ooh and aah at the glorious starbursts of fiery color above us, I let a frail, fragile hope buoy my soul. I let myself believe in it. I can get through this. I will fight my way to the other side, for my children's sake. I reach for Zoe's hand and as the fireworks continue to pop and explode, I lace my fingers through hers and hold on.

CHAPTER FIFTEEN

TESSA

"You look so pretty, Mom."

I turn from my reflection to smile at Katherine standing in the doorway of Rebecca's guest room. We've been getting ready for the club's cocktail party, and it made sense for me to do it over here. We've been spending more and more time in Rebecca's house, coming over right after breakfast, eating dinners out on the deck.

Coming back to our little cottage for bed sometimes feels like returning to real life—or a bad dream. We never stay very long, and we're always back here or at the club, letting this life be ours. And it is. For a summer, it is.

I smooth the silky material over my hips, enjoying the way it flares out around my calves, how sexy it makes me feel. How happy I am. "Thank you, Katherine." I reach for the crimson lipstick I decided to be bold enough to try. I feel daring, courageous, so different from my normal, shrinking self. I've been coming into myself over the last few weeks, in a way I had longed for but had never actually hoped would happen. And it has. By some miracle, it has.

This morning I called Kyle to ask him how the gig went last night. In addition to daring, I felt magnanimous; I hoped he had a good time. Maybe, with this new version of me, we can work our way back to each other again. We can meet each other on equal ground.

"It was great," he said, brimming with enthusiasm. "Paul played drums and I played bass. We did six numbers and they asked for another one at the end."

"Wow! That's wonderful." I vaguely remember Paul from our college days, and then a bit after—a guy who never grew out of saying "dude" or thinking a rock festival t-shirt was dressing up. "Will you play again?"

"Yeah, we might, next weekend. If they want us back."

"I'm glad, Kyle. It's great that you can get back into your music."

Kyle was silent for a moment; perhaps he doubted my sincerity. "Yeah, well," he said at last, and his tone was more reserved. "How are things up north? How are you?"

"Fine." I haven't told him much during our few brief conversations. He knows about Rebecca, and I've mentioned that the kids are taking swimming lessons, but I haven't wanted to go into the whole imbalanced dynamic between Rebecca and me—although perhaps it isn't as imbalanced as it was. I feel more in control of myself, on slightly more equal footing with Rebecca, money aside. Something has been shifting slowly over the last week, although I'm not even sure what it is. "I'm going to a party tonight, actually," I said, and I could feel Kyle's surprise, even through the phone.

"You? A party?"

"What?" I tried for a laugh. "I used to like parties."

"Used to," he repeated with emphasis. "You haven't gone out—anywhere—in years, Tessa." There was something quietly sad about his tone that caught me on the raw.

"There hasn't been much opportunity," I retorted. "But I'm going out now."

"I'm glad." He sounded sincere, almost fervent. "I'm glad you're going out."

I finished the call feeling uneasy. It almost sounded as if Kyle was blaming me for not going out, not having friends, and that thought rankled. Why does everything always feel like it is my fault?

Now I push the conversation to the back of my mind and focus on the positives. A night out. Yes, I'm a little nervous, but I like my dress and I've straightened my hair and I think I look good. I'm determined to enjoy myself.

"What are you guys going to do tonight?" I ask Katherine, catching her eye in the mirror as I put my lipstick on. "Watch a movie? Do your nails?" It still heartens me that Katherine has finally found a friend. I'm not so naive not to realize that, as with Rebecca and me, the relationship is a little bit unequal. Charlotte, with her aura of quiet authority, calls the shots, but that's okay. All friendships are like that, aren't they, to some degree? Nothing in life is perfectly balanced.

"I don't know." Katherine digs her toes into the plush carpet. "When will you be back?"

"Not too late," I say, even though I don't really know. "But you don't mind, do you, sweetheart? You'll have fun."

"Yeah," Katherine says after a tiny pause, and for a second she looks uncertain. "Yeah, I know. I will."

I give my reflection one final, satisfied look and then turn from the mirror. Downstairs the other children are milling around, waiting for us to leave. Kerry, the third sitter we've engaged, is sprawled on the sofa, also waiting for us to go.

"Where's your mom?" I ask Charlotte, and she shrugs, calmly indifferent.

"Upstairs, I guess. She's still getting ready."

A few minutes later Rebecca comes down in a drift of expensive perfume. "Tessa," she exclaims, "you look absolutely gorgeous! I knew that dress was perfect for you."

"You look gorgeous too, Rebecca," I say, but it comes out a bit awkwardly because the truth is, she doesn't, not exactly. She's still Rebecca... still tall, still elegant, her blonde hair swinging along the sharp line of her jaw. Her makeup is expertly done and diamonds glint at her ears and throat. Her dress is lovely too, the lilac a perfect foil for her pale good looks, the silky material skimming her body and swishing about her calves.

And yet, despite all that, Rebecca doesn't look gorgeous. She doesn't even look that good. Her complexion is pale and washed out, and even the expensive makeup she's expertly applied doesn't hide the deep, violet circles under her eyes. And while the dress is beautiful, it hangs off her skinny frame in a way that isn't flattering. She's lost weight in the last few weeks, and she definitely didn't need to, even by the Upper East Side's exacting standards. But more than any of that, it is the air of brittle fragility about her that I notice, as if she could break. Splinter apart completely.

"Well?" Rebecca says brightly as she reaches for a gossamer-like cashmere pashmina and tosses it over her shoulders. "Shall we go?"

"Yes, let's." I smile at Katherine, who is hanging back in the doorway, and then look for Ben, but he and Max have disappeared outside, which is something, at least. Better outside than huddled over some screen. "Have fun, everyone. We won't be back too late."

"Yes, we will," Rebecca trills as she grabs her car keys. "Don't wait up." She turns to the babysitter, who has barely looked at us. "Except for you," she adds with a smile, and then we head outside.

We don't speak as we get into Rebecca's SUV. It's a cloudy evening, the clear blue skies of yesterday now hidden behind dank, gray cloud. There's a smell of rain in the air, and the lake looks like a plate of tarnished metal.

"So much for our nice weather," Rebecca says with a little laugh. "At least the party's inside, except for the fireworks."

Her fingers—her new manicure is chipped, I notice—tap the steering wheel as she drives and I struggle for words to say. I can't pretend that something isn't going on with Rebecca, even though most of the time I try to because I don't know how to deal with it directly. Is it something with her husband? Her drinking? She presents such a positive image so much of the time, bright and cheerful and confident. Even when the mask slips I have trouble believing it might be just that—a mask.

Even now I wonder if I'm reading too much into everything, worrying about Rebecca simply because I have to have something—someone—to worry about. That's been my default lately, my way to feel as if I'm in control of my life.

But surely she's fine? She's *Rebecca*. She has, by her own admission, such a charmed life. And most of the time she's a whirlwind of bright, enthusiastic energy.

The other day, when we went shopping, I tried to get her to confide in me, but I could tell she didn't want to, and I didn't press. Sharing a little bit of my own story was hard enough. But tonight there is something urgent and raw about Rebecca, something pulsing and dangerous beneath her elegant exterior. A wave of trepidation laps at me as we pull into the club's parking lot, which is nearly full. Tiki torches flicker by the entrance and waiters brandish trays of champagne and Mojitos as we step through the doors. Tinkling music spills from a quartet set up in the lobby, and people are mingling and circulating, laughter drifting along the breeze.

As excited as I was about the evening, I tense up almost immediately, for my sake as well as Rebecca's. I don't actually know anyone besides Rebecca, and within the first few minutes I've seen a mom I recognize from the pool debacle of a few days ago, when Ben held that poor kid underwater. She clocks me and freezes before quickly, deliberately, turning away. I gulp my Mojito; Rebecca, I see, has already drained hers.

"This is fun," she says, plucking another glass from a tray, and I can't tell if she's being sarcastic or not. We didn't discuss who would be driving home; perhaps she assumed it would be me, since it pretty much always has been. I decide to stick to just one Mojito, even though I'm tempted to down several to ease my jittery nerves.

We move through the crowds toward the dining room, which has been cleared of tables, a band set up at one end. Some people are already dancing, but not many; that critical mass has not yet formed to get everyone planting hands on hips in a group Macarena.

Rebecca sidles along the wall, drinking her cocktail, her gaze darting here and there. She still seems edgy and out of sorts, and I'm not sure what to do. I was expecting her to take the lead, the way she always does, and yet as I stand with her on the edge of the crowd, both of us on the verge of becoming bona fide wallflowers, I realize that over the last week, she's been taking the lead less and I have more. It's a feeling that floods me with both surprise and confidence, a surge of power along with a deepening unease. What's really going on?

"Shall we mingle?" I suggest, and Rebecca looks at me as if I've suggested we strip naked.

"All right, fine," she says after a moment, and we start to shoulder our way through the crowd. Surprisingly, or maybe not, it doesn't take too long before a conversation starts up; the real surprise is that the woman addresses me, and not Rebecca. She grabs me rather tightly by the arm, pushing forward through the press of bodies.

"I just wanted to say, I saw what happened the other day with your son." She sees my wary expression, waving it away. "Oh no, no, no, I don't mean like that. I felt so sorry for you. I've been there, you know? Boys can be a little rough, and that Toby is always crying to his mom the minute things don't go his way. Seriously." She rolls her eyes, and a wave of relief pulses through me.

"Really?" I feel like I'm grabbing onto a lifeline.

"Totally. His mother needs to calm the hell down, if you ask me." She laughs, the sound raucous. I don't know whether to believe her, to trust her version of events, but I choose to because it's so wonderful to hear someone echoing my own hopeful thoughts. "Are you from the area?"

"No, just here for the summer, renting."

We chat briefly about schools and kids and going back to work—she seems overly impressed by my card-making business, such as it is—and when she moves on to chat to someone else I realize Rebecca has gone. I feel a frisson of alarm, both for myself, navigating this crowd on my own, and for Rebecca, wherever she is.

Then a red-faced retiree grabs me by both hands and tells me I must dance with him. I'm too shocked to do anything but obey, and we're soon on the dance floor, shimmying to the latest pop song. He's clearly drunk but fairly benevolent, and soon he dances away toward someone else, but by then I've been joined by several other people, and everyone seems to be getting into their groove.

It's been a long time since I've danced. In my art school days, confidence buoyed by alcohol, I used to get out on the dance floor and sway and twirl, a free spirit wannabe. But now I feel old and awkward, every movement disjointed, my limbs out of sync. And yet no one seems to mind. I catch another woman's eye and she smiles.

Suddenly I feel liberated enough not to care. I start to swish and sashay and even raise my arms above my head, getting into the spirit of the thing along with everyone else.

Before long I am laughing, carried away, filled with a sense of my own buoyant being, part of something greater than myself, the music pumping through me. It's only when the song switches over to a slow number that I look around and realize it's been an hour and I still can't see Rebecca. I order a glass of juice from the bar and stand and sip it while my gaze travels slowly around the crowded room, couples swaying to the music, others clustered in knots around the dance floor. She's tall enough that I should be able to spot her quite quickly, but I don't see her anywhere.

Something prickles along my skin, a shiver of apprehension that doesn't make sense. We're at a party. Rebecca is a grownup. She can do what she likes, just as I can.

And yet... I remember how edgy she seemed earlier, the barely leashed energy that felt different, dangerous. I leave the empty glass on the bar and walk out of the dining room; the lobby is half-empty, people drifting about, knocking back drinks or sneaking a smoke by the open doors. Rebecca isn't there.

"It's time for the fireworks," someone official announces, and as I stand in the middle of the lobby, feeling lost, everyone starts to head toward the doors to get a look at the firework display. Having seen some last night, I'm not too bothered, but I want to find Rebecca.

I follow the crowd outside onto the front lawn, but I can tell she's not there. I sense it, even amid the crowds in the dark. And so while everyone mills around outside, I go back in, wandering through empty rooms, past piles of discarded cardigans and purses and high heels, half-filled drinks abandoned on tables and trays, to the French doors that open onto the pool area. Moonlight glimmers on the placid water; the loungers are all folded up and put away and there is a ghostly feel about the place. In the distance, I hear the initial rat-a-tat-tat hiss and then the sonic boom of a firework going off, feel the thud in my chest. As the sound of the firework fades away, there is nothing but silence, and then—a small, muffled sound.

My scalp prickles and I keep moving forward. From the shadows someone kicks a chair, and it falls over with a loud, metallic clatter. I hear a suppressed giggle, a whispered "sssh". I should leave, I know that; I'm not dumb, I know what's going on—what has to be going on. And yet I don't. I keep walking forward, my heart thudding in time with the firework explosions. A particularly high-flying one sends a shimmer of green, otherworldly light over the whole pool area, and that's when I see it. Them. A man and Rebecca, pushed up against a pillar, her leg wrapped around his waist.

I freeze in shock, all my senses assaulted by the sight. Her head is thrown back, her eyes clenched shut, almost as if she is in pain. Her leg looks pale and bony, hiked up by his hip; he is all roving mouth and hands, and as I stand there, numb with shock, it occurs to me that he's not even good-looking. He's paunchy and middle aged; I can see his bald spot from here. *What is she doing?*

I am so shocked I simply stand still, rooted to the spot, speechless and staring. Has Rebecca done this before? Is this kind of thing why she's ended up in Upstate New York instead of the Hamptons? I feel naive and gauche and childish; I never expected *this*. I don't know what to do.

And then Rebecca lowers her head and her gaze locks with mine. For a second I see, or at least I think I see, such emptiness in her eyes that I am stunned all over again, but then it is replaced by a flash of rage—directed at me. She doesn't move, doesn't push the guy off her. She just stares at me as he continues to fondle and maul her, like some gazelle brought down by a mangy lion. The moment stretches on for far too long; I feel as if I've been standing there for minutes, hours. And still Rebecca doesn't look away.

Then, filled with both shame and something akin to horror, I turn away, nearly stumbling in my heels, and run back inside.

CHAPTER SIXTEEN

REBECCA

Shit. *Shit.* Tessa's look of shock and judgment is blazoned onto my brain as I press my head back against the brick pillar, hard enough to hurt, and squeeze my eyes shut. This stupid ass—I don't even know his name—doesn't even notice. He's so intent on his own pleasure that he hasn't seen Tessa—or me.

I am filled with a rolling, boiling shame, worse than anything I've felt before. *How did I end up here?* It's a question I keep asking myself, and yet I have no answers. I just keep sinking lower and lower, and in this moment I'm not sure there's much further to fall.

I'd been enduring his slobbery kisses, feeling nothing, for about ten minutes before Tessa came. Before her glare of startled condemnation shocked me awake. Now I feel the man's fingers slide under my skirt and I plant both hands flat on his flabby chest and push him off me. Hard. He stumbles back, his shirt coming out of his pants, revealing a patch of pale, hairy belly.

"What…?"

I don't bother explaining; I just walk away on trembling legs, straightening my dress as best I can. I have to find Tessa. The crowds blur around me; everyone is coming back indoors from the fireworks, talking and laughing, their voices too loud, ringing in my ears. Desperation leaks out of me like some toxic gas; my teeth are chattering. *I have to find Tessa.*

I have to explain… but how can I explain? The answers don't make sense, even to myself. *I wanted to see if I could still feel something. Anything. I'm on a mission of self-sabotage, because I don't know what else to do, and I've got to do something.* Tessa would look at me as if I'm crazy. Maybe I am crazy.

When I push my way through the crowds in the dining room, she's not anywhere to be seen. I feel dizzy with panic, with self-loathing. What was I doing, and *why*? I don't even know. I'm not sure I can even remember how I got out to the pool area with a guy I don't even know, and a middle-aged nobody at that.

I was standing on the sidelines, watching Tessa dance; she seemed so carefree and happy, tossing back her hair, laughing out loud, and there I was, knowing absolutely nothing could compel me out onto that dance floor. Nothing could make me look as I were having a good time.

These last few days I've been gritting my teeth and trying my best and what tonight has been telling me is, *it's not working.* I can't do this anymore. I can't pretend, I can't fake it until I make it, and I feel as if I'm screaming silently all the time and nobody, *nobody* hears.

I catch a flash of crimson in my peripheral vision, and I turn to see Tessa slip out the front doors. I follow, tripping in my heels, desperate to get to her even though I have no idea what I'm going to say. How I can possibly explain.

I catch up with her at the car; she doesn't have the keys, so she's just leaning against it, her arms folded, her head averted from me.

"Tessa…" I stop, hopeless, helpless.

"It's not my business," she says in a tight voice. "I know that."

"I'm sorry." I don't even know what I'm apologizing for. It's not as if I've hurt *her*. Just myself, over and over again, in as many ways as possible. "I don't… I don't know why I did that."

"You don't?" She turns to look at me; she's practically glaring. "What's going on with you, Rebecca? Why are you throwing away an amazing life, three great kids, a loving husband—"

"You haven't actually met Josh," I interject, and she shrugs angrily.

"He certainly seems loving, calling and texting you all the time. And you're throwing it away—for what? Some balding businessman in Upstate New York? I mean, seriously?"

"If he was good-looking, would it make a difference?" I honestly have no idea how I can make a joke in a moment like this. I feel as if I'm made of screws and bolts, all of them coming loose. Soon they'll be bouncing and rolling away on the ground, and I will be nothing but a pile of rusted, broken bits and pieces that nobody, least of all myself, will be able to put together again.

"I just don't get you," Tessa says.

"I never asked you to." I can't talk to her when she's like this, all prickly self-righteousness. There's no way I can make her understand.

"Fine. Shall we go home?" She nods to the car, holding out her hand for the keys. "I'll drive."

I almost keep hold of the keys, simply because her tone is so bitchy, but then I don't. I can't, I'm drunk. The world is spinning and I feel sick. I hand her the keys and we climb into the car silently.

"I didn't expect you to be so judgmental," I say after we've been driving in silence for a few minutes. I look out the window, at the darkened blur of lake and trees. "You don't know anything about my life, Tessa. You just think you do."

"Fine. Then tell me." I start to shake my head, because I'm not going to tell her anything when she's acting so holier-than-thou, but then Tessa hits the steering wheel with the palm of her hand. "Why won't you tell me?" she demands, her voice rising. "Something's clearly very wrong, and I have no idea what it is. How can I help you if you won't even say, Rebecca?"

"You want to help me?" I let out a laugh utterly devoid of humor. "Really?" Right now, she just seems as if she wants to disapprove of me, as if she's waiting for the chance to feel superior.

"Yes, of course I do," Tessa says, but she sounds uncertain. "Rebecca…"

"No one can help me," I state flatly. "No one."

"Surely it's not as bad as all that—"

"Why? Because I'm rich? Thin? Beautiful?" I say each word with a sneer. I feel as if I could explode or collapse, I'm not sure which. But one thing I know: I can't hold it together any longer. *I can't.*

Tessa pulls into the driveway and we sit there for a few seconds. It's only a little after nine; the kids might still be up. I know what she's thinking: she doesn't want them to see me stumble in drunk. I don't, either; of course I don't. Yet still I unbuckle my seatbelt and walk toward the house, putting one foot in front of the other as carefully as I can. Where else am I going to go? What else am I going to do?

"Rebecca…" Tessa hurries after me, tripping in her heels. With a muttered curse, she slips them off as I start up the stairs to the deck. I walk slowly, precisely, taking each steep, narrow step with care. My heart is pounding and my head feels light. I have no idea what I'm going to do when I get inside the house; it's as if I'm outside of my body, looking in, wondering. *Hmm. What is that crazy lady going to get up to now?*

"Rebecca," Tessa says urgently, and grabs my arm. "Wait." We both stumble, and for a second I think we're going to tumble down the steps to the concrete slab below. The world lurches dizzyingly and I grab onto the bannister, barely managing to right myself. Tessa stares at me with wide, panicked eyes; she's bloodied one knee and her dress, her beautiful dress, is torn, but at least she's kept her balance.

"Rebecca, please. Wait a second. Let's talk…"

"I'm fine," I say, and wrench away from her. I continue up the steps. Tessa follows; I can hear her labored breathing. I wonder what she is scared I'm going to do.

The house is quiet inside; I turn to see the sitter, whatever her name is, taking a pouting selfie in front of the fridge. Her eyes widen as she catches hold of me, her duck face morphing into a frown. "Sorry... I thought you weren't going to be back until late?"

"Change of plans." My voice sounds tinny and strange. Everything feels far away. "Where are the children?"

"Upstairs, watching a movie." She eyes me uncertainly. "Um, are you okay?"

"I'm fine." If they're upstairs, then at least they won't see me. Although if they don't see me... if I just go meekly to bed and wake up the next morning, every morning, endless, nothing changing, nothing ever changing... I feel like screaming at the thought of it. Screaming and never stopping.

"Rebecca!" Tessa's voice is high and frightened. It's only when she grabs me by the shoulders that I realize I *am* screaming. Loudly. "*Rebecca.*" She gives me a little shake, her face so panicked I almost want to laugh.

And then I am laughing—hysterically, the laughter welling up inside me and spilling out in bubbles and squeaks. I sound like I've completely lost it, and that's because I have. Out of the corner of my eye I see Kerry—I remember her name now—looking both fascinated and terrified.

"Rebecca, please." Tessa is still holding me, her face close to mine. "Why don't you..." She searches wildly for some plausible suggestion. "Have a bath? I'll run you a nice bubble bath..."

"And that will solve everything, will it?" Another laugh escapes me, wild and high. Tessa looks at me helplessly, her nails digging into my shoulders.

"It might help..."

"No. It. Won't." The words come out low and deadly. I jerk away from her, stumbling upstairs. Tessa follows me, even though I don't know where I'm going—there's nowhere to go. I end up at my bedroom door, but I stop because I can't go in. I can't curl up on my bed and make this all go away. It's too late for that. It's been too late for a long time.

"Rebecca…" I bat Tessa away like an annoying little fly, my flailing hand connecting with her face. She lets out a yelp. I don't even turn.

I take a deep breath. There's nowhere to go. No way out of this moment, of every moment. This is the rest of my life. I can't escape that; I can't escape anything. This is happening to me, and there is no way to stop it.

A low keening—a ghostly, ungodly sound—escapes me. I press my head against the doorframe, as hard as I can, the grooves in the wood starting to hurt, easing this terrible pressure inside me just a little bit.

Then I tilt my head back and hit my forehead hard against the door. Tessa yelps once more. My head throbs and my eyes water but the pain feels good, just like the cutting does. It distracts me from everything else; bizarrely, it makes me feel as if I am in control, even though I know I am not. Absolutely I know I am not.

I do it again. And then again, harder this time.

Tessa starts pulling on my shoulder. She's crying now, trying to get me to stop, and then I hear Charlotte's high, frightened voice, calling my name. And Zoe, my dear, darling, angry girl, yelling at Tessa to leave me alone.

The world has both sped up and slowed down, shrunk to this moment. My forehead. The door. Pain blazing through me, so I can't, thank God, feel anything else.

"*Mommy!*" I glance down and see Zoe staring at me, tears streaming down her cheeks, her fists grasping handfuls of my dress. "Mommy, stop. Please stop."

And then, at the sight of her terrified face, I finally do. I slide down to my knees, the world whirling around me, and not just because I am drunk. My head is pounding and my vision has started blurring at the edges. Have I given myself a concussion? Could things get any worse? How far do I have to fall to finally get to the bottom of this endless pit?

"Why don't you go upstairs," Tessa says to the children. Her voice is shaky. "Go upstairs, and I'll take care of your mom."

"No." This, of course, from Zoe.

"It's all right," I croak. I start crawling on my hands and knees to the bedroom, the world spinning and darkening around me. I hate the thought of my children seeing me like this, so much so that I can't bear to think about it. I try to blank my mind. "It's all right," I say again. "I'm going to be all right." I know it's a lie. Nothing is all right, and nothing is going to be all right, ever. But somehow I make it to my bed and heave myself up on it, curling into a ball. I hear whispers, people moving around, a choked cry. Pain blazes through me and I drift in and out.

Then, the click of a door, and the mattress shifts as Tessa sits down on the bed. She dabs a damp cloth to my forehead, making me wince. When I open my eyes I see it has come away bloody. I close them again, because everything hurts and I have no words.

"At least take some ibuprofen," Tessa says quietly. "And some water."

I hold out my hand and she tips two pills into it. I pop them into my mouth and grind them down, the bitter, acrid taste flooding my mouth.

"Water…" Tessa says softly, and presses a glass into my hand, guiding it to my lips. I drink, the water dribbling down my chin, because I am that helpless.

"I'm all right," I manage. "Just leave me alone. Please." Tessa hesitates, and I know she is worried about me. Concerned I might do something, hurt myself more. "I just want to sleep," I promise her.

"I'll check on you in a little while," she says, and then she tiptoes away. I curl up into as small and tight a ball as I can and scrunch my eyes shut, as if I can make the world go away. I can't, but at least, eventually, I fall asleep.

I wake to a blazing headache; it pounds through me with hammer blows, and I roll onto my side to retch onto the carpet. I empty out my entire stomach, my heart thudding along with my head. Never have I been so wretched. I don't know what time it is, but everything is quiet and dark and I'm sober enough to recall blurred images and words that make me cringe. I picture Zoe's frightened face and close my eyes. There's no coming back from this.

"Rebecca…?" Tessa calls softly, and then she comes into the darkened bedroom. She inhales sharply and then goes about cleaning up my sick while I lie flat on my back, staring up at the ceiling.

"Why don't we get you cleaned up?" Tessa suggests, and I realize how I must look—covered in blood and vomit.

"I can do it," I say, struggling to a sitting position even though it makes my head ache all the more, and my vision swims. "Really."

"Okay," Tessa answers after a pause. "I'll wait in here."

Somehow I stagger to the bathroom and turn on the shower. I strip off my dress, avoiding my reflection because I'm not ready to see myself yet, and then I step under the hot spray, sinking down to the bottom of the shower stall and pulling my knees up to my chest. I don't know how long I stay in there, letting the water wash over me, wishing I could drown.

Eventually Tessa knocks on the door, sounding worried. "Rebecca… Rebecca? Are you okay?"

How to answer that? "I'll be out in a minute," I call. After another indeterminable age, I turn off the shower and reach for a towel, catching a glimpse of my gaunt frame, the huge, purple lump in the middle of my forehead. I gasp involuntarily, shocked by the sight of myself.

"Rebecca…"

"I'm coming." I dry myself off and wrap myself in a thick terrycloth bathrobe. I open the door, avoiding Tessa's gaze as I cross to the bed and sink upon it. "Thank you for cleaning that up," I say, nodding to the floor. "And for everything else."

"It's no trouble." She makes it sound as if she's picked up some groceries for me.

"How are the kids?"

Tessa hesitates. "Sleeping now."

"Good."

Silence winds its way between us, heavy and expectant. "Rebecca… you need help." Tessa speaks quietly, imploringly, as if I'll disagree with her, insist that I'm fine, and tell her about one of my fabulous ideas. *I know, another spa day! That's what I need. A little pick-me-up.* I bet I could convince her, too, just as I have all along. Instead I let out a huff of hopeless laughter.

"You think?"

"I'm sorry. I should have…"

"This isn't on you, Tessa."

"I should have realized," she insists, "that something was wrong. That you had a problem."

She reminds me of Josh a few months ago, coming into the TV room. *Rebecca, we have a problem.* As if I didn't know. As if I wasn't living and breathing it every day. And that says it all, doesn't it? My problem. *Mine.*

"Don't blame yourself," I say tiredly. "It's not your fault."

"Still…"

"Seriously, Tessa." I close my eyes, blanking out her anxious face, the way her fingers are knotted together. I don't have the emotional energy to assuage her guilty conscience. Not now.

"I called Josh," she whispers. "He's coming up here."

She makes it sound as if she's called the principal, the police. *Uh-oh. Now I'm in trouble.* "When?"

"Now."

"Now?" I open my eyes. Tessa looks at me pleadingly, still needing some kind of assurance or absolution.

"Yes, he said he'd rent a car and come up right away." She checks her watch. "That was a little over three hours ago."

It's a five-hour drive from the city. He could be here soon. I let out a groan, because I'm not ready for that. I'm not ready for anything, but what choice do I have?

"I'm sorry," Tessa says, "if that wasn't the right thing to do, but I didn't know what else…" She trails off, and I don't bother to fill the silence. "I just thought he should know… he'd want to know…"

Actually, I'm pretty sure he *doesn't* want to know, hasn't wanted to know for months, but I'm not sure that even matters now. "I completely understand why you called him," I say dully. "Don't worry about it." I sink back against the pillows. "And thank you, Tessa… for everything." I think of all she's done for me in the last few hours, but I can't even summon the energy to feel embarrassed or ashamed. I'm empty.

"What time is it?" I ask. I must have knocked over the clock on the bedside table because I don't see it.

Tessa glances at her watch. "A little after two in the morning."

I think of Josh driving through the night, intent on getting here, and it's like probing a sore tooth that's been given a hefty shot of Novocain. I can't feel anything right now, but I know I will. It's just a matter of time, and I have no idea how I'll handle it when I do. "Thanks," I say again, and after an uneasy moment Tessa tiptoes away.

CHAPTER SEVENTEEN

TESSA

I can't sleep. I'm utterly exhausted, my eyes gritty, my mind a dazed blur, but I can't sleep. I don't even try. After I leave Rebecca curled up on her bed, I go downstairs and make myself a pot of coffee.

The house is silent, the night still. The children only dropped off an hour ago, too upset and confused to sleep. And I had no answers to give, although I offered what comfort I could. I felt completely out of my depth, and still do.

I pour myself a cup of coffee and take it out to the deck. It still feels damp outside, a muggy heaviness to the air that promises thunderstorms. I sip my coffee and stare out at the unending blackness of the lake, my mind reeling through the events of the evening, as I've been doing for most of the night, still trying to comprehend how we got to this place. How I didn't see how much trouble Rebecca was really having.

I remember the way she walked up the stairs to the deck, like a woman facing her execution. How she seemed so distant, almost as if she wasn't there. And then that unholy screaming, like her insides were being ripped out. Worst of all was when she started hitting her head against the doorframe and I couldn't stop her. I couldn't stop any of it. Why was she like that? What is so very wrong?

My hands are shaking at the memory and I spill coffee onto my fingers. I go inside to pour my coffee down the sink and run cold water on my hand. Everything in me trembles.

Perhaps worse than Rebecca hitting her head so deliberately and methodically was the children seeing her do it. Charlotte was shocked, her gaze transfixed on her mother, Zoe incandescent with terrified rage. Katherine, Ben, and Max had all hung behind, huddled on the stairs, eyes wide, faces pale.

When I finally got Rebecca to stop, I knew I needed to deal with the children first. What on earth were they going to think? They looked like a group of ghosts, huddled together, pale and silent.

"Come upstairs," I said. "It's all right, your mom is going to be all right."

"How can you say that?" Zoe spat. She gave me a look full of hatred, and I couldn't blame her. Her world was collapsing. No one should see their mother like that. For a second I pictured my own mother, lying in bed, unable to speak, barely able to move, her eyes full of torment, trapped in her body. No one should see their mother like that, either.

"I know this is strange and scary," I said as calmly as I could while five children looked up at me with expectant terror. "But it's going to be okay. Your mom is..." I stopped, unable to think of an explanation that would make sense to a child, because the truth is, I wasn't even sure what was wrong with Rebecca. Was she an alcoholic? Was she having a nervous breakdown? Surely something more had been going on tonight than having a few too many.

"What?" Charlotte demanded, her voice ragged. "What about my mom?"

"She's having a hard time," I said gently, and Zoe gave me a well-duh expression because it didn't take a genius to figure that one out. "Come on, guys." I motioned for them to follow me upstairs.

In the playroom I straightened out the rumpled sleeping bags and plumped pillows, trying to seem matter-of-fact. "I know this is hard, but try to get some sleep, okay? Your mom will be much better in the morning."

"Why was she hurting herself like that?" Max whispered. "Why was she banging her head against the wall?" He was always so quiet, sometimes he felt a little bit forgotten. I put an arm around his shoulders, giving him a gentle squeeze.

"I don't exactly know, Max. I think she's feeling sad and that…" I was fumbling in the utter darkness. "That made her feel better, even though it shouldn't."

"But *why*?" He looked heartbroken and mystified.

"I'm sorry, I don't know." I was so ill equipped for this moment. "Get some sleep, things will be better in the morning." No one looked convinced, but they all settled into their sleeping bags, and I sat on the sofa for over an hour, listening to their breathing slowly even out. Katherine, I saw, was sucking her thumb. Zoe was curled up in a tight little ball, knees hugging her chest.

Eventually I went back downstairs and checked on Rebecca; thankfully she was sleeping. I knew I needed to do something, but what? I ended up calling Kyle, even though it was after eleven.

"Tessa?" His voice was sharp with worry. "Is everything okay?"

"Yes… I mean, no…"

"What's happened?"

"I'm okay," I reassured him, my voice shaky. "And the kids are. But my friend… Rebecca… Kyle, I don't know what to do."

"Something's happened to your neighbor?" He sounded both incredulous and relieved.

Haltingly I explained the situation—her drinking, the episode upstairs, the kids. "What should I do, Kyle? She's in no state to deal with them…"

"Call her husband," he said flatly. "It's his problem, not yours."

"I'm her friend—" I retorted, stung, but he cut across me.

"Tessa, you've known this woman for less than a month. You're not her friend. Not her real friend. And you do not have the ability or even the right to deal with this situation." He sounded so certain, it was both comforting and an irritation. I didn't have the *ability*?

"Please, Tessa," he added more gently. "Call her husband. You can't handle this on your own. Surely you realize that?"

"Okay," I relented. Calling Josh did make sense, even if I felt reluctant to take Kyle's definitive instruction. "I guess that's the best thing to do."

"You're okay?" Kyle asked, just to check. "Everything's okay?"

He sounded so worried. "Yes," I reassured him. "I'm fine."

After we'd said goodbye I rooted around for Josh's number; Rebecca's phone had a password I didn't know and so I ended up creeping upstairs to get Charlotte's phone. She was still awake, staring at the ceiling, and without a word she swiped the screen and gave me the number.

"Go to sleep, sweetie," I whispered, touching her shoulder. "If you can."

She stared at me for a moment, her gaze both direct and opaque. "Why do you think my mom hurts herself on purpose?" she asked. "Does it help her somehow?"

I gazed back at her helplessly. "I think maybe she just… didn't know what else to do?"

"Some girls in my class are like that," she continued. She sounded musing rather than worried or sad. "They cut themselves. Some of them do it as a dare."

"I… I don't think that's like this, Charlotte," I said carefully. "But if girls are doing that sort of thing, they need help."

Charlotte didn't answer and I tiptoed back downstairs, gathering my courage for one of the most difficult phone calls I would surely ever have to make.

The phone rang several times and then switched over to voicemail. I left a halting message, explaining who I was and that Rebecca wasn't well and he needed to call me as soon as possible. Three minutes later, he called back.

"Hello?"

"Is this Tessa?" His voice was tense, tired. "This is Josh Finlay."

"Yes… I'm sorry to bother you, uh, Mr. Finlay…"

"Please call me Josh."

"Right, th… thanks." I was stammering in my nervousness. "The thing is, Rebecca is… she's had a bit of a… an episode tonight."

A quick intake of breath made me tense. "What do you mean?"

"She was quite upset…"

"What happened exactly, please?" He spoke politely, but also like a man used to giving commands. And so I explained, leaving out what I'd witnessed at the club, because that wasn't for me to tell.

"How much had she had to drink?" Josh asked flatly.

"I don't know. A few cocktails? She… she was drunk." I felt like I was betraying Rebecca with this information, and I had to remind myself that she needed help. That neither of us could get through this alone.

"Okay." Josh sighed heavily. He didn't sound surprised. "I'll drive up," he said. "I'll hire a car and leave tonight."

"Okay," I said. "That's probably best."

Back upstairs Rebecca was still sleeping and so I moved around aimlessly, sitting with the kids for a while—Charlotte and Zoe were still awake—until they'd both drifted off and then tidying up downstairs. I still felt shaky inside, unable to keep from reliving the evening over and over again, especially its worst moments.

And then Rebecca woke up and was sick, which was almost a relief. At least then I could be busy and useful. But she still looked awful, and not just because of the huge lump on her forehead. She looked as if some essential part of herself, some part of her soul, had been sucked right out of her. There wasn't even any sorrow anymore in her face, her eyes, just emptiness and indifference.

It's three thirty now, and my head aches. I pour another cup of coffee even though I know I won't drink it. I've checked on Rebecca twice more, and she's still sleeping. Everyone is.

I sit on the sofa and wait for Josh to arrive, wondering what will happen when he does. Will he take Rebecca and the children back to New York? It seems like the most sensible thing to do, and yet it fills me with regret. I can't imagine the rest of the summer without them, and yet now I can't imagine it with them, either. Not after this, but perhaps things will look better, or at least clearer, in the morning. My mind drifts over the last two weeks—the afternoons swimming at the club, skinny-dipping with Rebecca, the trip to Syracuse, all of us lying on blankets looking up at the fireworks only last night. So many memories have already been made, happy ones. I remind myself of them because I need to remember that they were real, that those things happened, especially in light of tonight's awful events.

A little after five in the morning a car's headlights cut through the early morning mist that hovers over the lake in gossamer shreds. I rise from the sofa, unsure if I've actually dozed for a little bit. I feel thick-headed, my eyes gritty, my body aching.

The steps to the deck creak under Josh Finlay's deliberate tread. When he appears on the deck, standing in front of the glass door, he is not at all what I expected, which I realize now was some big, bluff man with a red face, a loud laugh, a popped collar, and an ostentatious Rolex. Josh Finlay looks like a grownup version of Max—tall and slight, with rumpled dark hair and glasses. He waits for me to open the door, smiling tiredly.

"You must be Tessa."

"Yes…"

"Thank you so much for being here. For all you've done. I can only imagine how much it has been."

"It's no trouble. I've wanted to. Really. Rebecca and I..." I pause, feeling for the words. "We've become close over the last few weeks."

"Yes, Charlotte said your family was spending a lot of time with them. She's become good friends with... Katherine, is it?"

"Yes." I am gratified by his knowledge.

"Where's Rebecca?"

"She's upstairs, sleeping." He nods slowly, like a man absorbing a blow.

"Would you like a cup of coffee? I made a pot." Hours ago, but still. "You must be tired."

"Thank you, yes. A cup of coffee would be great."

I bustle around the kitchen, getting his coffee, feeling self-conscious because this is his house more than it is mine.

"I'm sorry you've been put in this difficult situation," Josh says as I hand him the cup of coffee, our fingers brushing. "It must be very upsetting for you, as well as for your children." His expression tightens, and I know he's thinking of the kids seeing Rebecca banging her head against the door. I can't get the image out of my mind.

"It is upsetting, but mostly because I'm worried about Rebecca. I've never seen her so..."

"I shouldn't have let her come up here on her own." Josh shakes his head, his face full of recrimination. "Tell me, how has she seemed to you over the last few weeks?" He gestures to the sofas in the adjoining family room, and we sit on opposite ones, as if it's a job interview. "Have you been worried about her before tonight?"

"Not... worried, exactly." I hesitate as I sift through the confused jumble of my feelings. "Sometimes it felt like something was wrong," I say carefully. "But it was only fleeting impressions... a moment here or there. Mostly she seemed so bright and animated..."

"And her drinking?" Josh asks quietly.

"She drank a… a fair amount, certainly." I can't deny that, and yet… "But it just seemed social. Cocktails at the club, or wine with dinner. She wasn't ever properly drunk, not really."

"Just a little bit drunk?" he fills in.

"A little buzzed, maybe, on a couple of occasions." I feel guilty, because I'm not sure this is just about the alcohol. How can it be? People with drinking problems don't scream the way Rebecca did. They don't bang their head against the door until they bleed. "She seemed like she had it under control. Like she had everything under control."

"She always does. She fools everyone, even me." He sighs and leans his head back against the sofa. "Especially me."

I feel a twist of pity for him, because he seems like a man with the weight of the world settled firmly on his shoulders. "There have been plenty of times when everything's been fine," I hasten to reassure him—as well as myself. "Most of the time she's been full of fun, always planning something to do…" I think of her dancing around the kitchen, jumping into the lake. Laughing and belting out pop songs, careless and yet full of energy and fun. I wanted to be like her, and now I have no idea what to feel, or even who to be.

"Rebecca has always had that ability," Josh interrupts my circling thoughts. "It's a gift. She makes everyone feel special and valued, and she's always been the life and soul of the party. It's one of the reasons I fell in love with her."

"I'm sure," I murmur, because I don't know what else to say. Rebecca made me feel special, certainly. I miss that now.

"But I've noticed," Josh continues, "over the last few months, she's seemed increasingly unhappy. Drinking a lot more. First, in private, and then also in public."

"She told me about the party," I offer, and he raises his head to give me a sharp look.

"Did she?"

"Just that she'd had too much Prosecco and was dancing. On a coffee table." I squirm a little, to recount the details now.

"Yes, that's the gist of it. But it was so unlike her. Rebecca loves a party, she always has, but she's never crossed the line. Everyone always looks to her for cues, for inspiration. It was as if, in that moment, she just snapped."

Kind of like she did tonight. "Did she say anything about it? Any explanation…?"

"Just that she'd been having a good time. But it didn't look like a good time. It didn't feel like a good time." He shakes his head. "It felt more… desperate than that. And yet desperation is one word I would never associate with my wife."

I nod, because I know what he means. In one form or another, I've felt that from Rebecca all summer. Like something is wrong in her world but I have no idea what it is. As if she's fighting an invisible enemy, some monster I never even notice.

"I shouldn't have let her come up here," Josh says heavily. "I know that now. I knew it then, really, but I wanted to believe she was okay. She wanted me to believe it too. It's so easy to deceive yourself, isn't it?" He smiles sadly. "So I let her because I thought a new environment might help, a chance to breathe and to be—and she was dead set against going to her parents."

I almost tell him how Rebecca put her parents off visiting, how she seemed, at one point, to dread their visit more than seemed right or normal. But I don't, because I already feel disloyal, as if I am betraying her with every word I say. Shouldn't he be having this conversation with his wife instead of with me?

"You should get some sleep," I suggest. "Since Rebecca is sleeping. Unless you want to talk to her now?"

"No." He smiles tiredly. "I'll wait. Thanks for the coffee, Tessa."

"Of course." I take our empty cups to the kitchen while Josh stands and stretches. I'm not sure what to do, where to go. It's not yet six in the morning, and the children might sleep for another couple of hours.

Josh puts a hand on my shoulder, making me jump a little. "Why don't you get some sleep, too?"

"I'm not sure I can," I admit, although waves of fatigue are crashing over me and nearly making me sway. Still, it feels weird to head upstairs with him. This isn't my house. It's not really his, either.

"Even if you just try for a bit," Josh presses. He takes his hand from my shoulder. "Close your eyes, at least."

I don't feel I can refuse, and I am tired. So, we do go upstairs together, Josh following behind me. I nod toward Rebecca's bedroom, the door mostly closed. "She's in there."

Josh pokes his head in and then steps back. "Still asleep," he whispers. "I'll go sleep in one of the kids' bedrooms till she wakes up."

"Max's room is there." I point across the hall, and Josh smiles his thanks. He looks so worn down and tired, I almost feel like giving him a hug. Of course, I never would.

Once Josh has gone into Max's bedroom, I head into the guest bedroom where I got ready for the party what feels like a lifetime ago. I'm still wearing my scarlet cocktail dress, I realize with a jolt. I haven't even considered changing. I wonder what Josh thinks of me, a crazy-eyed woman in fancy dress at five in the morning. Just all part of this bizarre and sad situation.

I strip the dress off and take a shower, grateful for the stream of hot water that both revives and soothes me. Then I pull on the pair of shorts and t-shirt I was wearing before the party and curl up on the bed. As tired as I am, I don't sleep.

CHAPTER EIGHTEEN
REBECCA

Sunlight is streaming through the crack between the curtains when I hear the door creak open, a careful, familiar tread. I roll onto my back and blink the room into blurry focus.

"Rebecca…?" Josh calls softly. My heart tumbles over. I don't reply. "Rebecca," he says again, and gently he sits on the edge of the bed. He takes in the sight of the lump on my forehead and draws a quick breath in, his face paling, his eyes roving over me as if looking for more damage. More clues.

I look at him—my husband of fourteen years. I was only twenty-four when we married, practically a kid. Josh was the same. We met at a boring party thrown by one of my college friends, a girl I didn't like that much. We both left after an hour and ended up walking downtown, talking for hours, and then having milkshakes at a deli near Times Square. We were married just a year later. It all felt so innocent and hopeful, a million miles from where we are now.

"Oh, Rebecca!" Josh's voice is choked. "What happened?"

"I hit my head," I reply, actually attempting to keep my voice light. This is what I do, my default. We can't get serious. Not even now. Because if we start to get serious, to truly talk, I'm not sure what will happen. What Josh will believe.

Besides, we've never really had that kind of relationship. We have always existed on a plane of easy, superficial happiness—

vacations, evenings out, movies in, children coming one after the other. How many people stop and really stare into someone's eyes, never mind actually say something important and real? So much of life is about skimming, and I was okay with that. It felt like enough. It was enough; it was all I needed. Who needs to debate the meaning of life every day of the week? Who needs to confess to their brokenness and jagged pain? Who *wants* to?

"Why, though?" He reaches for my hand. "Why did you do it? Help me to understand."

I stare down at our hands, our fingers intertwined. His are brown and lean, mine are pale and slender. There is an artistic wedding photo of our clasped hands, rings winking brightly. Now I noticed how ragged my nails look, my polish chipped. Josh's fingers tighten on mine.

"Rebecca."

He's waiting for a response, and the words, so many words, are burning in my chest and bottling in my throat. How even to begin? "It seemed like a good idea at the time," I finally say. Josh sighs; I've disappointed him. Again.

"You can't go on like this."

"I know." I take a deep breath, trying, still, somehow, to reach him. "I know, Josh. I know I can't. I feel like I'm going crazy inside, trying to figure myself out, and it's not working." Another breath, painful, buoying me. This is more than I've ever said before. "I need help."

"I know you do." I feel something almost like relief; maybe there is a way out, after all. A way forward. Maybe Josh can help me, guide me, through this morass. Then his next words freeze everything inside me. "I've booked you into a rehab facility, up here in the Finger Lakes. It's only twenty minutes away."

"Rehab…?" I stare at him, my fingers cold in his warm, sure grip.

"It's a very highly respected place, even in the city. Very private and discreet." Because God forbid anyone should know I have a problem. That I *am* a problem. I just stare at him as he continues doggedly, "This could be really good for you, Rebecca. They have a four-week program and then follow-up visits, as needed. It could all be sorted out and behind us by the time school starts."

I slip my fingers from his. I feel as if I am being tidied away. "Is that what you want?"

"I want you better," Josh says firmly. "And this is what will accomplish that."

"How can you be sure?" I am curious; I want to know what he thinks. Why he's so certain rehab is the answer, that alcohol is the problem.

"Because there will be professionals there to help you, Rebecca." He sounds as if he is talking to a child. "To get you well and sober again."

Sober. I fight an urge to laugh, which I know would not be a good response in this moment. If I stop drinking, does he actually think the problem is going to go away? Can he be so *stupid*? I open my mouth to say something of this, but then I see the closed, obdurate look on my husband's face and I realize there's no point. Josh has decided what the problem is and how to solve it, and I'm too tired to fight against his tide.

Besides, maybe he's right. Who am I to know what is real, what is right, what *works*? Maybe if I stop drinking, I'll feel better. Things won't seem so bleak as they do now, when the whole world is pressing down on me. When my own mind is a no-go area, a danger zone.

"A four-week program," I say slowly. "Outpatient?"

"No, residential."

I stare at him. He's locking me up? For a *month*? "And who is going to look after the kids while I'm away for that long?"

"I thought your parents—"

"No." The one word comes out vicious, certain.

Josh looks surprised. "I think they'd be up for it, Rebecca. I know they can be hard to manage sometimes, but—"

My fingers curl on the sheet, nails snagging on the cotton. "I don't want them taking care of the kids. Not for that long." Not at all.

"Why not? Do you mean, because you don't want them knowing?"

I stare at the ceiling. "That's part of it, I suppose."

"What's going on?" Josh asks quietly. "Is there something you're not telling me?"

Again I open my mouth. Close it. Until I can sort out my own head, figure out what is true for myself, until I'm *certain*, I don't want to tell Josh. I don't want him to dismiss my fears, or make them more real. I can't stand either option, which leaves us in this uncomfortable place. "Yes," I say finally. "There is something, or at least there might be, but I can't go into it now. I'm not ready."

Josh stares at me, looking skeptical, as if he's unsure whether to believe me, or whether to press.

"Please just let this go," I say. "For now."

"All right, then who can be with them? I could hire someone, a nanny, but it would be a stranger." He sighs heavily. "I could take a week off to get them used to somebody, maybe two for compassionate leave, but it's not ideal—"

"No." I can't ask that of him, and besides, I don't want to be in his emotional debt. I'm already feeling like I've let everyone down. Zoe's fearful face flashes through my mind and I close my eyes. How can she ever forgive me? How can I ever forgive myself? I open my eyes. Josh is frowning down at me, a look of concern on his face, along with a spark of something like exasperation. He's a problem solver, my husband. He wants this done and dealt with in the way he thinks best. I'm not meant to be so difficult, so time-consuming. I'm the one who manages his life—the clean house, the happy children, the dry-cleaning and the bills. I do it all, so he can make us money. That's how it works.

"I don't want some nanny looking after them. It's going to be tough enough, with me gone so suddenly." Panic seizes me. *I can't go, I can't leave my children.* "Can't I do something outpatient?"

"It doesn't work that way, Rebecca."

"I'm not an alcoholic, Josh." I feel like I have to say it. He does not reply. "Do you believe that?"

"It's just a word."

"But I'm not." I bite my lip, because I know he doesn't believe me, not really.

"Whatever your... condition, I think this will help. At the very least, it will give you some time to think."

But maybe I don't want to think. "I don't want to leave the children for that long."

"Rebecca, what the children really need is a mother who is completely there for them, present and healthy and whole." He takes a deep breath and continues evenly, "They need a mother who doesn't get drunk and hurt herself while they're watching." His voice rises and I recoil, shame and hurt flooding through me. "I'm sorry," he says in a lower voice. "I didn't mean... I'm sorry."

He's right, though. He could have said it more nicely but he's right: my children need me healthy. And I'm not getting better on my own.

"Why not your parents?" he presses again. "They know the kids, they love them—"

"No." And then it comes to me—reluctantly, yet with growing realization, with dawning certainty. "I know," I say. "Tessa can look after them."

"Tessa?" Josh looks blank. "But you've only known her for a few weeks..."

"We've become very close." That close, though? Do I know her that well? Do I trust her that much?

"That's a lot to ask of a friend, Rebecca, especially one you've just met."

"I know it is, but she's the best choice. And Tessa will do it."

"You trust her?" Josh asks. "With that much responsibility?"

"With my life." I let out a huff of sound, something between a laugh and a sob, because that might be what I'm actually doing.

Josh shakes his head. "I don't know…"

"It makes sense, Josh. The kids can stay here, keep on with their lessons, and I can see them on weekends. I'm allowed visitors, aren't I?" I'm not going to jail, after all.

"Yes…"

"It makes sense," I repeat more firmly. I feel more convinced, more reassured that this could work. "This is the right thing to do."

"Okay," he relents. "I suppose we can give it a try."

"Good."

"Do you want to ask her, or shall I…?"

"I will."

"If you're sure…"

"I am."

Josh nods slowly, and I close my eyes. "I'll let you sleep," he says softly, and I feel the mattress shift as he gets up from bed. A few seconds later the door clicks softly shut.

I drift into a doze, a foggy dreamscape where I keep seeing people's faces—my sister, my mother, my father, my husband, my children. I turn away from them all, too wretched to offer the atonement I know I need to. I feel adrift, bobbing alone in a foreign sea, and no one is close enough to reach out a hand, to save me. I need to save myself, and I'm not sure I know how.

Eventually I wake up and I blink at the ceiling, waiting for the dream to recede, but of course it doesn't. It's reality, and I need to face at least some of those people.

I feel like an old woman as I hobble around the bedroom, picking out clothes—a pair of capris that are baggy on me now, and a shapeless t-shirt. I put some loose powder on my bruise to make it look less lurid, without trying to conceal it completely, because of course I can't. And then I venture downstairs.

It is late morning and rain drums against the weathered wood of the deck and streaks the sliding glass door like tears. The lake is obscured by thick gray fog. Everything feels subdued.

"Hey." Tessa is in the kitchen, wiping the counters. Everything looks tidy and neat, and she looks exhausted. I wonder if she's slept at all.

"Hey."

She smiles, or tries to. "How are you feeling?" she asks as if I've had a touch of the flu.

"Okay, I guess. I've certainly been better." I perch on one of the bar stools. "Where is everyone?"

"The kids are watching a movie upstairs. Josh is working in the study."

"Ah." Of course he is. I haven't even been in the little snug off the living room yet, set up with a desk and a leather club chair. "Did Josh mention our… plans to you?" I ask after a moment. Tessa's blank look is answer enough. "I guess not."

"What plans?"

I hesitate, that moment of indecision before you take the swan dive, the flying leap. Do I really want to do this? Can I trust this woman that much? *Do I have a choice?* "He wants me to go into a rehab program for four weeks."

"Oh… okay." Tessa nods, looking startled, but I can tell she doesn't understand where I'm going with this.

"It's near here, about a twenty-minute drive." She keeps nodding. "It's residential, Tessa, so I'd have to stay there."

Her eyes widen. "Right…"

I take a deep breath. "Tessa, I'm asking if you'll take care of my children while I'm in there." Her jaw goes slack, and I plow ahead. "I know it's a big request. Huge. And I wouldn't ask you if I didn't—if I didn't think you were the best person for it." As I say it, I realize how true it is. Tessa has been closer to my kids these last few weeks than any of my friends from my so-called real life. "They know you, they like you." Still she doesn't respond, and I start to feel a little tense, a little desperate. "I wouldn't ask you if I didn't think it was a good idea," I add quietly. "The kids are all getting along, and you could move in here, so nothing would have to change. Josh can't spare the time from work, and to tell you the truth, there isn't anyone else…" It hurts to admit this. My bevy of friends from the city? Not a text all summer, and in any case I'd never ask a single one of them for something like this; I'd never admit my need or trust them that much.

"Right. Okay. Wow." Tessa is still nodding, more slowly now, thinking it through. "I didn't expect…" she says, and trails off. "Of course I want to help," she says at last, and with a shiver of disbelief, I wonder if she is about to turn me down—and I realize I can't let that happen. I might have reservations, fears, but this is the only real option I have. And I meant what I said. My kids know Tessa, they could stay here. This is really the best choice.

"If you need help from babysitters, whatever, you can do that," I say. "Sky's the limit, of course. Obviously. Order takeout every night. Hire a housekeeper. Whatever, Tessa, I mean it." Suddenly I am desperate, babbling. I don't even want to go to rehab, and yet here I am, begging, because I don't see any alternatives. I know I need to do something. "Please, Tessa, if you think there's any way you could do this… we'd pay you, of course…"

"Rebecca, I don't need to be *paid*." She sounds affronted, and so, reluctantly, I back off.

"Of course, if you really feel you can't do it, I understand. I'm sorry, I know I'm being pushy. You have to do what you feel is best for you and your kids."

At that, Tessa's expression crumples a little bit. "Oh, Rebecca! Of course I can do it. I *will* do it, I want to help you." She reaches for my hand, holding on tight. "I want you to get better."

"So do I," I say, and I don't think I've meant anything more.

*

It all seems to happen quickly after that, everything speeding up and by. The kids come down after the movie, circling around me warily. Charlotte gives me penetratingly thoughtful looks that I hate, while Zoe just looks accusing, and Max won't look at me at all. I'm overcome by guilt, and I have no idea how to make amends. I try, offering smiles, to play a card game, to braid Charlotte's hair. They accept my token offers as if they are humoring me.

When I lay the cards out for a game of Concentration, they act as if they are merely enduring the game as well as my presence. When I braid Charlotte's hair, she sits completely still, her face averted from mine. I want to cry, but I can't—everything is frozen inside.

That evening, we all eat outside, a motley group. The sky has cleared to a pale, fragile blue, and Josh has insisted on using the huge, stainless steel behemoth of a barbecue that I haven't touched all summer. The deck furniture is still damp, and Tessa brings out towels to sit on. She's made burgers from a package of ground beef, and they're lumpy and uneven, charred outside, a bit raw in the middle, but who am I to criticize? I owe her everything. *Everything*.

After we eat, I tell the children the plan. It feels like something out of a bad made-for-TV movie: cue the weeping violins, the confused expressions, the martyred mom, everyone being heroic and noble.

"So, I have to go away for a little while," I say, trying to keep my voice upbeat and matter-of-fact. "To get better."

"What's wrong with you?" Zoe demands, her tone bordering on rude. Charlotte's eyes narrow in silent assessment. Max slips onto Josh's lap and leans his head against his shoulder as if he is far younger than eight.

"I'm not very well," I answer Zoe. "I wish I was, but I'm going to a special hospital that will help me feel better." I wince at the infantile way I'm describing it all, and I don't think I'm fooling anyone, not even Max. No one says anything for a moment.

"When will you get back?" Max finally asks in a small voice. "And who will take care of us?"

"I'll be back in a few weeks, and Tessa will be taking care of you." I give them as bright a smile as I can. "Won't that be nice? Nothing will have to change." Except me.

"Tessa?" Zoe repeats, her voice ringing with scornful disbelief that is underlaid by fear. I know my girl—she doesn't like change, she doesn't like what she can't control.

"I know I'm no substitute for your mom, Zoe," Tessa says in an attempt at motherly concern for my kids, "but we'll manage, don't you think?"

Zoe merely shoots her a scathing look without bothering to reply, but I see her lips tremble and I long to hug her. I touch her hand, instead, and she jerks it away, hurting us both.

"Everyone's going to need to chip in and help," Josh says, stroking Max's hair. "It might be hard for a bit, but it's worth it, for Mom." I smile bravely, but I don't think anyone buys it. It's not as if I have leukemia or something, is it? And they know that. Even little children can see that much. They blame me, and I don't blame them for it—I can't.

Later, after the McIntyres have gone home and the kids have gone to bed, Josh and I sit in the living room, an overly formal room I've barely gone into, and hash out the prosaic and painful details. He gives me a brochure for the rehab facility—Lakeview Retreat. It looks like an upscale hotel, complete with a gym, indoor and outdoor pools, and a serenity garden, whatever that is. Residents are called guests and treated as such.

I skim through paragraphs about how I won't be treated as someone who is diseased, but rather a person of dignity, worthy of respect and capable of change. I almost believe their sugary PR, vague and fuzzy as it all sounds. I feel the tiniest lift of hope that this might actually work.

"I feel like I'm going on a vacation," I remark to Josh as I hand back the brochure. He looks at me over the top of his glasses, which I've always found strangely sexy.

"There's no need for it to feel like a punishment."

"I know, but it still seems a little decadent." Lakeview only has six guests stay at one time, and two gourmet chefs, plus a masseuse and manicurist.

Josh shrugs. "We can afford it, Rebecca. I want you to be comfortable."

"Still. It feels a little wrong. Unfair, at least, somehow."

Josh gives me an assessing look. "Maybe you're the only one who thinks you need to be punished for something."

"Am I?" The words slip out of their own accord, and the mood, which had been tentative but faintly hopeful, suddenly shifts to tension and simmering resentment on both sides.

"What is that supposed to mean?"

"Aren't you angry with me?" I try to keep my voice reasonable. "At least for the whole dancing-on-the-table thing?"

Josh takes off his glasses and rubs his eyes. "I'm not angry," he says with a tired sigh. "Although I admit I was at the time. Angry and concerned." He looks up. "I knew something was wrong, and now we can fix it."

And that feels like the end of the conversation, which is fine. It's not as if I want to rehash it all, anyway. Josh leans forward, an evangelical light in his eyes. "This is going to help, Rebecca. It's going to work. You're going to get better, and we're going to go back to the way we were." He makes these promises as if he is reciting vows, oaths he means with his whole heart. I stare at him silently, unable to respond, to reassure him, because the truth is, as much as I want him to be, I'm just not sure he's right.

CHAPTER NINETEEN

TESSA

The next morning, we pack up all our stuff in Pine Cottage. Josh told me he was taking Rebecca to the rehab place around ten, and so I am up at eight, my body aching with fatigue even as my mind buzzes with purpose. We need to take everything over to Rebecca's house. I debated whether we should leave our things at Pine Cottage and run back and forth; I didn't want to be presumptuous, invasive—but four *weeks*, and Josh is leaving tonight.

Last night, after we left the Finlays, I called Kyle and told him what was happening. He went a little bit berserk.

"Tessa, seriously? This is *not* your problem."

"I know it's not, but I want to help."

"You really think that's a good idea, considering?"

"Considering what?" I asked, annoyed and hurt by his tone, as if he didn't think I was capable of doing this.

He sighed heavily. "Just… don't we have enough to deal with?"

"You said that before. What do you mean exactly, Kyle? What are we dealing with?"

He was silent, and I waited, my heart beginning to thud. I wished I hadn't asked, hadn't laid down the gauntlet like that. Did I really want to know what he meant?

"Things haven't been easy, Tessa," he finally said. "You know that."

I felt a prickling sense of shame, as if this was somehow my fault. As if everyone's happiness had been my responsibility. And maybe it has. "I know they haven't," I whispered.

"I don't want to go backward, you know? Not after all this time."

"Backward?" *Back to what?* "We're not going to go backward, Kyle. Actually, things have been improving, despite what's happened with Rebecca. Katherine and Ben have made friends..."

"And you?"

"I have, too. I know things with Rebecca are bad, but this summer has been good for us, Kyle. It's what we've needed."

"Okay," he said after another long, uneasy pause. "Okay. But tell me if it gets too much, okay, Tessa? *Tell me.*"

"I will," I said. I felt startled by his intensity, after months of silent, unspoken accusation and hostility—or so it has felt to me. Why was he changing now? Was it because I'd changed? "You don't need to worry about me, you know."

"But I will," he answered rather grimly. "You know I will."

After the call, I scrolled through the last few months and even years in my mind, trying to figure out if something significant had happened without me quite realizing. When had this distance opened up between Kyle and me? In the last year, or before then? When my mother had her first stroke, and my focus transferred from my family to my mom? But it had to. I feel guilty, of course I do, but I also know I had no choice. My dad simply wasn't able to step up in the way he needed to. It was all up to me, and I was glad to be there for my mom, when she'd always been there for me.

Still, it hurts to remember it all; going back over the last year, the days and weeks blur into a mundane fog of simply doing—to and from school, the occasional card-making, meals and laundry and errands, rinse and repeat. But in the midst of all that... there were good days, surely? Nights out, Saturdays with everyone together, a vacation to Cape Cod a couple of years ago...

I get out my phone and swipe through photos to jog my memory. Ah, yes, there it is. In April we went to an Easter egg hunt in Prospect Park. In February we went bowling in Union Square. I stare at the photos of the four of us, Kyle in mid-swing, Katherine shyly proffering an Easter egg, and let these anchor me. Comfort me. Things haven't been as bad as all that, no matter how he talks.

I tell myself to appreciate Kyle's concern rather than be unnerved by it. And then I start packing.

By nine thirty we have lugged our suitcases over to the lake house, although after we've bumped them up the steps, I wonder at the timing. Should I have waited until Rebecca had gone? It seems tactless to move in while she's moving out, somehow.

I feel as if I am an interloper, intent on taking her place, as I leave the cases out on the deck. Rebecca comes downstairs, looking better than she has in recent days, and yet still awful. Her smile is a bright rictus, feverish spots of color on her thin cheeks. She's wearing a canary-yellow linen sundress and designer sandals, sunglasses slipped onto her head and bangles sliding down one bony wrist.

"I'm just about ready," she chirps to me, in a parody of her usual enthusiastic trill. "You wouldn't believe this place, Tessa—a spa and a hot tub and two gourmet chefs." She rolls her eyes. "Ridiculous, but who am I to complain?"

"Sounds like you'll be spoilt."

Rebecca takes a step toward me. "Take care of them all for me, okay?" she asks in a low voice. Her voice trembles as her hand skims my wrist. "I know Zoe will be a handful. She's angrier than ever and it's all my fault. But please... be patient with her."

"Of course I will." I feel near tears. "Of course I will, Rebecca—"

"And the others, too. Charlotte seems so tranquil, but I still worry. And Max is so quiet..."

"I know." I try to smile. "I know them, Rebecca. Not as well as you, but—"

"I know you do." She smiles back, the curve of her lips tremulous. "That's why I'm asking you, Tessa. Because I know you will care for them. And because I know I can trust you. We're friends, aren't we?" Her fingers clutch my wrist, her nails like talons.

"Yes," I say, a bit unnerved by her intensity. "Yes, of course we are."

Josh comes in, looking harried; they're running late. He takes Rebecca's single suitcase to the car and then the children troop down for goodbyes.

Rebecca hugs them each in turn, even Katherine and Ben. "Be good," she says, the threat of tears audible in her voice. "Have fun. I'll see you on the weekend… Daddy said you could come visit."

"I said maybe," Josh says quietly, and Rebecca hugs everyone again before heading down the deck stairs. Josh smiles at us, mouthing his thanks to me, and then slides the glass door closed, the sound making me feel as if we've been sealed inside a luxurious tomb. No one says anything for a few seconds; it's as if we're suspended in this moment, unsure of what comes next.

Then Zoe breaks it, predictably. She whirls on me, her hands on her hips. "What are your suitcases doing out there?"

I feel guilty, practically stammering my response. "We… we needed to bring our things over, Zoe…"

"You couldn't wait, could you?" she flings at me. "I bet you were dying to get out of that horrible little place you were living in!" She doesn't wait for my response, but runs upstairs and slams the door of her bedroom so hard we feel the thud of it downstairs.

I take a deep, steadying breath. I know she's hurting and afraid, I get that. I tell myself I'll give her some time and then I'll go up to talk to her, a prospect that feels incredibly daunting.

I can do this; I told Kyle I can do this, Rebecca believes I can do this. And so I can, and I will. "Ben and Katherine, why don't you help me bring the suitcases inside?"

"I'll help," Charlotte says quietly, and we spend a few moments lugging everything in. Max watches us apprehensively.

"Where are you all going to sleep?" he asks, and I hesitate.

Where *are* we all going to sleep? Charlotte and Zoe's bedrooms have two twin beds each, but Max's only has one, and then there's the guest bedroom, as well as Rebecca's room. I dither, wondering what is best, what will be least offensive, while the children wait for my verdict.

"Charlotte, you could share with Zoe," I suggest hesitantly. "And Ben and Katherine could share your room…"

"Zoe is *not* going to want to share," Max pipes up. Charlotte does not look enthused about having to change rooms, although she doesn't say anything. What a minefield this all is.

We end up having Katherine share Charlotte's room, and Ben takes the guest room. Max and Zoe keep their own rooms, and I go in Rebecca's room. I had wanted to avoid sleeping in Rebecca's bedroom because it felt too invasive, and besides, what about when Josh visits? But I don't really see any viable alternative.

I leave my suitcase by the door and knock quietly on Zoe's door. There is no answer, and gently, I turn the knob and open it a crack.

"Zoe…?"

"Go away." Her voice is muffled and I glimpse her lying face down on her bed, a pillow clutched to her.

"I will go away, but I just wanted to tell you I understand how hard this is, and I don't want to try to take your mom's place. I couldn't, Zoe, because she's so amazing." My voice wobbles; Zoe has gone still, but she doesn't say anything, and somehow this emboldens me enough to continue, "I just want to help you all, keep things going for when your mom comes back and everything is better than ever. That's all." But she still doesn't answer, and I wait, although for what I couldn't say. Do I really think Zoe is going to lower the pillow, beam me a smile, and say, *Thanks, Tessa, for understanding. That makes me feel so much better.*

No, she doesn't do anything. I realize she must be waiting for me to leave, and so I step out of the room and softly close the door. I tell myself that was progress, of a sort. She listened; she heard me.

By the time the rest of the kids have settled in their new rooms, Josh has returned, somehow looking older and more tired than he did when he left. The children rush him as he comes in the door, even Zoe, who has slunk out of her room and is studiously ignoring me. It gives me a lift to see the obvious love between them all. He meets my gaze over the tops of their heads.

"Thank you, Tessa."

"It's no trouble. You don't need to keep thanking me."

"Still."

"Did everything... go all right?"

"Yes, I think it's going to be good." He steps back from the children, smiling at them. "Now, do you all have somewhere you need to be?"

"Tennis," Zoe says reluctantly, "but we don't have to..."

"Best to keep to routines." He touches her head lightly. "But how about I meet all of you in town afterwards, for pizza?" He turns to glance at me. "Is that okay? I'll need to take off after that, but I'll be back next weekend."

"Yes, fine." What else can I say? Josh retreats to the study while we get ready to go to the club.

Everyone is remarkably docile as we troop out to the car, and no one says anything as I climb into the driver's seat of the SUV I've driven several times before. As soon as I turn on the engine, the radio blasts out, making me jolt in surprise. I turn it off quickly.

"Mom always leaves the radio on," Zoe says from the backseat.

"Sorry, it was just a little loud." I take a quick breath and turn it back on.

"And she sings along," Zoe adds, a challenge to her voice. Does she want me, or not want me to? I have no idea.

"I know she does, Zoe," I say as I reverse out of the driveway. "She's great that way, isn't she?" She doesn't reply.

I battle a thousand moments like that one over the course of the afternoon. If I do something differently to Rebecca, I'm doing it wrong. If I do the same, I'm trying to take her place. I can't win, especially not with Zoe, and so I tell myself to accept it and move on. It doesn't matter. Zoe is nine, and she's hurting. Still, I grit my teeth as Zoe flounces away from me to go to tennis, having accidentally on purpose hit me with her racquet as she'd turned. I'm not going to mind, I'm not going to let myself mind.

By the time we are driving down Geneseo's main street in search of the pizza place Josh had mentioned, I am feeling tired and frazzled and ready for a break, and I'm only a few hours in. I have an urge to have some time just with Ben and Katherine; I realize I haven't even checked with them that this is okay. I just assumed it would be, because they've all been getting along, but what if it isn't? What if this is all a huge mistake?

"Are you staying with us for pizza with Daddy?" Zoe asks, and I briefly close my eyes.

"Of course they are, Zoe," Charlotte scolds. "What else would they do?"

Which, as a sentiment, doesn't make me feel much better.

Josh is waiting in the pizza place, an old-fashioned Mom and Pop type of joint, as we head in. Zoe rushes him, wrapping her arms around his waist possessively, while Charlotte and Max—and Ben, Katherine, and I—all hang back. Josh's smile tries to include everyone.

"How was the afternoon? And more importantly, what type of pizzas should we get?"

I am content to let him take the lead and I sit on the end of the table for eight, sipping my Diet Coke and only half-listening to Zoe's excited chatter as she details the minutiae of the day while everyone else pushes greasy slices of pizza around on their plates.

Afterwards, while the children are examining an old-fashioned pinball machine in the back of the restaurant, Josh approaches me. "I have to leave tonight, but I wanted to make sure you have everything you need." He presses a card into my hand. "Here's a preloaded credit card to cover all expenses, anything you need at all, and I'll transfer more funds to it whenever it runs low."

"You don't…" I begin, before I stop and realize that of course he does. I can't afford to keep house for six people—certainly not in the style the Finlay children will expect—and I know neither Rebecca nor Josh would want me to. They offered to pay me, after all, something I know I can't accept. This is a matter of friendship, not business.

"I've also written down my cell, home, and office numbers," he continues. "They're back at the house, and please do call me if you need anything, or are worried… anything at all." I nod, swallowing hard. No matter what I said, I don't feel prepared for this. "And I'll be back next weekend," he finishes. It feels like an age away.

"Are you leaving now? I mean, from here?"

"Yes." He has the grace to look a little guilty. "I really need to get back…"

"Of course. We'll be fine." I watch as he hugs the children in turn, gives me one parting smile, and then he's gone.

Back at the house, everyone drifts around, seemingly waiting for me to tell them what to do. There is a Rebecca-shaped hole in our lives, and it gapes. I keep expecting to hear her cheerful trill, suggesting something fun—making smoothies or playing a game or getting out the paints. Rebecca was great at organizing, at energizing, I acknowledge—and then realize I am thinking about her in the past tense.

The kids all go upstairs, slumped in front of the TV. I head to Rebecca's bedroom, stepping inside quietly, feeling as if I am trespassing on a shrine. I left my suitcase by the door, and everything is untouched. Although Rebecca took a lot of her belongings with her, there is still enough here to feel her presence. I breathe in the ghostly traces of her summery perfume. I walk slowly around the room, my bare feet sinking into the plush, cream carpet, every step feeling forbidden.

There are a few cut-glass bottles on top of the dresser—expensive ones, octagonal in shape, some perfume I've never heard of. I take the stopper out of one and breathe in the scent. Then I open a drawer, surprised to see how many clothes Rebecca has left. Silky, lace-edged bras and pants, in various pastel shades, matching sets. I think of my own graying Playtex bras and underpants with frayed elastic, with a flicker of shame. Why didn't she take all these? I run a hand over the silky material and then quickly close the drawer.

In the bathroom, she has left many of her cosmetics, expensive cleansers and creams, and an entire bag of high-end makeup, the kind I could never afford. I am just about to open one of the drawers of the vanity when I hear Zoe's sharp voice.

"What are you doing?"

I jerk in surprise and turn to see her standing in the doorway of the bathroom, glowering at me as usual. I smile and step away from the vanity.

"Just putting some stuff away. Is it time to get ready for bed?" I walk quickly out of Rebecca's bathroom and bedroom, toward the family room upstairs. After an endless few seconds, Zoe follows me.

By nine o'clock, by some miracle, they're all in bed, if not asleep, and I wander around the downstairs, the house's emptiness reverberating all around me. I wonder what Rebecca is doing. What she's thinking and feeling. I wish I'd spoken to her more before she went, that I'd said something real and important.

Eventually, around eleven, I head up to bed, stretching out in the double bed with a feeling of unreality. The house is quiet, the night completely still. Somehow I fall asleep, only to wake with a sudden jolt, my heart thudding. I lie there for a couple of seconds before I hear it—the sound of crying—small, pitiful sobs. Disorientated, I stumble out of bed, forgetting I am not in Pine Cottage until I feel the plush carpet underneath my bare feet.

I hurry out into the hall, blinking in the darkness, a sliver of moon from the skylight lighting the stairs. I hear it again—those desperate tears. My heart thuds harder and I peek into each bedroom, calling softly. Ben is asleep, as are Max, Charlotte, and Katherine. I step into Zoe's room, my heart contracting at the sound of her sobs.

When I creep closer, I see she is still asleep—her eyes scrunched shut, tears streaking down her face. Her knees are drawn up to her chest, one arm wrapped around them. I hesitate, wondering if I should leave her. But how can I? She's nine, and she sounds as if her heart is breaking right in two.

Tentatively I put one hand on her shoulder. "Zoe… Zoe?" Nothing happens and I give her shoulder a gentle shake. "Zoe."

Her eyes snap open and within seconds she is glaring at me. "What are you *doing*?" she demands, making me feel as if I was being creepy.

"You were having a bad dream…"

"Go away." Her voice is a high-pitched hiss. "Go *away*. I don't want you here, I don't want *you*!"

"Okay, okay." I back away, my palms up, my body shaking from the extent of her anger and pain. "I'm sorry, Zoe. I only wanted to help."

She doesn't answer; she's already rolled onto her side, her shoulders hunched, her back turned to me. I pause, wishing I could help, but I know there's nothing I can do to make it better.

In fact, I'll only make it worse. So I leave her to her tears and creep back to bed, feeling more helpless than ever. Even though I'm aching with exhaustion, I don't fall asleep for a long time.

CHAPTER TWENTY
REBECCA

Lakeview Retreat doesn't look remotely like a prison, but it still feels like one. An hour after Josh has left me, kissing my forehead as if I were a child and telling me he'll talk to me soon, I remain in my oh-so comfortable room, staring out at the verdant meadow that runs down to the lake, and doing my best to keep my mind blank.

I don't want to be here. I wish I did; I wish I thought it could help. But I don't, and it won't, even if I came on the premise, the desperate hope, that it might.

Everyone has been so helpful and kind, of course. As soon as I arrived a staff member brought glasses of strawberry and guava juice, garnished with slices of lime, for Josh and me. We sipped them as she showed us all the retreat's amenities, from the four-poster bed in my room to the luxurious ensuite bathroom, to the common areas, which are all done in tasteful cottage décor. It really does feel like a hotel, and this could practically be a holiday. Except.

Except, after Josh has left, the same staff member—Stephanie—gives me a ream of literature. Group therapy. Individual therapy. Meal plans. All of it couched in positive terms, like these are options I can choose rather than realities I must face.

The literature also makes it clear that this is not a medical facility or a detox program. As Stephanie says so helpfully, "We want to help you discuss the futility of your decision-making patterns, not embark on a course of medical treatment." I almost laugh at that. *The futility of my decision-making patterns.* She must be a mind-reader.

It all sounds good, of course. Day excursions. Positivity exercises. Mindfulness. Wellness. Holistic. I know the terms. It's like stepping inside a self-help book and being trapped by its well-meaning pages. But I'm still trapped.

I stay in my room until dinner, having neither the energy nor the desire to see any of the other five guests—the place, Stephanie informed me, is fully booked—or make any kind of effort. But eventually I am roused out of my room by another smiling staff member, to be informed that dinner will be served shortly.

Whether I have a choice in attending, I don't know. I can't tell how much this talk of freedom and respect is cheery lip service and how much is real. If I wanted to walk out of here, could I? Would I?

I drift over to the sitting room, where a motley crew of inmates—or rather, *guests*—are enjoying pre-dinner mocktails. Besides me, there is a paunchy, florid-faced businessman who reeks of money, a pouty teenaged girl who emanates attitude, a weedy-looking man in his twenties who is clearly experiencing some kind of withdrawal, his knee constantly jiggling, his fingernails ragged and bleeding, and a dignified woman in her sixties with a gorgeous silver bob.

A woman my age, with the same blonde highlights and Botoxed forehead, walks in after me. We take each other's measure and then move to opposite sides of the room. I don't want to talk to any of these people, and judging from the silence of the room, they don't, either. We all look guilty. Several people glance at the bruise on my forehead and look quickly away, no doubt wondering just how much of a headcase I am.

Stephanie is moving around us, pouring drinks and murmuring small talk that everyone ignores. What a crowd. I wonder if it's always like this. Some of these people must have been here for a little while, surely.

I perch on the edge of a squashy armchair and sip my juice, trying not to make eye contact. I know there is no point in me being here if I'm not going to try, but I don't have it in me just yet, and no one else seems to, either.

We're called in to dinner, and we troop in obediently to the gorgeous dining room; a table for six is laid with fine china, damask napkins, and crystal wine glasses—although of course no wine.

The food is delicious—locally sourced and freshly made, naturally—but I can only pick at it. I've lost too much weight—most of it without realizing—but I can't make myself eat. My stomach is in knots and yet I feel distant from and indifferent to everything, which is better than some of the things I've felt, I suppose.

The elderly lady, whose name, I discover, is Gwen, attempts a bit of small talk. Her manner is dry and her humor ironic, and she comments on the meal with a little half-smile that I almost return. In another place, another world, I would like her. I would hope I might be like her, when I got to be sixty-something. As it is the most I do is make eye contact once before turning back to my guinea fowl.

After dinner, we're encouraged to socialize, and Stephanie gets out a few board games that everyone ignores. I have discovered, in staccato bursts of conversation over the course of the meal, the names of my fellow guests, at least. Chloe is the teenager, and she arrived two days ago. Gwen has been here for two weeks. Bruce, the businessman, didn't want to give details but I learn from Gwen that his wife checked him in and he's been here for a couple of days. Liz, my doppelgänger, is leaving soon. The twenty-something ex-junkie is Geoff and, judging from his behavior, I'm guessing he hasn't been here very long.

We all sit in a conservatory off the living room as daylight is leached from the sky, turning it first a fiery orange and then a deep violet. The ripples of the lake smooth out, leaving it looking like a dark, gleaming plate. Gwen and Liz have a stilted conversation about some book they've both read, Geoff drums his fingers against his leg, and Bruce and Chloe are both on their phones. Funny, I didn't even bring my phone—I thought it wouldn't be allowed, but apparently guests can have access to just about anything, except alcohol. I guess I really did think this would be like prison.

My thoughts turn to the children, and it feels like probing dark, gaping wounds. I wonder how they are, how they are coping. I trust Tessa to look after them, in part because I have to, and I tell myself they'll be fine; children are resilient. They're strong. Even so, my heart clenches with both fear and love, especially when I think of Zoe.

She doesn't like Tessa, which isn't saying all that much, because there are so many people Zoe doesn't like, or at least acts as if she doesn't like. But will she be *okay*? Will Tessa be patient and loving with her? Will we all be able to get past this, eventually? I try to see into the future, to envision a place where we're all a family together, happy and whole, but it's like trying to peer through a snowstorm. All I see is endless gray, a constant blur, no sunshine in sight.

I finally leave the others a little after nine and escape to the safe, if lonely, solitude of my bedroom. Twenty-seven more days to go, I think grimly as I get ready for bed. And then what? That's the worst thought of all. Maybe tomorrow I'll feel like trying.

The next morning Stephanie tells me at breakfast—fruit smoothie, scrambled egg whites, and turkey bacon—that I am "welcome to join" the group therapy session at ten. Her smile is so perky and expectant that I feel like I can't turn her down, and maybe I really can't. I murmur something positive in reply and drink my coffee.

At ten I find my way to the Group Room—what an annoyingly innocuous name—which is a comfortable room off in another wing of the house, furnished in the same cozy cottage décor as the other common areas. There are boxes of tissues placed in helpful spots, and the only concession to what we're doing here is a whiteboard with some catchy if well-tried slogans written on it in bright blue pen: "What Consumes Your Mind Controls Your Life" and "Start Where You Are. Use What You Have. Do What You Can."

I consider taking that advice and realize it would get me absolutely nowhere. I almost laugh out loud, and Gwen, who is coming into the room, catches my smile.

"Ridiculous, I know," she says with a nod at the board. "But they have to try."

"Yes, but do we?" The words pop out of their own accord. Gwen gives me a considering look.

"Pretty pointless being in here, otherwise," she remarks. "But I understand what you mean."

I cross my arms and look away, already uncomfortable. Gwen settles into the chair next to mine. "You're new," she says, and pats my hand. "It will get easier."

"You're halfway through?"

"Just about." She sighs, the sound one of both weariness and acceptance.

I want to ask her what got her to this place, what events in her life unfolded to lead her to this moment, but it feels way too personal and invasive. Besides, the last thing I want is for her to ask me the same question back.

Geoff and Liz have joined us, but Bruce and Chloe are noticeably absent so I guess group time is optional. Geoff is still jiggling his leg and Liz is on her phone. The atmosphere in the room is subdued, even slightly malevolent, but maybe that's just my imagination. Gwen gives me a reassuring smile.

"It's always like this at first."

Like what? I want to ask, but don't. A young woman in her twenties I don't recognize comes in, closing the door behind her and giving us all a wide smile.

"Hello, everyone," she practically chirps. "So glad you have all decided to join us today."

I want to leave already, and judging by the expressions on everyone else's faces, I'm not the only one.

"So, we have a new guest with us today…" Her gaze trains expectantly on me. "Rebecca? Would you like to introduce yourself?"

Um, no. The slippery grease of social ease has deserted me now, in this place where I'm so uncomfortable and utterly exposed. I'm spent and dry.

"I arrived yesterday," I say, clearing my throat. "I'm from New York City." And that's about all the information I feel like giving.

"Great, Rebecca, I'm Emily. And do you know everyone else?"

We all look rather furtively at each other, not quite making eye contact. "I think so."

"Great, then shall we begin?" Emily presses her hands together quietly, in an almost-clap. "Who feels like sharing first today?"

Silence. I can't believe this type of thing ever works. Does chirpy Emily actually think one of us is going to blurt out all our innermost feelings simply because she asked us to? Although I imagine a place like this attracts a certain number of over-sharers, there are clearly none in this group. We all have slightly pained expressions on our faces, as if we're enduring a minor dental procedure and hope it will be over soon. Geoff's leg jiggles even more manically.

Finally, Liz starts, spitting out sentences like bullets. I try to listen, but after only a few seconds it's clear she's simply ranting about her ex-husband and his refusal to let her two teenaged children visit her. She's so bitter and angry, it's hard to listen to her, even as a pit opens inside me. Might I become like this, hardened with a toxic crust of resentment forming over everything? Give me enough time, enough rope…

"Okay, Liz," Emily says, holding up one hand to stop her diatribe. "Let's try to flip this around. You can't control Dennis's choices, but you can control your response to them." Liz simply stares at her, grinding her teeth. Emily points to the board without an ounce of awareness that this might not be the most helpful approach. "What consumes your mind controls your life, Liz, and right now I'm hearing a lot of anger and bitterness." Emily gives her a beatific smile while Liz looks as if she wants to spit.

"So what am I supposed to do with my anger? Choke it back down?" she snaps.

"Depression is anger turned inwards," Emily says seriously. "So that's not the solution. We need to examine your anger, figure out where it's coming from, and then see what positive steps we can take in the future."

"We?" Liz repeats disbelievingly. "I know exactly where it's coming from. My fucking ex-husband."

After an hour of this we finally escape, leaving the little room with its pseudo-positivity that doesn't even paper over the cracks. I feel like patting Emily on the shoulder and telling her to consider other jobs, but of course I don't. I just murmur some kind of thank you and breathe a sigh of relief as I leave.

Somehow I find myself walking alongside Gwen, into the so-called serenity garden, which is a labyrinth of paving-stone paths amid winding rows of honeysuckle and wild roses. The day is warm and drowsy, a few bumblebees tumbling through the air.

"I'm really not seeing how that is supposed to help," I remark as we walk along. In the distance the lake glints blue on the horizon. I wonder, if I went to the shore, if I'd be able to see the lake house on the other side. Fancifully, I imagine I might glimpse the children across the expanse of blue, hear the faint echoes of their laughter.

"I think it's more of a place to vent than anything else," Gwen says. "The real work, I've found, happens in the individual therapy sessions."

Which I have the first of this afternoon. I consider it with nothing but dread. "You seem remarkably put together to be in a place like this," I tell Gwen, and she laughs, the sound one of genuine humor.

"Only on the surface."

"At least you have that." I already lost that battle a while ago, it seems.

"Doesn't do you much good, though. In the end, it's just another thing you have to let go of, in order to get to the real problem."

"You mean the drinking."

Gwen gives me a look that seems almost amused. "The drinking? No."

"Isn't that why we're all here?" This is a rehab place, after all. It's what Josh thinks is the problem, and how stopping will solve everything.

"Honey, drinking—or smoking or toking or popping pills, whatever it is that helps you cope—that's just a symptom."

I stop on the winding path, the sun hitting me full in the face as Gwen gives me a look of sympathy. I know what she means, of course I do, because it's what I've been feeling all along. And yet it's the first time someone has said it to me. It's the first time someone actually gets it.

"Then what do you do?" I ask, my throat raw with the effort of asking the question. "If you take away what helps you to cope, what do you do then?"

"Stare it full in the face, whatever it is. Name it, claim it, beat the hell out of it." She shrugs, smiling, although her eyes look sad. "Whatever it takes to put it to rest and move on."

Her simple statement has the power to make me tremble where I stand. *If drinking is the symptom, how bad is the disease?*

That afternoon I attend my individual therapy session. I go reluctantly, dragging my feet, my heart thudding, but I go. Some part of me wants this, even if I'm dreading having to talk about my feelings, like peeling off layers of skin and revealing the quivering nerve endings underneath.

My therapist is someone I've never seen before, a woman in her forties with curly gray hair and a brisk, matter-of-fact manner I find strangely reassuring. Her name is Diane.

"Rebecca, hello."

"Hello." I sit down on the sofa across from her. We're in a small room in another wing of the house, away from the living area and bedrooms. It's very quiet, so I can hear the rustle of her skirt as she crosses her legs.

"How are you finding it here?"

"A bit boring, if I'm honest." After my walk with Gwen I had a nap and then picked at lunch before watching some mindless TV. I'm not exactly having miracle breakthroughs here.

"Boring isn't bad," Diane replies. "Sometimes it can be helpful to have the opportunity to be still and empty out your mind. Get yourself into a place where you're ready to talk as well as listen."

"I didn't realize that's what I was doing when I was watching *Desperate Housewives of Atlanta*," I quip. I realize belatedly that I sound a bit snarky, but I don't really care. She must be used to it.

"Reality TV can serve many purposes," Diane replies with a faint smile. "Why don't you tell me a little bit about yourself, Rebecca?"

Immediately I'm on the defensive, tensing already. "What do you want to know?"

Diane spreads her hands. "What do you want me to know?"

Oh, not these word games. I shrug. "Not much, actually."

"All right, then." Diane smiles and says nothing else. We stare at each other, a battle of wills. I know I'm being childish; I feel like Zoe, stubborn, determined. And for what? Because just like my defiant daughter, I am spiting myself in this. Diane is here to help me, yet still my jaw locks and my arms fold. We wait.

Minutes tick by, taut and endless. Finally, Diane shifts in her seat. "I'd like you to do something for tomorrow," she says, and I blink. That's it? We're *done*? I've been here for about five minutes. "I'd like you to think about what you're most afraid of."

"I can tell you that now," I surprise myself by saying. I take a quick, sharp breath before I speak, my words a dagger thrust. "I'm afraid of being right."

Diane cocks her head. "And would that be worse than not knowing whether you are?"

"Maybe, but in any case I don't have the strength to deal with it if I am."

She nods slowly. "That's why you're here, Rebecca. To find that strength."

"And I find that by watching TV and wandering through some serenity garden, listening to another guest bitch about her ex-husband?" I lift my eyebrows in challenge. "Interesting methods."

Diane smiles; we both know I'm on the defensive, my back against the wall. I'm practically bristling. "Yes, they are, aren't they?" she says quietly.

And that's it. I am dismissed, more or less, although I suppose I could have stayed if I wanted to—I don't. I walk back to my room but I'm too restless to simply sit and so I end up outside, walking toward the lake. A warm breeze blows over me and as I leave the manicured lawn for the wilder meadow, the grass teases and tickles my bare legs. I walk to the edge of the lake, shimmering blue under the summer sun. The houses on the other side are a distant blur, and I know I can't see our rental from here. I know it's too far down the lake, around inlets and bays, impossible even to catch a glimpse of.

Still I imagine I can see it, that I can see Charlotte and Max and Zoe on the dock, looking out toward the water, waiting for me. Needing me. And I take a deep breath and wonder where I am going to find the strength to face the truth, because God knows I don't have it inside myself.

CHAPTER TWENTY-ONE

TESSA

The next morning, the first day we're all on our own, I wake up and decide to be different. We need to get out of the rut we've all found ourselves in, figure out a new way to do life, this unexpected grouping of six.

I bounce out of bed and quickly wash, enjoying the huge, walk-in shower with the power spray. I feel filled with purpose, even though I don't know what we're going to do yet. I just know it's going to be something different.

Downstairs Charlotte, Max, Katherine, and Zoe are all sitting morosely in the family room, looking as if they don't know what to do with themselves, and why should they? Everything feels strange; Rebecca's absence pulses in the air, a constant reminder. Still, I try to stay cheerful.

"Where's Ben?" I ask as I switch on the coffeemaker I prepped last night, and start getting out cereal boxes and bowls.

"He's still asleep." This from Charlotte, who is watching me with a cool curiosity, as if she is only vaguely interested to see how I'll step into her mother's space. Fill her elegant shoes.

"Well, why doesn't one of you wake him up? We're going to do something different today."

"Something different?" Zoe, naturally, sounds suspicious. "But we have our tennis and swim lessons."

"We can miss them for a day, can't we?" I turn to smile at her but it bounces off her as she continues to squint at me. "It's not as if it's school," I persist. "What if we did something really fun today?"

"Like what?" This from Katherine, sounding both hesitant and hopeful.

"What would you all like to do? What would be something really fun and different?"

"Can we go to an amusement park?" Zoe sounds as if she's throwing down a challenge she knows I can't meet.

"An amusement park..." I concentrate on pouring my coffee. "Is there one around here?"

"I'll check on my phone," Charlotte says quickly. A few seconds later she has a list of results. "Adventure Time... that sounds lame, just go-karts and trampolines... Family Fun is just bowling... ah!" She holds up her phone triumphantly. "Seabreeze Amusement Park has roller coasters and everything and it's only forty minutes away."

"Well?" Zoe demands. "Can we go?" She juts her chin out in classic Zoe style, clearly expecting me to back down.

"Sure," I say, surprising, I think, everyone. "Why not?"

Everyone motivates quickly after that, bolting down their cereal and throwing on clothes. I pack a bag with the necessities—sun cream, snacks, swimsuits, spending money. I feel a wave of excitement, a ripple of trepidation—I am branching out on my own, forging ahead. I think of texting Rebecca, but then I remember she left her phone here. I saw it on the kitchen counter after she and Josh had gone, and wondered if she'd meant to leave it. I don't even know the name of the place where she is. It feels almost as if she's vanished, as if she's never coming back.

We are on the road to Seabreeze Amusement Park by ten o'clock, the radio blasting and everyone in a good mood, even, it seems, Zoe. I feel buoyant with victory. I even sing along, although not in Rebecca's belting tones.

It's a beautiful day, hot and sunny, perfect for spending outside. After we arrive, I make sure everyone lathers up with sun cream, and insist on a buddy system in case we get separated—Ben and Max, Katherine and Charlotte, and, unfortunately, Zoe and me.

Then we head inside the park. The entrance fee is steeper than what I could usually afford, but I took out three hundred dollars from the account Josh set up in Geneseo, feeling strangely guilty, almost as if I was stealing. But surely Josh and Rebecca would okay this trip? I hope they would, and in any case, they're not here. I'm not going to think about them now.

The amusement park is old-fashioned, one of the oldest in the country according to the glossy brochure I picked up on the way in, with the classic rides from my childhood—a wooden roller coaster, a tilt-a-whirl, a log flume, a carousel. Beyond the rides there is a water park, with slides and splash pools, and then, in the distance, the deep blue-green of Irondequoit Bay, part of Lake Ontario. The air smells of popcorn and sun cream, and the sun makes the tarmac shimmer.

The kids argue about what to go on first, and we decide to ease our way in on the Music Express, with its gentle rolls and hills, and blaring pop music.

My stomach dips and whirls as the ride starts, with Zoe and me crammed into a two-seater, and the kids all scream with delight as we zoom up and down and around.

We go on several more rides, and when Zoe asks for cotton candy I say yes. I'm saying yes to everything, which I might regret later, but today feels like a yes day. A day for happiness, for forgetting; a day simply to be.

Zoe looks surprised, and even mutters thank you as I hand her the cone of pink spun sugar.

"Can we go on the Jack Rabbit?" Charlotte asks after about an hour. She has turned out, somewhat surprisingly, to be a bit of an adrenalin junkie. I glance at the rickety wooden roller coaster with some apprehension—it's billed as the oldest roller coaster in the country, and it looks it.

"Please?" Charlotte persists, and Zoe chimes in obdurately, "You can't come to an amusement park and not go on the roller coaster."

"Oh, is it a rule?" I keep my voice light. "Well, who else wants to go on?"

"Me, me!" Ben shouts, elbowing Zoe, who elbows him right back. "Katherine?"

"I guess so." Katherine glances furtively at Charlotte, wanting to keep up. I glance at Max, who is looking pale and unenthused. "Max?"

"I don't like roller coasters," he says in a small voice, and my heart contracts.

"Don't be a wuss," Ben returns. This is kindness from my son, the way he encourages. At least that's what I tell myself. Max blinks.

"Come on, Maxie," Charlotte coaxes. "We'll all go on, and then you can say you've done it."

Max looks as if he has no desire to say that at all. "I can stay out with Max," I say, and Zoe turns scornful.

"Don't be a baby," she tells her brother. "You're only a year younger than me and I want to go."

"It doesn't matter," I say as evenly as I can. "Not everyone has to like roller coasters. It's not about being brave, it's just what you enjoy."

I might as well not have spoken. Max peers around at everyone and then straightens his bony shoulders. "I'll go," he says. He turns to me. "But can I sit with you?"

"Of course you can," I say, and I can't keep from putting my arm around his shoulders and giving him an encouraging squeeze, even though it makes Ben snort and Zoe roll her eyes. He's just so *little*.

I am trying to stay upbeat as we board the ride, but Max feels as if he is shrinking next to me, and the wooden tracks look both steep and old. I'm feeling nearly as nervous as Max.

"This is going to be fun," I say for both of our sakes as we buckle up in our car. Ben and Zoe are in front of us, Katherine and Charlotte behind. Max sidles next to me, his small body pressed to mine.

The ride starts with an almighty judder and then we are jolting along, the wooden rails absorbing none of the shock, so I can't keep from being thrown around, my elbow banging painfully on the side of the car within the first few seconds of the ride. At one point I am helpless to keep from sliding down the seat, pinning Max to one side. Then the track twists and he is plastered to me on the other side. I can barely draw a breath before we are climbing up the steep hill with that awful tick-tick-tick of apprehensive expectation, and the endless pause at the top, Max clinging to me, before we plunge down the other side.

Everyone is shrieking, myself included, one arm wrapped around Max. It's awful. Worse than awful. I feel as if I'm being beaten up by a motorized monster. I manage to glance at Max; he is pale and trembling, his mouth open in a rictus of horror. This must be his worst nightmare.

And then we are going around again, jolting and juddering, tilting and climbing, and it's all I can do to endure. I loved roller coasters when I was young, but this feels like nothing more than two minutes of torture.

And then, just as we are finally slowing down, the ride blessedly over, Zoe turns around to say something. Her body jerks spasmodically, and she throws up bright pink cotton candy puke all over herself—and me.

"*Ugh!*" I glance back at Charlotte, whose face is twisted in an uncharacteristic sneer. "That is so disgusting. Isn't it, Katherine?"

Katherine's anxious gaze darts between Charlotte and Zoe, and then she nods. "Yeah, it is."

"That's enough." My voice comes out sharp. Tears glitter in Zoe's eyes, caught between misery and her usual fury. I take a deep breath, and then wish I didn't. "It's all right, Zoe. It could happen to anybody. Let's get you cleaned up."

I instruct the others to wait on a park bench while I take Zoe to the ladies' bathroom. She is surprisingly docile, even holding my hand. Standing at the sink, I realize paper towels just aren't going to cut it. We're both stinking and sodden.

"I'm sorry," she mumbles, her chin tucked low as I dab at her t-shirt.

"It's not your fault, Zoe. I think maybe I shouldn't have bought all that cotton candy." I smile, trying to make light of it, but when Zoe looks at me, her expression is wretched.

"Is my mom going to get better?" she blurts, and my heart melts like wax.

"Oh Zoe, she is. Of course she is." I drop to my knees to give her a hug, vomit and all, but she squirms away from me almost instantly. I suppose that was the total of our bonding moment.

I end up buying two overpriced t-shirts for Zoe and me from the park's gift shop and I bundle our dirty ones into a plastic carrier bag. There is still a faint whiff of vomit about both of us, so I suggest we head to the water park, where we can all cool off. Zoe's chin is tilted at its usual angle, and she seems even more intent on ignoring me. This time I don't mind.

While the other kids tackle the big slides, Max stays close to me, splashing in the shallows of the wave pool while I sit in the sunshine and try to keep an eye on everyone.

After a little while he comes and sits next to me, stretching his legs out along mine as the water gently laps at us.

"Do you think my mom is doing okay?" he asks in a small voice, after we've been sitting silently for a few minutes. It touches me that he, like Zoe, looks to me for reassurance—and it scares me too, because I realize more than ever that I need to *be there* for these frightened children.

"I think she's in the right place," I tell him. "And that she's getting better."

"What was wrong with her, though?" Max peers at me worriedly. "I don't understand that part."

I pat his knobby knee. "I don't really understand it either, Max. It's a grownup kind of thing, which I know is hard to hear because you want to understand. But the important thing to know is that she's going to be okay." I hope I'm not making a promise Rebecca can't keep. "And your dad is coming this weekend. I think he might take you to visit her." Another promise I'm not sure about, but Max brightens.

"Really?"

"Well, maybe," I allow. "You can ask him, though. He said he was going to call tonight."

"Okay." Max smiles and then, breaking my heart a little, he leans his head against my shoulder. We stay that way until the other kids come off the water slides, wanting lunch.

We stay at the park till dinnertime, when we are all tired and happy, our skin feeling tight from all the sun and chlorine, my body aching in places it hasn't in a long time from being thrown about on a variety of rides. Zoe won an ugly pink teddy bear playing Skee-Ball, and I gave in and bought another bag of cotton candy for them all to share, warning Zoe to take it easy this time.

Everyone is sticky-faced as we climb into the car; I toss the wet towels and the bag with our dirty t-shirts into the back and then roll down the windows as we make our way home, letting the summer breeze blow over us.

Back at the house I order everyone into the showers to rinse off; amazingly, there are enough bathrooms for all five children to bathe simultaneously, which seems a little bit crazy.

While they're all washing, I pop some pizzas into the oven and then let them eat in front of the TV, up on the top floor. Then I shower myself, letting the hot spray wash away the last, lingering scent of Zoe's puke.

Downstairs I take my own slice of pizza out to the deck and eat it while I watch the sun sink toward the placid stillness of the lake. I feel surprisingly at peace, even happy—despite the vomit, the spurts of bickering, the heat, it was a nice day. A good day. And, I acknowledge with a flicker of guilt, it has been a relief not to think of Rebecca too much today. I decide not to feel guilty about that. The next four weeks are going to be challenging enough without adding a guilt trip to the mix.

I have just finished my pizza when the house phone rings, and I go inside to answer it.

"Tessa?" Josh's voice is low and warm. "How are you? How are you coping?"

"We're fine, actually. We had a nice day today... I took everyone to an amusement park near Rochester for a change. I hope that's okay?" I feel awkward, mentioning money, but it needs to be done. "I know amusement parks are expensive, but I thought the kids could use a change of scene..."

"Of course it's okay," Josh interjects. "Anything you want to do, Tessa, is fine by me."

Something about the way he says my name, as if he really knows me, makes me feel... uneasy. And also, I realize, a little bit pleased. I walk back out onto the deck. "How are you?" I ask, echoing his earlier question. "How are you coping?"

"Oh, you know." Josh lets out a tired laugh. "Managing."

"This has got to be hard on you."

"It's hard on everyone." I think of Max leaning into me at the park. Yes, it is definitely hard on everyone, and perhaps the children most of all. "But I want to make sure you're okay," Josh continues. "I know you didn't ask for any of this, and this isn't at all what you expected your summer to be like…"

He sounds so concerned and understanding that a warmth spreads through me. His concern is so different from Kyle's, who acts as if he doesn't think I can manage anything, as if he's constantly expecting me to let him down. Josh sounds sure that I won't. "You don't have to keep checking on me, Josh," I tell him. "I'm fine, and I'll tell you if I'm not."

"I will keep checking on you, just in case," he returns. "But I'm glad you'll tell me. I want you to tell me if anything's too difficult or challenging."

"It won't be."

"You do seem to have them all in hand, even Zoe," he says with a laugh, and I find myself smiling.

"I'm not sure about that." There is a pregnant pause, the kind that hums, and my heart skips an uncertain beat. "How's Rebecca?" I finally ask, and it feels as if I've hurled a grenade into the conversation, such as it was.

"I haven't spoken to her yet. The facility suggests a few days without contact to start."

"But you're coming up this weekend?"

"Yes, planning to."

"So, you'll see her then?"

"Yes," he says after a tiny pause. "But mainly I'm coming up there to see the children. How are they?"

"Fine, I think—"

"Who are you talking to?" Zoe's screeching cry pierces my eardrums and nearly has me dropping the phone.

"Zoe—"

"Is that my *dad*?" she continues incredulously, and I feel myself start to blush, as if I've been doing something wrong.

"Yes, I was just telling him about our day at the park—"

"Why were *you* telling him?" she demands as she marches up to me. I am mortified, because I know Josh can hear our whole conversation—all of Upstate New York can. I don't have a chance to say anything to him, though, because Zoe has snatched the phone from my hand and presses it to her ear as she whirls away from me. "Daddy? Daddy? We went on a roller coaster today and it was amazing!" She doesn't mention the vomiting episode, I notice.

I walk into the house, leaving Zoe to fill Josh in on all the details she chooses. I tidy the kitchen mindlessly, half-listening to Zoe rabbit on outside as I go over my conversation with Josh in my mind. There was nothing remotely untoward about it. Nothing at all *flirty*. I can hardly believe I'm using that word, even in the negative. It feels wrong, and yet Zoe's look of outrage and suspicion has me on the defensive. Wondering.

Zoe comes back inside, marching by me with her nose in the air. "I'll give the phone to Charlotte and then Max, Daddy," she says loudly, and I feel like it's for my benefit. Family only. *I get it, Zoe, trust me.*

And yet after she's gone upstairs, I go back to remembering our conversation, the warmth in Josh's tone, and I find myself smiling all over again.

CHAPTER TWENTY-TWO

REBECCA

Three endless days go by and nothing really changes. Breakfast, lunch, dinner… lovely meals I try to eat while avoiding everyone's eye, which isn't hard because they're all avoiding mine. Everyone is here on sufferance, it seems, at least in public.

I take walks along the winding paths of the serenity garden, and spend hours in front of the TV, letting mindless reality television and talk shows wash over me in a soothingly meaningless tide. And of course there are my therapy sessions. The group ones continue to be torturously dull; if it's not Liz ranting about her ex-husband, it's Geoff complaining how unfair it was that he lost his job. At least his knee has stopped jiggling. Mostly.

I try to feel some empathy for my co-guests, but I can summon nothing more than a mild curiosity mingled with faint impatience. Everyone feels so aggrieved and hard done by, as if life has sucker-punched them when they weren't looking. I feel like taking them by the shoulders and giving them a good shake. *You want to talk about sucker punches? Don't you know this is your fault?*

And is it *my* fault? I worry this question over, like fingers smoothing fabric until it disintegrates beneath the touch. Guilt is my constant companion. Guilt for drinking so much, for worrying Josh so much, for letting my children see me in a way children should never, ever see their mother.

It corrodes my insides, the worst kind of emotional acid, and yet underneath it is something else, some sleeping sensation I'm not willing to prod awake, despite Diane's best attempts.

Every afternoon I sit in the cozy little therapy room and stare at Diane in silence. Sometimes she asks me questions that I'm willing to answer, usually innocuous ones about where I live, my children's ages—the flotsam of my former life. She seems content to wait, not to push, and for some reason that annoys me. I've been here nearly a week, a quarter of my total time. Shouldn't I be making some progress? Shouldn't she be making me make it?

"You have to want to," Diane says when I ask her that question on Friday afternoon. "I can't drag you kicking and screaming into emotional wellbeing, Rebecca. It doesn't work that way."

"If only it were that easy, right?"

"Right." She cocks her head and I brace myself for something deeper, some piercing assessment of my current mental state. "I would have thought you'd want to engage with me at least a little, for your children's sake."

And there it is. "I didn't think therapists were supposed to give guilt trips."

"Not a guilt trip, just an observation. I can tell you love your children, Rebecca."

"How?" I am curious; I've barely talked about them. I certainly have done my best not to show any excess or unnecessary emotion. I'm not going to turn *that* tap on, trust me. I'm not ready for the flood.

Diane shrugs and spreads her hands. "There is an intensity in your voice and face when you talk about them. The way your hands clench, your body tenses… it tells me all I need to know."

"I feel guilty," I confess. I can admit that much. "They've seen too much."

"All the more reason for you to help yourself. Let them see something else."

"If that's possible."

"It is possible, Rebecca. Because the least you could let them see is you trying."

I know she's right. I *know* it, and yet I still can't make myself take that terrifying leap off the ledge. I edge close to the precipice, I peer down into its endlessly black depths, and then I scuttle away. Too far. Too high. Too terrifying.

"Rebecca." The tiniest touch of impatience is audible in Diane's voice. "Your husband is visiting tomorrow, isn't he?"

"Yes." Josh phoned me last night to say he was coming for the weekend, and he'd see me on Saturday afternoon. I asked if he'd bring the children, and then he asked me if he should. And reluctantly I'd said no—I wasn't ready, I wasn't better yet. I did ask him to bring my phone, though, simply for the photos stored on it. At least then I will be able to see their faces.

"Are you looking forward to his visit?" Diane asks, and now I am the one shrugging.

"Sort of." I feel like Josh is going to be disappointed in me, that he's going to have expected some instantaneous, miraculous cure, to have the brand new—or rather old—Rebecca back again, and I'm not there yet. Not remotely. I'm still not sure if I ever will be.

"It would be nice if you could report some progress," Diane says mildly. "Some effort."

"I can. I haven't had a drop of alcohol in six days." I give her a toothy smile. Her expression doesn't change.

"You haven't had *access* to alcohol in six days, Rebecca, so while that is an accomplishment, it's not everything. What's going to happen when you leave Lakeview?"

"Good question."

"At this point in time, do you think you'll start drinking again?"

"I don't know." The funny thing is, I haven't even been craving it. I used alcohol to blot out the memories, but I don't even need it now. I feel so numb inside, so empty, like there's nothing to blot out. But talking to Diane makes me remember that there is.

Later, I wander around outside by myself. The air is stiflingly hot, like a physical force pressing down on me. Most people are inside, enjoying their air-conditioned bedrooms, but I feel the need to keep moving, to outrun my ever-circling thoughts.

Gwen finds me in the serenity garden, tracing the twisting paths, one foot in front of the other, as if I'm going somewhere. We've spent a fair amount of time together over the last few days. She'd told me how her husband left her last year, because of her drinking. It was the wake-up call she needed, but she didn't actually do anything about it for another eight months. I can relate.

"How are you not melting out here?" she remarks as she joins me on the path. "It's brutal."

"Better than just sitting around."

"Ah." There's so much understanding in her voice that I look at her sharply.

"What?"

"You're in that stage."

"That stage? What's that supposed to mean?"

"You're getting closer, Rebecca. You're circling, but you're getting closer."

I try to act as if I don't know what she's talking about, and yet still I ask. There are two forces inside me, a yearning and a fear, and they are in mortal combat. It's why I still go to the therapy sessions. It's why I answer some of Diane's questions, and it's why I press Gwen now. "Getting closer to what?"

She gives me a small, sympathetic smile. "The root, the bitter root of whatever it is that drove you to drink. Whatever brought you to the lowest point, and God knows it had to be pretty low, since you're here."

"It's kind of nice here," I point out. "Better than some of the health spas I've been to." Yesterday I had a massage and a manicure, just for something to do. I gaze down at my newly pale pink nails.

"Not that nice," Gwen says, and I decide to turn the tables.

"What brought *you* here?" I ask. "What was your lowest point, Gwen?"

She gives me a long look. "You sure you want to go down that road?"

"Why not?"

"Because if you ask me and I answer, then I get to ask you."

"I don't have to answer."

"You will, though, at least in part," Gwen shoots back. "You'll have to."

And I know what she means, because there's an unspoken code at times like this, in places like this. She's my friend and I can't just turn my back on her. So, like Gwen said, do I really want to go down this road?

I stare up at the bright blue sky; the air shimmers with heat and sweat trickles between my shoulder blades, down the small of my back. Somewhere in the distance a bird trills, a fleeting, melancholy sound. I'm so tired of stalling. Of feeling frozen. At some point I've got to let myself thaw out, and Gwen feels like the safest person to talk to. To tell. "Fine," I say, taking a deep breath and blowing it out. "Deal."

Gwen is silent, and I lower my gaze to look at her. She stares out at the lake, marshaling her thoughts. I wait.

"Five years ago my son committed suicide," she finally says, and it is a shock. Of course I knew there was something, but *that*...? My own problems feel petty in comparison. *Trifles.* And I realize how judgmental I have been, to assume Gwen and Liz and Geoff and all the rest aren't facing the same or worse than I am.

"He was thirty-one," she continues as she keeps staring out at the shimmering blue of the lake. "He'd been struggling with depression for some time, since his teens, but…" There is always a but. That much I know.

"You felt like it was your fault." She glances at me sharply, and I realize how insensitive I might sound, and yet I feel the truth of what I am saying deep within. "You felt you should have been able to do something, because you're his mother."

"*Was*. I was his mother." She nods slowly. "But yes. Yes, I felt that. I still do. Therapists tell me I need to let go of the guilt, but I can't. It's like it's become a part of me; it's twined all the way through me like some poisonous yet necessary vine. To let go of it would be to let go of myself."

"Yes." I release a long, low breath. "Yes, I can understand that."

"I started drinking just to blot out the memories. Remembering him well, remembering him at his worst. They both hurt. Alcohol became the only way to get through each day, moment by moment." She sighs, the sound shuddery. "But then it got out of control, as it does when you're not actually dealing with the hurt and the mess behind the addiction, and finally, my husband said he was leaving if I didn't stop." She pauses. "I didn't stop."

I feel an icy dread steal through me at the thought. If anything should compel me to try to heal myself, surely it should be the looming threat of *that*?

"And then?" I venture to ask after a few minutes when neither of us says anything. The bird trills again; fleeting, fluting.

"I blundered on for a while, because I couldn't face anything else. Drinking was the bandage I didn't want to rip off."

My fists clench of their own accord. It feels as if she is speaking right into my experience, and it *hurts*. "But you finally did."

"Only when I was thinking of doing the same thing my son did." Gwen closes her eyes and pinches the bridge of her nose. "I caught sight of my reflection in the bathroom mirror, a bottle of pills in my hand, a wild look in my eyes, and I suddenly thought, is this what I've become? Is this how it will end? *Me?* You know,

I was a human rights lawyer before all this. Not that it matters."
She lapses into silence as I absorb all her words. I feel as if she
has cracked open a door and peered into the jagged depths of
my soul, seen the ruins within.

Gwen glances at me with a faint smile. "Now it's your turn."

"Right." That was the deal, but I don't know where to begin.
How to begin.

"I imagine the details are different, but the story is the same,"
Gwen says. That crack just got wider, brighter, light flooding in,
so I long to shield myself from the glare. *How does she know?* I
wonder, even as I think, *of course she knows.*

"So, what was it?" she asks gently. "What are you holding so
close to yourself you're terrified to let it go?"

"A memory," I whisper, the word torn from me, leaving me
wounded and raw. Already I feel the threat of tears, of surrender-
ing to the pain that pulses deep inside. Gwen nods slowly.

"What kind of memory?"

"My…" I can't go on. That familiar bottleneck feeling catches
my throat. I've never got this far. Never said this much, and yet
I've barely said anything. Gwen waits. I decide to start again.
"Four months ago I was visiting my parents in Wisconsin. It
was Presidents' Day Weekend." I stop again and Gwen keeps
waiting. "We were having a fun time," I say stiltedly. "Card games,
charades, lots of food. My mom makes the most amazing meals,
three-course dinners every night."

"And?" Gwen asks eventually.

"And, right there in the middle of it all…" I close my eyes as
the memory bombards me. "I was tossing a salad at the kitchen
counter, right before dinner. My father came up behind me. He
was laughing, and then he whispered in my ear." A choked sound
escapes me and I draw a quick, steadying breath. "Something
about not liking anchovies. But…" I stop, not knowing how to
explain without sounding like I am completely crazy.

"But it reminded you of something?" Gwen guesses, and of course she's right.

"All of a sudden, this memory just—just *fell* into my head. Out of nowhere, like an asteroid from outer space." Causing a huge, terrible crater in my life. "I never had a hint of it before." I need to make that much clear. "*Nothing.*"

"Okay," Gwen says calmly. She is not surprised.

Do I have to go on? But of course I do. "It was a memory from when I was little," I whisper. "I'm not sure how old. Maybe six or seven…" Younger than any of my children are now. I feel sick, the bile churning in my stomach, rising in my throat. "He was whispering… telling me not to…" I shake my head. I can't put it into words. I *can't*. Because I love my dad. Because my memory *must* be wrong. Because if it's not, then everything I've known about love is the grossest misconception. Every memory I've ever had is false, fake, a life built on lies. I can't live with that. I *can't*.

"It's all right, Rebecca," Gwen says, and she touches my shoulder. I realize my eyes and fists are both clenched, everything in me resisting this memory, and the terrible truth of it. *Maybe.*

"It's not all right."

"No, of course it isn't," she agrees in that same calm voice. "I shouldn't have said that. Nothing is all right. But you can let yourself remember. You're going to have to, at some point. Because it will never go away otherwise."

"And it will go away if I do?"

"No, but you can learn to live with it. Deal with it. It's the only way, sweetheart. Trust me."

I nod slowly. I know it is, and yet I don't want it to be. I've been resisting giving in to this moment for four months now, four agonizing, endless months. Maybe this is finally the blessed and terrifying end of the road.

"You can imagine what I remembered," I say, my voice as leaden as my insides. My eyes open, my hands hanging limply at my sides, the fight gone out of me, which is both worse and better than anything I've ever felt before. "I remembered my father... touching me. Telling me not to tell anyone." My stomach churns as I say the words; I feel as if I am betraying everyone I've ever loved. Gwen squeezes my shoulder, but I don't feel like she understands. "You have to realize," I say, each word like a shard of broken glass in my throat, "that I love my dad so much. I always have. He's been the most amazing..." I stop, draw a ragged breath. My eyes burn, and so does my stomach. Everything hurting, because this can't be true—I can't let this be true. "You can't understand," I practically gasp.

"No, I can't," Gwen agrees. "But I understand how something that feels wrong and impossible can still happen, and it can wreck your world so much that you try to destroy whatever is left."

I let out a sob, and Gwen enfolds me in her arms. "You've taken the first step, Rebecca," she murmurs. "That first hard, horrible, awful step. But you've done it, and you can take another one. You can keep going."

"I don't know how..."

"Keep talking. Keep healing. You're seeing the therapist?" I nod. "Start talking to her. You've ripped the bandage off. Now it's time to staunch the bleeding."

By the time Josh arrives the next afternoon, I am feeling completely wiped out. Talking to Gwen was both good and hard, and she was absolutely right. The bandages are off, and I am bleeding. But it helped to talk to Diane earlier today, even if it was in staccato bursts, barely saying anything. I've *started*.

I told her a little bit about my memories, and how I wonder whether they are true. She hasn't said one way or the other, just asked me questions. Kept me talking.

But it feels like I have not just turned a corner, I have crested a mountain. There is a whole range of rugged peaks ahead of me, but at least I see the path now. A little bit. And when Josh comes into my room on Saturday afternoon, it feels as if I haven't seen him for a year. It's been less than a week.

"Rebecca." He bends to kiss my cheek, his lips cool against my skin. "You're looking well."

"Am I?" I've barely looked in a mirror all week; everything has been turned inward.

"Yes, definitely. The bruise has faded." He smiles as if to take the sting from the words, the reminder of where I've been, *who* I've been. I stare at him, feeling as if I've completely changed, or at least begun the metamorphosis, the shedding of old skin, and he can't see any of it. All he sees is a bruise that is now a yellow-green instead of a vivid purple. But can I really blame him? I've told him so little, and yet I've wanted him to understand anyway. *To know*.

"How are the children?" I ask as Josh sits down in my room's one armchair. I perch on the edge of the bed.

"They're all right." He sounds cautious, as if he isn't telling me something, and I have to brace myself.

"What is it? They are all okay, aren't they?"

"Yes, of course they are, Rebecca. It's just… this is hard on them." There is a faint note of reproach in his voice that I can't ignore.

"I didn't ask to be here." Josh's silence is eloquent. My hands clench into fists. I was making progress, such as it was, but now I feel as if I'm sliding inexorably back, into resentment and bitterness and fear. "Tell me what's been going on. How is Tessa?"

"Tessa's fine. Coping really well." *Coping*. The word catches me on the raw. She has to cope with my mistakes, my absence. I'm so much hard work.

"And Charlotte? And Max? Zoe?" I say their names eagerly, yet each one hurts. I miss them, I long for them. I've tormented myself all week with what they're doing, *how* they're doing. And now Josh is here, and he won't tell me. Why won't he give me details?

"They're going to be fine." Josh smiles, but it doesn't reach his eyes. I stare at him, and he feels like a stranger. Why won't he tell me more? What is he keeping from me? And then I remember all that I am keeping from him. How do we start to bridge this chasm of silence and secrets? How do we learn to trust each other enough to speak the truth? After fourteen years of marriage it seems ridiculous that we don't have a foundation of familiarity to build on. But maybe we lost it a long time ago. Maybe we never had it in the first place.

"Josh…" He raises his eyebrows, waiting. For a moment I consider telling him… something. Stumbling toward the truth, but I don't even know how. And Josh's faint, slightly superior smile unnerves me. He still thinks this is just about the alcohol. I'm not being the glittering and glossy Upper East Side wife and mother he thought he was getting, that he expected in exchange for a huge diamond ring and a lifestyle to which I have readily become accustomed. I know that's unfair; he's deeper and kinder than that, but I also know that he doesn't want this messy, broken Rebecca; that he doesn't know what to do with her.

He's not interested in the person I'm trying to be, someone who is uncovering terrible truths and trying to find a way to live with them. "Tell them hi from me," I say instead. "And that I miss them, so much. And give them my love."

Josh nods, that smug smile still in place—or am I imagining it? "Of course I will," he says.

CHAPTER TWENTY-THREE

TESSA

Over the next week we find our routine. It isn't easy or natural, but it works. At least, it starts to work. Twice that first week, Max wets the bed. He creeps into my bedroom in the middle of the night, waking me up with a gentle shake of my shoulder, tears streaking silently down his face. Twice I creep into his bedroom and change his wet sheets as quietly as I can, not wanting anyone else to see his mortification. Poor, sad little Max.

"I'm sorry, Tessa," he says with a hiccup as he steps into the shower to wash the urine off his skinny legs. "I'm so sorry."

"Max, you don't need to be sorry. These things happen." I hand him a thick, fluffy towel as he steps out from under the spray. "You know your mom is going to be okay, right?" I feel as if I am breathing truth into the words. He nods seriously. "And do you also know," I ask, "that *you're* going to be okay?"

His face crumples, and I pull him into a hug. He wraps his arms around my waist and holds on tight.

I savor that hug; Max's neediness is a balm to my wounded soul, an antidote to Ben's endless, indifferent energy. I feel a bit guilty for being glad that he needs me, that he looks to me for comfort. Just as I feel that same flicker of uneasy guilt when Charlotte plops next to me and asks if I will French-braid her hair before swimming, something Katherine has never, ever done. My daughter watches silently while I braid Charlotte's hair, and Zoe proclaims that her head now looks like a croissant. Charlotte gives both Zoe and Katherine a challenging, faintly patronizing look.

"I like it."

"It *is* a French braid," I say lightly, meeting Zoe's gaze, and get a glare in return for my pains. I never seem to get it right with her. Everything is an offense, and I wonder if I should just give up, but I keep trying. With all of them, I keep trying.

And somehow, through the days, we find our way. We settle into the same routines minus Rebecca, and a small, treacherous part of me feels like it's actually easier. I don't have to manage Rebecca's manic energy, not that I ever could; I don't have to pale in her shadow. At the club, I read a book while the children swim, and one day a middle-aged mom sits in the lounger next to mine and exclaims that she's just read the novel I've picked up—it had been on Rebecca's bedside table—and the next thing I know we're chatting away, and she's inviting me to a summer book club. Not that I can go, but I never expected it to be so easy to make friends. What have I been missing all along? Why didn't this happen in Brooklyn, when I've been so desperate for someone to reach out, to *notice*?

One day that week we eat lunch in the club's restaurant, burgers and fries as a special treat. Because we can. Because I am trying to be different, but not too different. Because we all need and deserve something just a little bit special.

Another day I get out all my card-making supplies and let the children go crazy with glitter and glue, cardstock and colorful markers. The materials are expensive, and they all use an excess of everything, but I don't mind. I want to take a snapshot of Zoe's face as she gleefully shakes glitter all over her card; I want to capture Ben's zeal as he draws a rocket ship and festoons it with fake jewels. I want to keep this memory close to me, savor it for a long time, because it feels so sweet.

One afternoon I take them all grocery shopping, and as a way to make it entertaining I give them ten dollars each and tell them to pick out enough food for one meal. They race around the store, filled with purpose, and return to me with arms full—vegetables and chicken for sensible Charlotte, a frozen pizza for Zoe, three boxes of Coco Pops for Ben.

"Seriously, Ben?" I roll my eyes. "We are not eating cereal for dinner."

"Why not?" he retorts. "You asked us to get something for dinner, and I did." He stares at me in challenge, arms folded, chin raised, and the other kids watch, waiting to see what I will do.

And so I shrug. Smile. I take the boxes from him and toss them into the cart. "Fine, we'll have cereal for dinner. See how everyone likes it." Ben grins, and the other children exchange looks of surprised delight. I feel like I made the right choice, like I *won.*

There are worse things, surely, than a bowl of Coco Pops? The old fears I once had, that I was doing it all wrong, that I'd missed some essential piece in this puzzle of motherhood, are slowly slipping away from me, like the shedding of an old, flaky skin.

Somehow, with Rebecca gone, with her children, I am becoming the mother I was meant to be. The mother I wanted to be all along.

We eat the Coco Pops that night, and Ben has two bowls. "Drink all the milk, at least," I order, and five children gleefully obey. As we are clearing the table, dusk settling outside, Zoe points toward the window.

"Fireflies!"

I turn to see one winking and bumbling through the air as soft, purple shadows fall over the lawn.

"Can we go out?" Charlotte asks eagerly.

"Can we catch them?" Ben interjects.

"Of course we can." Saying yes is easy. It's wonderful.

And so we leave the dirty bowls and spills of milk; I find a few glass jars in a cupboard and poke holes in the lids. As night falls we are all out there, chasing after the fireflies that dance through the air, longing to capture their winking lights.

I watch Zoe hold one so gently in her hands, and then carefully, so carefully, put it into her jar. Her face is alight, and my heart expands with joy. I love seeing her look like a child, carefree and happy, her world honed to this one exquisite moment.

As we are running about in the grass, jars in hand, our laughter echoing through the air, an older couple strolling along the road stop to watch us.

"This reminds me of my childhood," the man calls with a smile. "Are they all yours?"

"Oh no—" I give a laugh as I shake my head.

"Well, you're doing a good job," he says. I am still smiling when we head indoors. Of course, not everyone sees this the way I do. When Kyle calls one evening, he is full of caution and even disapproval.

"I'm glad you're coping, Tessa," he says, "but this still isn't your responsibility."

"It is now." I want to tell him I'm not just coping, I'm thriving. But I'm not sure I have the words to explain that to him.

"I'm just worried," he persists. "You found it hard enough back in Brooklyn, dealing with our two—"

"That's not fair." Instead of being heartened that he understands how difficult it was for me, I feel criticized and judged.

"How is it not fair?" There is a throb of feeling in Kyle's voice; it sounds almost like anger.

"Because maybe that was Brooklyn," I fire back. "Maybe that wasn't me. And maybe I can be different here."

Kyle is silent for a long moment. "You can be different?" he finally repeats. "How different, Tessa?" I don't know how to answer. I can't tell if he thinks I can't change, or that I shouldn't.

"Why don't you come visit?" I suggest, even though I'm not sure I actually want him to. "See for yourself."

"I can't come up until August."

Which is nearly three weeks away. Rebecca will be back then. "Is work crazy?"

"I have gigs planned." He sounds defensive. "That bar in the Bronx wants us to open every Saturday."

And clearly those gigs are non-negotiable and more important than anything else. I take a deep breath and inject a note of enthusiasm into my voice. "That's great."

"Thanks." We are both silent, listening to each other breathe. "As long as you really think you can handle this," Kyle says. He still sounds dubious.

"I can, Kyle. You don't need to worry."

"Okay." His voice is resolute. "I won't."

Rayha, too, seems wary. "It just seems so much to take on," she says when she calls one evening. "Three more children…"

"I love them," I fire back. "And they need me."

Rayha is silent; I sense her disquiet and it annoys me, so after dutifully asking about Zane, I end the call.

By Saturday afternoon I am feeling both peaceful and anxious, at war with myself. It's been a strange week, a good week, a strengthening and healing week, and yet… Rebecca. When I think of her, I feel guilty. I should think of her more. I shouldn't be enjoying this—her house, her kids, her life—the way I do. I know that, and yet…

I push the thoughts away. I choose not to think of Rebecca very much. And when Josh pulls into the drive on Saturday evening, having visited Rebecca before coming here, the children all rushing out to the deck to greet him while I stand by the sliding glass door, hands folded at my waist, beatific smile in place, I don't think of her at all.

I watch as the children fly down the stairs, Zoe nearly slip-ping in her haste to get to him first. He stops mid-way across the lawn to accept their group tackle, and then he hugs the children each in turn, their arms wrapped around his waist, heads burrowing into his stomach.

By the time he climbs the steps to greet me, I am feeling nervous, as if I have to justify my presence. "Tessa," he says in the same warm voice I remember from the phone. He grips my elbow in a reassuring squeeze. "How are you?"

"I'm well." I sound a little bit breathless. "Dinner's ready."

"You made dinner?"

I spent all afternoon slaving over it, not that I'd ever admit as much. But I am quietly proud of what I've accomplished—the table laid with neatly folded paper napkins and colorful pottery plates, a jug of fresh lemonade and a big bowl of tossed salad in the middle. The chicken parmesan is bubbling away in the oven, and the aroma of garlic bread scents the air.

"Wow!" Josh says as he steps into the kitchen. "Did you do all this?"

As if I've made a three-course, gourmet feast. I duck my head modestly. "It's just dinner."

"Thank you so much, Tessa. For everything."

"Why don't we eat? While it's still hot?"

Josh sits at the table with the children clambering for his attention while I bustle about, feeling strangely happy simply to move pots around, drain pasta and grate cheese. It isn't until I've put it all on the table that I realize Ben and Katherine aren't even there.

"Just a sec," I say as everyone prepares to dig in. "Let me find Ben and Katherine…"

I hurry upstairs, calling their names, only to find them curled up on the sofa on the top floor.

"Guys!" I am breathless and exasperated. "What are you doing up here?"

Ben shrugs and Katherine looks away. Guilt wars with annoyance within me. "What's going on, you two?" I sound like a school teacher.

"Nothing." This from Katherine, who still won't look at me, one leg wound around another.

"Ben, Katherine, it's time for dinner." I wait for them to get up and come downstairs, but neither of them moves. Now I am really getting annoyed. "Come on, you two. Mr. Finlay has driven a long way—"

"Oh, *Mr. Finlay*," Katherine says, rolling her eyes, and I stare at her, nonplussed.

"Katherine..."

"Fine, I'm coming." She gets off the sofa, and slinks past me, and with a groan Ben follows. Downstairs they are all waiting for us; no one has touched their food.

"Everything all right?" Josh asks as he raises his eyebrows.

"Yes, fine." I smile, trying to mask my irritation with Ben and Katherine's behavior. It's not their fault; I understand their awkwardness.

"So, tell me what you've all been doing this week," Josh invites once we've all started eating.

"The usual," Charlotte says. "Tennis and swimming."

Josh turns to me. "You haven't had trouble, with membership at the club? I didn't even think of that..."

Before I can think of a reply, Zoe jumps in. "Didn't you know, Daddy? Mommy paid for Tessa and her kids to have a membership at the club." Her eyes round innocently as she waits for Josh's response, and I squirm inwardly.

"That's good," Josh says, frowning slightly, clearly sensing some undercurrents.

"She paid for it weeks ago," Zoe states with emphasis. "Right at the beginning." I wonder if she even knows what she's saying, the effect it will have. How can a nine-year-old be so astute about the nuances of accepting money from a friend?

"Oh." Josh glances at me, his eyes slightly narrowed, and I try to keep from blushing.

"It was very kind of her…" I murmur, glancing down at my plate.

"Mommy offered to pay for sailing too," Zoe continues. She sounds viciously gleeful now. "And she paid for them both to go to Syracuse and have manicures and stuff."

Now my face is fiery. How does Zoe, all of nine years old, know so much about money, and who pays for what? I force myself to meet Josh's kindly gaze. "Rebecca has been very generous…"

"I'm glad it has worked out," Josh says after a pause. Fortunately, Zoe doesn't keep at it, and the rest of the meal passes uneventfully.

I tidy up while Josh plays with the kids upstairs, and then settles them into bed. Ben and Katherine drift around, and finally retreat to their rooms. I know they feel as awkward as I do, almost as if we shouldn't be here. And maybe we shouldn't.

Should I have offered to return to Pine Cottage for the night? I'm suddenly embarrassed that it didn't even occur to me, and even if it had, I know I wouldn't have gone. I want to be here, awkward as it is. It feels like my home too.

I haven't been back to our cottage all week, not even to check on things, and now a pang of guilt adds to the embarrassment. What would Kyle think, if he realized our rental is going to waste? All that money he was so resentful to part with.

I stand at the sink and stare out at the moonlit water, remembering how Rebecca and I swam out to the raft on one of my first nights here, how much of an enchanting enigma she seemed to me, elusive and interesting. I wonder how she is now, how she was with Josh. I'm not sure I should ask. Everyone skirted around mentioning her at dinner; it started to feel a little bit absurd, as if we were trying to pretend she didn't exist.

"They're all in bed, if not asleep."

I turn at the sound of Josh's voice. He smiles at me, and in an instant the mood shifts. I smile back.

"They're very glad to have you here."

"I'm glad to be here."

He pauses, one hand resting on the counter, while I lean against the sink, unsure how to navigate this moment, unwilling for it to end.

"You saw Rebecca this afternoon?" I finally venture, after a few taut seconds have passed. Outside the night is darkening to velvet shadows, and the house is quiet and still.

"Yes, I did." Josh runs a hand through his hair, rumpling it rather ridiculously. He's so not what I expected from a high-powered Wall Street exec. He reminds me of Max. "Would you like a glass of wine?" he asks, and I jerk back a little in surprise. "Maybe not the most appropriate thing, considering, but…" He spreads his hands. "I could use one."

"I… I don't know if there is any wine," I stammer.

"I brought a bottle with me." He walks over to the bags he left by the door and pulls out a bottle of red. "Courtesy of the liquor store in Geneseo."

"Right."

"I know it might seem insensitive or even crass, considering." He grimaces. "But Rebecca isn't here." His words hang in the air and then settle. Still, I say nothing, as ever uncertain. "Well?" He lifts one eyebrow, giving a weary smile, and a shaft of sympathy slices through me. Why shouldn't I accept? We're both adults. We're both tired. It's just a glass of wine. But I still feel a little uneasy, a little guilty, as I murmur my thanks and Josh uncorks the bottle with a satisfying pop.

I find two glasses and he pours, and I force myself to relax. It's been a good week, but it's also been a long, hard week. A glass of wine definitely won't go amiss.

Josh brings both glasses over to the adjoining family room, and then hands me one before sitting down. We settle in opposite sofas just as we did a week ago, when everything felt so fragile, so fractured. Now, although I am still tense, the mood is much better.

"So, tell me about the week," Josh says, and it makes me think that Rebecca, and his visit to her, is a no-go area.

"It's been good," I answer cautiously. I don't feel I can admit to Josh just how good it's been for me. I feel like some maternal parasite, feeding off the fear and grief of his children, so grateful to be needed, to feel useful, to know the right things to do and say for once. "We've had our fair share of bumps along the way," I add, thinking of Zoe on the roller coaster, Max wetting the bed, "but I think we're doing okay."

"Good. I'm glad."

"About the club membership…" I feel I have to say it. "Rebecca was very generous, and she paid for us to have a summer membership and swimming and tennis lessons," I explain awkwardly. My cheeks burn. "As well as some other things. Looking back, I realize I probably shouldn't have accepted so much from her. I'm sorry if it seems as if I was taking advantage." I lower my gaze as I take a sip of wine.

"Don't worry about it, Tessa. If anyone's taking advantage, it's me." He leans forward to put one hand on my knee. His palm is warm, and sparks shoot through me. I sit frozen, shocked. He doesn't mean anything by it, I know that—he's just grateful. And yet he doesn't remove his hand, and the moment spins on just a little too long. "Thank you," he adds in a low voice, "for taking care of my children."

I nod jerkily, and he finally removes his hand and sits back. Clearly, I read way too much into that small gesture. But the mood feels strained as we sit and sip our wine in silence. I can't think of anything to say.

"Rebecca didn't seem much better today," Josh says after a moment. "At least that I could see."

So, we are going to talk about Rebecca. Perhaps that's the safest area, after all. "What was she like?"

Josh shrugs as he takes a sip of wine. "I don't know. Distant. Brittle." He pauses, his face drawn in bleak lines. "I'm not sure she's trying all that hard, to be honest."

"Maybe that's part of it," I suggest hesitantly. "To get to a place where she can try…?"

"Then I wish she'd get there. It's already been a week." There is a note of irritated impatience in his voice that I don't know how to respond to. I feel sorry for Josh, but I also feel sorry for Rebecca. It's not exactly her fault, is it? Or is it? I remember her at the Fourth of July party, that guy's slobbery mouth on her, her head thrown back, and something hardens inside me. Josh is right: Rebecca could try a lot harder.

"Sorry," he says, turning back to me with an abashed, and rather endearing, smile. "I shouldn't be talking like this to you."

"It's okay." I'm conscious of the wine, and the darkness outside, the hushed stillness of the house. My knee still feels warm from where he touched it. "I guess you need someone to talk to."

"I do. I can't tell anyone about this back home. I haven't even wanted to tell Rebecca's parents, for her own sake."

"Do they know…?"

"Not really." He sighs. "I've told them a bit, but not much. It doesn't feel fair, though, to keep it from them. They love her so much."

"Rebecca seemed like she had some problems with them," I offer cautiously. "She didn't want them to visit."

"Well, we know why that is, don't we?" Josh sighs heavily. "They'd be on to her right away."

I sip my wine in silence, mulling that over. I don't think that can be entirely the reason, based on the way Rebecca has been acting, but what do I really know? The more I remember how Rebecca was, the less sure I am of what is real, what is true. Memories have a way of blurring and morphing into another, more pleasing shape; I'm not sure anything I can recall about the last month is really accurate.

"Anyway," Josh says with a smile. "Enough about that. Tell me about yourself. Rebecca mentioned you're from the city?"

"Yes, Brooklyn."

"Brooklyn's great. I used to bike along the Promenade."

"I love the Promenade!" I exclaim in surprise. It's one of Brooklyn's best-kept secrets, a sliver of green along the waterfront, with views of downtown Manhattan. When Katherine was a baby, I used to push her along there in the stroller; we'd watch the boats go by, taking the trash to Staten Island. Picturesque for New York City.

"And then I'd get pizza at Dellarocco's," Josh continues, and I can't keep from letting out a little exclamation.

"I love their capricciosa!"

"My favorite too," Josh says with a nod. "Shiitake mushrooms, artichokes, and olives. Delicious."

I shake my head in smiling disbelief, amazed we've found this little bit of common ground. "Yes, it's always been my favorite. I haven't been in years, though." I should take Ben and Katherine when we get back. All four of us, even.

"Me neither," he answers. "We should go together sometime." His words seem to hover in the air for a second, and he lets out a little laugh. "All nine of us, I mean. A city reunion. When all this is past us."

"Right." Of course that's what he meant. I'm embarrassed by the directions my thoughts insist on heading.

"Well…" Josh leans forward and takes my empty wine glass, his fingers brushing mine. "It's late. We should probably go to bed."

"Right." He stands and takes the glasses to the sink. I follow. "Thank you for the wine."

"My pleasure." He turns to me with a smile. I realize way too late that he has nowhere to sleep.

"I'm sorry," I say stiltedly. "I think we've taken up all the beds."

"Don't worry, there's a pull-out bed in the study. I'll be fine."

"Let me get you some sheets, then." I go upstairs, Josh so close behind me I can hear the whisper of his khakis. My pulse is pounding in my throat, in my ears. This is ridiculous.

I fumble in the linen cupboard for sheets and a pillowcase, Josh standing behind me, his breath practically fanning my ear. I am blushing hotly, the moment speeding up and slowing down at the same time. I am reading too much into this. I *must* be.

"Here." I turn around but he's even closer than I thought, and the sheets hit him in the chest, and catch me off balance. He puts his hands on my upper arms to steady me, and for a few taut seconds we engage in an awkward dance, trying to regain our footing, our bodies brushing.

"Daddy?" A sleepy voice has us both stilling, our gazes locked on each other's. Zoe stands in her doorway, rubbing sleep from her eyes. Josh's hands are still on my shoulders.

"Hey, Zo!" He drops his hands and steps back, but she's already seen. I can tell from the way her jaw drops and her fists bunch. My face is scorching, and I feel sick. Nothing happened, and yet…

"What are you *doing*?" she hisses at me, and I recoil involuntarily. Zoe's look is one of pure, unadulterated hatred, worse than any she's given me before.

"Zoe." Josh puts a hand on her shoulder. "Tessa was just getting me some sheets. Let me take you back to bed." He shoots me a quick, apologetic smile as he disappears into Zoe's bedroom. I still feel shaky and sick as I go to my bedroom—*Rebecca's* bedroom—my mind whirling. I don't know what to think.

"Mom?"

"Katherine!" I whirl around, one hand pressed to my chest. What did she see? "What is it, sweetheart?"

Katherine's hands are pleated together, knuckles showing white and bony. "Can we go home?" she whispers.

I stare at her, stunned. "Go home? You mean—to Brooklyn?"

"Yes." She bows her head. "Or at least back to Pine Cottage."

"Katherine…" I stare at her helplessly. This is the last thing I expect now. "Why, sweetheart? Why do you want to go?"

"Just because." Her gaze darts away. "It's all too… weird."

"I know it is, sweetheart." How could I expect her to feel otherwise? And yet I still feel disappointed. "But the Finlays need us, Katherine—" I put my hand on her shoulder but she shrugs it away.

"That's not what Daddy says. He says they're not our responsibility."

I press my lips together, trying to hide my annoyance at Kyle's interference. "Maybe not our responsibility, but they're still our friends. Mrs. Finlay is going to be away for another three weeks. We can't just leave them on their own."

She folds her arms, hugging herself as if she's cold. "They have their dad."

"He has to work, Katherine—"

"So? Why can't he figure something out?" Her chin juts mutinously.

"Katherine…" I am at a loss. "Aren't you having fun? You and Charlotte get along so well now…"

"I guess, but…" She looks away. "I still don't like it here." Her voice is low and I have to strain to hear it.

"Okay," I say after a moment. "I get that this situation is a little weird. And maybe, when Mr. Finlay is out tomorrow with Charlotte and Zoe and Max, we can do something together. The three of us." I inject a note of enthusiasm into my voice. "Wouldn't that be nice?"

Katherine stares at me hopelessly. "You don't get it," she says in a voice of quiet sorrow that sends a chill of unease through me.

"What don't I get?"

"Everything," she says, and turns away, slipping like a shadow through the doorway before I can ask her what she means. I think of following her, demanding answers, but I know that never works, not with Katherine.

I close the door with a sigh, feeling tired and old and confused. There are too many nuances to attempt to discern, too many uncertainties to leave me stumbling. I am just slipping into my pajamas when a soft knock sounds at the door.

Thinking—and hoping—it's Katherine to come back and explain herself, I hurry to open it and then gape when I see who is standing there, a wry, tired smile on his face.

Josh.

CHAPTER TWENTY-FOUR

REBECCA

I have been at Lakeview for almost two weeks when Diane asks me when I am going to take the next step.

"What next step?" I ask, my tone guarded despite my best intentions to stay open. I've had quite a few watershed moments over these last weeks. I've spent hours talking to Diane, sifting through memories, trying to discover the truth. The annoying thing about her is she never tells me if I'm right or wrong. She barely makes any suggestions. She just lets me stumble on, sometimes prompting me, sometimes encouraging me, never leading me. This is clearly my work, and it's hard.

But I've made some progress. I think. I've looked my memories in the face, at least, and I've told as much as I remember to Diane—fragments and shreds, like the whispers of a bad dream. The trouble is, I still don't know if I can trust them. If I want to.

"What if you spoke to your mother and father?" Diane asks matter-of-factly one lazy afternoon. Fleecy white clouds drift through an azure sky. It's Friday, and Josh has promised to bring the children tomorrow. I am desperate to see them.

"Spoke to them? You mean about—"

"Your memories." She speaks calmly, so unruffled about everything.

"I couldn't." The reaction is instinctive, absolute.

"Why not?"

"Because they'd both be hurt, horrified—"

"Rebecca, if your father did in fact perpetrate these—"

"Don't." Perhaps I haven't made as much progress as I thought. I still hate even to think about the reality of my memories, even as I continue to prod them, like poking at a sore tooth, waiting for the jagged lightning streak of pain. "I couldn't hurt them that way, in case it isn't true."

"Why do you think you've had such a memory fall into your head—your words, remember—if it wasn't true?"

"I don't know." I shift uncomfortably. I don't like thinking like this.

"What you've described of your memories, Rebecca, has been very specific. The smell of pine needles—"

My throat tightens. "It was Christmas."

"Your sixth birthday."

The acrid smell of candles being blown out. Why do I remember such vivid sensory details, while so much else remains shadowy? Perhaps because I want it to. "Still, it doesn't prove anything, and I've read about False Memory Syndrome—"

"Which usually happens when a patient has been involved in hypnosis or psychotherapy, with suggestions planted by an unprofessional therapist."

"Still."

"If you really think the memories are false, why are you so upset? Why do you drink?"

She's really pushing me now. Two weeks in and the gloves are off. I wish Gwen were here; she left yesterday, and I felt as if I were saying goodbye to my mom, or rather the mother I need in this situation. She squeezed my shoulders and kissed my cheek and told me she was always at the end of the phone, but I want her here, holding my hand, urging me on, making me feel brave.

"Because I'm afraid they're not," I say at last.

Diane nods, unfazed. "Then the priority for you is to discover if they're real or not. If you can trust them or not." She leans back in her chair and re-crosses her legs. "Memory is a very strange, subjective thing. Did you know the more times you recall a particular event, the less likely you are to remember the details accurately? In fact, with each retelling, the memory is likely to transform, even as you are more likely to be assured of the accuracy of your recollection."

"Seriously?" I am fascinated and appalled by this. I really can't trust myself, can I? "Why?"

"It's your brain's version of the telephone game. Every time you recall a memory, you are remembering the last time you recalled it—the situation you were in, the emotions you experienced, the sensory details, even the aspects of the memory you remembered then that weren't accurate. And so all these things become embedded in your subconscious, for the next time you access that memory."

"So, I really can't trust anything I remember?" I am properly horrified now. "I really might have made this all up?" Which makes me a complete nutcase. Why would I make up something so terrible?

"No, I believe you can trust your first memory," Diane says. She still sounds calm. "But each time you've gone back over that memory, you might have embellished details, distorted facts, all without realizing."

"So, what do I do?"

"That's why talking to your parents could help. They have memories too, Rebecca."

"I can't do that." I shake my head. "Besides, if it is true, my father won't just admit to it, surely?" My stomach cramps at the thought.

"Perhaps not, but talking to him face-to-face could help you. You might remember something else, you might see something in his face—"

"No." A shudder goes through me. I can't bear my father admitting to something so awful, but I can't stand the thought of knowing he is lying, either. "No, I'm sorry. I'm not ready for that."

Diane is silent for a long moment. I feel as if I've failed her. If I'd agreed to confront my parents, would I prove to her and everyone else that I really am making the progress I know I need to?

"There is another possibility," she says at last.

"What possibility?"

"There is a practice called guided imagery. It's a way to recall memories, usually of traumatic events in your past, that you have suppressed."

A ripple of apprehension passes through me. "You mean like hypnosis?"

"That's one way. Another is more of a relaxation technique, with a trained therapist guiding you to remember sensory details of the event, which often trigger more concrete memories." She pauses. "I should tell you, however, that this practice is generally not approved by most professionals."

"Why not?"

"Because of the possibility of implanted memories or imagination inflation. It's really quite amazing, how people are able to remember specific events that never happened to them, simply by the power of suggestion, either in the past or present."

"Is that what you think I'm doing?" *Why* would I dream up something so horrifying, something that has made a train wreck of my life?

"No, because—as I said before—of the nature of your first memory. And if you had a professional who was very cautious about any sense of suggestibility, it could be a profitable technique for you. If you wanted to explore that route."

Do I? I've spent the last two weeks peering into the dark hole of my memory, but I haven't actually clambered into it to see what's there. I haven't dared. And if I did… if I got down in the muck and the mire and was finally able to figure out what was true and what wasn't? Could I finally have some peace, some sanity? Could I reclaim my life—my husband, my children? Could I make it all go away?

"I don't know," I tell Diane. "I'll have to think about it."

"Of course. It's entirely up to you, Rebecca. It's just one way forward."

By Saturday afternoon I am pacing my room, all thoughts of guided imagery and recovered memories replaced by the one consuming need to see my children. It's been two weeks, longer than I've ever gone without seeing them before. I haven't even talked to them in all that time, and it feels like forever.

I glance in the mirror, thankful the bruise on my forehead has faded to a yellow mark I've covered with concealer. I look a little better; I've put on a little bit of weight, so I'm not quite so gaunt. There are lines on my face that wouldn't normally be there, and flecks of gray and silver amid the blonde strands of my hair, but there is a spark in my eyes that I know has been missing for a long while. I wonder if my children will notice. If Josh will.

And then they are there, a discreet tap on the door I don't have time to respond to before Zoe flings the door opens and barrels toward me.

"Zoe!" I cry, my voice choking as I wrap my arms around my fierce little girl. She burrows her head into my stomach, holding me as tightly as she can. My heart cracks and the love in it overflows. "I've missed you," I whisper, like a prayer. "I've missed you and I love you so much. So, *so* much!" Zoe hugs me tighter and I glance up to see Charlotte and Max hanging back a little; Max is looking shy, Charlotte speculative. Beyond them is Josh… and Tessa. Ben and Katherine stand behind her, looking uncertain and out of place.

I feel a jolt, like missing the last step in the staircase. I didn't expect Tessa to come; I'm not sure why she's here. And while I'm glad to see her, of course I am, my brain is ticking over, noticing details. How her hand is on Max's shoulder, as if he needs the steadying, the strength. How pretty she looks, with hair tamed into natural, glossy waves, her hazel eyes sparkling, her lips curving into a generous smile of welcome. She's wearing the floaty red sundress I bought her, and I watch as she and Josh exchange a quick, complicit look—nothing more than a smile, but something in me goes cold and still.

"Mommy, when you are you coming back?" Zoe tilts her face up to look at me plaintively and I turn my gaze to her blue, blue eyes.

"Another two weeks, darling. Not long at all."

"That's forever."

Yes, at the moment it feels like forever. I smile and stroke Zoe's hair. "Tell me what you've all been doing." I beckon to Charlotte and Max and they come forward, Max dragging his heels a little. "Come and tell me everything."

Max looks back at Tessa and she gives him an encouraging smile, gently prods him forward. He walks toward me slowly, shyly. My poor little Max, it hurts to see how unsure he is of me. How he looks to Tessa for comfort and guidance, yet what could I really expect? I wasn't there when he needed me. And he needed me because of what I'd done to our family, what I'd become.

"Come on, Maxie," I coax, and I hold out one arm. After an unbearable second's pause he comes forward and presses his head against my shoulder. I wrap my arm around him like I'm never going to let him go. Out of the corner of my eye I see Josh smile again at Tessa, and then touch her arm. It's barely a brush of his fingers, yet it feels like a slap in the face. I sense an undeniable, easy intimacy between them that is worse than anything I could have envisioned. Yet how could this possibility *not* have occurred to me, considering? And yet. *Tessa…* and Josh. I feel as if a fist has just plowed into my stomach.

"Why don't we take a walk outside?" I suggest. Zoe clambers off my lap and I beckon to Charlotte, who is still hanging back. "I'll show you the serenity garden."

"The what?" Zoe asks, and I smile and reach for her hand.

"Let me show you." I turn my back on Josh and Tessa; I don't want to think about them, they don't have to come.

And so they don't. I don't let that knowledge hurt me as I take the kids outside, slipping past Josh and Tessa, Ben and Katherine. I cling to Zoe and Max's hands, Charlotte walking behind us, as we head down the hall and then out the French doors that lead to the garden, the lake a blur of blue beyond.

The air is still and hot, so stepping outside feels like walking into a brick oven. The sun beats down relentlessly; already, just a little bit past the middle of the month, the grass is turning brown and dry and withered.

"Here we are," I say brightly as I head toward the winding paths I've traced step by step over the last few weeks, the low hedges interspersed with wooden benches, the smell of honeysuckle heavy in the air. "Isn't it pretty?"

My three children look at the little garden, nonplussed. "Can you see the house from here?" Charlotte asks, nodding toward the lake.

"I don't think so, but why don't we check?" I know we can't, but we all walk through the meadow, the dry grass whispering about our legs, toward the shore. I've come down to the lake a few times; I've even gone swimming, cutting through the cool water, letting it soothe me.

Now I sit on the edge of the water as Zoe yanks off her sandals and wades in up to her knees. Max sits next to me, and Charlotte wanders off a little way, gazing out at the water, her arms folded, her expression remote. No one says anything, but I tell myself that's okay. We need to get used to each other again. Simply being together is enough for me, right now. I try not to think of Tessa and Josh back in my room with Ben and Katherine.

"Mommy, do you like it here?" Max asks. I put my arm around his shoulders and snuggle him in close.

"This is a nice place, but I like being home with you much better."

"I don't understand why you can't come home." His voice is so small. "You don't seem sick."

"I'm not sick, not really," I say carefully. "I just have some things I need to think about."

"You can't think about them at home?" He peers up at me anxiously, and my heart both contracts and expands. How is an eight-year-old meant to understand this? The answer, of course, is that he's not.

"There are special people here who help me to think about them. But I'll be home soon, Maxie, I promise."

"Two *weeks*!"

"But Tessa is taking good care of you, isn't she?" I can't help but ask.

"I guess so."

"And Daddy's been there on the weekends?"

"Yes…" He sounds a bit uncertain.

"It's going to be okay, Max," I tell him. For once I actually, or at least almost, believe what I am saying. "It's all going to be okay." I will make sure of it.

I catch up with Charlotte as we head back to the house. She's barely spoken a word the whole time we've been outside, barely met my eye. "How are you, Charlotte? Everything okay?" I grab hold of her wrist, meaning only to stay her, but she yanks it back irritably.

"Don't."

This is so unlike Charlotte, my beatific, beautiful girl, that I still. "Charlotte…?"

"I'm fine." She rubs her wrist and that's when I see them: two ravaged, red lines running parallel on her inner arm.

"What are those?" I ask, my voice coming out harsher than I mean it to. I point to the cuts. For a second neither of us speaks. The moment feels taut and suspended. Charlotte turns her arm away so I can't see them. There is a disturbing glint of challenge in her eyes.

"I scraped myself on some briars," she says. I know she's lying, of course I do. I also know where she learned to do that to herself—from me. And I am so horrified by this, so overwhelmed with guilt, that for a moment it is all I can do simply to stand there. A bitter little smile twists her lips as my daughter turns away from me and walks inside.

Max and Zoe come up to me and slip their hands in mine, and we walk back to the house in silence, my mind spinning, my heart aching. I can't stand the thought of Charlotte hurting herself intentionally; I can't stand the thought that she feels she needs to. And I especially can't stand the thought that I am in this place, powerless to help her. I know I have to do something, but what?

Back inside the house, Tessa and her kids are sitting in the living area with Josh, sipping fresh juice one of the staff has brought. Josh and Tessa are sitting on opposite sides of the sofa, but there is something relaxed between them that catches me on the raw.

"Did you have a nice walk?" Tessa asks brightly as we come into the room.

"Yes, we did. A lovely walk." Because I haven't actually greeted her yet, I bend down to enfold Tessa in a brief hug. When I press my cheek to hers I inhale the scent of my Estée Lauder face cream on her skin. "So great to see you, Tessa," I say as I step back. She smiles, and I smile back; like the moment earlier with Charlotte, it feels taut. It goes on a little too long. Then Josh says something, and Zoe plops herself into his lap, and I try to listen.

My mind is still spinning, and at the center of myself a realization is crystallizing. I need to get better fast. I need to become strong and well again, before I lose my family—and my husband.

CHAPTER TWENTY-FIVE

TESSA

When I opened the bedroom door and saw Josh standing there, my mind started spinning.

"Do you need something…?"

"Not really," he answered, and I stared at him in confusion. The seconds ticked by and then he stepped inside the room, pulled me into his arms, and kissed me. It was both a shock and a delight, a romantic fantasy and a waking nightmare.

We kissed hungrily, urgently, with the kind of devouring desperation I hadn't felt since forever. It must have only lasted about thirty seconds or so, certainly no longer than a minute. Then, as reality started crashing in, I wrenched myself away, breathing heavily, and we stared at each other for a long, tense moment before Josh stepped back, raking his hands through his hair and shaking his head.

"I'm sorry. I shouldn't have… that shouldn't have happened." He looked so shaken and miserable, I would have given him a hug if we hadn't just been kissing. As it was, he stared at me for another endless moment and then he turned and walked out of the room.

I stood there gaping for a few seconds, wondering if that really happened. My lips burned. It took me hours to get to sleep; even then I startled awake at every creak in the house, every whisper of the wind, half-expecting and yes, half-hoping, to my shame, for another knock on the door.

The next morning my nerves are writhing with anxiety as I get dressed. What if he decides it's too awkward, and he has to leave—or we do? How do we navigate past such a poor decision? Because I know it was wrong, of course I do. So very wrong with both of us married, with Rebecca in rehab, with the children, the *children* who need us both so very much, sleeping all around us. Just thinking about all the reasons why not fills me with a corroding shame.

The kitchen smells of coffee and sunshine as I come down at seven in the morning, before any of the children are awake. Josh stands at the kitchen counter, freshly showered and shaven, holding out a mug to me.

"Tessa." That voice. Just as low and warm as ever, without a hint of awkwardness or embarrassment. Meanwhile, I am trying not to cringe or blush, or both. "Milk, one sugar, right?"

"Yes, thanks." I take the mug, trying to avoid touching his hand.

"So." He gives me a shamefaced smile, a ridiculously hangdog look, and somehow I start to laugh. I know it's not funny, but he's managed to lighten a moment I expected to be unbearable. "I messed up," he says quietly. "I'm sorry."

"So am I—"

"It wasn't your fault."

Those thirty seconds or so sort of were. I could have pushed him away a lot sooner, and I didn't want to. "Still…"

He holds up a hand. "Let's just draw a line across last night, okay? We were both feeling vulnerable." He gives another wry smile. "At least I am. I took advantage of the situation, and I let my emotions run away with me. Trust me, it won't happen again. The last thing I want is to jeopardize either of our marriages, our entire lives." He pauses, his voice thick with emotion. "Our kids."

"No, I don't, either." Especially not our kids. What if Zoe had seen? She would have thrown an absolute fit. Or even Katherine… I picture her silent, wounded look and everything in me shudders. How could I have been so *stupid*, risking so much, just for a few seconds?

"I really am sorry," Josh says. "I never should have abused your trust like that. I don't know what I was thinking. I *wasn't* thinking. Obviously."

I'm starting to feel like a martyr, when I know we were both complicit. As surprised as I was, part of me was waiting for that knock. "It's okay, Josh. Really."

"I love Rebecca," he says, a statement, and I nod. I know that. I've seen it in his face, heard it in his voice. Josh nods back at me. "We'll say no more about it."

"Okay."

We stand in silence, sipping coffee, and amazingly, it doesn't feel tense or uncomfortable. Somehow Josh has turned our guilty secret into a shared joke, except it's deeper than that. A shared grief, because we are united in our worry about Rebecca, our fear for all our kids, our desire to do the right thing. And that binds us more closely together than any kiss ever could.

The kids start trickling downstairs a little bit later, and I set the table while Josh dons an imaginary chef's hat and makes pancakes. It reminds me of when Rebecca made pancakes, when everything felt so bright and possible. It feels like a lifetime ago, and yet improbably, this morning starts to feel that way as well.

Josh is jokey and fun, and Zoe hangs on his every word. She is deliberately ignoring me, but I don't mind because she looks so happy. As we're mopping up the last of the syrup from our plates, she asks what they are going to do today.

Josh glances outside; the early morning sunshine has given way to dank-looking clouds, the air hot and muggy. "Why don't we all go bowling?"

The *all* jolts me, and Zoe clocks it as well. Her eyes narrow. "All?"

"All seven of us," Josh says easily. "It will be fun."

I can't hide my surprise. I expected Josh to take his three out alone today, for some exclusive Daddy time. I was also anticipating some alone time with Ben and Katherine myself, knowing we need it. Everyone could use a little break.

"Why do we all have to go?" Zoe demands.

"I want to go bowling," Ben returns, sounding obstinate. The other kids remain silent, sensing the undercurrents.

"We should probably stay here," I interject. "Tidy up…"

"Tidy up?" This from Ben again, sounding indignant.

"You deserve a break too," Josh says firmly. "It will be fun. And we can go for pizza after."

Zoe folds her arms, looking thunderous, and I, to my own shame, do not protest again. I should, I know I should, and yet there is a part of me, that same tiny, treacherous part that wanted Josh to return last night, that wants to go. That wants to be with him, because when he looks at me I feel desirable and confident, competent and wanted in a way I haven't felt in a long time. And it has nothing to do with a kiss, so I tell myself it's okay. It's allowed.

In the end, Zoe gets over herself and we all have a lot more fun than I ever expected. I am terrible at bowling, and Josh gives me pointers, and somehow it feels natural to have him stand behind me, his mouth close to my ear, as he instructs me how to hurl the bowl down the lane; it lands with a clunk, and we turn to each other, laughing.

Josh is expansive, buying snacks, smiling indulgently. When Ben starts messing around with the heavier bowling balls, pretending he's going to drop one on Max's foot, all it takes is Josh's hand clapped on his shoulder for him to put it down, and I am so grateful. Kyle has never been able to manage Ben. He ignores his outbursts, or he just gets angry. I know I'm not much better, but it feels good—no, it feels wonderful—to be with a man who can handle my son.

By the time we are leaving the bowling alley in Geneseo the rain has cleared and we end up at a Mexican restaurant on the outside of town, ordering a ton of tacos and a huge platter of nachos that the children devour in seconds while Josh and I look on, smiling.

I know everyone—from the attendant handing out shoes at the bowling alley to the waitress refilling our sodas—thinks we're a married couple. A blended family, perhaps, since we have so many kids the same age. A real-life Brady Bunch. And nothing Josh or I do belies that belief.

Not that we do anything obviously inappropriate, of course. We sit on opposite ends of the table; we never touch. And yet I catch Josh's smile, the shared joke in his eyes, and I feel complicit. I am part of something, and I like it. I tell myself it's not wrong, it's not cheating. We both need a break from the crap life has dealt us lately. I give myself a free pass, an excuse, an absolution. I almost manage to convince myself that I don't actually need one.

It is late afternoon by the time we return to the lake house, and the kids all disappear upstairs to the temptations of the playroom with its PlayStation and air hockey and foosball. I drift around the kitchen, pretending to tidy up.

"I should head back soon," Josh says with a glance at his watch. "At this rate I won't be back in the city till eleven."

"Okay." I nod, not knowing what else to do. I don't want him to go, and yet the thought of him leaving brings relief, too.

"Thank you for everything, Tessa."

"I'm the one who should be thanking you. We all had fun today."

"Good." He gazes at me for another moment until I feel I have to look away. "I'd better go pack up my stuff."

A few minutes later he brings his one bag into the kitchen, and then he goes upstairs to say goodbye to the children. I come out to the deck to say goodbye, and Josh turns to me, his bag on his shoulder.

"See you next weekend." Before I can reply he pulls me into a hug, my chin resting on his shoulder as I breathe in the expensive, woody scent of his aftershave. I am shocked but I don't pull away.

Josh releases me with one of his sadly wry smiles, the kind that is both apology and acknowledgment, and then he turns and heads down the stairs.

As I turn back to the house I see Zoe standing there, glaring at me, and my heart stutters.

"Hey, Zo!" I say as casually as I can as I come into the kitchen. "Do you think anyone wants dinner?"

"Why," she demands in ringing tones, "were you hugging my dad?"

"We were just saying goodbye." I sound guilty, I know I do. Why did Josh have to hug me? Why did I have to let myself be hugged? And yet it felt good—the human connection, the physical contact. The *chemistry*. I can't deny that.

"You're not *friends*." She spits the word. "You don't even know him."

"I've come to know him," I say, trying desperately to sound light. "Because of…" I can't finish that sentence. "Zoe, why are you so angry?" I try to soften my voice. "What are you so worried about, sweetheart?"

"Don't call me sweetheart," she snaps, and then turns on her heel and stomps upstairs. I feel shaken and guilty for the rest of the day, and I vow that next weekend I will keep my distance from Josh. No hugs. No Sunday afternoons spent together, no matter how much I enjoy them.

Except somehow it doesn't work out that way. All week we keep in touch, with phone calls at night when we talk each other through our days while I lie on the bed and stare at the ceiling, letting his low, warm voice steal through me like honey. Impromptu texts throughout the day, just checking in, usually with photos of the kids, to make it all seem and feel legitimate. Respectable. Because it is. He's checking I'm okay, and I'm talking about his kids. We never veer into overly intimate, personal territory, or at least not too much.

Josh arrives Friday night, and after a week of contact and familiarity, we relax into the evening like old friends, drinking wine and talking about our former ambitions. Amazingly, he once wanted to be a history teacher.

"You don't regret turning hedge fund manager, though, do you?" I ask teasingly. I can't imagine having the money he does.

"Investment banking," he corrects with a smile. "And yes, a little bit." He shrugs. "There's always the road not taken, isn't there?"

I don't let his words have any other meaning. In fact, I finally exhibit some integrity and tell him I should turn in. I walk quickly upstairs before the moment can become expectant. It takes a long time to go to sleep.

The next day Josh insists we all come to see Rebecca, the first time the children will have seen her in two weeks.

"I'm sure you all want some alone time…" I begin, but he shakes his head firmly.

"I'm sure Rebecca will want to see you."

It doesn't take much to make me agree. I am curious to see Rebecca, and of course I miss her as well, in a way. And part of me, I'm ashamed to admit, wants her to see me. Wants her to see how different I am, how self-composed and confident. I want her to notice how well I've taken care of her children as well as my own.

I've spoken to Kyle a few times over the course of the week, but the conversations are brief, tense. I keep feeling as if there is something he isn't saying, but when I ask him what it is, he always, aggravatingly, backs off.

"I just don't want you to overdo it," he says, making me sound like I am nine months pregnant and attempting to run a marathon, or else an invalid.

"I'm *fine*, Kyle. Really." And I am fine. Zoe might still as good as hate me, and Katherine has withdrawn a little into herself once again, but I'm *fine*. The truth is, I just don't want this interlude, this other life, to end.

Rayha texts a few times, but I sense judgment from her; I made the mistake of telling her about the bowling, and she sounded shocked. I can't hide anything, and I think she knows I'm attracted to Josh. When she leaves a voicemail, I choose not to listen to it, telling myself I'll get to it later, but then I never do.

As soon as I see Rebecca at Lakeview, I feel as if I've made a big mistake. I shouldn't be there; I really shouldn't be there. And yet I am, and there is nothing I can do about it. When she goes off with her three, Josh and I take Ben and Katherine into the living area, which is empty of guests. We play a quiet game of Chinese checkers, waiting for the others to come back. Everything feels off; I feel like the dreaded other woman more than I ever expected or wanted to. And when I meet Rebecca's eyes, I have the worst feeling that she knows it, and feels it too.

"I don't think I should have come today," I tell Josh that night, after the children are in bed. I am standing in the kitchen while he sits sprawled on the sofa, checking messages on his phone.

He glances up briefly before returning his gaze to the glowing screen. "Why not? It was fine."

"It felt… intrusive." I clasp my hands together; they feel sweaty. "I don't think Rebecca wanted me there." Josh just shrugs, and suddenly, surprisingly, I am annoyed with him. "Josh, Rebecca's health and wellbeing should be both of our priority."

"It is mine," he answers calmly. "Whether it needs to be yours is up for debate."

"I just feel…" I am wading into deep and dangerous waters, putting a name to whatever has been hovering between us. "Maybe we're spending too much time together."

Josh stares at me for a long moment, and I fight the urge to apologize, to take back my words. "Do you really think that?" he asks quietly, and I squirm. He sounds so sad. "We're just friends, aren't we, Tessa?"

"Yes, of course we are." I've been put on the defensive, and I'm not even sure how. "I just meant… I don't want Rebecca to get the wrong idea."

"She won't, because there is nothing to get the wrong idea about." Josh stands up. "But perhaps I should go work in the study." He says this with dignity, and I watch in silent misery as he scoops up his laptop and takes it into the snug off the living room. I realize I was looking forward to another evening together, no matter what I just said to him. We haven't done anything wrong, have we? Why did I have to go and ruin it?

As he leaves a voicemail pops up on my screen; it's from Rebecca, and she left it hours ago, right after we left Lakeview. My stupid phone is always delaying messages, but I have a feeling this is one I really don't want to hear.

With my stomach cramping, I swipe to listen to it.

"Tessa, look, about today—" Her voice is so strident, so angry and commanding, that I end the message before I hear whatever it is she was going to say. I tell myself I'll listen to it later, but I know I won't. I don't want to hear Rebecca's diatribe against me, which is what I'm almost certain that message is.

The next morning Josh announces that he's taking Zoe, Charlotte, and Max to a go-karting place near Rochester.

"Why can't we come?" Ben practically bellows, and I try to shush him.

"We can have a quiet day here, Ben. We don't have to go out every single day."

"You're welcome to come, of course," Josh says, neatly throwing the ball smack into the center of my court. Now what? He waits for my verdict.

"Please, Mom," Ben wheedles. I glance at Zoe, who looks away, affecting supreme disinterest.

"No, we'll stay here," I say at last. "We'll go swimming."

"We *always* go swimming."

"It's fine," I say, but all three of us have our noses nearly pressed to the glass as we watch them leave, and we spend the day moping about, no one really wanting to go in the water. We don't know how to be on our own anymore, and yet in two weeks Rebecca will come home. Her time at Lakeview is already halfway done. In two weeks, we'll be returning to our old lives, except I don't even know what those will look like anymore. I can't imagine them.

In the late afternoon, with the Finlays still gone, Katherine joins me on the deck. The air is still and hot, the only sound a motorboat cutting through the water in the distance. Everything feels drowsy and slow.

Katherine sits slouched in a deck chair, her knees tucked up to her chest. She's wearing raggedy cut-off shorts and a long-sleeve t-shirt that hides her hands, and she looks pensive and a little sad.

"You okay, sweetheart?" I ask, and she nods. I feel as if we haven't had a real conversation in weeks. Everything has been so busy, with so much to manage, and Katherine has been happy spending time with Charlotte. At least I think she has, but now I wonder. I worry, ever my default, although I've done my best not to worry these last weeks.

"You're feeling better about things?" I ask. "You don't want to go home anymore?" She hasn't asked to again, at least, which is something.

Katherine shrugs, her gaze on the lake. "I guess so. When is Daddy coming?"

"He said in August." After his music gigs finish, and we leave the Finlays. I can't even imagine it, and yet it is only a few weeks from now. "It will be nice to be all together again, won't it?"

Katherine shoots me a sudden, sharp look. "Do you think it will?" she asks, chilling me with her challenging tone. Maybe Zoe isn't the only who has been suspicious, who has noticed.

"Of course I do," I say, but she doesn't seem convinced, and the truth is, I'm not either.

CHAPTER TWENTY-SIX

REBECCA

On Monday morning, two days after Josh's visit with the kids—
and Tessa and co—I park myself in a chair in the therapy room
and level Diane with a steely almost-glare.

"I want to try the guided imagery."

She raises her elegant eyebrows. "Are you sure?"

"Yes." I am a thousand percent sure. I can't screw around
anymore, wondering if I'm strong enough, hemming and hawing
because I'm not sure I want to know. I've *got* to know. I *have* to
be strong enough. My family, not to mention my marriage, is
at stake. After seeing Tessa with Josh, the scars on Charlotte's
arms… I left a message with Tessa, asking her to keep an eye on
Charlotte, explaining as much as I could. I don't actually know
what I said; it was garbled, a demand and a plea, begging her to
keep all of our children safe. Now everything in me both hardens
and cries out. I simply *have* to get better.

But it's not as easy as wanting it, I soon find. My first experience
with guided imagery a few days later is a veritable disaster. I lie on a
sofa like something out of a Freudian caricature while the therapist,
a woman with a calming manner and a monotone voice, drones on
quietly. I'm sure she's saying things that are useful, helpful, but I
can barely listen to her encouragements to picture a peaceful place.

I am too anxious to lie still, to let the memories come. My
body twitches and I keep moving, re-crossing my legs, sitting

up, lying back down. I'm like a toddler who can't settle. We both concede defeat after a fruitless half-hour, but I am determined to try again.

I spend the rest of the day prowling around the house and grounds, trying to quell my restlessness. I'm annoyed with myself for not doing better, for not getting it right, although Diane cautioned me, saying I couldn't force these things.

"I thought that was the whole point," I snapped at her, unable to keep myself from it. "That you're forcing the memories to come back." So I could finally get past this, and move on. Recover my life, my family. My *husband*.

"None of this is about forcing anything or anyone, Rebecca," she said, a note of reproof in her voice that made me feel like a petulant child.

Back in the living room I fling myself on one of the chairs. The only other occupant is Chloe, the bored-looking teenager who arrived around the same time as me. Gwen, Liz, and Bruce have all left, replaced only by an anemic-looking woman in her thirties who bites her nails and smokes incessantly, which I half-think should be against the rules but isn't. The place feels empty, as if we're forgotten.

Now I glance at Chloe, who I haven't said a word to for over two weeks. She's pretty in a standard rich kid way—blonde hair expertly highlighted, dramatic eyebrows, too skinny. She's scrolling through Instagram on her phone, one thumb constantly pressing the likes, but she looks completely bored with the process and I wonder why she bothers. Why do any of us bother with these pointless social charades, day in and day out?

I think of the other mothers and wives waiting for me back on the Upper East Side—my bevy of so-called friends, none of whom has sent so much as a text to me this summer. They're distancing themselves from me, just in case. Word about the dancing episode got around, and who knows what else. I don't even care; it's all so absurd anyway. That life feels like nothing more than a pointless parody now.

Then my wandering gaze catches the pale, jagged line on the inside of Chloe's elbow, and another one on her wrist. For a second I want to cry—for Chloe, for Charlotte, for myself, for everyone. Why are we all so *broken*? Why is this world so hard, so brutal and unforgiving, that we can't navigate it without hurting ourselves? Why does trying to be helped and healed feel like scaling a mountain that just keeps getting higher and higher?

Chloe catches me looking and she shifts in her seat, shooting me a glare as she turns away so I can't see the ragged red scars criss-crossing her arms. I'm amazed I haven't noticed them before. Maybe I was too consumed with hiding my own.

And what about Charlotte's? I haven't been able to get the image of those awful, crimson lines out of my mind. It is a deep, physical ache inside me to know she is doing what I have been doing, and I can't hide from the fact that it almost undoubtedly has to be because she saw me doing it. Because I'm here, in this place, rather than protecting and guiding her. I pray with everything in me that Tessa can keep my little girl from hurting herself any more.

Charlotte. Just thinking of her sends a pang of pain through me. She was always my easy one, who glided through life without any worries, who smiles like an angel. *How can this be happening?*

The next day I am even more determined to get this right. I lie on the sofa and close my eyes, breathe in deeply and try my damnedest to relax, which is, ironically, hard work.

Annabel, my trained therapist, does her best to help, asking me to imagine a peaceful place. A month, a *week* ago, I would have snorted in laughter and rolled my eyes at this kind of psycho-speak, but now I concentrate.

I picture a meadow under an azure sky, the long grass waving gently in the breeze just as it did when I walked through it with my children. Annabel tells me to imagine the sounds and smells, the textures and tastes. I feel the whisper-scratch of the grass as I stretch out and stare up at the sky. The hazy heat, the lazy drone of a bumblebee. A butterfly flits across my vision, and the crumbly earth smells dry and sun-warmed. I tilt my head back against the sofa to catch the sunlight that is only in my mind, and I feel its healing rays on my face.

Then, slowly, the scene starts to change. Annabel's voice is quiet but sure, asking me to picture another place. Christmas— the smell of spruce, the on and off blink of lights on the tree. Laughter in the distance, sudden and raucous—someone is in another room. Grownups, having a private joke. I am stretched out beneath the tree: my favorite place, secret, special. I gaze up at its branches, breathing in the fresh scent of spruce, mesmerized by the twinkling lights.

"What do you hear, Rebecca?" Annabel asks. Her voice is quiet, almost lulling me to sleep. I tell her about the laughter, how I don't know what is so funny.

"What else? What do you hear that is closer?"

"Footsteps." The word slips out. "The crack of someone's knee. He's bending down." I feel myself tense but I cling to the memory now, this memory I've been trying to hide from for so long. My eyes are clenched shut; my fists by my sides, but for once I let the memory come. I let it roll over me.

"And now?" Annabel asks softly. "What do you hear now?"

"He's next to me… he stretches out alongside me, but he doesn't fit. It feels wrong. He smells of cigarette smoke." My nose wrinkles, as if I can smell it now, stale and acrid, a whiff that overwhelms me. "His sweater is scratchy. I feel it against my face." A visceral shudder goes through me. "He's whispering in my ear…" But his voice isn't my father's. He doesn't smell like my father, of bay rum and breath mints. He smells sour and old. I squirm away. His hand is on my leg.

I can't hear Annabel anymore. I am trapped in the nightmare; the winking Christmas lights like a mockery, a face pressed close to mine, the clenching terror in my stomach. I want to get away, but I can't. I'm trapped underneath the tree, and then I hear the click of my mother's heels.

"*Becky? Dan?*"

My eyes snap open and I feel as if I'm falling from a very high distance, spiraling down, down, down to the ground, where I will land with an almighty thud, a terrible splat.

"Rebecca?" Annabel's voice is calm, anchoring me. Reminding me that I am here, not there. "Take a moment."

I realize I am breathing hard. There are tears streaking down my face although I can't remember crying. I don't speak for a few minutes, just try to get my breathing and body under control, let the memory, crystalline in its clarity now, recede enough for me to be coherent.

"You remembered more details," Annabel states after a long silence. I nod.

"It was helpful?"

"Yes." The panic and fear and churning sickness is all still there, skirting the edges of my mind, threatening to swamp me. There is part of me, a large part, that still feels like a very scared six-year-old girl. But another part feels something surprising and oh-so sweet: *relief*.

Relief, because that voice, that hand, that body—they do not belong to my father. And I know with a sudden and absolute certainty that my father did not abuse me. And that is worth staring the memory in the face, feeling the confusion and horror and shame. I'm filled with grief, and yet I'm so *happy*.

I spend the rest of the day in a daze, and then I take a huge nap, and when I wake, I feel both new and revitalized, like this is the start of the rest of my life, but also about a thousand years old, sad beyond belief. I'm a walking paradox, a living and breathing oxymoron, trying to figure out how to make myself work.

"Annabel says your session was successful," Diane comments when I see her the next day.

"I remembered."

"What did you remember?"

I take a deep breath, letting the knowledge fill me, float me. "It wasn't my father." I feel close to tears, ones of relief as well as terrible sorrow. My body sags with the overflow of emotion. "It wasn't my father."

"You're sure of this?"

"*Yes.*" I tense, giving Diane an angry look, because she cannot start putting bullet holes in my brand-new memories. I won't let her. "The smell, the voice, everything was different."

"Then who was it, Rebecca? Do you know?"

"My uncle." I let out a deep, shuddery sigh, letting the knowledge flow through me. "Uncle Dan, my father's older brother." The words feel funny as I shape them. *Uncle Dan.* I barely remember him, haven't even thought of him in years, decades, and yet he was the architect of my own disaster. And his voice did sound like my father's.

"Your uncle," Diane repeats, waiting for me to say more.

"He visited on holidays and birthdays when I was small." Christmas trees and blowing out candles. "He was an alcoholic, although I only learned that later. I barely knew him." Or so I thought. I shake my head slowly, the realization still reverberating through me. *Uncle Dan.* I take another deep breath and stare straight at Diane. "He died at least twenty years ago. My parents had lost touch with him a long time before that—I don't think we saw him after I was eight or nine or so." And now I wonder if they had a reason for that, which is a whole different kind of betrayal, and one I'll have to deal with eventually. But at least it's not the one I feared the most.

*

That Saturday Josh visits me with the children. One week until my liberation. I feel like I've been through the wars; I have the scars, but I've survived. And yet he sees none of that as he bends to dutifully kiss my cheek and Zoe tries to clamber onto my lap.

"Where's Tessa?" I ask, and I can't keep a touch of acid from entering my voice, even though I told myself I wasn't going to be that way.

"She thought we could all use some alone time together." He doesn't bat an eyelid. "And I think she's probably right. One week to go." He makes it sound ominous rather than hopeful, and that hurts. He has no idea of anything, and while I know I can't really blame him because I haven't *said*, I wish he had the eyes—the heart—to see, or at least to wonder. To *care*.

Instead, as we walk along the lake, Josh asks me carefully coded questions about my return, whether I feel ready, how I'm going to be. He's mindful of the children and I'm mindful how absolutely *clueless* he is. As they race ahead at one point, I turn to him tiredly.

"If you're worried that I'm going to start drinking again, Josh, then let me put your mind at ease. I'm not."

"I'm glad to hear that, Rebecca, but—"

"But you can't trust me? You're still not sure? Well, let me straighten you out then. I'm not going to drink because I don't have a *reason* to drink anymore. I don't have any memories to blot out, any demons to exorcise, any longer." I hold my arms out, tilt my face up to the sky. "I'm finally free." Or at least starting to be.

Josh, however, is unimpressed. "Free, Rebecca? Free from what?" I can't miss the note of cynical skepticism in his voice. I know what he's thinking. Bored, rich housewife who had to drink her days away, despite everything he's given me. Is that how he sees me, how he's always seen me? I shake my head.

"Didn't you ever think there was more going on, Josh? When did I become such a caricature to you?"

He jerks back a little. "I never—of course I thought there was more going on. But you wouldn't tell me, Rebecca, even when I asked, and so naturally I had to assume—"

"If I didn't tell you, it was because I didn't think you'd believe me. Or maybe because I didn't want you to believe me."

He looks even more skeptical. "Believe you? Believe *what*?"

"And," I add starkly, "because I didn't think you really wanted to know." He opens his mouth to object and I roll right over him. "Tell me the truth, Josh. Didn't you want this all resolved neatly, tidied away before it got too messy? Isn't that what you still want—a Stepford wife who takes care of your dry-cleaning and hosts great dinner parties and still has time for sex three times a week?" Not that we've been having that, but the bitterness spills out, bitterness I didn't even realize I had. "I've always been your mannequin, haven't I? The perfect accessory. But maybe that's not who I want to be anymore. Maybe I never really was that woman, that wife."

Josh stares at me as if I'm a stranger, and the truth is, I probably am. I've never said anything like this to him before; I've never even thought it. I was happy, or at least I thought I was, which felt like the same thing. It's taken all this grief to realize just how shallow my life was. How shallow my *marriage* was.

"You have no idea what I want," he says in a low voice that throbs with resentment and anger, and then he walks away from me, toward our children.

CHAPTER TWENTY-SEVEN

TESSA

Rebecca is coming home today. I can barely believe it. Looking back, the last four weeks have flown by, a montage of bittersweet moments, a life I've stepped into that I'm not ready to leave.

I know I shouldn't feel that way. I should be glad to get back to normal, except I don't even know what that is anymore. I've spent the day cleaning and cooking; a big frosted cake is on the kitchen counter, with *Welcome Home, Rebecca!* in my best curlicue script. It glitters with sparkles and sprinkles; the kids went a little crazy. I look at it now, and then at the blue, blue sky outside; it's the beginning of August and it feels as if the summer has flown by—especially the last four weeks. The weeks without Rebecca.

Over the last few weeks Josh and I have found a gentle equilibrium, a balance of camaraderie and closeness that doesn't cross a line. At least I don't think it has. We've managed to navigate it successfully—no more kisses, of course, and less of the emotional intimacy that I found so tantalizing. We're friends, real friends. At least I hope we are.

I think the children have come to enjoy the few weekends we've spent together, this surprise of a family made from disparate parts. Now it's going to be wrenched apart, everything put right again. It just doesn't feel that way, because I don't want this interlude, this other life, to end.

And yet it is. Josh has already gone to get Rebecca. It's late afternoon, the day hazy and hot. The slightly charred smell of our neighbors' barbecue drifts in from the open windows. In the last week the lake has come to life; cottages that were empty for weeks suddenly springing into action. August, it seems, is the month to be here.

I glance again at the cake, breathe in the scent of lemon polish along with the aroma of barbecue. I've packed up all our stuff and moved it back to Pine Cottage, which after four weeks of disuse smells musty and old and unwelcoming. I left the windows open and aired the sheets, but going back there feels like stepping into a tomb. My old life. *I don't want it anymore.*

"Mom?" Katherine stands in the doorway of the kitchen. "Can Charlotte and I use the bathroom?"

I let out a little laugh. "You're not of the age where you need to ask, sweetheart."

"I don't mean that." She rolls her eyes. "I mean, the main bathroom, off your room."

She means Rebecca's room. Rebecca and Josh's room. I changed the sheets, bought fresh flowers, scrubbed *everything*, including the bathroom and all that white tile. "Why do you need that bathroom, Katherine? I just cleaned it."

"It's so nice and big, and we wanted to do our nails and hair and stuff, for tonight."

"Tonight?"

"When Mrs. Finlay gets back." Does she think there's going to be a party? Should I have bought champagne? No, obviously not. "Please, Mom?" Katherine gives me a beseeching look, all doe eyes and clasped hands, and I cave because she's been so quiet these last few weeks and it heartens me to think that she and Charlotte are still, on some level, getting along.

"Okay," I say, relenting. "But clean everything up when you're done." But Katherine is already gone, hurrying upstairs with light footsteps.

I tidy up the kitchen, even though it doesn't need it. I am restless, waiting. Last weekend Josh took the kids to visit Rebecca, and Ben, Katherine and I went to a movie, all of us feeling a little lost. Then on Sunday Josh suggested we all go to a public beach on the other side of the lake, a place with shuffleboard and paddle boats and an ice-cream stand. Simple pleasures, but I savored them because I knew this was our last day together, the seven of us, Josh and me.

Guilt creeps in at the memory. We're only friends; we've barely touched since that kiss three weeks ago now. And yet Josh has filled something inside my soul, because I've let him. Because I had an emptiness that needed filling.

It's no accident that I haven't called Kyle in over a week, even though he's coming up in a few days. I haven't even called Rayha, because I am afraid she's already figured out what was going on, and will tell me what to do—and what not to do. *This isn't your life, Tessa. These kids aren't yours, and the husband sure as hell isn't, either.*

I could almost hear her, her voice full of certainty and gentleness, understanding me, telling it to me straight. I didn't want that. I didn't do anything wrong. And so I didn't listen to her voicemails and I didn't read her texts, just as I didn't let myself listen to Rebecca's voicemail, and I told myself I'd get back to her soon. Soon, when this has all come to an end.

I don't know how long I've been simply staring into space when I hear the sound of a car pulling into the driveway, the motor being cut. My heart turns over, an unpleasant sensation. Before I can call to everyone that Josh and Rebecca are back home, Zoe barrels down the stairs and tears past me.

"They're here! Mommy's here!"

"Zoe, careful!" I call as she hurtles down the stairs, but she's past listening to me. I have officially become irrelevant, to Zoe most of all. I stay in the kitchen as Charlotte and Max come downstairs and hurry outside, Max giving me a fleeting, uncertain look, which I return with a smile.

Ben and Katherine have stayed upstairs, choosing not to be part of this reunion. Perhaps that's what I should choose as well, for Rebecca's sake, and yet I stay where I am.

I hear their exclamations from the driveway, and when I peek out the sliding glass door, I see Rebecca giving Charlotte a tight hug. Zoe is practically rugby tackling her and Max clings to one hand. Josh stands a little bit apart, his expression bland.

They start up the deck stairs and I take a quick step back, out of sight. My heart is thudding, which is silly.

A few seconds later they all burst into the kitchen, full of laughter and excited chatter. Rebecca is smiling, a smile that lights up her eyes, her whole face. I am struck by how different she looks. How different she *seems*.

She's still effortlessly elegant, her blonde hair falling in a sleek waterfall nearly to her shoulders. She's wearing a pair of lavender capris and an ivory t-shirt with silk embroidery around the neck, designer sandals on her feet. But it's not the clothes or the hair or her chicness that I'm drawn to. It's something else, something I don't think I've ever seen in her before.

There are threads of gray amid the blonde that weren't there four weeks ago, and deeper lines by her eyes, from her nose to her mouth. But that's not it either—it's her *stillness*. For once Rebecca doesn't pulse with that barely contained manic energy that has been so much a part of her.

Even as she moves through the kitchen, smiling and laughing, she is somehow still; there is a peace to her that I've never seen before, and in a lightning flash of realization I know I am envious of her in a whole new and unexpected way.

"Rebecca." My voice is wavering. "Hi."

Rebecca's gaze trains on me and her smile freezes for a second before deliberately widening. "Hey, Tessa."

"Welcome home."

"Thank you." I hear a slight coolness in her voice that makes me blush.

"It's great to have you here." As soon as I say the words, I know they're wrong. They sound proprietorial, as if I'm welcoming her to my house, not back to her own. Rebecca tilts her head, her gaze travelling slowly over me, a faint smile touching her lips.

"Thank you," she says again. It sounds like a dismissal, and I'm not sure what to do.

"We made you a cake. The kids and I…" I nod toward the cake on the counter. It looks sloppy now.

"Did you?" Rebecca glances at Zoe, who is still holding her hand. "Why don't you show me, sweetheart?"

I need to go. Everyone wants me to go. It's time to politely excuse myself, and let them all have this moment. I know this, and yet still I stay there in the kitchen. Josh meets my gaze from behind Rebecca and he gives me a sad, fleeting smile. It's only a second, but Rebecca swings around suddenly to stare at him, and then she turns to me.

"Tessa, you have been so amazing." Her smile curves, reminding me of the Grinch. "But I'm sure you want to get back to your own house, your own kids." A breathless beat where no one speaks. "*I* know," she adds, reminding me of way back when, when she'd have one of her fantastic ideas, "why don't the three of you come to dinner tomorrow night? A way to say thank you, and to celebrate."

"That… that would be nice." What else can I say?

"Great," she says, and this time it definitely is a dismissal.

"I'll just get Ben and Katherine." I am, stupidly, near tears. This isn't my life, this was never my life. I *knew* that, and yet it hurts all the same. I hurry upstairs without meeting anyone's eye. Ben and Katherine are up in the playroom, watching TV and looking tense and bored.

"Ben, Katherine…" My voice is terse. "We've got to go."

"Go…?" Katherine blinks at me like a deer.

"Go home. Rebecca is back and the Finlays want some family time."

My children stare at me with owlish uncertainty. They're going to miss all this as much as I will—not just the big house, the flat-screen TV, the air hockey and everything, but the camaraderie. The companionship. The charmed lives we were all leading for such a short time.

"Let's go," I say, impatient now, and silently, Ben and Katherine follow me downstairs. The Finlays have moved to the family room, and they are all sprawled out on the sofas like some perfect family photo shoot.

"Thanks, everyone," I call, practically chirping. As reluctant as I have been to leave, I want this moment over. "See you soon."

"Tessa…" Josh says, half-rising, but I ignore him, practically wrenching open the sliding glass door. I keep my gaze trained ahead as Ben and Katherine follow me out to the deck and down the stairs.

We walk in silence down the sandy path winding through the trees, and I fumble with the key for the front door. Then we step inside Pine Cottage, and it seems so unbearably small and dark and lonely that I don't think I can stand it. Ben kicks the sofa and Katherine curls up on a chair, watching me silently. *Welcome to the rest of your life.*

For the rest of the day and evening I tell myself it's not that bad. I make spaghetti with canned sauce, and after dinner we go outside for an evening swim; it's still hot and sultry, and the lake feels tepid, like bathwater. Ben and Katherine paddle around a bit, and then get in a splashing fight that goes too far, and finally, I herd them back inside to get ready for bed.

"This bed's uncomfortable," Ben complains as he tosses around theatrically. The bed *is* narrow, little more than a camp bed with a thin mattress and rusty springs. The house still smells musty, forgotten.

"You didn't complain before, Ben."

"That was different."

Yes, it was. A gusty sigh rises from my depths but I suppress it. I knew living at Rebecca's house wasn't permanent or real, yet it amazes me how easy it had been to adjust to it. Not just to the wealth and luxury, although those were certainly nice. To the feeling, the belief, that I was different there. That we all were.

Restless, I go outside as twilit shadows settle over sand and lake, and sit down by the water, drawing my knees up to my chest. I cannot keep my glance from flitting over to the Finlays' house. Earlier, while we were eating, I heard Zoe calling from the deck, the smell of the barbecue.

By the time we went swimming, they'd gone back inside, but occasionally I saw figures flit across the picture window, like characters on a stage. I heard Charlotte or Zoe screech "Daddy!" and I thought how they must all be having such a wonderful time.

Now the lights are on in the family room, but I can't see anyone and I tell myself to stop looking. I'm turning into some creepy stalker, and so I decide to call Rayha. I feel guilty for ignoring her texts, and I need someone to talk me down from this ledge I've scrambled onto without realizing.

"Tessa." Rayha sounds surprised, and not that pleased. "Nice to hear from you at long last." The sentiment comes out hard.

Guiltily, I think of the phone calls I haven't returned, the text messages I ignored. "I'm sorry, Rayha, it's been so busy."

"Yeah, it must be." She doesn't say anything else, doesn't offer an opener or throw me a line to grab onto.

"Rebecca is back from rehab," I say. "So we're back at Pine Cottage." Of course she can't know all that means, all it feels like.

"That must be a relief."

"Oh yes, it is. Good to be back in our own place." I sound utterly unconvincing. "How are you?"

"Not great, actually." Rayha lets out a wobbly sound that is something between a laugh and a sob. "Zane's been in and out of ER for the last two weeks. He's having trouble swallowing and his consultant thinks he's going to need a feeding tube permanently."

"Oh, Rayha…" Misery swamps me along with the ever-increasing guilt. I am such a bad friend.

"I always knew this was going to happen. This is the way it goes with CDD, and especially now he's been diagnosed with…" She trails off, and I realize she is crying, noisy gulps that make me ache.

"Oh, Rayha. *Rayha*…" Tears spring to my eyes. I can't believe I ignored her texts; I can't believe I let myself act so selfishly.

"Leukodystrophy," she gasps out. She's mentioned it before, I think, but I have no idea what it is. "The degeneration of white matter in the brain," she explains dully. "Which eventually leads to a vegetative state and then death."

"Oh, no. Oh, *no*." Despite having lived with Zane's diagnosis for six years, I am shocked. The best outcome of CDD was to reach a certain point of stability, low as it might have seemed. But *this*… "Rayha, I'm so, so sorry."

"Are you?" Her voice comes out harsh now, almost spiteful. "Because you didn't seem it when you were busy living it up in your neighbor's house, Tessa. I left you three voicemails and sent a bunch of texts and I got nothing in reply. *Nothing*."

I close my eyes, wave after wave of shame rolling over me. "I didn't realize…"

"So you didn't even listen to my voicemail, the one where I was crying and saying how things had become really bad with Zane, and how much I needed to talk to you? You missed that one?"

"I really am—"

"You know what? Just forget it! Life is shit enough without having to deal with friends who can't be there for you. Who choose not to be, because their own lives are so fucking important.

Especially when you were there for them, over and over again, when *their* life was shit and they couldn't even hold it together for one second. Do you remember that, Tessa?"

She's switched tactics so quickly that for a second I am confused. "You mean when…"

"When your mom died? Or have you conveniently forgotten how much I was there for you then, day after day, even though my life was falling apart at the same time? How I held things up for you even though I was dying inside? You know what? Never mind. I get it. You've got a new best friend, another life. You're busy living it up at the golf club or on a yacht, or wherever it is you are. Go for it, Tessa. Enjoy the high life." She disconnects the call, leaving me reeling.

I sit on the sand for a long time, the phone in my hand, as I stare out at the darkness, my mind spinning in empty circles. I can't believe I might have lost my best friend, my only friend. My gaze flits over to the Finlays'. I've lost two friends, and it's all my fault. The realization thuds through me, and I can't escape it.

By the time we head over to the Finlays' the next evening, the fog of sadness and regret over Rayha's phone call hasn't lifted. We spent the morning mooching around the house before heading over to the club for lessons, although I debated whether to go at all. Maybe my membership would be revoked; I wouldn't even blame Rebecca for that, not really.

Ben and Katherine, however, were insistent they have their lessons—a fact that almost made me smile, considering Katherine's initial reluctance. So much had changed, and yet so much hadn't. We didn't see the Finlays at the club, which filled me with both relief and disappointment, in equal measures.

In Geneseo I buy a box of chocolates to take over, eschewing the more usual bottle of wine. I get ready carefully but not so much that eagle-eyed Rebecca will notice that I'm taking care. My hair is curly and natural, and I wear my old clothes, my real ones—a swishy summer skirt and a matching top. I use a discreet amount of makeup. It feels important to get the balance right, to convey a message.

Katherine flits around me, anxious and impatient. "Aren't you ready yet, Mom? Let's *go*!"

"Why are you so impatient?" I ask lightly.

"I want to see Charlotte."

"I'm glad you guys are getting along again." I meet her eyes in the mirror as I put on my lipstick. "It seemed like you weren't, for a little bit."

"Oh, that." Katherine's gaze slides away. "That was nothing."

"Okay." I'm not sure I believe her, but I decide to accept it for now. I cap my lipstick and try for a smile, even though everything in me feels leaden. "Let's go, then."

I have no idea what to expect as we climb the stairs to the deck. Will Rebecca be back to her usual self—all glittering, high-octane energy? I can't picture her otherwise, but as she opens the sliding glass door, I see right away that she still possesses that quiet air of self-contained calm she had last night, and it is matched by a steely purpose that unnerves me.

"Tessa, you shouldn't have," she says as she takes the box of chocolates from me. "But thank you."

"How are you?" I ask as I step inside. "Settling back in all right?"

Her eyebrows rise. "Yes, fine, thanks." There is a repressive note to her voice that makes me feel like I shouldn't have asked that question. I shouldn't have come at all.

"Great."

Rebecca turns to Ben and Katherine. "The others are upstairs, if you want to find them."

Ben and Katherine are gone in a flash, and Rebecca and I are alone. "Where's Josh?" I ask brightly, and then realize that is something else I shouldn't have said.

"He's run out to Geneseo, to get another bottle of propane for the barbecue. We used the last of it last night." Rebecca places her hands flat on the granite counter and turns to me with something like a smile. "I realize this is all a bit awkward, Tessa." I shrug, not knowing how to reply. "I owe you a huge debt of gratitude, for taking care of my family for an entire month. I know I can never repay that."

"I didn't mind, Rebecca…"

"I know you didn't." She speaks with a matter-of-factness that makes me blink. "I am quite aware of how much you enjoyed it, actually." Her steady gaze meets mine without a flicker. I feel trapped, and it takes everything I have not to look away. "But that's all in the past, isn't it?" she continues pleasantly. "All of it."

I lick my lips. "Yes…"

"The rest of the summer is going to be very different. *I'm* different, Tessa. Maybe you've noticed."

"Y-y-y… yes." I can't keep from stammering. "You seem like you're in a really good place, Rebecca."

"I am. At least, I will be, with time." She takes a deep breath. "So anyway, I just wanted to say thank you. I owe you a lot." *But not that much* hovers in the air, the real message. I nod slowly.

"I was glad to do it," I say, and Rebecca nods at me. *Yes*, her cool gaze seems to say. *I know you were.*

The sound of steps on the deck has us both turning. Josh opens the sliding glass door, holding a bottle of propane aloft. He smiles brightly.

"Shall I get this party started?"

CHAPTER TWENTY-EIGHT

REBECCA

I almost feel sorry for Tessa. She looks trapped and miserable, and no wonder. Clearly, she's been getting a little too used to my life. *A little too used to my family.* As Josh turns away to fit the propane to the barbecue, I can't miss the longing in her eyes and any vapor of pity I might have felt for her vanishes. Just how much did Tessa McIntyre steal from me? I haven't asked Josh yet. I haven't wanted to know, but he seems guilty, and so does Tessa. *Something* happened, I'm sure of it.

Last night Josh and I barely spoke to each other, first involving ourselves with the children so there was no need to talk, and then, after they'd gone to bed, moving around each other politely, like strangers stuck in an elevator together.

In any case, I wasn't ready to talk to him, not seriously. There were too many other important things to deal with. When I'd tucked Charlotte into bed, something I hadn't actually done for a few years, I took hold of her hand. She stilled, eyeing me warily.

"Charlotte." Gently, I turned her arm over and ran a fingertip along the faint lines that were still visible. At least there weren't any new ones that I could see, so perhaps I have Tessa to thank for that.

Charlotte tried to yank her arm away but I held on fast. "Why?" The one word was little more than a whisper.

"Why not?" she flung back at me. "You're one to talk, Mom."

"But…" My mind whirled. "What reason would you have to…?" I didn't even know how to begin.

"What reason do *you* have? Is taking care of us that hard?" Is *that* what she thought?

"No, of course not. That's not it at all, Charlotte, I promise you—"

"Then what is it?" Charlotte yanked her arm again and this time I let her go. "Never mind. I don't care, anyway."

She rolled over onto her back, away from me, her knees tucked up to her chest. I tried to think of what to say, how to explain in a way I wanted my eleven-year-old daughter to understand. There was still so much I didn't want her to know.

"Charlotte, I went away because I was sick. I know I didn't seem sick, not the way people normally do, but I was. And the—the cutting was part of that." Tears stung my eyes. I hated admitting to it. "But the last thing I'd want, the very last thing I'd *ever* want, is for you to do that, too. It was wrong of me, sweetheart. So, so wrong, and when you're older, I'll try to explain it better—"

"You know what? I really don't care, Mom." The tremble in her voice belied her words and I stared at her helplessly. When I rested one hand on her shoulder she flinched away.

"You won't do it again, will you?"

She turned to look at me, rolling her eyes, something she hardly ever did. "It was just a stupid dare, Mom. I'm not sad like you."

The scorn in her voice was like a stab wound, but I knew I deserved it. It would take a long time to make things better between us. A lot of hard work.

"Just a dare," I repeated slowly. "Who dared you?"

"It doesn't matter."

I couldn't see Katherine daring Charlotte to do anything. Was she lying to me? Could I be sure of anything, even this?

A new, unwelcome thought hammered through me. *What if I was wrong?* Could I really trust a single memory recalled under dubious, enforced circumstances? I'd looked guided imagery up online and it definitely seemed questionable.

What if I *wanted* my abuser to be someone other than my father, so much so that my subconscious manufactured a memory of an uncle I barely knew? Wildly, I wondered if Uncle Dan had even existed. I couldn't actually remember my parents speaking about him in years. Ever. What if everything, *everything*, was a lie? The possibility filled me with terror; I felt as if I were drowning, scrabbling to hold on to any surface, any certainty that I could.

"Charlotte, the other week, before… before I went away, you seemed as if you didn't want Granny and Grandad to visit." I hesitated, knowing I needed to ask even as I dreaded the answer. "Was there… a reason for that?"

Charlotte rolled back over to face me, her eyes narrowed. "What is that supposed to mean?"

"I'm just wondering."

"Why wouldn't I want to see Granny and Grandad?" Her voice rose, so unlike my usually serene daughter. "What have *they* done?"

"Nothing. Nothing, of course." I backtracked quickly, my mind in a ferment. "I was just wondering, because you seemed…"

"I didn't *seem* anything. I wanted them to come, I still do." And then she rolled back over, the conversation clearly finished.

I rose from the bed, my mind still spinning. Did I misread that moment, along with so many others? Maybe Charlotte hadn't seemed reluctant. Maybe everything I've ever thought I've seen or heard has been framed by own perspective, my own fear. I was reminded of what Diane said about memories, that our recall is affected by the last time we remembered them, like taking dolls off a shelf and twisting them into a different shape.

When it came to our lives, accuracy was a myth and absolutes were a joke, and yet I craved something solid to stand on with every fiber of my being. I still do.

A day later and I still haven't spoken to Josh, still haven't said anything worth saying. I am picking through the wreckage of my family, trying to put the pieces together. A hug for Max. Reading a book with Zoe. Getting up early to make pancakes. Reminding them all that I am here, that I will always be here, even though I wasn't before.

And now Tessa. Do I really want to know how much she and Josh got up to, and which one of them do I want to ask? Neither, it seems, at the moment.

"Why don't you toss this salad?" I ask, handing her a bag of lettuce and a wooden bowl. It feels like a kindness, to give her something to do.

I take a platter of marinated chicken breasts out of the fridge, peeling off the plastic wrap like a second skin. Tessa is mixing the salad with methodical movements, her head bent. Neither of us speaks, and I feel a flicker of sorrow for the loss of our friendship, such as it was.

I admit, I didn't have the clearest or most honorable motives in befriending Tessa McIntyre back in June. I was scared and lonely and half out of my head, needing a distraction, a *reason*. But over the course of the time we spent together, we grew closer. At least, I thought we did, but maybe like everything else in my past, that is a mirage, made hazy by memories that may or may not be real. Maybe I can't trust even that.

Outside Josh is whistling tunelessly and I hear some bumps and thumps from upstairs. Guilt needles me, along with the doubt; am I being unfair to Tessa? She stepped in at a second's notice and took care of my kids. Held my family together when I couldn't. Saw them through some very difficult times, and I'm not exactly thanking her, am I?

But then a voice whispers inside me, sly and insistent, *Yes, and she enjoyed your house. Your bed. She put your lotion on her face and she cozied up to your husband. What exactly would you be thanking her for?*

I have just taken the chicken out to Josh when Zoe flies into the kitchen, her face red, hands planted on her hips.

"Ben," she announces, managing to sound both furious and triumphant, "made Max cry!"

Considering that is something Zoe does nearly every day, I'm not too worried, but I head upstairs, Tessa on my heels. When we arrive in the playroom, Max is sitting on the sofa next to Ben, sniffling and tear-stained, while Ben hunches over his device, thumbs moving rapidly.

"What happened, guys?" I ask lightly.

"Nothing." This from Max. "It's okay."

"Ben?" Tessa asks quietly. He shrugs, looking down, and she walks forward and in one calm movement yanks the device from his hand. He looks up, a surprisingly chastened look on his face.

"Mom…"

"What happened?" she asks again, her voice low and serious, like she's really not going to take any crap this time.

Ben shrugs and she waves the device, still utterly in control.

"You're not getting this back, Ben, until you tell me what happened."

He presses his lips together. "Max got in the way and I got killed."

"On this." She brandishes it again and he nods, looking faintly abashed.

"I was on my highest level, though, Mom—"

"So, what did you do?" Tessa's voice is controlled. "Hit him?"

"I was in the way," Max interjects in a small voice.

Tessa shakes her head. "No, you weren't, Max. Ben, you know that hitting someone is not okay. Ever. Apologize."

To my surprise Ben hangs his head and darts a quick glance toward Max. "Sorry," he mutters.

"You're off this thing for the rest of the evening," she says, and he groans.

"*Mom*, that's so unfair—"

"No, it's perfectly fair. Come downstairs and set the table."

"*What*—"

"Now."

She marches downstairs without waiting to see if Ben is coming, and after a second he slinks down after her. I am reluctantly impressed by her sudden snap into discipline; the calm, controlled persona she exhibited is so far from the anxious, uncertain worrier I remember. Is this something she learned over the last month?

"Sorry about that," she says after Ben has set the table, slamming the silverware down, and then gone outside. She presses her lips together as she resumes mixing the salad more than necessary. "Ben doesn't know his own strength sometimes. And he's obsessed with that game."

"Have you considered having him assessed?"

"Assessed?" Her eyes narrow. "What happened to 'boys will be boys'?"

I shrug. I realize Tessa thinks I was trying to score a point, but I wasn't. Things feel different now, everything more tenuous and fragile. There isn't time to assume things will work themselves out, to hope for the best. And my experience tells me that the best is something you have to fight for. Hard.

"It might be worth it, just to see. Maybe something could be done…"

Tessa sighs, leaning her arms on the counter as she stares out at the bucolic scene—the blue lake, Ben and Max sharing the tire swing. Sort of. "We did have him assessed, a couple of years ago. Different doctors recommended different things. Kyle didn't want to go down the medication route, not when he's so young. And if I'm brutally honest, I don't think he has ADD or ADHD, or whatever the doctors sometimes say. I think he's just the result of lazy parenting." She grimaces. "Something I've been trying to change."

I nod. I know how easy it is to slump into bad habits, never mind having a catastrophic fall like I did. Tessa and I, in our different ways, are both trying to clamber out of the holes we inadvertently dug for ourselves. I just hope there is still time.

At least we have, by silent agreement, managed a truce as I call the kids to dinner and Josh brings in the chicken. It doesn't last long, though. I watch with narrowed eyes as he pulls out Tessa's chair. Seriously? He didn't pull out mine.

All through the meal I watch them covertly, observing the tiny, silent signals that show they have a deeper relationship than they want anyone to know. Nothing too incriminating, but it's enough. He smiles at her warmly, the way he used to smile at me. When he hands her the bread, their fingers brush. Am I overreacting? Am I *crazy*? All the same something hardens inside me, flinty and cold. This time, I don't think I am.

After dessert, an ice-cream cake bought in town, the children scatter. Ben and Max head outside, Charlotte and Katherine slip upstairs and lock themselves in my bathroom, and when I shoot Charlotte a questioning look, she smiles sweetly. "I'm going to do Katherine's nails and makeup."

"Okay." I nod, keeping her gaze, trying to both reassure and enforce. Zoe stays in the kitchen, her gaze darting between all the adults. Something simmers in the air, and I try to ignore it.

"Zoe, why don't you go outside?"

"I don't want to."

"Daddy could push you on the tire swing." There is a firm note in my voice that even Zoe knows not to contradict. An idea has fomented inside me: I am going to talk to Tessa. I need to know.

"Sure, Zo," Josh says as he rises from the table. "I'll push you really high." He glances at me, and then at Tessa, a slight frown between his brows.

"All right," Zoe finally agrees, and I watch as she and Josh head outside. The silence in the kitchen crackles, expectant, electric. After a few seconds Tessa starts clearing plates, her head bent low.

I feel firm with resolve now, an almost heady sense of expectation building in me. I *want* to know the truth.

"Why don't you just tell me what happened, Tessa?"

Tessa jerks, nearly dropping a pile of plates. Carefully she places them on the counter. "Sorry...?" She turns to me, trying to smile.

"Between you and Josh." She flinches, and I know I'm right. Something *did* happen, and the knowledge weighs heavily inside me, a stone in my gut.

"Rebecca..." Tessa sounds so miserably half-hearted. She doesn't know how much to admit. Her gaze flits to the window, where we can both see Josh pushing Zoe on the swing, a picture of familial bliss.

"I haven't spoken to Josh yet, if that's what you're wondering." My voice is still conversational, friendly. "But it's obvious that something happened between the two of you. So I'm wondering what it was. How much it was." I fold my arms and wait, trying not to tremble. I'm not sure I want to hear this anymore.

"Nothing happened," Tessa says, but I don't believe her. I don't even bother saying so, because it's so obvious to both of us she's lying. "Look," she tries again, "it was kind of an intense month, you know? You were just *gone*."

"You knew where I was—"

"What I know is you handed your whole family over to me and you expected me to pick up the slack, no problem." Tessa's voice rises to match my own. "You assumed I would, Rebecca. You barely waited for me to say yes."

"And that gives you the right to steal my husband?" I am stunned by her take on events, even as I acknowledge the partial truth of her words. Yes, I may have assumed, a *little*. I knew she'd do it. But was that a bad thing?

"I didn't *steal* Josh."

"Just took him while the going was good?"

"Doesn't he have any responsibility in this?"

"So, something did happen." Our voices climb higher and higher, making me dizzy. I feel sick.

"No." Tessa closes her eyes briefly. "Not exactly," she says quietly.

"Then what?" I lower my voice, as well. "What happened, Tessa?"

"We... we... kissed." A blotchy flush spreads across her face and throat. "Once. Only because things were so... everything felt so..."

"Don't excuse it." I try to sift through my emotions to discover how I feel about this admission. A kiss. Was that really it? Do I feel relieved it wasn't more, or angry that it was as much as that?

"We became friends," she states, and with a cold flash of realization I see that here is the real infidelity, the true betrayal. My husband started to fall in love with Tessa McIntyre—the Tessa I helped to create, confident and pretty and sensual.

"Friends." My eyebrows lift. "What does that mean, exactly?"

"Nothing—just that we became close. We were both feeling lonely and worried and overwhelmed, and we started to... depend on each other a little. But it never went anywhere physical, Rebecca, after that first kiss."

I stare at her incredulously. "Is that supposed to make me feel better?"

"I don't know. I guess not." She bites her lip, looking miserable. "I'm sorry. I never meant to take anything from you. I only wanted to help..."

"I think you're a liar." She blinks at how cold I sound. "I think you meant to take *everything* from me. My clothes, my face cream, my *kids*. I think you walked right into my life and *loved* it, Tessa, that's what I think. Am I wrong?"

Tears fill her eyes, turning them to glassy pools that spill onto her cheeks. I feel cruel, because I know I'm right: I handed her my life and she took it. I'm not even surprised. Poor, dumpy Tessa with the awkward kids and the indifferent husband, the walk-up apartment in Bumblefuck, Brooklyn, and the shabby little cottage on the lake, the shabby little *life*. Of course she took what she could; she gobbled it up.

"I'm sorry," she whispers. "I was trying to help. Honestly, I was trying to help."

"Were you helping when you were screwing my husband?"

"We never—"

"You know, what you're confessing to me is worse than some sordid one-night stand," I spit. "I could just about handle that. But this—this *closeness*? You came into my family, my life, you took over, and then you wrecked it."

Her eyes widen and anger flashes in their hazel depths. "Rebecca, if anyone has wrecked anything—"

"You want to blame me?" I am shaking with rage. "Blame me because I needed *help*?"

"All I'm saying is—"

"This is your fault, Tessa. *Yours*. You never should have made a play for my husband."

"I didn't!" she shrieks, her voice torn from her lungs, echoing through the kitchen. She presses her hands to her cheeks, her whole body trembling. "I didn't steal anything from you that you didn't just chuck away. Because if you really cared about your husband, Rebecca, if you really cared about your kids, don't you think you could have tried a little harder to stick around?" I reel back as if she's struck me, yet she's not saying anything I haven't thought myself. Repeatedly. "Do you know that Max wet the bed every night for a week after you left? Do you even *care*?"

She takes a step closer to me, thrusting her face next to mine, her eyes glittering. She's as angry as I am now. "Or did you care that Zoe had bad dreams and woke up crying? I was the one who dealt with all that. I was the one who's been their mother, Rebecca, for the last—"

"*Stop!*" The shriek has us both stilling, and the ice of horrified realization radiates through my body as I turn to see Zoe standing in the doorway, her fists clenched, her little body shaking. Outside Josh is wrestling with Max and Ben, oblivious. How long has she been there? How much has she heard?

"Zoe…" Tessa begins, and my daughter's eyes narrow to ice-blue slits.

"Shut *up*! Everything you've said is so *stupid*. It's so wrong! We never wanted you, we never liked you. *You're not my mom!*"

Tessa steps back, one hand fluttering at her throat. "I know I'm not—"

But Zoe cuts her off with a violent shake of her head, tears spilling down her cheeks. "Is it true? You and my dad?"

She heard that? I remember my ugly words, *screwing my husband.* "Zoe, we were having a grownup argument—"

"Everything's grownup when you don't want me to understand it," she cries. "But I *do* understand. You think I don't, but I *do*."

"Zoe—" We both call out at the same time, our voices rising in a plaintive, desperate chorus, but she refuses to listen to us. She backs away from the door, shaking her head, determined to get away. A sudden, formless panic seizes me.

"Zoe, *stop*—"

But it's too late. She's taken another step backward, and then another, and then she slips on the top step of the stairs. In front of our horrified gazes, my daughter falls backward, her eyes widening, her arms windmilling, her mouth open in a soundless O, as she tumbles helplessly down the steep set of stairs and then lands at the bottom with a sickening thud, followed by a far, far worse silence.

CHAPTERTWENTY-NINE

TESSA

For a single second that seems to go on forever, everything is still with a stunned, breathless silence. Then, as if someone has suddenly pushed play, we spring into action, or at least Rebecca does.

She hurtles down the steps and then Josh sprints over while the boys watch on, quiet and fearful. I stay rooted to the spot, still shocked at how quickly everything has spiraled out of control. My ears are ringing with the ugly words spoken, with that awful, awful thud.

"Call 911," Rebecca shouts, and I turn inside to look for my phone. I feel numb, my mind blank and buzzing. Josh and Rebecca are both crouched over Zoe. I see an ever-widening circle of crimson pooling around her head and I can hardly believe it—it feels like something out of a play, a bad movie.

My fingers tremble as I stab the numbers on my phone. "There's an emergency," I croak once the calm-voiced operator answers. "A nine-year-old girl has fallen down some stairs outside and hit her head. She's unconscious… there's blood…" An unruly sob escapes me and my legs nearly crumple underneath me. I grab hold of the deck railing to anchor myself.

"We'll send an ambulance," the woman says, her manner no-nonsense and steadying. "Can you please tell me your name and give me your address?"

I've just disconnected the call when Charlotte comes down the stairs, her face pale, her eyes wide. She must have seen from upstairs. I give her a sickly sort of smile, as if I can offer reassurance.

"It's going to be all right, Charlotte," I say, even though I have no idea if it is or not. "Don't worry…"

"Tessa," she says, and her voice is full of panic. "It's Katherine."

It takes me a few seconds to make sense of what she's saying. She's not looking so frightened because of *Zoe*. "Katherine…?" I repeat blankly. I have no idea where this is going, what Charlotte could possibly be trying to tell me, but I really don't like the look on her face.

"She's upstairs," she says. "She's—she's hurt herself." And then Charlotte starts to cry.

Panic lurches through me as I follow Charlotte upstairs to the luxurious bathroom off Rebecca's bedroom. I stop on the threshold, sway. Katherine is lying on the floor, the blood pumping out from a deep slash on her wrist. Crimson splashes decorate the white tiles. I can barely take it in. First, Zoe, and now Katherine…? It feels like a macabre joke, all this happening at once, except it's *real*. My daughter is lying on the floor, lifeless, as blood pools around her in dark swirls.

"Call 911," I manage through numb lips as I grab a couple of hand towels and wrap them tightly around Katherine's arm. We will need two ambulances. There is a deep and jagged slash on her wrist, and then I see a blood-soaked razor blade on the floor next to her. My whole body twangs with horror. I can't believe what I'm seeing; it makes no *sense*. Next to me Charlotte simply stands and stares. "Charlotte!" I snap. Katherine's face is pale and gray, her skin beaded with sweat. "Call *now*!"

"Okay." When she speaks to the 911 operator, the second one in a matter of minutes, she sounds terrified. "We need help… um… something has happened…"

With one hand still holding Katherine's wrist to staunch the blood, I grab the phone from Charlotte with the other and tell the operator exactly what is going on.

Then I toss the phone to the ground, careless of the clatter, and gaze down at my daughter, willing her to be strong. *There's so much blood.*

My mind is reeling, still trying to make sense of what I'm seeing, what has happened. I take in the disparate elements—the splashes of crimson blood against the white tile, my daughter's ragged wrist, that damned blade. I cannot make myself put them together.

"Katherine, hold on. Hold on, sweetheart." My voice catches on a sob and I force myself to sound steady. "Help is coming."

Katherine's eyelids flutter closed. Charlotte lets out a muffled sob, her fist held to her mouth. The towels I'm pressing to her wrist are soaked scarlet.

"What happened, Charlotte?" I ask as calmly as I can. Inside everything in me is racing, *raging.* "How did this happen?"

"We…" She starts to cry. "It was an accident. We were just… daring each other. You know…" No, I definitely do not know. They're *eleven.* "We never meant… the blade slipped…"

I close my eyes, fighting nausea and a deep, unending sorrow. How did my little girl, my shy flower, end up cutting herself with a razor blade for a dare? "Why would you do that?" I whisper, although I know there's no real point to the question. The tragedy has already happened, but I pray the worst won't happen. It skirts the edges of my mind, a black fog that threatens to take over.

"Hold on, Katherine…" My words ring in the silence because she has fallen unconscious. I hear the wail of sirens in the distance, and I realize they are probably for Zoe. Zoe, who is downstairs, as unconscious as Katherine. Two little girls whose lives might forever be altered, if not worse. *How did this happen?*

The question keeps ringing through me, with no answers, or at least with answers I don't want to give.

"Go outside," I instruct Charlotte. "You'll have to tell the paramedics where we are." As she leaves, I realize she doesn't know about Zoe. But it's too late to tell her now—she'll see for herself.

I stare down at Katherine, the blood now soaking my hands, turning them crimson, and whisper wordless prayers to keep her alive.

Charlotte comes what is surely only minutes later, but feels like ages. "They're coming. Zoe... Zoe and my mom and dad have gone..." She bites her lip, her eyes huge. It feels like far too much for one eleven-year-old girl to take in.

"Zoe will be okay," I say, trying to keep my voice from trembling. "And so will Katherine."

The next hour is a blur; the paramedics arrive and take over. I step back reluctantly and yet with relief—I don't want to leave Katherine's side but I'm so glad the professionals are here.

They load her onto a stretcher and take her to the ambulance outside; she looks so limp and lifeless, my heart squeezes painfully with fear. I follow them out, and in my dazed state, it takes me a moment to realize Rebecca, Josh, and Zoe have all gone, leaving me with Ben, Max, and Charlotte. Did Charlotte tell them about Katherine? When I ask her, she shakes her head, looking scared. I don't blame her, with everything that has been going on, but I still feel resentful, helpless. What am I going to do with all these children?

I end up having them all pile into the car while the ambulance goes on ahead to Dansville. They barrage me with questions—*Where is everybody? What happened to Katherine? What happened to Zoe?*

"They got hurt," I say tersely. My lips feel numb. "We'll know more at the hospital." I call both Rebecca and Josh on their phones, but neither of them answers. I feel impotent, angry rather than afraid because somehow that is stronger. But it isn't really; snapping at a couple of terrified nine-year-olds is hardly a show of strength.

At the hospital, I burst into the emergency room, only to be told to wait my turn, which enrages me all the more. The nurse at the triage station is calm to the point of indifference, and I want to shake her by the shoulders. I want to scream. I don't see Rebecca or Josh in the waiting room; *they*'ve already been seen, apparently. *Where is my little girl?*

After ten endless minutes a doctor finally sees me. I tell Ben, Max, and Charlotte to sit tight and I walk toward him on jelly-like legs. He gives me a brisk yet sympathetic smile and takes me into a little waiting room—the kind of room where, in the movies, people get bad news. You see it from a distance—the doctor's sorrowful shake of the head, the mother or wife or friend collapsing into herself.

I taste the acid of bile in the back of my throat and I start to feel dizzy. *I'm not ready for this.*

"What…?" My voice is a croak.

"I'm Dr. Wessel. The patient is your daughter?"

"Yes, Katherine McIntyre. She's eleven years old." I knot my clammy fingers together. "Is she… is she…?"

"She has lost a great deal of blood," he says calmly. "She severed the radial artery in her right wrist." I swallow hard. "At the moment she is unconscious, but we are preparing her for a blood transfusion, which will hopefully help matters a great deal." He smiles, and the first faint hope flickers through me.

"She'll be… all right?"

"As I said, she's lost a lot of blood. At the moment, we're considering this a class four hemorrhage, which is a loss of over forty percent of a patient's blood."

Forty percent. I think of the splashes on the tiles, the soaked towels. "And then…?"

"We'll know more once the transfusion takes place, which I hope will be in the next hour. Try not to worry." Which is like saying try not to breathe. "Do you have someone to stay with you?"

I think of Rebecca, and then I think of Kyle. "My husband," I say after a moment. "I'll call him. Can I... can I see Katherine?"

"Let's wait until after the transfusion," Dr. Wessel says, "as she's being prepped for it now. But really, Mrs.—?"

"McIntyre."

"Try not to worry. I know blood loss looks terrifying, but really even a class four hemorrhage tends not to be life-threatening. In a few hours you won't believe how much better she is." His smile is kind, with a touch of pity. "The real concern here is how your daughter ended up cutting herself in the first place."

Which feels like a rebuke, even though I know he means it kindly. His eyes are full of compassion. I nod jerkily, and a few minutes later, I'm back in the waiting room, with the children clamoring for answers.

"I think Katherine is going to be okay," I tell them.

"What about Zoe?" Charlotte's voice is high and thin.

"I don't know about Zoe." I try to stay calm when I feel like screaming that I don't *care* about Zoe. But I do, of course I do. I think of the events that led up to Zoe falling—Rebecca and me, our raised voices, the ugly accusations. *This is our fault.* And then I think of Katherine, hiding in the bathroom with Charlotte, daring to take a razor to their wrists. Is that our fault too? Where did they get such an idea? Guilt eats away at my insides, until I will be nothing but rust. I realize I need to call Kyle.

"Stay here," I instruct the three children. They are huddled together, woebegone, as they nod silently.

I go outside to call Kyle, my heart beating hard. The air is humid and sticky, with people hurrying by, looking anxious. This is the ER, after all. He answers on the first ring.

"Tessa?" Already he sounds concerned.

"Kyle, something's happened..." I stop, unable to go on.

"What? What's happened?" His words are sharp, urgent. "Tessa?"

"It's… it's Katherine." A sob escapes me and I close my eyes. I don't want to say any more. I don't want to make it more real than it already is.

"What's happened?" his voice rises raggedly. "Tessa, *tell me*."

And so I do, giving him the bare facts—the razor blade, the wrist, the blood. "But the doctor says this kind of hemorrhage is rarely life-threatening, so at least there's—"

"Life-threatening?" His voice is filled with both disbelief and pain. "Our daughter *cut* herself? What was she trying to *do*?"

"Charlotte says it was an accident—"

"With a *razor blade*? Tessa, what the hell is going on up there?"

"Kyle, please." I start to cry in noisy gulps. I can't hold it together any longer. "Please. I'm trying. I don't know…"

"I'll come up. Where are you?"

I give him the name of the hospital. He says he's leaving now. When the call ends, I close my eyes and lean my head against the wall. I know I should go find Rebecca and Josh, find out about Zoe, but I feel as if I can barely move from where I stand. I tell myself Katherine is going to be all right, and yet I know she isn't. Yes, her wrist might heal, her blood will replenish, but there are deeper, unseen scars that I never even knew about. How will those heal? How can I help her?

The minutes tick by and eventually I walk back into the waiting room, where Charlotte, Ben, and Max all sit, still huddled together. I try to smile but I can't—I feel as if I never will again.

"Okay." I take a deep breath. "We should probably find your mom and dad." I go back to the blank-faced woman at the triage desk and ask her about Zoe, but she won't tell me anything because of HIPAA laws.

"I have the other children here," I press. "They don't know where their sister is."

"I'm sorry." The woman's face is a mask. "Why don't you try calling one of the parents?"

As if I haven't already done that. I grit my teeth and turn away. An hour passes with agonizing slowness. There is no news of Katherine, no sign of Rebecca or Josh. I feel as if we are suspended in a purgatory of ignorance. Just for something to do, I buy a bag of Doritos from a dusty vending machine and let the kids share them while all of us watch the hands of the clock seem to stay still.

And then finally something happens. Josh rounds the corner, looking rumpled and tired, deep lines scoring from his nose to his mouth, and my heart clambers into my throat. I rise from my chair and Charlotte and Max rush him.

"*Daddy!*" Their voices ring through the hushed and strained atmosphere of the waiting room. He embraces them, closing his eyes.

"How is Zoe…?" I venture.

"She's in a coma." I blink in shock and tears run down Max's little face. "Medically induced for now, to assess the damage to her brain due to a hemorrhage when she fell." His voice chokes and then evens out. "We won't know anything until they take her out of the coma, hopefully in the next few days. How… how severe the injury is."

"Oh, Josh." My voice catches. I can barely believe it. "I'm so, so sorry…"

"She could have a complete recovery." His voice is hoarse but determined. "That is still a possibility, the doctors said."

"Of course it is…"

"We just have to wait and see." He smiles at me, but it looks hopeless. He doesn't believe what the doctors say, and I'm not sure I do, either. "Thank you for bringing the children."

I realize he doesn't know about Katherine. It doesn't feel right to tell him now, when she is surely going to be okay and Zoe's future is so unknown. And yet how can I not tell him?

"I didn't bring the children here to see you…" I pause. Josh frowns. "I'm here because of Katherine."

"Katherine…?"

"She… she had an accident, the same time as Zoe." He stares at me incredulously; it sounds so strange, so horrible. Two accidents in the space of a few minutes? Two little girls whose lives hang by a thread, and yet I have this horrible, creeping sensation that it's all related, all tangled; that both Katherine and Zoe are where they are, *how* they are, because of Rebecca… and me.

"Katherine did? What happened?"

"She cut herself." I press my lips together as I feel a spurt of unreasonable anger for Charlotte. Did she *dare* Katherine to do it? To slice her own wrists? I can't see Katherine being the instigator of that terrible game. But *why*? Why would two eleven-year-olds mess around with razor blades? I am afraid to think of why.

I remember how Katherine asked to go home, how she said she didn't want to be there anymore. Was this why? And I ignored her, more or less. I dismissed her concerns. I can't bear to think about it now, and yet I do. It torments me.

"She's going to be all right, though?" Josh asks me. He doesn't sound particularly concerned, and I can't say I blame him. It sounds as if Katherine sliced her thumb and needs a stitch or two, and I don't want to disabuse him of that notion. I don't want to admit the terrible truth.

"Yes," I say. "She's going to be okay."

Josh nods and smiles, the moment already moving on. Katherine is not his concern, and horribly, I understand that.

"Right, I should get back to Rebecca and Zoe." He pauses, glancing at Charlotte and Max. I jump in before he can ask me to take care of his kids for the nth time.

"I really need to be with Katherine now," I tell him as firmly as I can. "Kyle's on his way—"

"Kyle?" Josh looks startled. "Is it serious, then?"

"Kind of." I turn away, not wanting to talk. "Let me know how Zoe is."

"I will—"

I think of Zoe backing away from us in the kitchen. "And Josh, I'm sorry."

His eyes narrow as if sensing my guilt. "Sorry…?"

"I need to go." I grab Ben's hand and hurry away, in search of my daughter.

CHAPTER THIRTY

REBECCA

I sit by Zoe's bed and watch the faint rise and fall of her chest, her body barely a bump under the sheet. Bandages swathe her head and golden lashes fan her round, child's cheeks. It's so strange to see her so still. My Zoe is always in motion, a blur of determined activity and emotion, yet now it's all been leached out of her, and I can't bear it.

I long to see her running again, shouting, crying, bickering with Max. Anything but this terrible stillness. In my mind's eye, I picture that suspended moment as she stepped backwards and I knew, I absolutely knew, she was going to fall. I felt it before she stumbled, before her arms flew up and her mouth dropped open in a silent scream of terrified realization. Before both of our worlds shattered.

"Zoe." I rest my hand lightly on top of hers. "Zoe, sweetheart, I love you. You know how much I love you, don't you?" My chest squeezes with the pain of it, and it hurts to breathe. Did she—does she—know? Will I ever get to tell her? If I'm given the chance, I'll spend the rest of my life telling her—and showing her.

The doctors were terrifyingly noncommittal when she was rushed into the ICU a few hours ago. She's had a bleed on the brain, that much we learned. But whether it will cause lasting or serious damage, it's impossible to say, or so the doctors tell us. No one wants to make promises they can't keep, but I yearn for some hope to hold on to, something to keep me afloat.

I can't bear to think that this is all my fault, and yet that thought beats through me in a relentless tattoo. There I was, screaming at Tessa like a harridan, mindless of the children nearby, or how it might look to them. What happened to all my new-found serenity and acceptance? I spent the last four weeks working toward that and in a moment, a *second*, I threw it all away—and for what? To score a few sour points off Tessa McIntyre? I close my eyes against the thought; I am filled with shame and regret, too much to bear, and yet there is more to come.

"Rebecca." I open my eyes to see Josh coming into the room. He closes the door quietly behind him and joins me by Zoe's side. "Any change?" We both regard our daughter silently.

"No, no change." I take a deep breath. "The doctors did say it could be a while before she comes out of the—the coma." I hate saying the word. I'd never even known about medically induced comas, or the necessity of them. *Give the body time to heal itself,* the doctor explained with a reassuring pat on the arm. *The brain is an amazing organ.*

"Rebecca, Charlotte, and Max are here."

"What?" My voice rises a little, and I drop it to a whisper even though I don't think it matters. "Why did Tessa bring them?"

"She had to, because Katherine has hurt herself somehow. She's being treated in ER."

"Hurt herself?" I feel a shiver of premonition, along with an irritation that whatever Katherine is facing, it can't be as bad as this. "How?"

"I don't know. She cut herself, apparently." Josh shrugs, dismissive, but I turn cold. *Cut herself.* I think of Katherine and Charlotte, closeted up in my bathroom. *Why* did I let them go there? Why didn't I think about what they might be doing? I'd been so intent on Tessa, on confronting her, that I ignored my daughter. *Tessa's daughter.*

"Do you know how she cut herself?" I ask quietly.

"No."

"I should see Tessa." I look back at Zoe, lying there as still as ever. How can I leave my daughter? I can't keep from thinking that if I stay here, I can somehow imbue her with my strength, such as it is. Conversely, if I leave, I feel like I will hurt her. She will open her eyes and I won't be there. Again. But she *will* open her eyes, I have to believe that.

"If you want to," Josh says. He sounds surprised, a little diffident. I take another deep breath.

"Josh, I have to tell you something."

"Okay." Now he sounds guarded.

"Zoe fell down the stairs because she overheard Tessa and me arguing." Best to state it plainly, like ripping a Band-Aid off a wound with one swift yank.

"What were you arguing about?"

"You." He has the grace to look away.

"Rebecca…"

"I know the two of you kissed."

He closes his eyes and sighs heavily. "I'm sorry, it was one unguarded moment. It never should have happened. I regretted it immediately after."

I wonder if that is supposed to make me feel better. Then I wonder if it does. "That's not all it was, though, was it?" I ask steadily. He turns to look at me.

"Rebecca, do we have to do this now?"

"It all relates, Josh." More and more, with a deepening sense of regret, I am realizing how everything is related. How all our stories, all our tragedies, entwine and tangle into a terrible Gordian knot. How will we ever undo it all? Perhaps we can't.

"How could it possibly relate?" he asks, a strident note entering his voice.

"Because Tessa told me how close the two of you'd become."

"How *close*?" He looks startled, and I wonder if she made more of their connection than there actually was. Why would she do that—to make me jealous? To hurt me? Or was it just her wishful thinking?

"Do you deny it?"

"I won't deny that we became friends, but it wasn't... inappropriate."

"Even though it started with a kiss?"

"I told you, that was a mistake." There is an edge to his voice, and I wonder how he can feel aggrieved in this situation. But then I remind myself why I am telling him this.

"Josh, Zoe overheard us, Tessa and me. We were both angry, blaming each other, saying ugly things..." I swallow hard. "She got upset."

Josh's eyes widen. "And then she fell?"

"And then she fell." The words fall into the stillness like stones. I stare at the motionless form of our daughter and my eyes sting. *And then she fell.*

Josh shakes his head slowly. He looks dazed. "How did this happen?" he asks, but I don't think he wants an answer. "How did we get to this place, all of us?"

"There's something else I need to tell you."

He turns to me with a swift, searching look. "There's *more*?"

A lot more. "About why I started drinking. What..." My breath hitches. "What happened to me." He stares at me, his eyes widening, and I finally tell him the truth, total, terrible. I start out slowly, my voice halting, the words coming in a jumble, every syllable feeling both unfamiliar and right. Josh doesn't say anything, although a couple of times he shakes his head or wipes his eyes. Fear clutches at me, that he doesn't believe me. Sometimes I'm not sure if I believe myself, and yet I have a deep certainty that those memories are real. *Aren't they?*

Finally, I lapse into silence, the only sound the ticking of the clock, the steady hum and beeping of the monitors connected to our daughter. "Do you believe me?" I whisper.

He swings his head around to face me. "*Believe* you?"

"Yes. I mean… I know how it sounds…"

"How do you think it sounds, Rebecca?"

"Incredible. Impossible. I mean, I know my father wouldn't do that, and he *didn't*, yet for months I was so terrified he did. It consumed me, Josh. It ate me right up inside until it felt as if there was nothing left." Tears spill onto my cheeks. "And I let it." That is something I don't know if I can forgive myself for. "For months I let it." I let it overwhelm me, I let myself check out from my marriage, my children. And everyone suffered as a result.

"Rebecca, that's… that's understandable. I can't even imagine…" He shakes his head slowly. "Why didn't you tell me?"

"Because I didn't know how. I didn't want it to be true. And I wasn't sure you wanted to know." The words are painful to say.

"Why wouldn't I want to know?"

"Because you like to solve problems, Josh. Quickly. And I suppose because I've felt like…" I search for the words. "A useful accessory to your busy, successful life. And if I stop functioning…"

He stares at me, his mouth open. "Is that really how you've seen our marriage?"

"Isn't it how you've seen it, if you're honest?"

"*No.*" He rises from his seat and paces the room like something caged. "No, of course that's not how I've seen it. I admit, we might have fallen into a slump the way most marriages do. We have busy lives, a lot of kids… sometimes it's all you can do to just keep things going—work, home, school."

"And when I started drinking?" I ask quietly.

Josh breathes out heavily. "I suppose part of me was… angry. I'm not proud of that, but I couldn't understand why you were sabotaging yourself, our marriage, our whole life together. That's what it felt like to me."

"I know." I can't blame him for that; I know I can't. "I'm sorry I didn't tell you, but I was afraid, Josh. I was so afraid."

We lapse into silence, all the words we've said lying in broken pieces around us. Can we fix this? It's not a question I want to ask, not with Zoe lying so still. Not when so much is so uncertain, so important. *We have so much to lose.*

"I should see Tessa," I say. "Where are Max and Charlotte?"

"Outside in the waiting room."

"I'll talk to them, too." I nod toward Zoe. "Tell me if anything changes. The very minute…"

"I will." Josh's face is drawn in stark lines; he's thirty-eight but suddenly he looks old. "Of course I will." As I walk past him to the door he grabs my hand and holds it tightly. "Rebecca, I'm sorry."

"So am I," I say in a choked voice, and as I leave the room I wonder what we were asking forgiveness for. I look back at Zoe once, but she doesn't move, not so much as a flicker, and with a clutch of fear, I wonder if my baby girl will ever open her eyes again. In that terrible moment, I fear that she won't; that this will be the punishment for my sins. This will be my justice.

In the ICU waiting room, which is a hushed, private sanctuary compared to the frantic chaos of the ER reception area, Max and Charlotte are huddled together, watching a talk show on mute.

I gather them both in my arms and we cling together, a buoy of comfort in a drowning sea.

"Is Zoe going to be okay, Mom?" Charlotte asks, her voice trembling with anxiety.

"I hope so. The doctors will know when she wakes up."

"When will she wake up?" This from Max, pulling back from me a little.

"Soon, I hope." He burrows against me and I close my eyes. This feels like too much to hold, to bear.

After a few seconds I open my eyes and gaze at my oldest child, her pale, tear-splotched face, her worried eyes. She knows what I'm going to ask.

"Charlotte," I say quietly, "what happened with Katherine?"

"It was an accident," she whispers. Her face is pale, so pale, and her lips tremble. I ache for her, but I ache for Tessa and Katherine too.

"Were you…?" I can't say it in front of Max, and I don't want to say it at all. In any case, I don't need to. Charlotte nods, her gaze sliding away from mine.

"*Why?*" I ask, my voice rising to a soft wail. Charlotte shrugs helplessly.

"It was just a dare," she whispers. "Other girls do it, you know. At school. It wasn't just you."

I want to cover Max's ears. "But…"

"She didn't want to," Charlotte confesses, as tears spill onto her cheeks. "But I pushed her into it… I told her I wouldn't hang out with her anymore if she didn't."

"Oh, Charlotte!" I am helpless in sorrow. Why would my beautiful, calm, confident daughter do something like this; why do any of us do the things we do? Because we're all broken. Some of us hide it better, some of us struggle along. But inside, where it matters? *Broken.*

And now needs to be the time of healing. "We can talk about it later," I say quietly. "I need to see Katherine now."

"She'll be all right, won't she?" Charlotte asks. "I mean… it's not too serious, is it? Tessa said she thought she was going to be okay."

"I hope so."

"And Zoe?"

"I… I hope so." I stare at them both, not wanting to make false promises. "I hope so."

It takes some doing, asking, coaxing, and downright begging various nurses and orderlies, but I finally make my way up to the pediatric ward, where I find Tessa in a private room, sitting next to Katherine's bed. I tap on the door and she looks up in surprise, her face haggard, shoulders slumped. We've all aged in the space of a few hours; lifetimes come and gone.

"Tessa?" I whisper. I glance at Katherine, who is lying in bed, sleeping. "How is she?"

"I think she's going to be okay." Tessa releases a shuddery breath. "She's just had a blood transfusion. She lost over forty percent of her blood, the doctor said."

I jerk back at that, shocked by the huge amount. *From one little cut?* I glance at her wrist, the thick white bandage.

"She severed her radial artery," Tessa explains. "The razor blade slipped. That's what Charlotte said."

"Tessa, I'm so sorry."

She looks up at me with blank, tired eyes. "I can't believe how this has happened. My mind keeps going round and round in circles, wondering how we all ended up in this hospital, with two little girls—" Her voice breaks. "How is Zoe?"

"There's been no change. I don't know when she'll wake up." My voice wobbles. "*If* she'll wake up."

"Oh, Rebecca…"

"Tessa, did you—did you know Charlotte and Katherine were doing this?" The dazed look on her face makes me think she didn't.

"No, I had no idea. I still don't understand…"

"I left you a voicemail message." My voice is urgent; I try not to sound accusing. "A couple of weeks ago. Saying that Charlotte was cutting herself. I saw the lines on her wrist when they visited. I asked you to…" I stop, because this isn't her fault. If it's anyone's fault, it's mine.

"A message?" Tessa's eyes widen. "I didn't listen to it."

"Why not?"

She shakes her head. "I… I thought you were angry with me over… everything, really. Coming to Lakeview with Josh…" Her face crumples and she wraps her arms around herself, bowing her head. "What have I done?" she whispers brokenly. "What have I done?"

"It's not your fault," I say quickly. "If it's anyone's, it's mine. I should have told you in person, I should have told Josh. And… the reason Charlotte was cutting herself in the first place was because of me."

"What…?" Tessa looks up, her gaze startled.

"She did it because she saw me doing it."

"*You…*"

"Charlotte found me in the bathroom one evening, before I went to rehab." Tessa waits, looking dazed. "I… was cutting myself."

"What?" She shakes her head. "Why… why would you…?"

"It was all part of it. The… illness. I've been in such a bad place this summer. Drinking was only the tip of the iceberg, nothing more than my anesthesia of choice. But I shouldn't have dragged you into my life. My problems. And the last thing I'd ever want to do is have our children suffer as a result." But they have. And neither of us knows how deep their wounds are, or how long the healing process will take—if they heal. If we can still walk out of all this whole, if not unscathed.

"But I don't understand," Tessa says. She sounds lost, like a little child. "What is—was—wrong with you, Rebecca?"

So I tell her, just as I told Josh. Haltingly, the words chosen with laborious care. And when I finish, Tessa stares at me, appalled. "I had no idea…"

"Why would you?"

"I thought your life was so perfect." She lets out a sob and presses her fist to her mouth. "I've been envious of you all summer, Rebecca, as you said. I suppose I did try to—to steal your life, even just temporarily, because it felt so much better than my own. I let myself get lost in it, and everyone suffered."

"You can't blame yourself when I was the one—"

"Should I blame you, then? It would be easier." Tessa closes her eyes and gives her head a little shake. "But I can't just blame you, Rebecca. I didn't listen to your message, I tuned out whatever it was I didn't want to hear or see. Our daughters are in this place because of both of us. Because of what we did, how we acted, all summer. I can't escape that."

I shake my head, unable to deny the stark and terrible truth of her words. "I know. I can't, either."

"Katherine asked if we could go home weeks ago. *Weeks.* Was she—were they—*then?*"

I hate to think of it. "Maybe," I admit.

"And Zoe… she was like a ticking time bomb, waiting to explode. I knew that and yet—"

"You can't just blame yourself—"

"I know I can't." She sounds savage. "I blame you, as well. And Josh, and even Kyle. The children are innocent, because they're *children.*" Her voice chokes. "But as for us… it's all a tangled web and we all played a terrible part. But I never wanted to end up here."

"None of us did."

She lets out a laugh of pure sorrow, her gaze on Katherine's slight form. "I wanted to be different this summer, that's why I came up here. Things at home had become so unbearable—Kyle and I barely talking, the other moms at school avoiding or ignoring us. Kyle always acted as if he blamed me for something—maybe his mediocre life, I don't know. I hated it. I felt like I was living under a shroud. I wanted to break out somehow, and I thought this was the best way. But I wasn't different up here, or maybe I was—I was *worse.*"

"Tessa…" I let my voice trail off because I have nothing more to say. She blames herself; I blame myself. How do we move past that? And yet we have to, for the sake of our children. We have to find a way somehow to live with our mistakes—to learn from them, to heal, and to grow.

"Katherine is going to get better," I tell her, although I know I can't make such promises. "And so is Zoe." I try to paint a picture of a future we can live with, one we can hold onto now. "We are all going to move past this."

"*How?*"

I think of Gwen, back at Lakeview. "By staring this in the face and naming it. By looking into our weaknesses and failures and finding the strength to admit when we were wrong, and then to change."

"If we can."

"We can. Trust me, we can." Gently, I rest my hand on her shoulder. "It's going to be okay. It might be a long, hard slog, but it's going to be okay." I think of Zoe's still form, the eyes that have yet to open. What if it *isn't* going to be okay? What if Zoe has some kind of lasting brain damage? What if something happens to Katherine? There are no guarantees, no certainties. Everything hangs in the balance, and I can't bear it.

And then there are all the other worries. Will my marriage to Josh survive? How will I talk to my parents? What kind of help does Charlotte need? Like Tessa said, it's an endless tangle. How do we unpick all the knots? How do we even begin?

"Is Kyle coming?" I ask, and she nods.

"He'll be here in a few hours."

"Can I do anything…?"

Tessa gives me a sad smile. "We've done enough for each other, don't you think, Rebecca?"

I freeze, my hand still on her shoulder. I think of all the ways we helped each other—the clothes and beauty treatments, and far more importantly, the friendship and the laughter, the moments we had when it felt as if we really understood each other. The month she spent acting as mother to my children. We needed each other this summer… in so many ways. And look where we are now.

"Yes," I agree softly. "I suppose we have."

I don't like leaving Tessa alone, but I know I can't offer her anything more and I need to get back to Zoe.

"You will tell me if you need anything?" I ask, and she nods.

"Yes. I'm sure she'll be awake soon. The doctor said she might be up and about in a few hours." She speaks bravely, and I'm not sure she believes it. "Let me know how Zoe is."

"I will." Zoe, I know, will not be up and about in a few hours. The doctor said it could be days or even weeks before we know the extent of her injuries.

Slowly, I walk back to the ICU ward, everything quiet and hushed save for the murmur of voices behind closed doors, the intermittent beep of some important machine.

I check on Charlotte and Max, and after ascertaining that Zoe is still asleep, I take them to the hospital cafeteria for hot chocolate sipped in morose silence. It's nearing midnight and they're both exhausted, but I can't go home yet. Back upstairs, they curl up on the sofa and watch an episode of *Drake & Josh* on the TV in the waiting room. I hug them both, just because I can and it feels important.

Then I stand in front of the window that looks into Zoe's room. Josh is sitting by her bed, one hand gently holding hers. He looks so beaten down and yet so full of love, and I am reminded that once upon a time, a long time ago, we loved each other. And maybe it will be enough.

I walk into the room and he looks back at me with a tired smile and eyes full of sadness.

"Any change?"

He shakes his head. "No."

I sit next to him and he reaches for my hand, twining his fingers through mine. The simple gesture touches me more than any hapless words ever could. We sit in silence for a while; minutes or hours, I've lost track. It feels like we will wait forever, and in some ways that is better than knowing the worst. At least in waiting there is hope, there is a maybe.

And then, in the midst of our silence, the monitor Zoe is attached to starts beeping, and seconds later, a nurse rushes in, a panicked look on her face. I watch, transfixed, terrified, as I feel my whole world start to collapse.

CHAPTER THIRTY-ONE

TESSA

I feel as if I've been waiting forever, even though it's only been an hour since Katherine's blood transfusion. She woke up, apparently, while they were giving her the blood, and then fell back asleep. It's late, and she's exhausted, and I tell myself it's going to be okay. I repeat it like a promise.

Ben has fallen asleep in the waiting room of the pediatric ward, tucked up under a blanket by a kindly nurse. Kyle texted me to say he should be here in an hour or two. My body aches with fatigue and my eyes are gritty. I can still smell the faint, lingering scent of Rebecca's perfume, and her words, her confessional, echo through my mind. The memories and sorrow she tried to suppress. So much brokenness. And unfairly, terribly, it's our children who suffer the most.

I stroke Katherine's hand, and then the mouse-brown hair away from her forehead. My quiet, shy flower, longing and waiting to bloom. Why couldn't I see how much she was struggling? Why didn't I listen to her more closely when she said she wanted to go home? Because I didn't want to. Because I was having fun. I wasn't strong or wise enough to realize what was going on… in so many ways.

"Mom?"

Katherine's voice is a croak and I lean forward as an incredulous, joyful laugh bubbles on my lips even as tears spring to my eyes. "Sweetheart… it's so good to see you awake. To hear you."

She licks dry lips and I pour a glass of water, raise it to her mouth so she can take a sip.

"Thanks. I feel dizzy."

"As you probably should. You've had a blood transfusion."

Her face clouds as the memory returns and shadows enter her eyes. "Are you… are you mad at me?"

"Mad? *No*. No, Katherine, I am not mad at all." I squeeze her hand gently, longing to imbue her with my love and acceptance. "If anything, I'm mad at myself for letting this happen."

"It's not your fault."

"But I'm your mom." I try to smile but my lips tremble. "I'm meant to keep you safe."

"It was stupid." She closes her eyes and sighs, a whisper of regret-laced breath. "I was stupid."

"No, sweetheart, don't say that. You're amazing." And I haven't, I realize painfully, told her that nearly enough. For so long I focused on the parts of my children that left me dissatisfied. I've only considered the ways I wanted to help them be better, rather than simply accepting them for who they *were*. But I don't want to do that now; I don't want to do that ever again.

"I'm sorry," she whispers, and I squeeze her hand again.

"Don't be. We're going to get past all this, Katherine. We're going to get better, all of us."

"You don't need to get better."

"I think I do." In a whole new way. I don't want to take on someone else's life, I want to fix my own. I want to figure out what isn't working, what needs to change. And this brush with disaster, with death itself, has galvanized me the way nothing else could. "I haven't been the mom I've wanted to be to you, sweetheart, and I'm sorry. So sorry."

Katherine smiles faintly, her eyelids already starting to flutter. "I love you, Mom."

"Oh, Katherine! Sweetheart, I love you. I love you so, so much, and Daddy does, too."

"I know." She is smiling as she falls back asleep. I remain where I am, clinging to her hand, making so many promises to myself, to Katherine.

I am still in that position when Kyle comes through the door, looking tired and haggard and wonderful all at the same time. I am surprised by how fiercely glad I am to see him. There may have been a distance opening up between us, but this near-tragedy closes it, at least for this moment.

Kyle comes toward me and pulls me into a tight, wordless hug. I bury my face in his shoulder, breathing him in as I relish the feel of his arms around me.

"I should never have let you come up here." His tone is fierce.

"You couldn't have prevented this, Kyle—"

"I could have." He draws back a little, his gaze flicking to Katherine's sleeping form, flinching slightly as he takes in the thick white bandage on her wrist. "How is she?"

"She's okay." I give him a shaky smile, the post-adrenalin rush of relief lapping at me in waves. "She had a blood transfusion a couple of hours ago and she woke up for a little while. We spoke together. I think it's going to be okay, Kyle." The words fill me with hope, with fragile happiness. We can get past this.

We break apart and he draws up a chair next to mine and sits there, elbows braced on his knees. "How did this happen, Tessa? How did we let this happen?"

The *we* heartens me, but it's still a question with too many tangled answers. "I don't know." I gaze at Katherine, drinking her in. "But we're going to get past it."

"We need to, Tessa." Kyle's voice is both grim and heartbroken. "We need to, this time."

"This time?" I feel an unexpected chill at the emphasis in those words. "What do you mean by that, exactly?"

Kyle sighs heavily as he rakes his hands through his hair before dropping them wearily, with a shake of his head. "You don't even realize, do you?" he says, and my chill deepens, settling into my bones. "You don't remember."

"Remember what?"

"How bad it's been for us."

I struggle to stay composed, reasonable. "I know things have been kind of hard lately, Kyle, but it's a two-way street, surely? I mean… we've both become a bit distant over the last few months…" Or years, even—but he just shakes his head.

"I don't mean that."

"What, then?"

"Tessa…" Kyle leans forward. His face is full of compassion now, which alarms me for some reason. I have no idea what he's going to say. "Tessa, sometimes I think you've blanked out that year of our lives."

"That year…?"

"The year your mom died. Do you remember how hard it was? Do you remember what happened?"

"I remember I was grief-stricken." I feel myself prickle defensively. "I loved my mom, Kyle. You know that—"

"Of course I know that. What I'm saying is… Tessa, things were *bad*. For everyone. It was as if you blanked us for months— me, Katherine, Ben. It was almost as if we didn't exist."

"What are you talking about?" My voice sounds too loud. I can't believe he's talking about this now. It was two years ago, and I'd lost my *mother*. "Look, Kyle, I know I was sad, but my mom died. And that was two years ago now—"

"It wasn't two years ago."

"I think I know when my mother died."

"Yes, I know you do, but Tessa, it lasted a lot longer than that. It lasted for months, a whole year. Rayha helped a bit, but…" He shakes his head, and Rayha's words on the phone the other day run through my mind. *Especially when you were there for them, over and over again, when their life was shit and they couldn't even hold it together. Do you remember that, Tessa?*

I try to think back to that time, but pain and grief have blurred it into a hazy montage of sleepwalking moments. All right, yes, I know I checked out for a little while, but I was still *there*. I got through the days, I took care of my children.

Didn't I?

"Kyle, what are you saying, exactly?" I am suddenly seized by a panicky need to know. "What happened?"

He looks at me wearily. "You were diagnosed with severe depression, you were on pills."

"I remember that." I took Zoloft and it made me feel as if I were viewing the world from behind a hazy curtain, but not that bad, surely…

"You stopped showering, eating, talking even… you'd forget to pick up the kids from school, or do anything. You lay in bed for hours at a time. You cried all the time. You walked out of the house and didn't come back for hours… Sometimes I'd find you, sitting in the park, just staring into space, like you didn't even realize that you'd gone, that you'd left the kids alone."

I am cold, utterly cold. Katherine would have only been nine, Ben seven. I think of my daughter's scorn, the flash in her eyes. *Seriously? You're telling me this?*

"I ended up taking three months' compassionate leave," Kyle says heavily, "to try to help you."

"You did?" Why can't I remember *that*? How did I not realize? That whole year is fogged over in my mind, a place and time I never let myself think about. "And then what happened?"

"You spent a week in a hospital. A mental hospital."

I open my mouth to object. I would have remembered that. *Of course* I would have remembered that. But then I picture a white room, a metallic smell, a soothing voice. I feel jolted, as if by an electric shock. "And then?" I whisper.

"It seemed a little better after that. We soldiered on, more or less. I wanted you to go back to work, just to get out of the house, have something to do—"

I shake my head. "No, you wanted me to go back to work for money—"

"The money wasn't ever that important, Tessa." He speaks so wearily that I believe him.

"I started my card-making business…"

"Yes, and that gave you some focus. But Tessa, you've only sold a handful of cards."

A prickly flush breaks over me. "More than a few…"

"Not really."

I feel humiliated somehow. Have I really been that delusional? Kyle reaches for my hand. "Tessa, I'm not trying to hurt you by telling you this. I want you to know because more and more, I realize how much you've forgotten, or chosen not to remember, because that's the only way to cope. And if Katherine has hurt herself…" He glances back at the bed. "Then I want to make sure you can handle it. That we can all cope, together, this time, or that I can… I can give you the help you need."

I feel as if he is rewriting my entire story. "What about when we moved to Park Slope?"

Kyle looks at me warily. "What about it?"

"How was I then?" I have a sudden memory—standing in the schoolyard, tears running down my face while other mothers looked away. Was it really like that? Am I making it up?

"You were still in a hard place. We moved to try for a fresh start, but…"

"But what?" The words are ripped from me. Kyle shrugs.

"It was hard, Tessa. You still cried a lot. And instead of blanking the kids, you became obsessive about them, always… always picking on them. Nit-picking, like you were never satisfied. It was another coping mechanism, I guess. Something else to focus on. I know it's not your fault. I should have tried harder, figured something out—"

I shake my head. I feel as if with every word he says, Kyle is twirling the kaleidoscope of my memories, creating a new, unwelcome picture, and one that I am dimly beginning to recognize. I think of the way the other mothers ignored me in the schoolyard, the birthday party invitations that tailed off, the looks exchanged over my head. And it was because of *me*. Me—not Ben's boisterousness or Katherine's shyness. *Me*.

"What about Katherine?" I whisper. "And Ben?" Kyle doesn't answer but he doesn't even need to say it. I stand up abruptly, needing to get away from the memories that are creeping into my mind like a morning mist, except they are giving me clarity rather than obfuscation. I picture Katherine's tearful face, Ben hitting a wall. Because of *me*. Because, just as Rebecca did this summer, I checked out. I turned away, because I couldn't handle life anymore. And I didn't even remember doing it.

"How long?" I whisper. "How long was I like that?"

Kyle is silent for a long moment. "About a year," he says at last.

A year. A whole year. Is *this* why Ben acts out? Why I feel the yawning chasm between Katherine and me? I remember her anger, her sudden looks of scorn, and it all starts to make terrible sense. The last two years haven't happened the way I thought they did. At all.

"I'm sorry," I whisper. "I'm so, so sorry."

"Tessa, I didn't say any of this to make you feel guilty." Kyle reaches for me and I let him hug me, closing my eyes against the hot press of tears. "Hell, I'm guilty too, because I got so tired. If you felt there was distance between us, and I know there was, it was because I was tired of trying. And I was angry, which I know isn't fair. When you suggested going away this summer, I agreed even though I wasn't sure I should, just because I wanted a break."

"I thought you didn't want us to go because of the money."

"The money never mattered that much, Tessa. I know we're not rich, but we do okay. I was worried about you, but… I let you go. I let myself get caught up in my music. I let this happen as much as anyone else did."

"Oh, Kyle…" I am rewriting the narrative of the last few years with new, stark lines. Two years ago, my mother died. A year ago, I started to come out of the fog of my grief, but I hadn't realized how bad I'd been… how bad I still was.

"Maybe I should have got you more help," Kyle says. I remember a therapist I only saw a couple of times, because talking felt like it made it worse. "I should have been better about everything, too. I didn't handle it well, I know I didn't."

Still, I can't shake the blame. I think of Rebecca, so doubtful of her own memories. And here I was, so sure of mine. Can anything be trusted? Can we ever trust ourselves? Or do we need another person to show us the way, to remind us of the truth? Thank God I have Kyle.

"The point is," he continues, his arms coming around me, "we can be different now. Maybe all this happened to shake us up, bring us together. We can choose to face this as a family, Tessa, together. We can choose to be different, to be stronger."

Just as I was all summer, on my own and making a mess of it. "Yes," I say, and wrap my arms around him, returning his hug with all of myself, my soul. "I want that, I want that very much."

We are still standing with our arms around each other when the monitor connected to Katherine starts to beep.

CHAPTER THIRTY-TWO

REBECCA

"What's going on?" My voice is high and thin as a nurse checks Zoe's stats and that awful monitor continues its steady, anxious beep, reminding us that something is wrong. Something is very wrong.

"I'll get the doctor," the nurse murmurs and then she hurries away, leaving us alone with our daughter. I clasp Zoe's hand gently in my own, feeling completely terrified and utterly helpless. She is so, so still, and I am more afraid than I've ever been in my life that this might be it. I can barely get my mind around the possibility, even as it hammers through me.

"Josh…" My voice comes out in a pleading whisper.

"I'm going to go look for the doctor—"

"No, don't leave her." My voice trembles. "Don't leave her, not when—" I stop, because I don't want to put it into words. I *can't*.

"I won't leave, Rebecca." Josh crouches down on the other side of Zoe and holds her other hand. We wait, suspended in this awful moment, the beeps reverberating through me, each one worse than the last, but at least they are telling us she is still alive.

Then the doctor bursts through the door, and everything is a whirl of awful activity.

"She's had another hemorrhage," he tells us. "And it looks like it is putting pressure on her brain. We can do a scan to confirm, but I think she will need surgery." I stare at him blankly. *Brain surgery…?* "It would be better to perform the surgery as soon as possible, before the pressure becomes too great. We would drill a small hole in her skull," he continues, and I can't listen anymore. I feel as if I'm going to faint.

I hear the doctor talk about parental consent, and Josh's low voice asking questions. Then Josh turns to me: "Rebecca, do you permit them to operate?"

Do I? I simply stare, my mind spinning too much. "This is her best chance," he says, and I want to argue with him. Her best chance? *When did this become about chances?*

"All right." I speak through numb lips.

Moments later, we are taken to a waiting room, and Zoe is wheeled toward surgery, which will take several hours. Hours of unknowing, of being suspended in this terrible ignorance; I can't bear it.

"I'm going to go see Tessa," I say, and Josh looks at me in surprise.

"Are you sure…?"

"I've got to do something."

Upstairs, Tessa is huddled close with a man who must be her husband in the waiting room, looking as dazed and stricken as I feel. Ben is stretched out on some chairs, asleep. Tessa's eyes widen when she sees me.

"Rebecca…"

"Zoe's in surgery," I blurt. "She's had another bleed on her brain." Tessa looks at me, seeming barely to take it in. "How is Katherine?"

"There's been a complication with the transfusion," she says, her voice sounding disbelieving, distant. "I don't really understand it…"

"Oh, Tessa."

"They're going to be okay, though, aren't they?" She looks at me almost desperately for confirmation we both know I can't give. "You said they're going to be okay."

"Yes." I will make promises, because maybe then I can believe them. "Yes, of course they are, Tessa."

Back downstairs, Josh is waiting with Charlotte and Max; Max is asleep and Charlotte is leaning against Josh's shoulder and the sight of them all makes my heart squeeze with painful love. My family. *My family.* The most important people in the world to me.

"Any word?" I ask, and Josh shakes his head. It's far too early.

The next few hours pass in a blur and yet with agonizing slowness. My eyes feel gritty, my whole body aches. My mind trawls through memories that are now achingly precious. Zoe as a baby, red-faced and screaming, already angry at the world. As a toddler, precocious and fiercely independent, pushing my hands away when I tried to help her to walk, determined to tackle absolutely everything by herself. Zoe in first grade, memorizing the longest poem in the class just so she could. Always so fierce, so full of fire; my darling, defiant, difficult child. I can't lose her. Not after all the progress I've made, all the ways we've struggled. I can't; I won't allow it. But of course I don't have any choice.

And then the surgeon comes into the waiting room, looking weary and haggard. My heart leaps into my throat and Josh and I half-rise, waiting, terrified.

"The surgery was successful," the surgeon tells us with a tired smile. "Your daughter is awake."

It feels like an utter miracle to walk into the recovery room and see Zoe's eyes opened. Yes, they're unfocused, and her speech is slurred, but the doctor tells us that is most likely from the anesthetic and not the injury. While they still don't know the extent of her injury, my little girl is alive. She has survived, and I am so, so grateful.

"Mommy."

I reach for her hand, blinking back tears. "Yes, darling?"

"I want to go home."

CHAPTER THIRTY-THREE

TESSA

As the monitor starts to beep, Kyle draws away with a slight frown and I turn to look at our daughter. She looks paler than she did even a few moments ago, and her breathing is now coming in faint gasps. Kyle moves closer.

"What's going on…?"

Before I can answer, a nurse comes into the room and glances at the monitor, frowning.

"What's going on?" Kyle asks again, his voice rising, but she doesn't answer him.

"Let me get the doctor," she murmurs, and hurries away. I take Katherine's hand; is it my imagination, or does it feel cooler than it did a few moments ago? She was talking to me less than an hour before, sleepy and smiling. *I love you, Mom.*

A doctor comes in, someone new on the ward—a nameless stranger. Kyle and I watch in breathless alarm as he checks Katherine's stats, listens to her heart, shakes his head.

"What's going on?" This time Kyle's voice is low and surly with fear.

"I'm afraid it looks as if there's been a complication with the blood transfusion," the doctor says tersely. "We need to deal with it now."

"What kind of complication…?"

"Could you leave the room, please?" He gives us the barest of sympathetic smiles. "A nurse will come and get you when things have stabilized."

Stabilized? But I thought things were already stabilized. Katherine woke up; I *spoke* to her. Everything had turned a corner. *Everything.*

We let ourselves be shepherded out of the room even though everything in me clamors to stay. Back in the waiting room Ben is sprawled on the sofa, asleep. I pace the room, shivering with cold and shock, my mind racing in circles.

"What's happened to her?" I ask Kyle, even though I know he doesn't know. "She was fine just a little while ago. She was talking to me, she had some water."

Kyle shakes his head. "They'll tell us soon," he says like a promise, but it means nothing.

It's another two endless hours before someone comes to tell us what's going on. It's another doctor, kindly-looking, with gray hair and glasses.

"I'm afraid Katherine has developed a complication from the blood transfusion," he says. He looks alarmingly serious. "It's called transfusion-related acute lung injury, and it happens in very rare cases, when pulmonary edema is caused by the presence of leukocyte antibodies in the transfused plasma."

He might as well be speaking a foreign language. We stare at him dumbly and he tries to rephrase. "She has respiratory distress from a bad reaction to the transfused blood. We're doing everything we can." If that's meant to reassure us, it doesn't. *We're doing everything we can* means that it won't be enough.

Once again I'm spinning in a void of incredulity, except it's so much worse this time—*How did we get here?* I thought we were past the worst of it. We were on our way up as a family, facing this together. Katherine was *okay.*

I'm too stunned to cry; Kyle looks dumbfounded. "Can we see her?" he asks the doctor, who shakes his head.

"Soon."

Another hour passes. We pace, drink cold coffee, watch the muted TV with gritty eyes. My mind plays a torturously sweet montage of Katherine's childhood—her tiny newborn body, cuddled against my own. A chubby toddler, wrapping her arms tightly around my neck, burrowing her body next to mine.

Memories that have been buried for so long rise to the surface like bubbles. Katherine aged four, about to blow out the candles on her birthday cake, but two-year-old Ben got in there first. She didn't even mind; she just laughed and gave him some icing off her finger. I remember how she read stories to Ben with him on her lap; an enormous baby, he was practically as big as she was. She was only three and yet she'd read to him from her storybooks, making up the words.

How had I forgotten that, how generous and patient she was with her brother? How *happy*? She wasn't always the wary, worried pre-adolescent she's become, but it's as if I've forgotten everything that's gone before, as if the present has obscured the past. Now I want to remember—I need to.

I don't know how much of Katherine's quiet shyness now is due to her age and personality and how much is due to me not being the mother I wanted to be, but what I am sure of, with all my heart, is that I want a second chance to get it right. I will get it *so right* this time.

Another hour drags by and then yet another different doctor comes in. He looks even more serious, so much so that the breath freezes in my lungs, questions caught in my throat.

"I'm sorry," he says. "We're doing everything we can, but she's not responding to treatment."

Kyle and I stare at him blankly, both of us refusing to accept what he surely cannot be saying. "What do you mean...?" Kyle finally whispers, even though we both know what he means—and yet, surely, surely, he can't mean *that*. It can't happen this way. It can't *end* this way. She's *eleven*; she was talking to me just a few hours ago, telling me she loved me.

"Come and see her," the doctor says, and numbly, we follow him back to Katherine's room.

So much has changed in such a short space. Her breath comes in frothy gasps and tubes snake from her nose and mouth. Her head lolls against her chest and her face is pale and puffy, her fingers too. She looks so different, as if something vital has already left her, and I can't stand the thought.

"Katherine…" I whisper her name brokenly, a plea she can't hear. My baby, my only girl, my darling dream child. *How can this be happening?*

Tears run down Kyle's face as we sit on either side of her and hold her poor, swollen hands. She barely stirs; her eyelids don't even flicker. I feel as if she's slipping away from us, second by second, and there is nothing we can do but hold on, and even that won't be enough. We can't keep her here; no one can.

I remember how I sat like this with my mother and watched her life ebb away, like a receding tide as she sank deeper and deeper into unconsciousness. By the end I almost wanted it to happen, welcomed the final moment, because waiting was so hard.

But I don't feel that way now, at all. Now I cling; I hope; I pray. It can't end this way for Katherine. For us. It *can't*. I want to rail, scream, *fight*. Anything to resist this moment, and far worse, the next one. Everything in me insists it can't go this way, this isn't the way it's meant to happen. There is still so much I want Katherine to be able to do and see, to become. And now none of it will happen.

Time moves on, inexorable, relentless. Doctors come and go, and then one takes us aside, tells us the truth that is so terribly

342   Kate Hewitt

plain to see. Her lungs are filled with fluid; she's literally drowning inside her body, and there's nothing they can do. Nothing they've tried has worked.

"Blood transfusions are normally completely safe," the doctor says, looking a bit shell-shocked himself. "This is very, very rare." Which hardly makes us feel better. In fact, it makes us feel worse. *Why Katherine? Why us?* It should have been simple, an easy fix—at least physically. We should have been checking out of the hospital tomorrow, spending time as a family, trying to heal. Not this, never this.

The doctor leaves us alone. I ask Kyle if we should wake Ben, but he is deeply asleep and we decide it would be too upsetting for him. And so Kyle and I sit by her side and hold her hands, limp in our own. The only sound is the persistent beep of a monitor, reminding us that she is still alive. I would do anything to change this. Anything at all. I long to rewind the whole summer, take back the last two years. There is so much regret, so much disbelief, and yet amid it all is the knowledge that I can't let it end like this, a silent surrender. Not for my sake, or Kyle's, or Katherine's. Not for Ben's. I will fight this, the only way I know how—the only way I can.

And so I talk to her; I tell her everything I've wanted to say, everything I should have said—how much I love her, how wonderful she is, how the sound of her laughter makes me smile. I tell her how proud I am for who she is—her quiet sense of humor, her delight in books, her sensitivity, her kindness.

I tell her all the things I want us to do together, how I will be there for her, time and time again, whenever she needs me. I talk until I am hoarse, and Kyle talks to her too, in broken words, in desperate promises. We give her all of our love, and I hope and pray she hears it. She feels it, and somehow, *somehow* that is going to have to be enough.

As dawn breaks, flooding the hospital with pale, pink light, her hands still in ours, her body lets out one long shudder before going completely still. I've seen death before, but it feels so very wrong in a child. My daughter. My dear, dear daughter.

Kyle and I exchange silent glances, tears running down our faces, as that persistent beep turns to a drone and our daughter slips from this world like a shadow.

CHAPTER THIRTY-FOUR

REBECCA

One year later

Petaluma, California, is a small town suburb of San Francisco's North Bay, and it looks like it's been transplanted from a Norman Rockwell painting or a Brady Bunch set, with its old-fashioned brick buildings that make up its downtown, the ranch houses in neatly tended yards, kids riding bikes on the sidewalk, their laughter ringing through the still, clear air.

In some small way, it reminds me of Geneseo, which reminds me of last summer. Of grief and pain, hope and healing. *Of Tessa.*

We have been living in Petaluma for eight months. It's been a long road this last year—first, helping Zoe to heal over the course of the summer, giving Charlotte the support she needs, rebuilding our marriage, but all of it has given me a focus and a purpose that I've needed. I am determined now. So, so determined.

It took Zoe several months to get over her brain injury. Long, painful months of headaches and forgotten words, gaps in her memory that frustrated her and yet made her more determined. My strong, strong girl. By autumn she was mostly back to normal, and now, a year later, I am thankful it looks like she has made a complete recovery.

In September Josh resigned from his job, and took a far less stressful part-time position in San Francisco. He makes a lot less money, but we have savings and it seems so much less important now. The children are in public school, and I'm in therapy.

At Christmas I finally worked up the courage to confront my parents, and their tortured looks told me everything I needed to know. And then the confessions came out—how my uncle Dan was an alcoholic, how they became estranged from him when they discovered disturbing pornography in his room one Christmas. They were wretched with guilt, but I didn't have the energy or the heart to blame them, even though I still felt desperately hurt and betrayed. There had been too much blame and guilt already, and we cannot change the past. The important thing is, we're still here. And we're healing.

Now, as I stand on the deck of our split-level ranch and watch the morning mist rise in ghostly wreaths off Sonoma Mountain, I think of Tessa, who lost so much more than I did. I didn't see her for a few days after Zoe came out of surgery. We were practically living at the hospital, caught between exhaustion and excitement, hope and fear. We'd hired a round of babysitters for Charlotte and Max, checking in when we could, desperate to discover if Zoe was really going to be okay.

Then, when I was back at the lake house to shower and change and check on the kids, I saw her packing up her car. I watched as she walked toward the lake and stood on its edge, her arms wrapped around herself, looking like the loneliest person in the world. I hadn't seen her since I'd checked on her in the waiting room, and she'd told me there had been a complication. If they were leaving the lake, I figured it must have worked out okay.

So I walked outside, carefully down the deck stairs, and down the little twisting path between our cottages.

"Tessa."

She turned slowly, her stare barely taking me in. Her face was hollowed, her eyes blank. She looked at me as if I were a stranger.

"I'm sorry we haven't seen each other," I said. "We've been so busy with Zoe, at the hospital."

She nodded slowly, dully, and didn't ask about Zoe, which, to my shame, rankled me a little. "How are you all? How is Katherine? You'd mentioned something about her lungs…?"

"You don't know?" Her voice was flat, toneless, as if it didn't even matter. Nothing did. I tried to smile, waiting for whatever came next. "Katherine died, Rebecca." Tessa said the words starkly, and they hit me with hammer blows, making me physically flinch. "She died two days ago."

For a few seconds I couldn't take it in. I just stared, my mind spinning blankly. "But… but *how*?"

"That problem with her lungs? She basically drowned inside her body. She was gone within hours. The doctors said it was a very rare response to a blood transfusion."

"Tessa. Oh my… I can't…" I stared at her, unable to hide my complete and utter shock. "I'm so, so sorry," I said after a few painful moments. "I had no idea…" My mind blanked and blurred; I simply couldn't take it in. I had no idea how to respond. Katherine… little Katherine, with her shy, hopeful manner, one leg twisted round the other, Charlotte's shadow. *How…?*

"It's okay." Tessa shook her head, her gaze sliding away from mine. "I don't blame you."

Her words rooted me to the spot as I realized that she *should* blame me. That I played a part, even a crucial part, in this tragedy. If I hadn't… if Charlotte hadn't… Katherine never would have taken a razor to her wrist by herself. I *knew* that, and the weight and pain of that knowledge nearly crippled me. "Oh, Tessa." My voice choked. "I don't know what to say. I'm so, so sorry…"

"I know." She nodded toward the car. "We're going back to New York. The funeral will be there, in a few days. My father's coming." The comment seemed strange until I remembered that she had been semi-estranged from him.

"We would come," I began awkwardly, "of course we would, but…"

"No, you have Zoe to think of. And honestly, it's better this way, isn't it?" Her words seemed to hang in the air. "Goodbye, Rebecca." The words sound horribly final. "I hope you and your family are able to get past all this somehow." She turned away from me, dismissing me from her life, and of course I couldn't blame her. If I were her, I didn't think I'd be able to act with nearly as much composure and grace.

Compared to what she had to deal with, Zoe's injury seemed like nothing. *Nothing.*

"Tessa…" I began, although I didn't know what I would say. What I *could* say, considering.

But she'd already started walking away, and she didn't look back when I spoke. We never saw each other again.

I've looked her up, though, on social media sites. She hasn't updated anything, and her card store is closed down. I think of writing her, but I don't even know her address. I texted her once, but I got a message saying the number was not in service. She has completely disappeared from my life, and yet I think about her nearly every day. I wonder how she is, and I pray that she, Kyle, and Ben have somehow all managed to survive this, to struggle on.

And Katherine. *Katherine.* I was so dismissive of her petty problems, thought how easily they could be fixed. How little I knew. How self-absorbed I was. And how different I am determined to be now.

From behind me the screen door slides open and then Zoe steps out to join me on the deck. My dear, determined little girl.

Moving to Petaluma was good her, for all of us; the slower pace, the easier life. Except now I know nothing is easy. That is one lesson I've learned, at least. Mothering, marriage, life itself—none of it is easy or simple. It's hard, so hard, and yet it's also so worth it; to keep struggling on, fighting against the brokenness. Letting ourselves be healed.

"You sleep okay, sweetheart?" I ask as Zoe rests her head on my shoulder. She's taller now; her head nearly reaches my chin.

"Yes, I'm okay." I feel as if we are always reminding ourselves of that truth. *We are okay.*

"Good." I kiss the top of her head and say a silent prayer for Tessa and her family, as I do every morning, and together, Zoe and I watch the last of the morning mist melt away with the sun's healing rays.

CHAPTER THIRTY-FIVE

TESSA

I am sitting on a park bench on Brooklyn's Promenade, where I used to take Katherine as a baby, watching Ben feed the seagulls. I know he shouldn't—they are an urban menace—but he is enjoying scattering the breadcrumbs and I am enjoying watching him chucking handfuls with gleeful abandon while the birds flutter and peck.

It is a warm day, the sky a gentle, benevolent blue, boats bobbing on the East River, Manhattan's skyline hazy in the distance. It has been thirteen months since Katherine died.

I still mark every day without her, think of her constantly, remember her, treasure her. The pain is part of me, pulsing through every vein and artery of my body, like blood. I can't imagine life without it, and yet I am slowly, so slowly, learning to live with it. Letting it simply be a part of me.

She truly is my dream child now. And while the grief is as natural to me as breathing, it is Katherine's legacy—I am making sure of it—that Kyle, Ben, and I live life to the fullest. That I am to Ben the mother I always meant to be to both my children.

Kyle and I have worked tirelessly over the last year to give Ben the support he needs. Grief counseling, and help with learning, since it turned out he had an undiagnosed case of mild dyslexia no one ever caught. We've also enrolled him in several afterschool sports clubs and activities, to help with that manic boy energy that used to frustrate me so much.

Now I revel in it, in him, this child of mine who is still here, who is turning into a beautiful boy with humor and kindness, *who always was one*, if I'd just had eyes to see him. If I'd been different enough, healthy enough, happy enough.

But I'm not going to play that destructive blame game anymore, even though sometimes I am so tempted. I know now it only hurts. I accept the part I played last summer, and even before then; I acknowledge my weakness as well as my guilt. And I move past it, one heart-wrenching step at a time.

I've been in counseling too, and so has Kyle. We all need it. We're all battered and wounded, covered in scars, fighting to survive when Katherine didn't. *Because* Katherine didn't. Because we've all come to realize the only way to honor her memory is to take this day and every day after as a blessing, a gift, even when it still hurts so much.

I've made mistakes, more than I could ever count, and while they can still hurt, I believe in forgiveness and healing and hope, and I know Katherine did, too. I think of her last words to me, the assurance that she loved me, and it feels like the most important thing that has ever been said to me. I am thankful that she died knowing I loved her. That last conversation we had is the sweetest treasure to me now; I replay it in my head almost every day.

We've had help, so much help, in the last year. At Katherine's funeral, I reconciled with my father, both of us in tears, hugging each other silently. We see him nearly every weekend now; he moved to New Jersey, to be closer to us and especially to Ben. Sometimes we talk about my mom, and that helps, too. He admitted that he handled her stroke badly, that he didn't know what to do when she was so helpless, that he hurt both of us by not giving her the care she needed, and forcing me to do it instead. I forgave him, willingly, more easily than I ever expected to.

And Rayha, dear Rayha, forgave me just as easily, even though I knew I didn't deserve it. When we came back from the lake she was waiting, arms opened wide, and I stepped into her embrace, so grateful for her friendship, her love. Zane is in a full-time facility now, needing constant care. I visit him as often as I can, and I make meals for Rayha; I show up because that's what she did for me, what we do for each other. We all need to live under grace.

The mothers who once blanked me on the playground have come to our aid, at least some of them. There have been casseroles and cards and invitations to playdates and birthday parties. Not a stream, but a steady trickle, *enough*. And I have responded; I have chosen to engage in so many ways, even when I don't want to, when I feel like I can't stand one more minute of anything, because I will not let grief get the better of me this time. I will not let it win. And Kyle helps, encouraging me on, supporting me, just as I do my best to support him, even though sometimes, sometimes often, we mess up, we argue, we hurt each other. We also forgive.

None of it is easy; some days I struggle to find the strength or the will just to get out of bed. Some days I don't get out; I give myself time to wallow, to rest, to *be*. But we go on, and more importantly, we go on together. I am learning to find a fragile peace in moments like these—in sunshine, in a smile, in a memory of Katherine I'd forgotten that I now hold like a gift, painful and perfect. In life itself, which will always be a gift if we only choose it to be.

Some days I think of Rebecca, and I wonder how she is. If Zoe has made the progress they hoped for. I hope they've moved on, that they have found a way to be happy. I wonder if we will ever see each other again, and I think we probably won't. And like so many things about last summer, I let it—her—go.

"Hey, guys!" Kyle calls to us as he strolls down the promenade; he'd agreed to meet us here after work.

"Hey, Dad!" Ben grins at him before releasing the last of the breadcrumbs, spreading his hands wide as he gazes out at the river. Kyle smiles back at him.

"No more bread?" he asks.

Ben turns to us with a philosophical shake of his head, pushing the shaggy hair out of his eyes. "Nope. And no more seagulls."

Silently we watch the birds lift into the sky, soaring on pure white wings, elegant and graceful, until they are no more than distant specks in a blue, blue sky. The sun dazzles. The river shimmers. Ben reaches for my hand, and with my other hand I lace my fingers through Kyle's. I take a deep breath, and then, together, the three of us head for home.

A LETTER FROM KATE

Dear Reader,

Thank you so much for taking the time to read *The Secrets We Keep*. I am so pleased that you did and I really hope you enjoyed it. If you did, and want to keep up to date with all my latest releases, just sign up at the following link: www.bookouture.com/kate-hewitt Your email address will never be shared and you can unsubscribe at any time.

The idea behind *The Secrets We Keep* actually came to me a long time ago—back when I was a mother of young children, living in New York City. I noticed (and experienced myself!) the competitiveness that can emerge between mothers, especially in that kind of high-pressured, urban environment, but also how lonely and isolating motherhood can feel sometimes, and I wanted to write a story that explored these themes.

But even more importantly, I wanted to write a story about forgiveness and grace, because as parents we are trying our hardest to do right by our beloved children, and sometimes—even often—we make mistakes. Sometimes those mistakes have consequences, even terrible ones, but I do believe there is still grace and hope to be found, and ultimately that is what *The Secrets We Keep* is about.

Once again, I hope you enjoyed the story, and if you did I would be so grateful if you could spare a couple of minutes to write a review. And please do also sign up to my newsletter for updates on my forthcoming new releases.

You can also get in touch via my Facebook page or Twitter account using the links below, or join my Facebook page 'Kate's Reads', where we discuss all sorts of books.

Thank you for reading my books!

Happy reading,
Kate

 @katehewitt1

 @katehewittauthor

ACKNOWLEDGMENTS

I'm so thankful to my editor Isobel and all the wonderful team at Bookouture for working to make my book the best—and most successful—it can be. Thank you to my lovely friend Jenna, for always cheering me on, and to the fabulous writers in various Facebook groups who provide great emotional support and encouragement. Also, thanks to my husband and children for putting up with me when I'm racing against a deadline. Lastly, thank you to my readers. You are so wonderful for being in touch, letting me know how my books have affected you, and most of all, for reading them. Thank you!